JANIS REAMS HUDSON

APACHE PROMISE

ZEBRA BOOKS
KENSINGTON PUBLISHING CORP.

For Billie Jean Val Bracht,
so she won't beat me up.

ZEBRA BOOKS

are published by

Kensington Publishing Corp.
475 Park Avenue South
New York, NY 10016

Copyright © 1992 by Janis Reams Hudson

All rights reserved. No part of this book may be reproduced in any form or by any means without the prior written consent of the Publisher, excepting brief quotes used in reviews.

Zebra, the Z logo, Heartfire Romance, and the Heartfire Romance logo are trademarks of Kensington Publishing Corp.

If you purchased this book without a cover you should be aware that this book is stolen property. It was reported as "unsold and destroyed" to the Publisher and neither the Author nor the Publisher has received any payment for this "stripped book."

First printing: December, 1992

Printed in the United States of America

Praise for Janis Reams Hudson's APACHE PROMISE:

"For realistic Western flavor, accuracy, power, and passion, Janis Reams Hudson is one of the best. APACHE PROMISE fulfills Western readers' dreams." (4 +)

— Kathe Robin, *Romantic Times*

"Since her first book was published two years ago, Janis Reams Hudson has enjoyed the acclaim most writers wait years to achieve . . . APACHE PROMISE mesmerizes the reader from the first to last page . . . with enough action, thrills, intrigue and adventure to excite [any] fan, and an unusual romance between the two lead characters that makes this piece a tremendous treasure."

— Harriet Klausner, *The Anastasia Gazette,* St. Augustine, FL

A GAME OF DESIRE

"No," Angela begged. "Don't look at me like that." Was it his eyes that started that tingling sensation down deep inside her?

"Like how? Like you've been looking at me all night?"

"No!"

"Oh, yes." He advanced another step. "You haven't been able to keep your eyes off me, and you know it."

"You're crazy!" She backed away, embarrassed, confused. Heat flushed her skin.

"Am I?" He advanced.

"Yes! I never did any such thing." She raised her chin in the air and took another step back. When she did, she stumbled, and Matt grabbed her, pulling her to his chest. The sudden contact startled them both.

Matt tightened his arms around her and lowered his lips toward hers. She twisted her face away, and he brought a hand up to hold her head still. His lips came nearer.

"No," she whispered.

"Ssh. It's all right. Don't be afraid."

She felt the deep vibration of his voice clear down to her toes. Her eyes locked on his lips, and she swallowed. She tried to deny the soft, languid feeling that poured through her like warm honey. One more time she whispered, "No."

Then his lips met hers, softly at first, and she melted in his arms. At his urging, she opened her mouth to him, and the warm honey in her blood turned to hot, molten lava as desire erupted within her for the first time. . . .

CAPTURE THE GLOW OF
ZEBRA'S *HEARTFIRES!*

CAPTIVE TO HIS KISS   (3788, $4.25/$5.50)
by Paige Brantley

Madeleine de Moncelet was determined to avoid an arranged marriage to the Duke of Burgundy. But the tall, stern-looking knight sent to guard her chamber door may thwart her escape plan!

CHEROKEE BRIDE   (3761, $4.25/$5.50)
by Patricia Werner

Kit Newcomb found politics to be a dead bore, until she met the proud Indian delegate Red Hawk. Only a lifetime of loving could soothe her desperate desire!

MOONLIGHT REBEL   (3707, $4.25/$5.50)
by Marie Ferrarella

Krystyna fled her native Poland only to live in the midst of a revolution in Virginia. Her host may be a spy, but when she looked into his blue eyes she wanted to share her most intimate treasures with him!

PASSION'S CHASE   (3862, $4.25/$5.50)
by Ann Lynn

Rose would never heed her Aunt Stephanie's warning about the unscrupulous Mr. Trent Jordan. She knew what she wanted—a long, lingering kiss bound to arouse the passion of a bold and ardent lover!

RENEGADE'S ANGEL   (3760, $4.25/$5.50)
by Phoebe Fitzjames

Jenny Templeton had sworn to bring Ace Denton to justice for her father's death, but she hadn't reckoned on the tempting heat of the outlaw's lean, hard frame or her surrendering wantonly to his fiery loving!

TEMPTATION'S FIRE   (3786, $4.25/$5.50)
by Millie Criswell

Margaret Parker saw herself as a twenty-six year old spinster. There wasn't much chance for romance in her sleepy town. Nothing could prepare her for the jolt of desire she felt when the new marshal swept her onto the dance floor!

Available wherever paperbacks are sold, or order direct from the Publisher. Send cover price plus 50¢ per copy for mailing and handling to Zebra Books, Dept. 4005, 475 Park Avenue South, New York, N.Y. 10016. Residents of New York and Tennessee must include sales tax. DO NOT SEND CASH. For a free Zebra/ Pinnacle catalog please write to the above address.

LAND OF PROMISE

Westward they came
by the hundreds,
by the thousands,
leaving the old,
seeking the new.
Some rode,
some walked;
all hoped
to find something
or perhaps
lose something.
So westward they came
by the hundreds,
by the thousands,
heading toward dreams
or leaving a nightmare.
Hero and coward,
man, woman and child,
they came
to start over,
begin a new life
in a new land.
A land of promise.

—JRH

Prologue

October 12, 1866
Cochise's Stronghold
Dragoon Mountains, Arizona Territory

Everything was ready. The place was perfect. Tahnito had located it earlier in the week. For what he had in mind, his timing had to be precise. He glanced over at Little Bear, his enemy, and concealed a grin behind thin lips. The blood in his veins sang of victory. This was it. Now!

Tahnito tripped convincingly and stumbled against Little Bear. Both boys tumbled from the steep hillside onto a wide rock shelf. On his way down, Tahnito shifted a small rock with his foot, then rolled quickly away. The rock was the only brace holding a large boulder in place. With its removal, the boulder slipped, then rolled. Dust clouds and chips of rock flew through the air. The grating crunch of rock against rock echoed along the hills.

Little Bear tried to scramble out of the path of the boulder, but Tahnito was quicker and blocked the way, making good his own escape.

The big, round boulder dropped a final six feet, crashing onto the shelf where the boys had landed. The shelf held, but the boulder cracked and broke into dozens of large chunks and small fragments, showering the shelf and the boys with its jagged remnants.

When the air cleared, Tahnito brushed the dust from his face and glanced around for his companion. A pile of rubble shifted; a dusty, gray hand appeared from beneath the debris. While Tahnito watched, more pieces of broken boulder moved and tumbled as Little Bear struggled to rise.

Little Bear levered himself on cut elbows, coughing and spitting dust and chips of rock from his mouth. Dirt and rubble sprinkled around him as he shook his head. He felt cuts and bruises in a dozen or more places, but no sound left his lips, not even a moan, for an Apache does not cry out his pain.

The crunch of feet on gravel drew his gaze to Tahnito, who came to stand over him. Little Bear looked up and saw that his companion had somehow escaped without a scratch. It was no wonder, the way Tahnito had put his foot in Little Bear's back to scramble for cover. Little Bear shook his head in disgust.

He tried to get up, but discovered his foot was trapped beneath the largest chunk of boulder. When he attempted to pull himself out, the worst pain he'd ever felt in his life shot up his leg. Broken, jagged pieces of bones ground against each other in his ankle. His head felt light and the world momentarily went black, but again, he did not cry out.

Through the fog of pain in his brain he heard a deafening roar. When his vision cleared, Tahnito's black head was disappearing around the bend to freedom. From above and behind Little Bear came a low snort and growl, accompanied by the shuffling of large feet on loose rock.

Little Bear was trapped. He couldn't get up. He couldn't even turn to see what was behind him. With his foot still firmly caught beneath a rock that outweighed him two or three times over, he had to twist around at the waist to see what was happening.

Squinting against the glare of the afternoon sun, he didn't see anything at first. Then a shaggy, massive, brown head came around the rock that had him trapped. The huge brown bear snapped its jaws, showing long, sharp teeth, and growled deep in its throat. Little Bear reached for the knife at his waist, praying it was still there, even though he knew the knife wouldn't help. With his foot trapped, he was as good as dead, and he knew it.

Frustration, anger, and fear combined to form a bitter taste in his mouth.

He was only fifteen. He thought of his family, his home, and knew he didn't want to die. He wasn't one to give up, but neither could he fool himself about the danger he was in. The bear probably weighed at least six hundred pounds, and it was mad about something — it was in the eyes, that anger.

Little Bear gripped the hilt of the hunting knife his father had given him and snarled at the bear. "Come on, *shash*," he taunted. "Let's see how much of you I can carve up before I die."

Chapter One

April 2, 1872
Memphis, Tennessee

"Get to bed now, dear. Tomorrow's the day. We have to get up before the sun."

"I know. I will." Angela Susanna Barnes kissed her mother on the cheek and smiled. "Good night, Mama."

When Sarah Barnes left for her own room, Angela changed into her nightgown and took down her hair. She brushed the hip-length, blond curls and thought how strange it seemed to be leaving Memphis. She'd been born and raised here, never traveling anywhere. She had slept in this room over her father's store for as long as she could remember. Yet tomorrow they would be off on what her father called "a grand adventure." Joseph Barnes had been wanting to go west since the day he'd limped home from the war, when Angela was ten, and found the hated Yankee blue all over his beloved Southern city.

He'd slowly resigned himself to the sight of blue uniforms over the years; he realized they would be present now no matter where he went. But he still wanted to go. Three months ago he'd made the final arrangements to sell his store. He would start another one in Tucson, out in Arizona Territory.

Angela's mother had not been thrilled in the least to

realize they were headed for Apache country, but Joseph just kept telling her everything would be all right, trust him, and hadn't her doctor said she should be living in a drier climate anyway?

So they were going. Tomorrow. Tomorrow it was their turn to ferry their wagon across the Mississippi and head for the unknown West.

Angela sighed and began rebraiding her hair to keep it out of her face while she slept. She didn't know yet how she felt about this move to Arizona, except that she would miss her friends terribly. But Mary Lou was engaged now, and Jennilee had married last winter; so Angela figured they probably wouldn't miss her nearly as much as she'd miss them. That thought hurt more than she cared to admit.

Then she smiled and chuckled. Jennilee's marriage had been a surprise to everyone, including Jennilee herself. The girl had pined over Ralph Comstock for months, never dreaming he returned her affections — until that evening at the Harrisons' party last fall.

Jennilee had been flirting with her dinner partner just to see if Ralph, seated at the far end of the table, would react. She got more of a reaction than she'd bargained for. Ralph shoved back his chair, threw his linen napkin down on his half-eaten dinner, and called her name down the length of the table.

Angela giggled, remembering Ralph's embarrassed blush and Jennilee's shocked expression when Ralph, right there in front of over twenty dinner guests, demanded Jennilee stop fooling around and marry him.

It was positively the most romantic thing Angela had ever heard of. Of course, she'd die if anything like that ever happened to her. Imagine baring one's deepest emotions so publicly! Yet, oh, to have a man love her that much!

With a sigh, she turned out the lantern and stood before the window. Just to feel the soft Memphis air one more time, she raised the window and gazed out over the rooftops. The fog had already seeped up from the river, but it wasn't heavy tonight, just a light mist. Would there be fog in Tucson? Surely not. It was in the desert, wasn't it? She'd heard the town was smaller than Memphis, and wondered what kinds of people lived there . . . what her new life would be like.

Try as she might, she couldn't draw a mental picture of herself in Arizona. With a troubled sigh, she reached up to lower the window. From the alley below came a crashing and scuffling. She leaned out, expecting to see a dog or cat scampering away. Instead, she saw a man, clearly illuminated in the lantern glow from a downstairs window. He lay sprawled on his back in the dirt next to the woodpile. Another man loomed over him.

"I thought I told you I was gonna scout for Hargrave's wagon train," the standing man growled.

The man on the ground rolled to his side, then stood. "Yeah, Miller, ya told me. 'Cept Hargrave hired me, not you."

Angela caught her breath. They were talking about Mr. Hargrave, the man who would be leading the seventeen wagons, including hers, westward tomorrow.

"That was supposed to be my job, Johnson, and I plan to take it," said the man called Miller.

"Too late, buster, 'cause I already got it. We head out tomorrow, as soon as the last wagon crosses the river."

"We'll see about that." Miller swung his fist and knocked Johnson to the ground, then grabbed a stout length of firewood from the woodpile. Swinging it like a club, he brought it down with all his considerable strength on Johnson's shin.

Angela jerked, wide-eyed. She heard the simultaneous sounds of a man's scream and a bone snapping.

"*Now* it's my job, Johnson. Nobody gets in my way. Remember that."

Angela gasped.

The man called Miller straightened and glanced around. He scanned the doors and windows lining the

13

alley. Angela ducked back into her room. Had he seen her?

"If ya know what's good for ya, you'll keep quiet," the man said in a low, menacing tone. "What happened to him can happen to you."

Angela was so scared she shook all over. She'd always feared violence of any kind. Sheer terror held her immobile until long after the man named Miller left. When she finally worked up the courage to peek out the window again, the injured man, Johnson, was also gone. The alley was empty.

Had the man named Miller seen her? Had he been speaking directly to her? She slammed the window shut and threw herself on the bed and buried her head under the covers.

Her breath came in fast little gasps as she huddled there in the dark, terrified. How could people do that sort of thing to each other? It was beastly! But what should she do? What could she do?

Nothing, that's what.

Her father was the brave one of the family. She and her mother were both self-confessed cowards. Many were the times during the war when they had crouched in the cellar beneath their store and hidden from the enemy. They'd been lucky not to have the store burned down around their heads. But their entire section of town had been spared, probably because it was a merchant district and the Yankees had need of their goods.

"Let them take what they want," her mother had said to her. "We'll just stay here and keep out of their way. If we do that, maybe they won't hurt us."

It had kept them alive, but had ruined the business. The Yankees had taken what they wanted, and when Joseph had come home after the war, the store was nearly bankrupt. Angela had found that out much later, when she started doing some of the book work.

Suddenly it all came together in her mind, the reason for this move west. They were broke! Selling the large store in Memphis to start a small one in Tucson had got them out of debt. That's why her mother wasn't resisting this move!

What difference does it make now? she scolded herself. None of that helped her decide what to do about what had just happened in the alley. She should tell someone. Her father. He would undoubtedly go to the sheriff, and Miller would be arrested.

But what if Miller got loose? Criminals got loose all the time, didn't they? Just last week three bank robbers had busted out of the town jail. If Miller got loose, he'd come after Papa! Maybe even her, too!

"Coward," she hissed to herself in the darkness. She admitted it then. She wasn't going to tell anybody anything.

But this was absolutely the last time, she promised herself. This was the last time she would allow herself to be a coward. Everybody needed one last time at something, didn't they? Well, this was hers. She'd be safe and cowardly this one last time; then, the next time something happened, she'd be brave. She was seventeen, wasn't she? She'd be eighteen soon. She could make her own decisions.

So she decided.

Coward now — heroine later.

Abraham Miller Scott — no, he was Abe Miller now, he reminded himself, and he'd best not forget it — gave a final glimpse at the open second-story window up the alley, then shrugged. If somebody had seen him, the sucker was obviously too chicken-livered to do anything about it.

Dismissing the possible witness with a sneer, he whacked Johnson over the head to shut up that godawful groaning, then hoisted the man up and over his shoulder. Damn heavy bugger, Johnson was.

With a grunt, Miller staggered down the street, hat

low over his face should anyone bother to look his way. He headed for the edge of town, a nice dark alley he knew of, where he could make sure Johnson never bothered him again.

In the darkness, Abe Miller smiled with grim satisfaction.

Chapter Two

August 27, 1872
Camp Bowie
Apache Pass, Arizona Territory

A string of tension threaded its way from wagon to wagon as the westbound travelers neared the most dangerous point of the trip—Apache Pass. They'd already sweated through Doubtful Canyon, so named because it was said that once you entered it, it was doubtful the Apaches would let you leave. There had been no trouble, no sign of Apaches. But now it was time to worry again. According to rumor, Apache Pass was more dangerous, even with the U.S. Army stationed there.

Abe Miller, the scout for Ward Hargrave's wagon train, had disappeared up the trail over an hour ago. The anxious eyes of the passengers scanned the dusty, broken terrain. A colorful collared lizard raised up on its hind legs and ran for cover as the first wagon neared. Beside the trail, a jack rabbit waited until the last possible minute, hypnotized by the approach of man, then bounded off for cover. From beneath the stingy shade of a scraggly shrub, an old black crow scolded, its voice drowned out by the clink and rattle of dozens of chains and harnesses, the creak and groan of wheels and axles.

But as far as the eye could see up the almost indiscernible gap between the Dos Cabezas and Chiricahua mountain ranges, there was no sign, no small cloud of dust, nothing to tell the worried travelers their scout was on his way back. If the pass was safe, wouldn't he return and tell them so? If it wasn't safe. . . .

Perched on the high seat of the seventh wagon in line, Angela gnawed on her lower lip. She and her mother usually walked beside the wagon, but the threat of danger persuaded them to ride for now. Angela glanced repeatedly at her father as he handled the reins beside her. Tension snapped and crackled all around him, as thick as the ever-present dust in the air. He was worried. They were all worried. Not that Angela cared a flip about what happened to Miller. If he'd met with some unfortunate end, it was no more than he deserved. But did that mean they were riding into a trap? Were there Apaches lurking just around the next hill?

Angela shuddered. For once she was glad they weren't in first position today. She'd rather eat the dust of the six outfits in front of them than be the first to meet up with Apaches. At least this way they might have some warning. For whatever that was worth.

At a shout from up ahead, Angela gripped the edge of the seat till her knuckles turned white. The cry echoed back from one wagon to the next.

"All clear! All clear!"

Angela wilted with relief. Her father visibly relaxed. Her mother, riding inside the wagon, poked her head out the back flap over the raised tailgate and passed along the message. "All clear!" There was a smile in her voice. They were safe.

The seventeen wagons, led by wagon master Ward Hargrave, passed the small clearing amid the yuccas and granite boulders where the old Butterfield Stage station stood, out of use these past ten years, and pulled up at Camp Bowie just before noon. So far,

18

their luck had held. Gossip had it that Ward Hargrave was the luckiest man ever to lead a wagon train, and the sixty-plus people he led now thought his reputation well-earned. They had made it clear through Indian Territory, Texas, and New Mexico along the old Butterfield Mail route, all the way here to Apache Pass. By the end of the week they'd be in Tucson, and not one bit of Indian trouble yet. Some of the men took to calling him Lucky Hargrave, and Hargrave, he didn't mind a bit. The next group of wagons he led west, he'd probably charge more.

All the wagons looked pretty much alike, with a blue bed, red wheels, and white canvas curved up over the top. But by now the red and blue paint was faded, cracked, and peeling, and the only place the canvas was white was somewhere in the dim memories of the travelers.

Angela climbed down from the high wagon seat and shook what dust she could from her limp, blue gingham dress. She helped her father unhitch the mules, then went to the back of the wagon. Her mother had already opened the tailgate and set out a pan of water and a sliver of soap. Angela tossed her bonnet onto the tailgate and rolled up her sleeves. It felt good to wash away the dust and grime of the morning, even if the water was warmer than she wished.

But then, everything was warmer than she wished. It was down right hot!

"Hey, Angela, you comin'?" Sudie Mae called out from the next wagon. "Me an' Ma's goin' to the trading post for a look-see. I ain't been in a store in a coon's age. Pa wouldn't let me go that time you and your ma went back at The Pass in Texas, but this time he says it's okay. Bet they've got peppermint sticks in there. Pa give me a penny so's I could get me one."

As Sudie Mae rattled on, Angela bit back a sigh and finished drying her face. She looked up to see her mother in the back of the wagon. Sarah winked at her, aware that Sudie Mae could get on anyone's nerves without even trying. Sarah grinned and handed Angela a few coins to spend at the store. "Have fun," she whispered.

Angela groaned and rolled her eyes, then took the coins. She knew they didn't need any supplies. The money was for whatever she wanted to buy, and peppermint sticks did sound good. They would have sounded a lot better if it weren't for Sudie Mae. The girl could out-chatter a jaybird.

Sudie Mae had been talking nonstop the whole time. "Ma! I think Angela's ready. Miz Whaley was gonna go with us, but she done went and changed her mind. Don't know why she'd pass up a trip to a store. Must be feelin' poorly. Not me! Don't care how poorly I might feel! Remember that place in Fort Smith we went in, Ma?"

And so it went. As Angela walked with Sudie Mae Latimer and Mrs. Latimer, Sudie Mae recalled every trading post and store she'd either seen or missed all along the trail.

When the women reached the corrals, halfway between the wagon grounds and the store, Mrs. Latimer wrinkled her nose as if shocked to smell manure, even though they'd all been smelling tons of it for months.

"Shooowee!" Sudie Mae hollered, interrupting her own monologue. "Shore do stink, don't it?"

"Lands-o-goshen!" her mother said in agreement. "Look! Over there past the hospital. That's the post there."

Between the corrals and the post, walking toward them as if he didn't have a care in the world, was Abe Miller. As he passed them, he pushed the brim of his hat up with the open mouth of the brown bottle he carried.

Angela ground her teeth and averted her gaze. He'd left them all to wonder and worry over what to expect in Apache Pass, not bothering to let them know it was safe, so that he could drink a beer! She couldn't think of a bad enough name to call him.

The three women angled off toward the store, thereby avoiding the parade ground and most of the fort. The entire area was dry, dusty, and desolate, the gravelly ground broken only occasionally by a struggling clump of bear grass or thriving cactus. The only portion that looked like it got any care at all was the officers' quarters, where someone had planted a few trees and flowers that all seemed to be wilting in the mid-day sun.

Angela, too, felt a little like wilting. Even the mountains beyond looked hot. Why hadn't she worn her bonnet? She stepped under the thatched overhang in front of the store and breathed a sigh of relief.

"Shade, at last!" Sudie Mae carried on. "I declare, I don't know when was the last time I saw shade. Oh, my," she said as they entered the store. "I'm sure it's nice in here, but after all that sun, my poor little ol' eyes just can't see a thing."

Angela rolled her own "poor little ol' eyes" and wished for some cotton to stuff in her ears. It was dim in the store, but her eyes adjusted after a few seconds. She let Mrs. Latimer and Sudie Mae browse through the merchandise while she stayed near the door.

She'd already spotted what she wanted, and it was right there on the counter, the same place it was in most stores—a great big jar full of peppermint sticks. She was going to get a stick for each of her parents, too, for she knew they loved them nearly as much as she did.

She stood with her back to the door and eyed the jar. A large shadow fell across the counter as someone entered behind her. In the next instant, Sudie Mae actually stopped chattering, but only long enough to draw breath. Then she let out an ear-piercing scream.

"Eeeee! Indians! Help, somebody! We're bein' attacked! We're all gonna die! We're gonna be scalped!"

21

Angela spun around, as did the three men in the far corner and the man stocking the shelves behind the counter. In the doorway stood a coppery-skinned man and two children. The man's thick, black hair hung past his shoulders. It was held back from his face by a red bandanna wrapped around his forehead. He wore a Yankee blue flannel army shirt, light blue trousers with a breechcloth hanging over them to mid-thigh, and tall moccasins. He had the coldest, blackest eyes Angela had ever seen.

At each elbow stood a child, same thick, black hair, but with lighter skin and sky blue eyes. The boy's hair was short, and the girl's had a streak of white at her temple. They both looked like they were fighting back a severe case of the giggles.

The man was definitely an Indian, and the children were probably part Indian, but Angela failed to see anything even remotely threatening about the trio, except for the man's cold, hard stare directed at the Latimer women.

Sudie Mae and her mother still shrieked from their corner, and the man behind the counter joined in the commotion. "What the devil do you think you're doing, Shanta? I may be forced to let you in here 'cause you work for the Army, but I by God don't have to let them there half-breed nits in here. Go on! Out with the lot of ya. Can't you see you're upsettin' these ladies?"

A blank, emotionless mask dropped over all three of the dark faces. The women in the corner finally stopped their screaming long enough to breathe, and in the total silence that reigned, Shanta and the children turned and left.

"Well, I do declare!" Mrs. Latimer cried, marching up to the counter. "Just what kind of place is this where decent white folks have to be scared out of their wits by a bunch of dirty, stinkin' Injuns?"

"Real sorry you were so scared, ma'am, but you

needn't be," the man behind the counter assured her. "Shanta's an Apache scout—"

"An Apache!"

"Yes, ma'am. He scouts for the Army."

"And I suppose those dirty little breeds are the result of him forcing himself on some poor, defenseless white woman?"

"Oh, no, ma'am. If that was the case, the Army wouldn't have nothing to do with him. No, the twins live on a ranch over near Tucson. So ya see, you weren't really in any danger."

"Well, I should hope not!" Mrs. Latimer's bosom quivered with indignation. "All the same, we decent folk appreciate you getting them out of here. Imagine! Half-breeds runnin' around here like they was white folk!"

Angela cringed with each exchange of words. She held her tongue as long as she could, then had to speak. "They were only children, Mrs. Latimer."

"But, Angela, dearie, they're half-breeds. Dirty little half-breeds."

Angela frowned. "You mean because they have mixed blood?"

"Well, of course it's mixed! What ever are you thinkin', girl?"

"I was just trying to understand why their mixed blood is such a problem, when mine doesn't seem to be. Or Sudie Mae's, for that matter."

Mrs. Latimer straightened like a starched sheet in a stiff wind. "My girl's no breed, missy. And neither are you!"

"Why not? I'm half English and half heaven-only-knows-what. And since you're Dutch and Mr. Latimer's German, that means Sudie Mae's got mixed blood, too. I was just trying to figure out the difference. Could I have five of those peppermint sticks please?" she added to the astonished clerk.

Angela's heart pounded. Her knees threatened to

buckle. She had no idea why she'd spoken out like that, except it angered her to see those poor children treated that way.

The clerk glared at her while he fished the candy out of the jar. Angela placed her money on the counter, took her peppermint sticks, and walked out the door. She spotted the two children—twins, the clerk had said—standing next to the hitching rail, wearing identical wooden expressions.

A man ran toward them from the direction of the corrals. A big man, with blond, wavy hair and a scar on his cheek. Something grisly hung from his neck. It looked like some sort of animal claws. Angela shivered. He reached the twins before she did; anger radiated from him in tangible waves.

"What the hell's going on? They probably heard that screaming clear in the next county."

Angela screwed up her courage, stepped in front of him and shouted, "Leave them alone!"

The man halted and stared at her like she'd lost her mind. He glanced sharply from her to the twins, then over to the scout, Shanta, who leaned negligently against the side of the store. "I asked what the hell is going on," the blond man repeated.

"Just keep away from them," Angela warned. "They've been through enough for one day. They don't need the likes of you calling them any more dirty names." She turned from him to kneel before the twins, forcing a smile for their benefit.

The little girl tilted her head to one side and said, "Why did you take up for us in there?"

Angela blinked in surprise, not having expected them to speak English—and such perfect English it was. "Because they were wrong," she said.

"No they weren't," the boy answered. "We are half-breeds."

"So? One of your parents is white and one's Indian.

24

What does that have to do with anything? I didn't get to choose my parents either."

The twins' looks of amazement matched that of the big blond man who now stood behind them and faced Angela. She ignored him. "I, uh, came to buy a treat, but I bought too much. Do you suppose you could help me?" She held out her handful of peppermint sticks. "I only needed three. If you each take one, then my father won't yell at me for buying too many."

The twins looked at each other, then up at the blond man. "Can we, Matt?" the little girl asked.

Angela was confused as she looked up at him. Why would the girl ask permission of the man who'd just been yelling at them? What was he to these twins? For one brief instant her eyes met his. His gaze trapped hers, and she felt like she was drowning in warm, brown velvet. Something light and wonderful fluttered in her chest. A question played across his eyes, then something else. Something almost like gratitude. Then he smiled, a slow, devastating smile that took her breath away, and nodded. "Thank the lady."

Angela wanted nothing more than to go on staring into his eyes and return that smile. Instead, she forced her attention back to the twins and gave them each a peppermint stick.

"Thank you, ma'am," they said in unison.

The constant background noise from inside the store erupted as the two Latimer women emerged. "I do declare, Sudie Mae, would you look at that! Consortin' with heathens."

"Yeah, Ma. A body just never knows about some people."

"Ain't it the truth," Mrs. Latimer said as she huffed past Angela and marched back toward the wagons. "Just wait till her pa hears about this!"

Angela shook her head at their backs. "Don't pay any attention to them," she told the twins. "They just don't know any better. Some people can only feel good

25

about themselves by pretending they're better than others. People like that aren't worth worrying about. How's the candy?"

She waited until each one took a lick, then rose to her feet. "I'd better get back now. You take care." When she was halfway to the corrals, she turned back for a final wave. The four of them — the twins, the blond man, and the scout — were standing there, staring at her.

Chapter Three

The wagons nooned at the cottonwood-lined crossing of the San Pedro River, taking advantage of the available water and shade. It was their third day past Camp Bowie.

In the wagon belonging to Joseph Barnes, things weren't going well.

"She's awful sick, Papa. She needs a doctor," Angela whispered. Keeping her voice low was pointless. Sarah Barnes was delirious with fever and couldn't hear a thing. Angela whispered anyway, more out of fear than anything. "There was a doctor back at the fort. Couldn't we take her there?"

Joseph felt his wife's heated face. He chewed his lower lip a moment, then said, "I'll go check with Hargrave and see which is closer, the fort or Tucson."

While he was gone, Angela continued sponging her mother's face. The heat inside the wagon was stifling. It felt like there was no air at all, only this terrible, unremitting heat. Even the horsefly buzzing around the front opening seemed to be panting.

A gunshot echoed off the encircled wagons. Angela jumped, nearly knocking over the bowl of water beside her mother. Excited voices called questions back and forth outside. Angela poked her head out the back end of the wagon.

"Never mind folks!" Hargrave hollered. "It's just Miller, doing a little target practice."

Angela's mind barely registered anything beyond the fact that nothing serious was happening. She breathed a short sigh and resumed her seat in the wagon. Her thoughts were totally occupied by her mother. As far as Angela could remember, Sarah Barnes had never been sick, except for an occasional lung congestion. Now she lay there helpless, delirious with fever, struggling for every breath, and Angela was scared.

A few minutes later Joseph returned, his gaze going directly to Sarah while he spoke to Angela. "It's as far to Tucson as it is back to Apache Pass. Ward says the last time he was in Tucson, they didn't have a doctor. I can't chance that. I told him when we break camp in another hour or so, we'll be heading back for Camp Bowie while the others go on. We should make it by ourselves just fine. How is she?"

"She's a little quieter now, but the fever's still high." Angela's chin quivered. She lowered her eyes to hide the stinging moisture from her father, but he saw.

"Don't fret, honey," he said, putting his arm around her. "We'll get her to the doctor and she'll be fine. You'll see."

Even in the stifling heat, her father's arm around her felt good. Strong and comforting. To change the subject, she asked, "What was that shooting about? What did Miller shoot this time, somebody's laying hen?" Angela shuddered, remembering the Hilmers' dog.

The Hilmers had five children from ages ten to two, and one hound dog. At least, they used to have a dog, till the night Miller accidentally stepped on its tail. The dog had yelped, then leaped for Miller and grabbed a mouthful of pant leg. Miller kicked the growling hound away, calmly drew his pistol, and shot the dog right between the eyes—in front of all five Hilmer children.

And it wasn't a shooting that was hushed up, either. After the crying was over, the Hilmer children gathered up all the youngsters in camp, and there were plenty. They carried the dead dog to a low hill, and cried and pleaded until Ward Hargrave himself was persuaded to come and say words at the graveside service.

Angela's lips twitched at the memory of the tongue lashing Hargrave gave Miller after having to face all those crying children.

In spite of her humor at his expense, however, she was still terrified of the man. Every time she saw him, she heard again the sound of snapping bones. She'd never told anyone about what she'd seen in the alley that night. She was still too afraid.

"No," Joseph answered. "No, this time it was an Apache, or so he says."

"An Apache! Are we under attack?"

"I hardly think so, Angie Sue. He was probably just shooting at shadows. He went out and scouted across the river and couldn't even find any tracks. If there was someone or something out there, it's gone now. I think he was just showing off for that Swedish girl — what's her name?"

"You mean Helga?"

"That's the one."

Angela was relieved to hear Miller was interested in someone else besides her, but she'd have to warn Helga, who was a silly girl, and not too bright. (Helga considered Sudie Mae Latimer her best friend.) Mr. Miller was not above taking advantage anywhere he could — like the night before they reached Fort Smith, when he'd caught Angela alone at the wagon. He'd come up behind her and pinched her fiercely on the buttocks. Angela had shrieked, and without even thinking, she had turned quickly and struck him across the cheek so hard her hand had stung all the next day.

Stunned surprise had wiped the grin off Miller's face, only to be followed by a mean, vicious glare. It was a look that said he'd get even some day. From then on, Angela made sure she was never alone.

"This water's too warm, Angie Sue," her father said, interrupting her thoughts. "Why don't you take the small pail to the river and get some cool, fresh water for your mother?"

Angela took the bucket and climbed from the back of the wagon. It was good to be able to stretch her legs for a few minutes.

"Watch the heat, honey," her father called out to her. *Watch the heat.* That was the trouble. She *could* watch the heat. It rippled up from the ground in liquid waves. She could almost see her skin drying out under the burning rays of the sun, and she could certainly feel it. Memphis had been hot in summer, but nowhere near this hot!

The trees along the river offered shade, and the gurgle of running water gave the impression of coolness. Wanting privacy, Angela walked a half mile upstream. She knelt beside the river in the shade of a giant cottonwood and brushed loose tendrils of pale blond hair off her damp neck. She ran a hand along the single braid wrapped in a coronet around her head and rearranged a pin or two to keep it snugly in place.

Leaning over, she splashed her face with water, then, with her eyes still closed, turned her face into the slight stirring of air not quite strong enough to be called a breeze. The water evaporated from her skin almost instantly. It left her face feeling tight and dry.

Was Tucson this hot and dry? Heaven forbid!

She sat still and tried to think cool thoughts. It didn't help. Instead, her mind wandered. She worried about her mother. She worried about Miller. But try as she might to clear her mind, a soft pair of warm brown eyes came to her, unbidden, behind her closed lids.

Matt. The girl had called him Matt.

She'd thought about him a lot since leaving the fort. Him and the twins. What was he to them? When she and her father took her mother back to the fort, would the tall, blond man still be there? Were the twins still with him?

Even after three days, she could still feel the fluttering in her stomach and the stumbling of her heart whenever she pictured his eyes. And his smile.

Her reminiscing was abruptly interrupted when a large, dark hand swept from behind and clamped over her mouth. Another arm snaked around her waist and held her firmly against the rock-hard wall of a man's chest. Panic assailed her. The scream that couldn't escape her constricted throat nearly strangled her. She struggled to free herself, but her kneeling position made movement difficult.

"Be still!" a harsh, accented voice whispered in her ear. "If you help me, and don't scream, I won't harm you. If you scream or try to run, I'll kill you. Do you understand?" When she didn't answer immediately, the man squeezed her waist tighter, cutting off her breath. "Do you understand!"

Panic stricken, Angela tried to nod her head. It was nearly impossible, considering the grip he had on her, but she managed to let her assailant know she understood. His grip relaxed slowly. When she could, she took in great gulps of air. She didn't care how hot it was now, at least it was air.

Her captor forced her to turn around, and she stared into the blackest eyes she'd ever seen. The man's skin was coppery brown, and his thick, black hair hung well past his shoulders. He reminded her of the scout at Camp Bowie, the only real difference being his clothes. Except for a loincloth and a pair of tall moccasins, this man was totally nude. The sight of all that dark, bare skin terrified her.

"Bandage my leg," he ordered.

"Wh-what?"

"If I'm going to get out of here before that trigger-happy fool comes looking for me again, I need my leg bandaged."

Angela had heard about people going into shock before, and now she figured that's what had happened to her. All she could do was sit there and stare at the man, and vaguely realize that her panic was subsiding.

"You're an Apache!" she blurted out. But if he really was an Apache, and he certainly fit the description, why wasn't she still terrified?

"You figured that out all on your own, did you? Well, right now I'm a wounded Apache, and I'd appreciate your help. If I don't get back to the others soon, they'll come looking for me, and then there'll be trouble. I'd like to avoid that if possible. If your man was a better shot, or a better tracker, I'd be dead by now."

"My goodness! You certainly don't talk like an—" Angela swallowed the rest of her words, realizing how offensive they would have sounded.

But the man before her had obviously been around. He seemed to pick her unsaid words right out of her brain. "Like an illiterate savage?" he supplied.

"I didn't—" Angela's tongue stammered to a halt. Her face heated to an unbearable degree that had nothing to do with the sun or the temperature.

How could she even think to call him such a thing after what had happened at the fort! She lowered her eyes in shame and confusion. That was when she noticed his leg. "You're bleeding!"

"Keep your voice down," he warned. But his harsh tone was softened by the totally unthreatening look in his eyes.

Tending wounds was nothing new to a girl who'd grown up during the War Between the States. Young as she'd been, every available hand had been needed to tend the wounded when the Yankees came to town.

The Apache had piled green leaves over the twin holes in the front and back of his thigh to try to stop the bleeding. Angela peeled them away and set to work cleaning the wound.

"What's your name?" she asked as she tore a strip

32

from the one petticoat she wore. Her question surprised both of them.

"Why do you want to know?"

She shrugged. "Well, in case our train is attacked by Apaches, I can say I know you, and maybe they won't kill me." In spite of the possibility that just such an attack could occur, Angela felt herself smiling at the man.

"I'm not sure it would work, but my name is Natzili-Chee."

Angela struggled to pronounce it and failed miserably.

"Just call me Chee," he suggested. "It's easier, and that's what my friends call me."

"Where did you learn to speak English so well?" she asked as she continued working on his leg. He winced once when she had to pick out a piece of leaf from the raw flesh. "Sorry."

"It's okay. You're just full of questions, aren't you?"

"I guess so." *It must be his eyes,* she thought. They were wary, yet friendly. Something in them told her she had nothing to fear from this Apache, so she simply forgot to be afraid. She shrugged and tore a longer strip from her petticoat to use as a bandage. She blushed again, realizing what a view of her legs she'd just given him.

Chee chuckled softly. "When I was a boy, I worked on a ranch over near Tucson. They taught me English."

"They taught you well. There. I'm finished," she said, tying off the bandage securely. "You'd better go now. I've been gone too long just to fetch water. Someone might come looking for me."

Chee stood and tested the strength of his leg. He gave a grunt when he put his full weight on it. Next to his foot lay a long, stout limb. Angela picked it up and handed it to him. "Try this," she offered.

Chee asked her name, and she gave it. Then he thanked her for her help, apologized for scaring her, and turned to head farther upstream.

Before he even got three feet, a loud, metallic click

brought him up short. With a gasp, Angela spun around and stared into the cold, gray eyes of Miller. Behind her she heard Chee turn slowly to face the threat.

"Step aside, Angela," Miller ordered.

She knew what he intended. He intended to shoot Chee, and she stood directly in his line of fire. From somewhere inside her the answer came. "No." Her eyes grew as wide as Miller's. Her own daring stunned her, but she meant it.

"What?" Miller croaked.

"I said no."

Behind her back she motioned for Chee to go, but he waited. "He doesn't have a gun, Miller. It would be murder," Angela said, still motioning frantically for Chee to leave.

"Murder! For Christsake, girl, he's just a stinkin' Apache! But then after the way you took up for them little half-breed brats back at the fort, the whole damn train knows you're nothing but an Injun lover. At least the nits were only half scum. This'n here's *all* scum."

"He's a man, Miller. I thought you only shot dogs," she taunted.

Miller took a step toward her. She backed up. If he got his hands on her, he could shove her out of the way and shoot Chee. Behind her, she finally heard Chee limp away.

"I thought your method with men was to knock them down in some dark alley and take a club to them," she taunted. "That's more your style, isn't it?" She couldn't believe what she was doing.

Miller stopped in his tracks and narrowed his eyes to menacing slits. "What the hell are you talkin' about?"

"You know exactly what I'm talking about. I saw you that night. I know you broke that man's leg so you could get his job."

He drew his shoulders back, chin up, and waved his pistol in the air. "You don't know what you're sayin'."

"You know I do. And if you don't let this man go, I'll

34

tell Mr. Hargrave just what happened to his last scout. You'll never work on another wagon train again, he'll see to that."

"Why, you little bitch. You been lordin' it all over the place how you were too good for the likes o' me, and you're nothin' but a schemin' little Injun-lovin' blackmailer."

"At least I'm not a thug and a bully who makes little children cry." She had to hold his attention no matter how scared she felt. His eyes kept straying over her shoulder, and finally she heard a crashing in the brush and the sound of hoofbeats pounding away from them.

"I could silence ya right here and now. What's to stop me?"

Angela swallowed hard. There was nothing to stop him. Nothing, and no one. He could shoot her here and now and claim the Apache did it.

This was worse, much worse than watching from the safety of her upstairs window while he hurt some stranger. This time it was her life on the line! Why, Lord why, hadn't she told someone what she'd seen that night? Miller would have been thrown in jail, and none of this would be happening. Why had she been such a fool and kept quiet?

Wait! Miller had no way of knowing she hadn't told anyone! Could she bluff her way out of this? Maybe. Just maybe.

She took a deep breath and forced a bravado she was far from feeling.

"What's to stop you? Not much, I guess. Except I told my father what you did to that man in the alley, and Papa knows where I am right now. He probably saw you come here, too. I imagine if anything happens to me, he'll know who did it."

The look in Miller's eyes told Angela she'd won, but she'd made an enemy for life out of one Mr. Abe Miller, wagon train scout and shooter of dogs. She grabbed up her bucket, filled it with water, and ran back to the relative safety of the wagons, her breath coming in frantic little gasps.

The enormity of what she'd just done began to sink in, and her knees nearly buckled. She'd helped an Apache! She'd tended his wound and talked with him like they were old friends. She'd even sided with him against a white man. This was entirely different from the incident at the fort.

Good heavens! She'd even threatened Miller, and she was ten times more afraid of him than of the Apache.

An hour later, Lucky Ward Hargrave called an end to the nooning. Men hitched up their teams and made ready to leave. When the wagon train moved out, one wagon stayed behind. A short time later, it, too, moved out, but it headed back to the east, back toward Camp Bowie in Apache Pass.

Neither Angela nor her father saw the lone horseman light out in their same direction shortly before they left. If they had known the man called Miller was riding to Camp Bowie to report the sighting of the Apache, they might have taken precautions. But for the time being, their biggest concern was Sarah. She was getting weaker.

Chapter Four

They camped that night among the rugged rocks of
Texas Canyon, still two days away from the fort and
the much-needed doctor. But the next morning when
Angela awoke, stiff and sore as usual from sleeping in
her cramped place near the front of the wagon, the
doctor was no longer needed.

There sat her brave father, hero of the Confederate
Army, with tears streaming down his face,
holding. . . .

"Papa?"

He didn't hear her.

"Papa? Papa! No! Oh, noooo! Motherrrr!"

They buried Sarah Jane Barnes in the rocky ground
amid huge boulders beside the trail. Joseph made a
wooden marker, burning her name and the date into it
with a piece of hot iron. He and Angela knelt beside
the grave and clung to each other in sorrow. Finally,
Joseph stood, ran his sleeve across his damp face, and
helped Angela to her feet.

"You go on back to the wagon, honey." He cleared
his throat before going on. "I'd like to be alone with
your mother for a bit, this one . . . last time." His
voice cracked over the words.

Angela stumbled back to the wagon, her arms and
legs like lead, her tears finally dry. The anguish was

too great for mere tears. She climbed onto the front seat of the wagon and watched her father kneel beside her mother's grave. She could see his shoulders shaking. His head was bowed.

A slight stirring of air brought the faint rustle of grass and a low murmur to her ears. He was talking to her mother, saying good-bye, but Angela couldn't make out the words. She was glad; she didn't want to hear such private thoughts as this final good-bye.

Angela was numb. This was surely no more than a bad dream. In the morning she'd wake up and everything would be fine. Her mother would be there, smiling at her. Her sweet, loving, gentle mother.

It was a nightmare. But it was devastatingly real. Her mother was dead. The quiet sob that came from her father told her how real it was. Angela couldn't imagine anything else on earth that could make her father cry.

Joseph's shoulders stiffened, and he stared past the marker toward the rocks. His hands balled up into tight fists at his sides. He spoke again.

But that wasn't her father's voice! Following his line of sight, at first Angela saw nothing. Then a gleam of light bounced off something shiny in the rocks. Someone was there! She couldn't see who it was, but obviously her father could. She strained for a better view, then saw the other person. Or at least part of him, a very small part. What she saw was a man's right hand, and it held a pistol pointed directly at her father! Brush and boulders hid the rest of the man.

The numbness she'd been experiencing still held her in its grip. What should she do? What *could* she do? With a start, she remembered the pistol her father kept in a leather pouch beneath the seat. Her hands shook violently as the numbness receded and terror took its place. Straining her ears to hear past the thundering of her own heart, she heard voices, harsh

38

and angry, but couldn't make out the words or identify the stranger in the rocks.

With fumbling fingers, she hurried to find the gun. She choked back a sob of panic. Where? Where! Oh, God, where was it? She felt her father's rain slicker; a splinter jabbed into her palm; she cursed; she prayed. There it was! She grasped the smooth leather and hauled it up into her lap, banging it beneath the seat once on the way.

Hurry hurry hurry! her mind screamed at her fingers. The drawstring was knotted. A whimper escaped her throat as she struggled with the stiff knot and tore off two fingernails before it finally came loose. The pistol was heavy and cold, a deadly thing, made for a deadly purpose. Her father always said a rifle was for killing food; a handgun was for killing men.

She'd never fired a rifle or a handgun in her life, but she'd seen it done. Shaking so badly she had to use both hands, she raised the pistol straight out in front of her and managed, by using both thumbs, to pull the hammer back. This was no time to be a coward. Her mother was dead, and someone was holding a gun on her father!

She didn't think about the promise she'd made to herself that last night in Memphis. She didn't think about being brave or heroic. She only knew she had to do what was necessary. This time she had no right to cower in some dark corner and hide until danger was past. Her father was unarmed and grief stricken. He was in no shape to defend himself. It was up to her.

Dear Lord, please let this thing be loaded!

The next instant was one she would remember for the rest of her life. It was over in a second, yet took a lifetime to happen. The man in the rocks pulled his trigger. Angela stared in horror as her father dropped to the ground, sprawling across her mother's grave. The shot echoed dully in her ears and seemed to reverberate right down into her very soul . . . a deafening thunder she would hear in her sleep for as long as she lived. Trying to deny what she'd seen, Angela squeezed her eyes shut and pulled the trigger. The gun barked and bucked in her hands.

She heard a sharp cry. Her eyes flew open. It was either pure accident or the hand of God, but she'd somehow managed to hit the only part of the man she could see — his gun hand.

Then he disappeared in a loud crashing of brush, followed a moment later by the sound of receding hoofbeats.

The gun dropped from her numb fingers. Frantic, she scrambled down from the wagon, her eyes never leaving the inert form of her father. When she reached his side, she rolled him over, calling his name. He didn't answer. Her mind knew he was dead, but her heart refused to accept it. Until she saw the small blue-black hole in the center of his forehead.

Stunned, she removed her hand from behind his head, and it came away covered in blood and something else. She didn't want to know what else. She began to scream. And she screamed, and she screamed, and she screamed. She screamed until she had no breath left with which to scream. Then she buried her face against her father's lifeless shoulder and sobbed for what seemed like forever.

She must have passed out or cried herself to sleep, for it was late in the day when she next looked around the little clearing. The mules still stood there, hitched to the wagon. The sun was past the noontime halfway mark. And her father lay dead across the fresh mound of her mother's grave.

Sweat ran down her face and body unnoticed. Blisters formed, burst, then formed and burst again, unnoticed. Dirt clung, skin burned. Muscles screamed with the unaccustomed effort of digging a grave. Angela's only thought was that she must dig this grave, and she must do it right. She must lay her father to rest beside her mother, so they could be together here in this small clearing beside the trail that lead nowhere but to death.

She worked to some secret rhythm, bending, shoveling, tossing, bending, shoveling, tossing. She'd never used a shovel before in her life. Sweat rolled down her face. Words came to her lips — long-forgotten words from some long-forgotten poet.

" 'To these whom death again did wed, this grave's the second marriage-bed. For though the hand of Fate . . .' " *What? The hand of Fate. . . . What did it do? The hand of Fate . . .* " 'For though the hand of Fate . . . could force 'twixt soul and body a divorce, it could not sever man and wife, because they both lived but one life.' "

Somehow, eventually, it was done. Her parents were together now, in the ground, in their "second marriage-bed," in heaven, or wherever people went when they left this earth. At least they had each other.

Angela now had no one. She was alone. Totally alone in the middle of nowhere.

Slowly, in a soft, quavering voice, she began to sing.

"A-ma-zing grace, how sweet the sound
    that saved a wretch like me."

The skin on the back of her neck prickled.

"I on-ce was lost, but now am found . . ."

Someone was watching her! She could feel it in every nerve, every pore of her body. Her muscles tensed. Her throat constricted, but she managed to choke out,

"Was blind, bu-ut now I see."

The feeling of being watched grew stronger. She even imagined she heard breathing. The empty gun lay on the wagon seat yards away. The shovel, too, was out of reach. She'd left it leaning against a boulder beyond the graves. Not knowing what else to do, she kept on singing.

" 'Twas grace tha-at taught my heart to fear,
    and grace my fears re-lieved;
How precious did that grace a-ppear
    the hour I first be-lieved!"

Was it him? The man who'd killed her father? The one she'd shot? Had he come back to kill her, too?

"Thro' ma-ny dan-gers, toils and snares,
    I have al-ready come;
'Tis grace hath bro't me safe thus far,
    and grace wi-ill lead me home."

Doggedly, as if her life depended on it, as if the very words could keep her safe, she kept on singing:

"The Lord hath pro-mised good to me,
    His word my-y hope se-cure,
He wi-ill my shield and por-tion be,
    as long as life en-dures."

Surely God wouldn't allow her to be murdered while she sang her mother's favorite hymn!

"When we've been there ten thou-sand years,
    bright shi-ning as the sun . . ."

Oh, Lord, oh, Lord. This was the last verse she knew! What then? What then?

"We've no-o less days . . ."

The song should comfort her, make her strong. But it didn't.

"To si-ing God's praise . . ."

She ended on a sob,

"Than when we-e first be-gun."

With trembling fingers, she dabbed at her moist eyes, then squared her shoulders. She would turn, and he would be there, her father's murderer. And he would kill her.

A strange calm settled over her. She noticed for the

42

first time what a beautiful day it was. The sky was a deep, clear blue; the air was fresh and clean. From a nearby bush, a blue jay scolded, sending two small sparrows fluttering away.

Slowly, with the anxious twittering of the sparrows still in her ears, Angela turned to face her father's murderer.

For less than an instant, relief surged through her veins. It wasn't him!

Then she gasped as her dazed mind leaped to life, warning her she was in even greater danger than she'd imagined.

Indians!

Directly before her unbelieving eyes, three savage-looking Apaches swayed drunkenly on shaggy horses. Angela knew instinctively that these Apaches were nothing like the one she'd met yesterday. They were dressed the same, breechcloth and moccasins, and they had the same coloring, some of the same facial features. But Chee had only wanted help. These men wanted something more. Much, much more.

For a long moment nobody moved. Angela stood frozen in shock, unable to even breathe. Then, as if on cue, all three Apaches kicked their horses forward and started circling her, yelling wild cries that sent shivers of dread down her spine. A nearly empty whiskey bottle sailed from one pair of hard, brown hands to another as the riders circled closer. Every time she tried to dodge away, a horse was there to nudge her back into the center of flashing hooves and leering faces. She whirled repeatedly, gasping for breath, looking for a way out as the encircling savages drew closer and closer. Dizziness made her stumble.

Suddenly a pair of hard, cruel hands grabbed her from behind and slung her facedown over a horse, in front of the rider with the thin, smirking lips. The breath left her lungs upon impact. Someone tied her

43

hands and feet tightly, cutting off her circulation. She parted her lips to scream, but a dark hand shoved a dirty rag into her mouth.

The horse turned. Angela screamed behind the gag. Draped helplessly across the animal's back, she swayed and bobbed with every flex of its muscles, fearing more than anything that she'd slip to the ground and be trampled by those fierce, sharp hooves.

When the horse stilled, Angela raised her head and watched in horror as the other two savages unhitched the mules and set fire to the wagon. Their drunken cries of victory curdled her blood.

In minutes they were pounding away through the rocks, mules in tow. Angela's heart pounded in rhythm to the drumming of the hooves. Her ribs and belly slammed into the horse's back again and again. Twigs and limbs slapped her legs and head as the beast crashed headlong into the heavy brush toward the east.

God in heaven, she begged. *Let me die quickly.* Then something large and solid struck her head. A deep, welcoming blackness engulfed her. She thanked God for answering her prayer so swiftly.

When Angela came to it was dark, and she was lying on the ground. She lay there a moment and tried to figure out where she was. She tried to move, and couldn't. She tried to swallow, and couldn't. She tried to remember, and couldn't.

Then it all came flooding back. Her mother, her father, the gunman. The Apaches! *Oh, God.* She wasn't dead after all. She assumed her hands and feet were still tied, but she couldn't feel them at all. The gag in her mouth was still there, and she now understood why it was called a gag as her throat convulsed in a futile attempt to dislodge the strangling cloth.

Her captors removed her gag and untied her long enough for her to drink and relieve herself. For the latter, they gave her no privacy. She thought she might die of embarrassment, except she was sure her fear would kill her first. She was able to take one last gulp of water before they tied her again and stuffed the gag back into her mouth.

She hurt so bad she didn't think she could stand it. Her head throbbed with every beat of her pulse. Her arms and shoulders screamed with pain because her hands were tied behind her back. Her legs had buckled beneath her when she first stood. Now they were tied again at the ankles. She knew her feet were still there, but only because she could see them. With every breath she took, her stomach and chest hurt from pounding against the bony, unyielding back of that sweaty, smelly horse.

She was spared that indignity the next morning, but the savages had a new torture for her. The thin-lipped one smirked as he untied her feet then slipped a rawhide noose over her neck and forced her to run behind his horse. Angela concentrated on putting one foot in front of the other, but it was a long time before the numbness left and she could feel the ground beneath her again.

Then she wished fervently for the numbness to return, for her thin-soled slippers were not made for the terrain they crossed. Over rocks and gravel, through cactus and sage, sharp ravines and dry creek beds, she plodded. Many times she stumbled and fell. But the unrelenting pull of her leash forced her to scramble painfully to her feet time after time. It was move or be dragged to death.

She wanted to die; she knew that. But somehow, she could not simply lie there and let herself be cut to ribbons by the sharp rocks and cactus. So she kept moving. And moving. And moving. The Apaches didn't

45

stop for a nooning, like the wagon train had done. They just kept right on.

Her skin burned beneath the savage rays of the Arizona sun. Her eyes burned from the bright glare. Her lungs burned from inhaling air that felt like it came straight from a blast furnace . . . or hell. But her mind did not burn—it was numb.

Angela remembered the fear that had engulfed her when she'd first seen the three warriors, but she didn't really feel it any more. It was still there, she was certain, but she was too tired and in too much pain to concentrate on fear. She didn't have the strength to spend on it.

Finally, at dusk, they stopped. Angela might have been able to walk farther, since putting one foot in front of the other was the only thing that kept her from falling flat on her face. But when they stopped, she stopped. Her eyes closed, and she was asleep before she hit the ground.

Sometime during the night she was awakened by rough hands grabbing at her. She moaned and tried to turn away, unwilling to leave the sanctuary of sleep. But the hands wouldn't leave her alone. Sharp voices uttered deep, guttural tones. Whiskey fumes pinched her nostrils just before something was thrown over her face. A cool breeze teased her legs.

But if there was a cool breeze, why couldn't she breathe? She struggled from the dark stillness of her sleep and opened her eyes to more darkness. She came to her senses when she realized it was her skirt that covered her face, and the men—no they were animals!—were laughing.

She felt something cold and sharp running down first one thigh, then the other; then her drawers were yanked from her body, leaving her totally exposed from the waist down. With her hands still tied behind her back and her skirt over her face, Angela found the

46

strength to be afraid. She began to kick and scream.

The men laughed harder. Greedy, calloused fingers crept up her thigh. Hands grabbed at her ankles, her waist. She kicked out blindly, connecting with something firm, like a man's chest. But the hands kept coming, grabbing, pulling, pinching.

A shot rang out and echoed through the darkness. It must have struck nearby, for sharp sand sprayed across Angela's bare legs. The Apaches released her. It was dead quiet. Then the stillness was broken by the slow plodding of a tired horse approaching.

Angry Apache voices broke out all around her. After a moment, her skirt was jerked back down over her bareness, and Angela stared at the black silhouette of a fourth Apache squatted next to her. Moonlight revealed his face. It was Chee.

Chapter Five

Angela leaned her head wearily against the rough bark of an oak, the only tree in this little hole in the rocks where they'd brought her. The four Apaches — her three captors and Chee — had been arguing since they made camp an hour ago. She knew she must be the subject of the disagreement. She wished desperately she understood their language.

She'd never been so glad to see anyone in her life as she'd been last night when Chee showed up. He had untied her and made her promise not to scream or run, then gave her food and water. She'd been allowed to ride on the back of his horse today, too, instead of being forced to run and walk again. It was a good thing, for she doubted her ability to walk another step, much less run. Of course, after a day of straddling the back of a horse, she was certain she'd never be able to move again, anyway.

She'd never actually ridden a horse before, but she'd been too frightened and too exhausted to notice the new experience. She'd wrapped her arms around Chee's waist and concentrated on hanging on. Maybe she should have tried walking instead. No one needed to worry that she might scream or run; she wasn't capable of either.

There'd been a few minutes last night, after Chee's arrival, when the fear relaxed its hold on her, but the respite had been brief. Chee's arrival did not guarantee her safety, she knew. After all, what did she really know about him? He was an Apache. Her captors were his friends.

While the four of them argued, she succumbed to exhaustion and fell asleep, in spite of her fear.

Chee felt like howling in frustration. "Fools!" he spat. "You know Cochise has forbidden all raiding for over a year now. What were you thinking to capture a white girl? What do you think he'll do when he finds out?"

"He won't find out, unless you run to him and announce it," Tahnito said heatedly through his thin lips.

"We're not taking her into camp. We're not that stupid," said Mahco.

"We're going to keep her here for our use. No one needs to know about her." Caje, the youngest of the trio, looked to the other two for confirmation.

"Here? An hour away from camp? And you expect no one to find out? I was right!" Chee cried, throwing his hands up in disgust. "You are all fools! You know Cochise wants peace. That's why there's been no raiding. You say you found her only a few hours from Apache Pass. What do you think *Los Goddammies* at the white man's fort will do about it? They'll know who took her. Our band is the only one in the area. Nobody else raids around here. You'll bring the bluecoats down on us and ruin Cochise's chances for peace. He will kill you."

The three younger warriors were silent, uneasy, beginning to realize the trouble they may have created. Chee thought rapidly. There was only one way out of this mess, but as far as he could see, it was perfect. They couldn't return Angela to her own people because her family was dead. She had nowhere to go, no one to provide for her. But suppose. . . .

"Listen to me, my friends. I have thought of a way out of this trouble for all of us, including the girl. You may not like the idea at first, but if you think about it, you will see it will be a good thing."

Tahnito narrowed his eyes, wondering what Chee was up to. "What are you suggesting?" Tahnito was the leader of the other two, and Chee was the friend of a man Tahnito hated. He was not eager to pacify Chee in the least, but he now realized it had been foolish to take the girl. The simplest thing to do would be to use her, kill her, and hide the body. Then no one would know. But Chee would never go along with that, because the girl had helped him once.

"We give her to Bear Killer," Chee stated.

Tahnito clenched his fists in anger. "No!"

"Hear me out before you say no. You know he'll be here any day now, and you know what happens when he comes. You've all seen the way your sisters and the other girls look at him when he walks through camp. Don't try to deny it. You know they all want him."

Mahco started to interrupt, but Tahnito motioned him to silence and nodded for Chee to continue.

"If Bear Killer had a wife—a white wife—they'd stop following him around quick enough. None of our girls would want to be second wife to a white woman, not even for Bear Killer. And besides, Bear Killer will only take one wife—you know that. So we get the girl off our hands, and at the same time, your sisters and sweethearts will stop following Bear Killer around. Think about it."

Tahnito frowned. It was true what Chee said about the girls. Bear Killer's blond hair and Anglo features attracted too much attention. The men would like to see him married, but not, Tahnito thought, to one of their own. Tahnito's own sister, Alope, was always talking about Bear Killer this and Bear Killer that. It was enough to drive a man crazy. He and his sister had had more than one argument about that white man. Tahnito would never allow her to marry the one she wanted.

"How will this keep Cochise from finding out how she got here?" Caje wanted to know.

"How will he know?" Chee asked. "I'll ride out and meet Bear Killer and get him to agree to come for her. She'll ride into camp with him, and I think in exchange for her life, she will keep quiet. We can leave that up to Bear Killer."

"What makes you think Bear Killer will want her? Why should he go along with any of this?" Tahnito asked.

"You know how he is about white captives," Chee said with a shrug. "Remember what happened to Woman of Magic when our warriors took her? He'll take the girl to save her from that. Besides, by white man's standards, she's very beautiful when she's cleaned up."

Tahnito thought for a moment. The idea had merit, but he still had reservations. "Maybe we will think about it." His two cohorts nodded their agreement. "Maybe he can have her when we're finished with her."

"No!" Chee was adamant. "If he finds out about it, you know he'll go straight to Cochise. And I will go with him."

The argument continued. Tahnito wanted very much to have this white girl to himself for a while, even if it meant sharing her with Caje and Mahco. He'd been a long time without a woman. Apache laws and customs forbade fraternizing between single men and women. With no raiding for the past year, therefore no captives, a man's opportunities were limited.

Unless there happened to be a cooperative widow in the band. If she was agreeable, it was considered all right to slip off into the bushes with her, and no one thought badly of either one of them. But with over a year of peace behind them, there were no new widows these days. No young ones, that is.

Still, a woman, especially a white woman, was not worth his chief's wrath. Tahnito agreed to let Chee talk to Bear Killer. Mahco and Caje reluctantly decided to go along. It was, Tahnito decided, the only thing to do, but it rankled him to be party to anything that might bring pleasure to Bear Killer.

A hand on her shoulder brought Angela awake with a scream in her throat. She relaxed slightly when she recognized Chee.

"I will be away for a day or two, maybe longer," he said. "You will be safe while I'm gone."

Panic rushed through her veins. He was abandoning her! "Don't leave me here with them, Chee," she begged. "Take me with you."

"Angela, I can't. Trust me, will you? You helped me once; now I'm trying to help you."

"Then take me with you!"

"I can't," he repeated. "Until and unless they decide to take you into camp, you belong to them. But I have a plan, and they've agreed to it. Now I must set it in motion."

Hope rose in her heart. "A plan? To get me away from here?"

"If it works, yes. But much will depend on you."

"Anything," she cried. "I'll do anything to get away from them."

52

"Will you, Angela? Will you marry a friend of mine in exchange for your life and freedom?"

Angela quailed. The hope in her heart withered. Marry an Apache? Live with these savages for the rest of her life? Or at least until she could escape. *Dear God!* She looked over at her three captors, all eyeing her carefully. She knew what they had in mind. It was impossible to misinterpret that searing look in those hot, black eyes. A fierce shudder ripped through her. Could she accept one of them to avoid having to submit to them all? Could she not?

"One of them?" she asked, her lips trembling, her mouth dry.

"No. The man I have in mind is my friend, Bear Killer. He is a good man, Angela, and he's your only choice. Do you agree?"

She trembled at the sound of his friend's name. To have a name like that, a man must be vicious and savage. She swallowed heavily. "What you're saying is . . . it's this Bear Killer or all of them. Is that it?"

"That's it, Angela. But don't worry. I think you'll like him, and I know he'll like you."

In spite of Chee's smile of reassurance, Angela felt her stomach shrivel into a tight knot of fear.

Chapter Six

Matt Colton pulled back on the pinto's reins and cocked his head to listen. Behind him, the twins halted their own mounts and looked alert. There it was again, the sharp whistle of a pintail duck.

For half a second Matt started to look to the sky in search of the bird, then stopped himself with a grimace of disgust. It was too early in the year for pintails to be this far south, and the only reason one would be here at all was to pass through on its way somewhere else. This was not duck country.

Since it wasn't a duck, and it wasn't a known Apache signal, that left only one other possibility. Chee.

It was a game they'd played with each other since boyhood — each one always trying to catch the other off guard. This time it had almost worked. If Chee had whistled five minutes ago, he'd have caught Matt daydreaming about a pair of brilliant green eyes in a small, oval face encircled by a pale golden braid. Green eyes wavering between fear and outrage when they looked at him, but gentling into compassionate softness when settling on his stepbrother and stepsister.

Actually, "step" was a term others used. As far as Matt and the rest of the family were concerned, there was no "step" to the relationship. Pace and

Serena were his brother and sister just the same as Spence and Jessica were, even though the twins were sired by someone other than Travis Colton, Matt, Spence, and Jessica's father. Even the law acknowledged Travis as the twins' legal father.

Travis Colton had married Daniella, Matt's stepmother, shortly before she gave birth to Pace and Serena. When the twins were barely a week old, Travis had adopted them, despite the fact that their sire was some unknown Apache rapist.

The entire family and all the Triple C employees stood firmly behind Matt's father and his decision to raise his wife's half-breed children as his own. Friends and acquaintances had swiftly learned to keep any and all criticism to themselves.

Talk still ran rampant, Matt knew, but not within earshot of a Colton. Only a few people with loose tongues and careless attitudes toward reaching old age had slipped up, and all had lived to regret the mistake.

But even close friends of the Coltons had never been loyal enough to actually take up for the twins against prejudiced attitudes. Most whites in the territory hated all Apaches, the Chiricahua in particular, with a vengeance. And most especially, they held the twins' adoptive grandfather, Cochise, in total abomination and no small amount of fear.

So who was that green-eyed beauty in blue gingham who'd been prepared to defend his own brother and sister from him the other day?

He'd wanted to see her again, but had been forced to spend the rest of that afternoon confirming head counts and signing contracts on the Triple C mustangs the Army was buying. By the time he was free of his duties for the day, it had been dark. He'd strayed over near the wagons, but hadn't caught another sight of the girl.

He told himself he only wanted to thank her. After all—it wasn't every day a white girl stuck up for half-breeds.

He hated taking the twins to the fort—for their sakes, not his. But they knew what could happen and had chosen to go anyway. That way they could get to their grandfather's stronghold for their twice-a-year visit a week or two sooner than if they'd had to wait for Matt to return home and get them.

What made it particularly bad this time was that they'd had to stay at the fort several days longer than just that one afternoon. They'd had to wait for the Army paymaster to show up before receiving payment for the herd. Matt had sent the money back with the ranch hands, then finally headed out with the twins. Chee had probably expected him several days ago.

Matt leaned an elbow on his saddle horn and shifted his weight, the creak of leather so loud it nearly echoed off the surrounding rocks. Nothing moved. Not the wind, not a bird, not even a lizard. A moment later Chee appeared, soundlessly, as if by magic, from behind a boulder several yards down the trail. He nudged his horse into a walk until he was beside Matt.

"Howdy, pardner," Chee drawled.

Pace and Serena giggled. They'd known Chee all their lives, but no matter how often the fierce-looking warrior let loose with one of his white-man phrases, it always took them by surprise.

Shanta, who now scouted for the Army, and Chee, who rode with Cochise, had worked at the Triple C on and off for years right after the twins were born. Cochise had sent them to his adopted daughter, Daniella, whom the Apaches called Woman of Magic because of the white streak in her black hair. The Chiricahua chief wanted the two

56

young apprentice warriors to learn as much about the white man as they could, and share that knowledge with their people.

Cochise did not consider the whites and Mexicans at the Triple C his enemies, but they were the exception. All the other non-Apaches in the territory were trying to kill him and his people. Cochise did his best to return the favor.

He'd believed by learning more about his enemies his victory over them would come swift and sure. For ten years he'd waged a war in southeast Arizona that had brought white man's growth and development in the area to a virtual standstill.

But one of the things he'd learned from the whites, through Shanta and Chee, was that his cause and his people were doomed. His enemies were too many. No matter how many he killed, there were always more. Too many more.

Because of the things Shanta and Chee told him, Cochise had been thinking a great deal about peace lately. So much so that for the past year he'd persuaded his warriors to stop all raiding.

Chee had stayed with Cochise, and Shanta had joined the Army scouts in an attempt to determine, by keeping his eyes and ears open, if Cochise's dream of peace had any sort of chance.

Matt prayed for the dream to come true. If Cochise could maintain control of his warriors and keep the ban on raiding in effect, it just might.

Deep in thoughts of peace for the Chúk'ánéné, Matt didn't realize how close they'd come to Cochise's winter *rancheria* until Chee reined his horse to a halt. Coming back to the present, Matt eyed his friend carefully, wondering why Chee had stopped. At the look on Chee's face, Matt told the twins to ride in alone.

When Pace and Serena left the two men there

among the sage and rocks, Matt turned to Chee and said, "All right. What's up?"

"Why must something be up? Can one friend simply not wish to speak to another?"

Matt nodded in acknowledgment. "Of course. But that isn't what you want. What's happened?"

When Matt heard what Tahnito and the others had done and what he, himself, was expected to do, he swore viciously. "What in the hell were those fools thinking of?"

Matt absently fingered the scar on his cheek and felt the scars on the rest of his body tingle. He'd have to kill Tahnito some day, he knew that. He'd known it since The Day of the Bear, as he referred to it privately. Matt had never told anyone about the trap Tahnito had led him into that day. Only Tahnito knew. And Matt somehow sensed that because the plan had failed and Matt had lived, and because Matt hadn't told anyone what had happened, Tahnito hated him even more.

"Because they're all hotheads. You know that," Chee answered. "And you know what they'll do to the girl if you don't go along with them."

"Yeah, I know. What I'm wondering is, why me? Who brought my name into it?" Matt eyed his best friend, watching him shift uncomfortably on his handmade Apache saddle. "You? Goddamn, Chee, why me?"

"Why not you?" Chee asked defensively. "You need a wife anyway. Those three, and others, would love to see you married, especially to a white girl. That way all our unmarried girls, and some of the married ones, I'm sure, would stop following you around all the time."

"You exaggerate."

"Ha!"

Matt finally agreed to go with Chee, hoping he'd

58

be able to talk Tahnito and his friends into just letting the girl go. But it was only a small hope. He knew Tahnito too well.

Angela huddled at the base of the oak and tried to make herself as small and inconspicuous as possible, without much success. As the day wore on, her three captors began to stare at her more and more often, sending rivers of fear coursing through her.

She fought to hold her tears at bay. Chee hadn't even been gone a full day. How was she to survive until he returned? He said she'd be safe, but he must have known that as soon as he left there would be nothing to keep these three from taking advantage of his absence.

Why did you leave me here with them?

What if something happened to him? What if he didn't come back? What would happen to her?

Dear God, she knew what would happen, and she wanted to die. She wouldn't be able to defend herself if they came at her. They had tied her hands as soon as Chee left this morning.

And it was only a matter of time before they did come at her. She could see it in their eyes, feel it in her bones. A scream of pure terror threatened to rip loose from her throat.

Except for her captors and Chee, there wasn't a soul on earth who knew — or even cared — where she was. She was alone. Totally, completely, terrifyingly alone. There was no one to help her, no one to know or care what happened to her in this arid, blistering hole in the rocks.

From where she sat it looked like there was no way out of the tiny piece of ground surrounded by towering rock walls. Entrance to the hidden place was a narrow passage around the side of a boulder.

From time to time one of the Apaches would crawl to the top of the rocks and scout the area to make sure no one was near.

The young one with the crooked teeth—Caje, Chee called him—had just climbed back down from the rocks. Now he approached her. Angela stiffened. It was too soon! The sun was just going down! She was supposed to be safe until Chee got back!

Her braided coronet had long since fallen, to hang like a thick rope down the middle of her back. Caje took hold of the braid and said something to his two friends. Her heart began to pound in her ears. Her mouth went dry. Her muscles quivered with terror.

Tahnito and Mahco came forward. The three savages stared at her hair as if just now noticing she had any.

"No!" Angela screamed. She jerked free of Caje's hold and sprang to her feet, only to be caught and held by Mahco, the one with the broad, flat nose. Tahnito found the rag and stuffed it into her mouth. She struggled to get loose but was no match for their strength.

Their laughter terrified her as much as their obsession with her hair. Her heart threatened to pound its way right out of her chest, if it didn't stop beating altogether. She'd feared being raped and killed, but it only now occurred to her . . . *Indians take scalps*.

She screamed behind her gag just as Caje finished unbraiding her hair. She screamed again as all three men ran their hands through it, fanning it out, tugging on it, and laughing . . . always laughing. Angela went crazy. She kicked out at them and butted one in the stomach with her head. Her sudden actions won her an instant of freedom, but only an instant. When she whirled to run, her hair fanned out behind her. Tahnito caught his hand in it, yanking her back against his chest and nearly knocking the wind from her.

Suddenly a deep voice shouted, *"Bíni'!"* An arrow twanged into the tree just inches from Tahnito's head. He leaped back beside the tree and pulled Angela in front of him as a shield.

Angela looked up and saw it was Chee who'd shot the arrow. He was back! She sagged in Tahnito's arms and choked down a sob of relief while her vision blurred.

Chee shouted something that sounded like a demand. An angry demand.

Tahnito released her with a shove. She stumbled away, tripped on the hem of her dress, and fell. Gasping for breath, she watched her three captors confront Chee and another man. Her eyes widened. A white man!

Matt.

She blinked rapidly and tried to peer through the hair streaming across her flushed face. Surely she was imagining him, simply because she'd thought about him so much since that day at the fort. A white man wouldn't just ride into an Apache camp. And he wasn't trussed up like a captive.

Even as she denied his presence, he swung down from the back of his big pinto and stepped toward her captors. He was without a doubt the same man from the fort. The one who'd stood behind the half-breed twins and gazed at her with such soft brown eyes.

Those brown eyes had yet to look at her closely.

A heated argument broke out among the men. Angela was stunned to see the white man back the other three down, in their own language! Who was he? What was he doing here? Surely he could get her away from here; he seemed so . . . self-assured.

With a confidence bordering on arrogance, the

61

man called Matt turned his back on the Apaches and walked over to her. He knelt beside her and scowled while he untied her hands and removed the rag from her mouth. His touch was almost gentle when he held her face up and looked at her closely. His eyes widened with surprised recognition. He swore softly, then went and got his canteen.

Angela tried to gulp down the cool water.

"Easy, there. Not too much at once," he cautioned. "Just sip it."

When arguing with the Apaches, his voice had been cold and hard, but now, when he spoke to her, it was soft and gentle, the way he'd spoken to the twins. It created a tiny spark of warmth where only coldness and fear had been before. Could he save her?

"Who are you?" She handed the canteen back with shaking hands. "Can you help me? I need to escape. They're going to kill me, I know they are, and I'm so frightened! Help me, please!"

"Just take it easy," he said. "No one's going to hurt you now. I'm Matt Colton. What's your name?"

"A-Angela," she stammered. "Oh, please, you've got to help me! If these men don't kill me, then they're going to make me marry some horrible savage named Bear Killer. Please! Please help me!" she begged. She glanced up and realized Chee could hear every word she said. She blushed with shame at her choice of words to describe his friend.

Oddly enough, Chee didn't seem offended. He was laughing!

"Horrible savage?" Matt asked.

"I didn't mean—I-I mean. . . ."

Matt turned to Chee. "You didn't tell her?"

Chee shrugged. "I thought I'd let you do that."

Matt shook his head and turned back to Angela, a slight smile curving his lips. "Well, I guess I've been called horrible a time or two, but I've never really thought of myself as savage."

Angela's battered mind made no sense of his words. She simply stared at him, confused.

"I'm Bear Killer," Matt explained.

Her confusion gave way to stunned surprise. "You? You're Bear Killer? But I thought . . . I mean, you're not . . . those children called you . . . you said your name was . . . Matt." She stammered to a halt, confused again. Then she noticed the necklace around his throat. Bear claws! The import of his words dawned on her. *He's Bear Killer!* "Does that mean you can get me away from here?"

"In a way, yes." The smile in his eyes and on his lips faded. "But we have to do it their way."

"Their way? What do you mean? You wouldn't let them—"

"No!" Matt said. "They won't hurt you now, as long as we stick to their agreement."

"Their agreement?" Angela swallowed. "I-I don't understand."

"You said it yourself a minute ago. It's either them or me. I'm afraid those are your only choices."

She met his eyes squarely, remembering what Chee had told her. "You mean . . . we . . . you and I have to . . . get married?"

"It looks that way."

She turned her head until she was looking at him out the corner of her eye. "You'd do that, marry me? Why?"

Matt shrugged. "I need a wife." His eyes softened as he gazed at her. "Besides, I owe you something for the way you took up for the twins, and right now it looks like I'm your only way out of this mess. If you agree, we'll ride into camp tomorrow and the *diyini* will marry us."

"The what?"

"The *diyini*. The shaman. He's like a preacher, a doctor, and a soothsayer, all rolled into one. Some call him a medicine man."

Angela shifted uncomfortably on the hard ground. Her eyes flashed to the bear claws around his neck. She shivered. "Are you trying to tell me you . . . live with the Apaches?"

"No. At least not all the time. I come here two or three times a year. But I am a member of this tribe; they adopted me when I was a kid. And I have a half-breed brother and sister, the twins, who come to visit their grandfather. They're here now, so we'll have to stay. We'll be here for a month or more."

"A-a month? With them?" Her gaze darted toward Tahnito and his friends. *I can't do this! I don't want this! I want my mother! Mother! Papa! Where are you? We should be in Tucson by now, at our new store. You shouldn't be buried in the ground and I shouldn't be here!*

"It'll be all right," Matt assured her. "They won't bother you."

It was amazing how just his voice could soothe her raw nerves. "What happens when we leave here?"

Matt glanced around. Angela followed his gaze and noticed Chee had moved away and was building a fire.

"Look, Angela, I know you're in a tight spot here. I'm your only way out." He lowered his voice. "We'll pretend to go along with them and get married. We'll have to act like it's real. As soon as we leave here, we can have the marriage annulled, and you can be on your way to wherever it is you were going. If you need help with money or anything, I'll take care of it."

"You'd do all this . . . just to help me? Why?"

"It's only partly for you," he said. "I've seen girls in your situation before, but I've only known of one

64

who lived through what those three have planned for you. I'd do just about anything to spare someone from that. But there's more to it. Have you ever heard of an Apache named Cochise?"

"Of course," she said, her body tensing with new apprehension. "They say he's terrorized the Southwest for years now, and killed hundreds of people. What does he have to do with this?"

"What you've heard about him is mostly true. But now he wants peace. He's the chief of this tribe, and none of his people have raided or caused any trouble in over a year. If he finds out what these three fools have done to you, there'll be trouble. It could split the tribe and start the war all over again." His fists clenched at his sides. His voice hardened. "It's up to the two of us to see that doesn't happen."

The change in his voice frightened her. "What do you mean?" She licked her lips nervously and watched, fascinated, as his eyes followed her tongue, then darted back to her face.

"I mean you have to promise me you'll never tell anyone how you got here," he said fiercely. "We'll say we've been secretly engaged and you were coming to meet me. Chee found you and brought you here so we could be married. Like I said, I'll get you out of this mess, but you have to swear to anyone who asks that you came here on your own. Do you agree?"

"But what about them?" Angela asked, nodding to the three who had captured her.

"Don't worry about them," Matt said. "My guess is, by now they wish they'd never thought of taking you in the first place. They know what Cochise would say about it. They won't talk, and if by some chance they do, you can leave them to me. What do you say? Will you marry me, and can you make it look real to everyone?"

She stared at him a long moment thinking, *This*

isn't happening. I'll wake up soon and be back in the wagon with Mother and Papa. But as she clasped her hands together over her dusty, blue gingham skirt, a dozen raw blisters made their presence known. Blisters formed while digging — She swallowed and forced the thought away. "I . . . guess I really don't have much choice, do I?"

"No, you don't," Matt said coldly.

Good heavens! She'd just insulted the only man who could possibly help her. "I didn't mean that like it sounded, honestly!" she cried. "I'm very grateful for what you're doing for me."

With a short nod, Matt rose and joined the other men. Angela watched the sure, confident way he walked, with his shoulders back, his head high. A thousand questions buzzed through her mind. Who was he? Where did he come from? If she understood him correctly, all she had to do was pretend to be his wife for a month. It was too easy.

She had tried to prepare herself mentally to accept an Apache named Bear Killer. The reality of Matt Colton was a little hard to comprehend. He was every girl's dream of a young, handsome suitor, and he was going to be her husband. Was he real?

Angela was too exhausted to think anymore. She leaned her head back against the rock wall and fell asleep. Sometime later she roused briefly to find herself in Matt's arms. He carried her near the fire and laid her down on what must have been his bedroll, covering her with a blanket. She dozed again. In her sleep, she imagined she was a child once more, and her father had come to say good night and tuck her in. She smiled.

Chapter Seven

Although they were already in the Dragoon Mountains and Cochise's *rancheria* was only a mile away, as the crow flies, from where they'd camped, it still took Matt, Angela and Chee over two hours the next morning to get there because of the winding, backtracking trail through rocks and canyons. Tahnito and the others took a different route and wouldn't arrive until later in the day.

Angela spent the entire trip torn in a dozen different directions. She was somehow confident that once they arrived, Matt would keep her safe, yet she couldn't shake her fear. She tried to concentrate as he told her about the stronghold and what she'd see there, what would be expected of her.

But most of her energy was spent being terrified she would tumble to the ground with every step Matt's pinto took. Matt had lifted her sideways onto the saddle and told her to hook her right knee over the horn. He'd then mounted behind her and reached around her with both hands to grasp the reins.

What was she supposed to hang on to?

With the horse's first step, she swayed dangerously and gripped the front edge of the saddle. Matt's arms brushed against hers, and even through the soft cotton of his shirt and her dress, her skin tingled. When the horse scrambled up an incline, Angela fell back against Matt's chest. A moment later, they plunged down the bank of a steep wash, and Matt wrapped an arm around her waist to keep her from sliding off.

Once more on level ground, he settled her against his chest and kept his arm around her waist, talking all the time about life in the Apache camp. He was so casual about it, Angela felt certain he had no idea how closely he held her, but surely, any minute now he'd hear her heart pounding and feel her skin burning where he touched her.

Matt's thoughts weren't too far from hers, but "casual" was the farthest thing from his mind. His easy, gentle touch was brought about only by force of will. Not that he didn't want to hold her. On the contrary! She felt right, somehow, resting there in his arms. She was so delicate, so lovely, he had to struggle to keep his eyes on the trail. He left the task of keeping an eye out for trouble to Chee while he concentrated on his bride-to-be.

Strange to think in a matter of hours he'd be married to this girl. Lately he'd been thinking about finding a wife, but he hadn't expected to end up marrying a stranger on a temporary basis. What was she like, this girl? He already knew she was kind and beautiful, and not afraid to help those in need. And she was strong, too. Stronger than even she knew, to have withstood Tahnito's abduction so well.

He kept up a steady stream of talk to take her mind off all she'd been through.

Matt's deep voice helped soothe Angela's frazzled nerves. Feeling more secure with his arm around her, she finally relaxed somewhat.

When they rode into the *rancheria,* Matt shifted

his weight, straightened his back and raised his head. Angela tensed. He carried her before him like some conquering hero returning with his prize of war.

Matt had tried to describe the camp to her, to prepare her, but it was so far removed from anything she knew that she stared, wide-eyed, at everything and everyone.

And everyone stared back. Matt was nothing new to these people, but that he should ride in with a white girl on his lap was apparently something else again. Mouths gaped, and excited voices spread the news.

The men were dressed as she'd expected—barely at all—in breechcloth and tall moccasins. Some wore shirts, most did not, and a few wore hats. White men's hats. Slouch hats, high hats, bowlers, and Stetsons, with a Mexican sombrero or two among them for good measure. Angela preferred not to think about how the Apaches had acquired those hats.

The women came as a total surprise to her. She wasn't sure what she'd expected, but with all the men strutting around half-naked, she had not expected the women to be wearing buckskin dresses or colorful blouses and long, cotton skirts.

The young girls all wore their hair just as did the men and boys—long and straight, hanging loosely down their backs. But most of the older women had their hair twisted up at the nape and held in place by some sort of hourglass-shaped piece of leather.

Next to these women Angela, with her ragged braid, dirty face and torn, smudged, blue gingham, felt like a street urchin. But there were too many new sights unnerving her to allow much room for worry over her appearance.

69

There were dozens of grass huts, which Matt called wickiups, arranged in small groups and spread out everywhere. Every place there was a clearing in the trees, there was a group of wickiups. The ground around them was hard-packed and bare, the grass having been beaten down and worn away by hundreds of feet over the years. Dogs and children ran everywhere, dark, copper-skinned children and mongrel dogs of every conceivable description.

Several men called out exuberant greetings to both Matt and Chee. A few of the women smiled shyly. Angela was eyed with a disconcerting mixture of curiosity and suspicion.

Several yards ahead, a middle-aged man and woman emerged from a wickiup. Chee waved farewell to Matt and Angela, rounded a bend, and was out of sight. Matt reigned in when he neared the older couple. He swung to the ground, then lifted Angela down and took her hand. She tried to return his reassuring smile, and succeeded to a small degree.

These would be his adoptive parents, Angela thought. Matt had told her about them. He spoke to them, and she knew what he was saying even though she couldn't understand the language. If Angela hadn't been so run through with horror at losing her parents, terror at being captured, and bewilderment that she was soon to marry a total stranger, she might have smiled at the comical expressions the surprised couple wore. Matt tugged on her hand and pulled her forward.

"Angela, this is *shimá*—my mother—Huera, and *shitaa*, Hal-Say. They welcome you."

Angela smiled shyly at the couple. Huera stepped forward and embraced her lightly. Hal-Say and

Matt nodded their approval. It could have been a bad thing if Matt's adoptive mother was not willing to accept his wife.

"Come on," Matt said, tugging on Angela's hand again. "Let's go find the old man."

"The old man?"

"Dee-O-Det, the shaman."

Huera called after them with an anxious tone in her voice. Matt threw a reply over his shoulder without breaking his long-legged stride. Angela had to practically run to keep up with him.

Near the center of the compound they stopped at a wickiup whose door faced east. In fact, it appeared all the doors faced east. But this wickiup had a ring of stones surrounding it, whereas the others didn't.

Matt called out something toward the wickiup, then turned to Angela. "These are sacred stones," he explained. "No one is allowed to cross them to Dee-O-Det's wickiup without his permission."

A moment later an old, gray-headed man stepped through the door. His face was a collection of wrinkles and folds. When he stood still, Angela would have sworn he was the oldest living thing on earth. Except he stood straight and tall, not all stooped over like so many old people. Then he came toward them, and Angela blinked in surprise. His step was lively, his bearing proud, and his eyes sharp.

"Matt!" A high-pitched voice called out breathlessly from behind them before the old man could speak.

Angela watched, astonished, as the beautiful, young half-breed girl from the fort ran toward them, dodging baskets and fire pits, people and dogs. At the fort, she'd been shy and quiet . . . wary even. Now she was sparkling, alive with excitement and curiosity.

Matt greeted her with an indulgent look. "Hi, princess."

"Matt, is it true?" the girl demanded breathlessly. "Is she your wife? Did you get married without even telling anybody?"

"Hello, Serena," Matt said with exaggerated politeness. "I'm fine. Thank you for asking. And how are you? You remember Angela, don't you?"

"Matt!" the girl cried. "Of course I remember. She stood up for us when that old windbag—" She flashed a sheepish grin at Angela, who tried desperately to keep from laughing. "Uh, I mean . . . when that . . . lady . . . started screaming. Are you married?" she asked again, glancing back at Matt.

"Not yet. We seem to have been interrupted."

"Matt," the girl pleaded.

"All right," he relented. "Angela and I are getting married. Angela, this little busybody is my sister, Serena. And this," he added, indicating the young boy who'd quietly joined them, "is Pace, my brother."

He'd told her before that the twins were his brother and sister, but surely he and the twins had only one parent in common, for no part of Matt gave hint of Apache blood. Where he was blond, the twins' hair was black, except for the startling streak of white sprouting at Serena's temple. Matt's eyes were dark brown; theirs were bright pale blue. They were both beautiful children. Their Indian heritage showed in their skin and hair, but not their facial features or their eyes.

They were Matt's family. He had made it plain to her earlier that even they must not learn the truth about this marriage.

When she'd originally promised to keep silent

72

about her abduction, she hadn't realized the lies she would have to tell. But she had promised, so there was nothing to do but make the best of it. She held out her hand first to Serena, then Pace. "How do you do? I'm pleased to meet you."

"Do Mother and Dad know?" Serena asked.

Mother and Dad? Angela thought frantically. Did Serena mean Matt's real parents? Would Angela have to lie to them, too?

"I haven't told them yet," Matt answered easily. "But you know that doesn't mean anything."

"You mean Mother might have seen," Pace said.

"Maybe. Who knows?" Matt said. "If she doesn't already know, she will when we get home, so don't worry. I'm not trying to keep any secrets."

Mother might have seen what? Angela wondered.

Matt then introduced Angela to Dee-O-Det, the old shaman. The two men began speaking in Apache, and Serena gave Angela a running account of the discussion.

"Matt's asking Dee-O-Det to perform the wedding *gutál,* or ceremony, for you, because white people always have a ceremony. Dee-O-Det is reminding him that for the Chúk'ánéné—that's what this band of Chiricahua call themselves—Chúk'ánéné. Anyway, for them a wedding ceremony is rare. Usually, when two people get married, they don't have a ceremony, they just move into a wickiup together and say they're married."

"They do?" Angela asked, beginning to feel uneasy. Would she be expected to just live with Matt that way, and call it marriage? But then, she reminded herself, it really didn't matter, since they were only pretending anyway.

Dee-O-Det finally agreed to perform the ritualistic ceremony for Matt and Angela when Matt

73

pointed out that his stepmother, Woman of Magic, would expect it, since she and Travis, Matt's father, had the ceremony performed for them, and by Dee-O-Det himself, some ten years ago.

Huera approached the group at a fast walk. With her were two women about her age, and a younger woman. *"Shiye'!"* she called. "My son!"

Angela stood bewildered as Matt was swamped by the women, who all seemed to be arguing with him. Did they not want him to marry her? Would Matt give in to them and return her to her captors?

"Serena, what's going on?" she asked during a lull in the chaos. "Who are these women?"

"Huera is Matt's *shimá*, the woman who adopted him. The other two older ones, Nali Kay deya and Tesal Bestinay, are my grandfather's wives."

Wives? My goodness!

"And the younger one, Nod-ah-Sti, is Tesal Bestinay's daughter-in-law. They're telling Matt he can't marry you until you have your own wickiup, and until you've had a chance to rest and get cleaned up. Nod-ah-Sti says he's mean and terrible if he expects you to get married in a torn dress."

Angela looked down at herself in dismay. She must look a fright. It had been days since she'd bathed, combed her hair, or changed clothes. But she had no other clothes, only the blue gingham dress she was wearing.

Matt finally threw up his hands in surrender. Again Serena translated.

"He says all right, but he's not real happy about it. He says they can have you today and tomorrow, but that tomorrow night you get married. They're saying that's not enough time, but he won't change his mind."

Angela glanced uneasily from the women, to

74

Matt, to Serena. "What does he mean, they can have me?"

"They'll help you build your own wickiup and get you some more clothes, things like that," the girl told her.

"Me? Build a wickiup? Women don't build houses, even huts of grass like these. Matt can do that, can't he? I wouldn't have the faintest idea what to do."

"Matt can't do it, Angela," Serena explained. "An Apache man only hunts and fights, and while he's here, Matt is an Apache. Everything else is done by the women. Don't worry. We'll all help you," the young girl offered. "You're getting off lucky, really. There should be two wickiups—one here in the compound, where you'll live, and the other out in the woods somewhere for your honeymoon."

Angela swallowed uncomfortably. "Honeymoon?"

"An Apache marriage is supposed to start with a ten-day honeymoon, when you go off by yourselves, just the two of you. It's supposed to get things off to a good start, or something. But Matt says there won't be a honeymoon. Don't you want one, Angela?"

"N-no. It's not n-necessary."

In the next moment, the women hustled Angela away, with Serena along to translate. Angela glanced back at Matt. He just grinned and shrugged, as if to say, "What could I do?"

His grin was wonderful. For some silly, unknown reason, it made her heart beat faster and brought an exciting flutter to her stomach.

Serena pulled Angela into Huera's wickiup to show her what she would be building. It was a round, dome-shaped grass hut, roughly seven feet high in the center, and about eight feet across.

75

Around the bottom there were thin, wooden poles sunk into the ground. The tops of the poles were bent toward the center and tied together, leaving an opening for the smoke from the fire pit in the middle of the floor. Only it wasn't a real floor, just dried grass laid on top of the dirt. Bundles of dried grass covered the entire structure, but Angela couldn't figure out for the life of her just how those bundles were held in place. She had the uneasy feeling she was about to find out.

"I really have to build one of these?" she asked Serena.

"Sure," Serena said. "Every woman builds her own wickiup when she gets married. Don't worry, we'll help you. It'll be easy, you'll see."

Easy?

If Angela thought crossing the country in a covered wagon was hard, hot work, it was nothing compared to what she went through during that day and the next.

Huera chose a sight for the wickiup right next to her own, and they set to work.

To speed things along, Matt and Hal-Say went down to the stream to a grove of willows and cut the poles for the women. While they were gone, the women rounded up enough digging sticks so that everyone could work on the holes, to have them ready when the men came back with the poles.

As she knelt there in the dirt between Serena and Huera, Angela paused to look around. When she and Matt had ridden in this morning, the only thing she had hoped for was to be allowed to live, and then later, to leave. She had not expected to be welcomed by these "savage" strangers.

Of course, they were doing this for Matt. She understood that. But still, she felt their friendship

76

and drank it in. As they set to work sinking the poles in the ground, a strange, primitive feeling swept over Angela. She imagined herself a young native girl in some long-forgotten land, preparing a home for her mate, who would soon come striding up with the day's kill slung over his shoulder. She would cook the meat over the fire. Later, they would embrace each other on their bed of furs.

Bed of furs, indeed! she thought. *It's the sun, that's what it is, Angie Sue—too much sun can make you crazy.*

She pushed the strange thoughts away and went back to work. But they returned with a rush later. The sun was sinking low, and she and the women had already started tying on the bundles of dried buffalo grass, when Matt walked up. Draped over his shoulders was the carcass of a young deer.

. . . the day's kill slung over his shoulder.

Angela's breath caught in her throat. Her eyes drifted slowly down over his bare, tanned chest, along the thatch of blond curls that stretched from nipple to nipple, then narrowed until it passed his navel and disappeared beneath a rectangle of brown hide.

Good heavens! He was dressed like an Apache! The breechcloth ended at mid-thigh, leaving nothing but bare legs clear past his knees. Knee-high moccasins covered his calves and feet.

Her gaze traveled slowly back up his length. A tingling began in the pit of her stomach when she realized how narrow the breechcloth was. It left the sides of his hips bare. From the top of his moccasin up, the only thing that broke the expanse of bare skin along his side was the rawhide cord that held up the patch of hide covering his private parts and his buttocks. He was almost as dark as an Apache, from head to . . . knee. And that skinny little cord

77

was no wider than a shoelace.

Good heavens, he's magnificent! Beautiful! When his eyes met hers, it was as if he could read her thoughts, for a slow, lazy grin curved his lips. She felt the heat of her blush and turned quickly away. It was at least an hour before her hands stopped shaking.

Chapter Eight

Angela and Serena slept that night with Nod-ah-Sti, since Tahza, Nod-ah-Sti's husband, was off somewhere with his father, Cochise.

With the five women and Serena all working steadily the next day, the wickiup was finished by mid-afternoon. It was somewhat of a record for the tribe. It usually took a minimum of three days to construct one. But then, a woman didn't usually have so much help.

Huera brought Matt's belongings, and the other women contributed baskets and jugs and such to complete the furnishings. They showed her how to make a *téesk'e'*, a bed, consisting of nothing more than dry grass piled along one wall. Angela covered it with the blankets from Matt's bedroll.

During all the hours of work, Angela depended greatly on ten-year-old Serena to help her understand what was happening, what was being said, and what she was supposed to do. When Huera, Angela's future mother-in-law, declared the work finished, Angela noticed Serena had lost her excitement for the coming wedding.

"Serena, is anything wrong?"

The young girl heaved a heavy sigh and stared off into the trees. "No."

"Come on, Serena. You've been such a big help to me, I know I couldn't have done a thing without you. Have I done or said something to make you look so sad?"

Serena just shook her head and walked away. When Angela turned she saw Pace standing nearby with a large bundle draped over his shoulder. He watched his sister leave. There was a look of disgust on his face.

"Pace, do you know what's bothering her?" Angela asked. She hadn't seen much of the boy since she'd arrived, but maybe he could tell her something.

"I know," he said solemnly.

"Well?"

Pace studied Angela a moment, then looked back to Serena's retreating figure. "I told her this would happen. This is what was supposed to happen. But, well, pardon me, but sometimes girls are just plain dumb."

Angela blinked in surprise. "What are you talking about?"

"Rena thought when she grew up Matt would marry her. Now here you are, and he's gonna marry you. I told you it was dumb. A girl can't marry her brother, even if he is just her stepbrother."

"Stepbrother? But I thought . . . never mind. I understand. Thanks for telling me, Pace. Do you mind that I'm marrying your brother?"

Pace seemed to look right through her, an uncanny, faraway look in his pale blue eyes. "No, I think you're supposed to marry him." Before she could ask what he meant, he thrust his bundle at her. "Matt said to give you this. It's to sleep on."

She took the weight of it in her arms and found it surprisingly heavy. As soon as she had it, Pace disappeared.

Temporarily dismissing Serena's problem and Pace's odd words from her mind, Angela carried the bundle into her new wickiup and dropped it on the *téesk'e*.

If her friends in Memphis could see her now, she thought with a chuckle.

That primitive feeling washed over her again as she gazed around the tiny hut. Pride rushed through her veins—pride in her own accomplishments. She had taken pride in things before, but making a dress or arranging merchandise neatly on the shelves of her father's store was a far cry from building a home.

It wasn't much of a home, to be sure, and she hadn't done it alone, but she was still proud. Those primitive women of long ago would have understood her feelings, just as she knew the women who helped her build it understood.

She bent down and unrolled the blanket-wrapped bundle. No wonder it was so heavy! Heat washed over her as she ran her hands through the thick fur of the huge bearskin, which Pace had said was "to sleep on."

. . . *on their bed of furs.*

Vivid pictures flashed through her mind and made her blush. Two naked bodies entwined in a lovers' embrace, surrounded by dark fur. One body was small and feminine—hers. The other was the large, muscle-bound form of Matt Colton.

Angela gasped and forced the pictures away. Whatever had possessed her to think of such a thing? Good heavens! This was going to be a marriage of convenience, an arrangement, a . . . a business agreement. It wasn't going to be real!

A tiny, irritating little voice in the back of her mind whispered, *But with a man like Matt Colton, don't you wish it was?*

"No!"

Angela nearly ran from the wickiup. She left so fast the buckskin flap over the door gave an audible snap in her wake. Gradually her thoughts quieted and her mind calmed. She went in search of Serena, but couldn't find her. Instead, she found Nod-ah-Sti, who

81

took her to the women's bathing pool. The water had been warmed by a day in the sun. It soothed her skin and her mind.

Nod-ah-Sti showed Angela how to pound yucca root to use as shampoo. When Angela was scrubbed clean, Nod-ah-Sti wrapped her in blankets from head to toe so that no one could see any part of her.

They went to Nod-ah-Sti's wickiup, and the other women were there to help with the final preparations. Serena came in while the women were removing the tangles from Angela's waist-long hair, and Angela motioned for them to stop.

"Serena," she said softly. "I talked to Pace earlier, and he told me what was wrong." She knelt down in front of the girl. "Oh, Serena, I'm so sorry. I didn't know you wanted Matt for yourself."

Serena jerked. Her eyes darted around to the other women. She blushed beneath the deep tan of her face.

"It's all right," Angela said. "They can't understand, can they?" The girl seemed to relax a bit. "If I'd known how you felt, Serena, I wouldn't have agreed to marry Matt. I never thought we'd be hurting anyone this way. But I gave my word. You wouldn't want me to go back on my word, would you?"

Serena lowered her eyes. "No," she whispered. "I guess not. I guess I knew I was too little for him anyway. It just kinda, well, it kinda hurts a little, you know?"

"Yes, honey, I do know." Angela paused a moment, then asked, "How old are you?"

"Ten. Why?"

"Well, I'll tell you a secret. When I was ten, I had a problem just like yours, almost. I didn't have any brothers, but I had an uncle. He was the most wonderful man alive, next to my father, of course," she said with a sad smile. "I remember asking him one time if he would marry me when I got older."

"What did he say?" Serena asked with interest.

"He said he'd be honored to marry me." Angela's mouth twisted in a wry grin as she remembered the episode. "Then he patted me on the head and sent me back to the other children. A month later, he married somebody else."

"What did you do?" Serena's eyes were big now, their pale blueness shining with curiosity.

"Well, I remember crying a lot at first. But then, something happened that made me forget all about wanting to marry a man so much older than me."

"What was that?"

"I discovered boys. Boys my own age, that is."

"Boys?" Serena asked, a note of skepticism in her voice.

"Boys," Angela assured her, smiling. "Of course, they could never compare to my uncle, but I realized it wouldn't be fair of me to ask him to wait till I was old enough to get married, and if I really loved him, I'd want him to be happy. So I made friends with boys my age, and you know what? It was fun."

"What happened to your uncle? Was he happy with his new wife?"

The other women were growing restless. The sun was down now, and she knew they felt she should hurry; but Angela ignored them. Right now Serena was more important. "Yes, he was. She made him much happier, I'm sure, than I could have."

"How did she do that?"

Angela chose her words carefully. "Well, I think it helped that they were close to the same age and had a lot in common."

She cringed inwardly at what she was doing. She was trying to convince Serena that Matt would be happy with this marriage, when the whole thing was just a pretense, a lie. When it was all over and Angela left for wherever it was she would go, Serena would

83

hate her. But that was better than having the girl be hurt now by wanting something she'd never have.

"I suppose you're right," Serena admitted. "Anyway, please don't tell Matt," she begged. "He'd just think I was silly. Besides—he needs a wife now, and I'm still too little." She thought for a minute longer, then giggled.

"What's so funny?" Angela asked, her own lips curved in a smile. It looked like the crisis was over.

"If Matt was a real Apache, instead of just an adopted one, I could be his second wife when I got old enough."

"Would he do that?" Angela asked, alarmed. Not that it mattered to her. This marriage was only a pretense, after all.

"No. Not Matt," Serena said. "But anyway, it's okay that you're gonna marry him. That way you'll be my sister. I always wanted a big sister."

My goodness. How was it possible to become so attached to someone so quickly? Angela already knew she would miss this child when she and Matt went their separate ways. She hugged the girl to her chest, feeling a hard lump grow in her throat. "And I always wanted a younger one."

When Angela turned back to the other women, the frenzied preparations for the wedding resumed. The mock wedding, which everyone assumed was real. She wondered what kind of ceremony these people had, then remembered they usually had none at all.

Why would a perfectly normal, decidedly handsome man like Matt Colton choose to spend his time among these savages?

Angela immediately regretted the thought. So far, these people had been nothing but good and kind to her. The only thing she had to base her low opinion of Apaches on was rumors and newspapers back home. Her father had always told her to believe none of what she heard and only half of what she saw. In the case of the blood-thirsty, savage Apaches, it seemed her father's advice was justified, except for Tahnito and his friends.

It was dark by the time Angela was dressed in her borrowed clothes. And what clothes they were! How very generous of Nali-Kay-deya, mother of Cochise's youngest son, to loan out her own wedding dress! Angela had always dreamed her wedding gown would be soft, but instead of the satin or silk of her dreams, she wore buckskin. But it was soft. Soft as butter.

Dyed a soft, muted yellow, the fringed skirt and poncho-style top were decorated with rows of colorful, delicate beadwork. Hundreds of metal cones—bugles, Serena called them—each no longer than the first joint of her little finger, jingled and tinkled with each breath Angela took. A musical dress. A magical dress.

For an instant her eyes closed, and that primitive feeling washed over her again. Indeed, she did feel primitive, and even a little wicked, for she wore absolutely nothing beneath the dress, not even her own petticoat.

On her feet she wore an exquisitely beaded pair of moccasins. Serena called them *kébans*. She could see the circular, upright tabs on the toes as they poked out from beneath the bottom fringe of her skirt.

Her hair hung loose around her shoulders and down her back. The women had placed a soft doeskin headband, dyed the same muted yellow as the dress, around her forehead.

With a start, Angela realized it was time to go. She took a deep breath to steady her nerves. Why should she be nervous, anyway? It was all a charade, wasn't it? For show? To convince the tribe that Matt was married, and to prevent trouble not only between Cochise and his hotheaded warriors, but between the Apaches and the Army.

It was important, but it was still only for show. There was nothing for her to be nervous about. She was just going to go out there and marry a white man who ran around dressed like a half-naked Apache, that's all.

The mere thought of the last time she'd seen Matt, with that deer draped over his shoulders, was enough to turn her knees to jelly.

Dear Lord, please let him have some clothes on.

Chapter Nine

Matt approached the ceremonial log, outwardly calm, inwardly agitated. He wished the women would have stayed out of it. He'd wanted to get this over with as quickly and quietly as possible, but the events surrounding the wedding had slipped beyond his control. The entire *rancheria* was here for the ceremony. Meat had been roasting since yesterday, and a feast and celebration were planned for immediately afterward.

"This is ridiculous," he muttered under his breath.

"Come on, Bear Killer, she's a nice enough looking girl. Just relax and enjoy. Having a wife around all the time does have its compensations." Chee gave him a leering wink.

"It isn't like that, and you know it," Matt said. "It's not like it's for real. It's only temporary, just to get her out of this mess. It wasn't supposed to be such a big deal."

Natzili-Chee studied his white friend closely. So that was the plan, was it? A white man's temporary, uncomplicated marriage for convenience? *Oh, my friend, that won't do at all.* What good would all this careful maneuvering do if Bear Killer showed up next spring with no wife? The trouble would simply start all over again.

No, it just wouldn't do at all.

Dee-O-Det approached and the crowd quieted. When Angela stepped from the wickiup, all talking ceased. The flames in the central campfire crackled and popped, and off in the distance a coyote begged the moon to send him a mate, but there were no other sounds.

Matt's breath halted as he stared at the vision approaching him. His heart pounded a slow, steady accompaniment to the beat of drums and the bell-like jingling of a thousand tiny bugles that kept time with her footsteps.

She had no parents to walk beside her, so she walked alone. He thought he detected a slight trembling. Her borrowed clothes, so carefully prepared and donned, went unnoticed by the groom as Matt studied his bride.

She wasn't "a nice enough looking girl," as Chee said. She was beautiful! Her skin was a soft, golden tan, with a faint sprinkling of freckles across her nose and cheeks. Her face was slightly oval, with a daintily pointed chin and a pert, short nose. Her lips were full and lush. Her bright green eyes, almost emerald, were wide with apprehension.

Was she blushing? His eyes roamed over her face slowly, and then were drawn, spellbound, to her hair. He'd never seen such hair in his life. It hung loose and thick, clear down to the tops of her thighs. Firelight danced off it, turning it a golden bronze, but he detected pale, sun-bleached streaks here and there. More than anything in the world, he wanted to bury his face in those long, wavy tresses and lose himself there.

Dee-O-Det cleared his throat; Matt breathed again, then turned to face the shaman. He was suddenly glad he'd put on his best buckskins for the occasion. It wasn't a suit and tie, but he'd been told he looked good in the form-fitting buckskins. Angela's eyes roamed over him as if studying the close fit of the garments, the bulges and contours of muscles beneath, and his chest swelled a little.

He was twenty-one, financially well-off, and a beautiful girl was practically devouring him with her eyes. And she was about to belong to him!

His chest swelled a little more.

Angela, her heart pounding, approached slowly and stood at Matt's left, where Dee-O-Det pointed. Serena stood at her left elbow to translate. Angela glanced at the girl, and this time it was Serena who gave her assurance. Angela didn't know what she would have done without her.

The crowd, having begun to murmur, quieted again. Angela's knees trembled so hard she feared she might fall. The bugles on her dress tinkled with every tremor of her body. But Matt was there, this stranger she was about to marry. Or pretend to marry, she reminded herself. She felt heat and strength emanating from his body, and it comforted her.

The drums increased their rhythm, and so did her heart. She hadn't noticed the drums before. The shaman chanted to himself, then picked up a bone-handled silver knife and held it high.

The drums stopped, and with them, her heart. Nothing seemed real to her. A wedding was held in a church, or maybe a parlor. This wasn't a wedding. Not her wedding. It was some kind of strange, primitive dream. Everything was happening in slow motion. A loud buzzing filled her ears.

Dee-O-Det held the knife over his head, and Angela felt herself sway. Matt shifted his weight until his arm pressed against hers, steadying her. She wanted to look at him, to smile her thanks, but didn't. She couldn't take her eyes off that knife. Firelight danced along the shiny, silver blade, turning it gold, orange, red, then silver again.

The old man lowered the knife to the log that separated him from Matt and Angela, then picked up a long stick with pine needles on one end and waved it over their heads. A cool puff of breeze released the pleasant aroma of pine. Some kind of golden powder dusted down on their heads and shoulders.

Dee-O-Det knelt on his side of the log. Serena stepped forward and took Angela's right arm, holding it toward the shaman, wrist up. At the same time, Pace, who had been on Matt's right, took his brother's left arm, pushed up the sleeve, and held Matt's bared wrist next to Angela's.

When Dee-O-Det picked up the silver knife again, Angela followed it with her eyes, her heart thundering in her chest. He held her hand and quickly made a small incision on the inside of her wrist, then did the same to Matt.

Angela stared at their wrists, transfixed by the sight of the blood welling from both cuts.

Dee-O-Det turned Matt's arm so that the cuts were pressed to each other, then bound their wrists together with a wide strip of cloth.

Whose pulse was that pounding to the beat of the chant raised around them? His, or hers? Angela couldn't tell. Serena's voice came to her as if from a great distance.

"They're singing for you," the girl said. "They're singing:

"Now for you there is no weather;
For one is shelter to the other.
Now for you there is no fear;
For one is protection to the other."

The people kept chanting, and Dee-O-Det sprinkled Angela and Matt again with his golden dust. He raised his hands in the air, and silence reigned in the clearing. The snap and crackle of the central campfire echoed in the stillness.

Serena translated the shaman's words:

90

"You have two bodies, yet now there is but one blood, and you are one and the same person."

With a flourish, he whipped the binding from their wrists. *"Nzhú!"* he cried. "It is good!"

The drumbeat picked up again. People surged forward, shouting and laughing, pounding Matt and Angela on their backs. The couple was carried along by the crowd as nearly everyone moved toward the food. A few broke away to begin a dance.

Stiff pieces of hides, used as plates, were piled high with food and handed to the newlyweds. While Matt spoke with friends, Angela, with Serena at her side, picked a chunk of meat from her plate with her fingers. Her stomach was in such knots that food was the last thing she wanted, but people were watching. It would be rude to refuse her own wedding feast. With something close to panic, she bit off a piece of meat and chewed. It was tough, but surprisingly flavorful.

"You like it?" Serena asked.

Angela smiled and nodded. "It's delicious. What is it?"

Serena grinned. "It's m—"

"Ahem!"

Angela turned to Matt at his interruption that seemed deliberate. He scowled at Serena.

"Oh! It's . . . *jaandeezi.*" Serena grinned first at Angela, then at Matt.

"What's going on, you two?" Angela asked. "What is *jaandeezi?" And why do I get the feeling I'm better off not knowing?*

"It's—"

"Ahem!" Matt's scowl deepened.

Serena rolled her eyes. "It's how it's cooked," the girl said. "Special herbs and things. It's a favorite around here."

Angela would have asked for details, because the meat was truly delicious, but Serena dashed off into the crowd.

The party grew boisterous when someone began passing around the *tiswin*. Pace explained that it was homemade brew, and that it tasted terrible. The smell of it was enough to convince Angela not to try it.

Singing, dancing, and laughter whirled all around them for what seemed like hours. Matt and Angela had both eaten their fill, but had yet to speak to each other as husband and wife.

Matt noticed the slump to her shoulders and remembered what she'd been through during the past several days, not to mention putting up a wickiup in record time. "You're tired, aren't you?"

The sound of his voice jarred her from her daze, and she jumped. "What? Oh, no, I'm fine, really."

She was nervous. When she looked at him, he thought he detected a note of fear in her eyes. She was probably worried he wouldn't stick to his part of the bargain and leave her alone. He sighed heavily, thinking of the long, restless night to come; the *many* long, restless nights to come.

He hadn't thought, when he'd agreed to this plan, that she'd have such an effect on him. He hadn't anticipated this uncontrollable rush of blood through his veins every time he looked at her. He'd never been driven wild by the mere sight of a woman before, but he could feel it happening now, and it worried him. He had to keep away from her and leave her alone. He'd promised her an annulment, and a Colton never went back on his word, damn it.

"There you two are," Chee cried, a wide grin splitting his bronze face. "You've got to try this new drink I made." He held up a pitch-covered jug and two drinking gourds.

"Angela's tired, Chee. We're turning in."

"Just one drink," Chee insisted. He poured Matt and Angela each a gourdful of his brew, then raised the jug high in the air. "To your marriage, my friends! May it be long and fruitful!"

92

Matt and Angela refrained from looking at each other, but Matt wondered at Chee's choice of words.

Angela must have been thirsty, for she finished her drink in a hurry. Matt wasn't quite finished with his when he suddenly lowered the gourd and sniffed its contents. Something tickled his memory, then he knew.

He grabbed for Angela's gourd, but it was empty; she'd already drained it. "Damn you, Chee," he swore.

Chee grinned wickedly. "You might as well finish it all. She did."

Angela looked from one man to the other in confusion while Chee laughed and Matt growled and swore. Matt finished off his drink, then threw the gourd at Chee's head and swore again. Chee ducked out of the way, howling with laughter.

"Guneedligu 'águnasi, shik'is!" Chee called. "Have a good time, my brother!"

Matt scowled, grabbed Angela by the arm, and practically dragged her to their new wickiup. Someone had lit a small fire inside, and shadows danced along the grass walls.

"Matt, what's wrong? Let go! You're hurting me!" She winced when he tightened his grip on her arm. Real fear flashed across her face.

Matt swore again, then released her. "I'm sorry. I didn't mean to hurt you." He began pacing the narrow confines of the wickiup, ducking his head occasionally to accommodate the sloping walls and roof, which allowed only a few steps in any direction for someone of his height.

"What's happened, Matt?"

He didn't answer. How could he tell her?

"Is it—are you—is it because you had to marry me?"

He turned to her in surprise. "No, of course not. Look, I've got something to tell you, and you're not going to like it."

"It was Chee's drink, wasn't it?"

"What makes you say that?"

"I saw the way you looked at him, but I don't understand. I thought it was delicious, and it was nice of him to go to all that trouble for us."

Matt rubbed the back of his neck and rolled his head to ease an ache. "You won't think so when I tell you what was in it."

But he wasn't going to tell her what was in it. He knew that. He had to tell her what would happen, but if she knew she'd just drank the powdered remains of a certain species of European blister beetle — well, he didn't want to be around for her reaction to that bit of news. Especially if she ever found out that *jaandeezi* was the Chiricahua word for mule. And that the particular mule she'd just eaten was one of her own.

At the look of fright in her eyes, all he said was, "He's drugged us."

His calm, matter-of-fact statement plainly stunned her. "But why would he—? What kind of drug?" She looked up at him with wide eyes the color of summer leaves on the cottonwood outside his bedroom window. "Are we going to die?"

"No! Angela, no, it wasn't poison. We aren't going to die, I promise."

"Then, what was it? What will it do to us?"

"What will it do?" he repeated, staring at her from across the tiny fire. "I don't know quite how to say this, except to tell you that long before tomorrow morning, we won't have any grounds for an annulment."

Chapter Ten

It took a moment for his meaning to sink in. When it did, all Angela could do was blink and stare at him as a suffocating heat crept up her neck.

"Do you understand what I'm saying, Angela?"

"No!" She lied, and she knew he knew it. "No," she repeated. "You can't mean it!"

He did mean it; the look in his eyes told her so. But she refused to acknowledge it. "You're lying!" she cried. "I've seen the way you've been looking at me all night. You're just trying to trick me. You've been lying to me all along, haven't you?" Her panic grew with each ragged breath she took. "There wasn't anything in that drink at all. You just want me to think there was so I'll go along with you. Well, it won't work, Colton! You just stay away from me, you hear?"

As she backed away, he shook his head slowly, but remained where he was. "I'm not lying, Angela. But you'll find that out in a few minutes, when the drug starts working on you. In the meantime, I suggest you take off those borrowed clothes before something happens to them." He stepped around the fire. The flames seemed to leap from the ground and dance in his eyes.

"No," Angela begged. "Don't look at me like that." Was it his eyes that started that tingling sensation down deep inside her?

"Like how? Like you've been looking at me all night?"

"No!"

"Oh, yes." He advanced another step. "You haven't been able to keep your eyes off me, and you know it. Some of the looks you gave me out there were so hot I thought my buckskins were going up in flames." He took another step.

"You're crazy!" She backed away, embarrassed, confused. The tingling grew and intensified until it centered in that most secret part of her body. Heat flushed her skin.

"Am I?" He advanced.

"Yes! I never did any such thing." She raised her chin in the air and took another step back. When she did, she stumbled on the edge of the low, grass bed and waved her arms wildly, trying to keep her balance. Her borrowed dress jingled in agitation. When she was just about to go over backward, Matt grabbed her and pulled her to his chest. The sudden contact startled them both. Her heart fluttered; her skin felt prickly. The tingling in her loins turned to a warm, moist throbbing.

They stared at each other for long minutes, their eyes locked, their breaths mingling, their hearts pounding rapidly against each other. Angela looked away first and struggled to free herself from his embrace.

Matt tightened his arms around her and lowered his lips toward hers. She twisted her face away, and he brought a hand up to hold her head still. His hand was so big it held her head easily. His lips came nearer.

"No," she whispered.

"Ssh. It's all right. Don't be afraid."

She felt the deep vibration of his voice clear down to her toes. Her eyes locked on his lips, and she swallowed. She tried to deny the soft, languid feeling that poured through her like warm honey. One more time she whispered, "No."

Then his lips met hers, softly at first, and she melted in his arms. At the urging of his tongue, she opened her mouth to him. The warm honey in her blood turned to hot, molten lava as desire erupted within her for the first time.

Matt had never taken the drug before, but he knew people who had, so he knew what to expect. He knew that as soon as it took hold of him he'd become no better than an animal. He didn't want to do this to Angela. She was too young and innocent to be treated that way. But he also knew that in a matter of minutes it would be too late.

Her arms came around his waist, and she sank her fingers into his back like claws. She moaned, deep down in her throat, and Matt knew it was already too late. Her response was driving him crazy. His one comforting thought was that she, too, had taken the drug.

He tore his lips away and looked down into her flushed face. Her eyes were fevered, fueled by the same fire that roared through his veins. "Angela," he breathed.

She gazed at him with liquid eyes, her breathing ragged. "I feel so strange, Matt. What's happening to me?"

"It's all right." His hands trembled as he released her head and stroked her back beneath the heavy curtain of her hair. She moaned again and leaned into him. This time when he kissed her there was no trace of tenderness, only demand that she yield him everything.

And she did.

His kiss was savage, as savage as she had once thought it would be from a man called Bear Killer. But now there was no room in her mind for thought, except for the thought of more. She wanted more.

Even through their clothes she felt the hardness of his desire against her stomach. She ground herself into it, raising on tiptoe, trying to put the pressure where her body told her it belonged.

She had no idea how it happened, nor did she care, but she suddenly found herself standing naked before a naked Matt. All she could think was, *Yes . . . oh, yes! Let me touch his skin. So much skin.*

Then suddenly they were touching, body to body, mouth to mouth. They gasped together; they groaned together; they trembled together.

All Angela wanted was to be able to crawl inside his skin and become a part of him. But there was an emptiness in her, and she knew that somehow she wanted him to crawl inside her, too.

Their lips never parted as Matt swung her up into his arms and carried her to the bearskin. When he lowered her to the dark fur, there were no loving looks, no soft sighs or tender touches, as a man and woman might share on their wedding night. There was only fire and need.

Angela's eyes opened wide in surprise when she felt his hand run down her bare stomach and clutch frantically at the pale yellow curls at the juncture of her thighs. His mouth released hers, then lowered again and took in her gasp as his hand slid lower and firmly cupped her womanhood. Her hips thrust up of their own accord, and she pressed herself into his hand.

His fingers caressed her warm, moist depths, and she knew she was dying. But she didn't care. If this was what it was like to die, she would gladly go.

But first she wanted more.

A growl rumbled in Matt's throat when he felt how hot and wet and ready she was. He withdrew his hand, and she whimpered in protest. He pushed her legs apart and lowered himself between her soft thighs. The last remnants of control fled him when she moved her hips beneath him. With one brutal thrust, he plunged into her, feeling the delicate membrane of her maidenhood tear as he went, knowing he was hurting her, yet powerless to stop.

But the drug had its affect on Angela, too. The sharp, unexpected pain was gone in an instant, and it was nothing compared to the pleasure of having that aching void inside her filled at last. She clung to him desperately, the only solid thing in her spinning world. Her head felt light, and her blood pounded in her ears. Her hips thrust up to meet his, jerkily at first, then more smoothly and fiercely as she caught his rhythm and matched it.

Matt was surprised when she started to move against him so soon. He both cursed the drug and praised it, assuming correctly that it had lessened her pain. Then all thought but one fled his brain, that one being that he must find release from this tormenting pleasure.

On and on they thrust. Her legs found their way around his hips, and her arms, his chest. Her fingernails sinking into his back only added to his pleasure.

He raised up on his elbows to relieve her of some of his weight and to increase the pressure of his thrusts. He lost himself in her smooth, warm depths time and time again.

Angela protested the loss of his lips with a groan. She raised her head, trying to find some part of him to taste. When her mouth came in contact with his firm, rounded shoulder, she tried to devour it. She licked, she sucked, she even chewed on his flesh. She tasted the saltiness of his sweat, and felt drops of it fall from his face to mingle with her own.

The pressure built, and Angela didn't know what would happen; she only knew she felt ready to explode. Her breath came in ragged gasps.

Finally, minutes, hours, maybe years later, they both found what they'd been seeking, what Angela hadn't even known existed. Matt threw back his head and uttered a sharp cry, and Angela sank her teeth into his shoulder as wave after wave of relief slammed into them. The spasms went on for an eternity, and they shuddered together, gasped together, cried out together, as the intensity of their mutual climax held them in its grip.

The first thing Angela became aware of as she slid down from that peak of pleasure was the sound of harsh breathing, his and hers. She opened her eyes slowly and found Matt watching her intently. Neither spoke while they stared into each other's eyes. Then Matt lowered his lips to hers and kissed her with a fierceness that sent her heart pounding even before it had a chance to calm.

He tore his lips away and burned her with his gaze. "No annulment, Angela," he said. Then he kissed her once more, smothering any reply she might have made, had she been capable of thought.

Drug or no drug, Matt couldn't believe Angela's responsiveness. She was incredible, this stranger who was his wife. Before he could tell her how right this intimacy with her felt, before he could even catch his breath, it began again, that burning, driving need. That was the curse of the drug: it prolonged the pleasure, postponed relief; then, when release came, it hissed and flamed again, like a fire newly fed, building the hunger rapidly, denying the rest so sorely needed, denying any time to enjoy the release.

Matt had tasted of her mouth, but now he needed to taste her flesh. His lips and tongue traced a hot moist path down her throat to her breasts. When his tongue lapped at a dusky peak, the nipple was already hard. Angela writhed beneath him and cried out her pleasure. His lips closed over the taut bud, and he suckled gently at first, then harder as he felt her response.

Angela had no need to wait for that piercing instant of pleasure when he entered her, for he'd never left.

He was still buried deep within her, and her legs were still wrapped around his waist. Muscles she'd never used before tightened around him.

His mouth trailed fire in a path from one nipple to the other. He nipped at it, teasing it with his teeth; then he groaned out loud as she moved her hips in a circular motion beneath him.

Matt wanted to laugh hysterically with his pleasure. Angela wanted to cry from hers. But there was no room for his laughter or her tears when he began to move inside her, and she moved with him. The sweat hadn't yet dried on their bodies, and now it was pouring again.

The last tiny flame of the fire beneath the smoke hole died out, leaving nothing but a few embers in the darkness. But the fire on the bearskin rug flamed on. All night it blazed, being fed anew each time it flickered out. The man and woman it burned could do nothing to thwart it. No matter how exhausted they were, or how their muscles protested, they joined again and again, each time finding release, only to be tormented by the flames of desire before they could fully savor it.

There was no time for Angela to learn the finer points of making love. There was only the frenzied, clawing search for release, followed again and again by the building pressure, then brief, so brief, respite.

As the sky above the smoke hole turned from black to gray, Matt knew his final release had come. The drug had let him go. He collapsed beside Angela and pulled her into his arms, then fell asleep.

When he woke, the gray was turning pink, so he knew he hadn't slept long. His mind groped for a reason for his waking, and found it instantly. Angela's grip on his shoulders was bruising in its strength. Her face was pressed against his chest, and she squirmed against him as she straddled his thigh.

"Angel?"

101

She whimpered and pressed her face harder against him.

"Angel, look at me." When she didn't respond, he placed a hand on her chin and forced her face up. It was barely light, but he could see the fiery blush, the gathered tears, the exhaustion, the mingled look of frustration and embarrassment. The drug hadn't worn off for her yet.

She twisted her head away and sobbed, "Don't look at me!"

"Angela, it's all right." He held her tightly when she tried to push away. "Ssh. I'm sorry, I'm sorry. Don't cry, Angel, don't cry." He raised his thigh between her legs, increasing the pressure where she craved it.

"Yes!" she cried. "Oh, yes!" She rocked herself against him, harder and harder, until she cried out her climax and collapsed on top of him.

But before she could even catch her breath, it came at her again, that driving need. Matt saw it in her eyes. He wanted to be able to give her what she needed, but his body was spent beyond belief. His manhood lay limp and unresponsive to his will and her need.

He rolled her onto her back, and she clung to him, taking him with her. He slid his hand down between her thighs. When his fingers slipped inside, she winced.

"Am I hurting you, Angel?"

"It doesn't matter," she gasped.

He started to withdraw. "It does matter."

"No!" she cried. She grabbed his wrist with both hands and clenched her eyes shut. "Don't stop! Please!"

Matt relented and tried to be as gentle as he could while still giving her the pleasure she craved. But he knew how sore she must be. His flesh, too, was raw.

Again she cried out her release, and again, it was

102

only temporary. Matt swore beneath his breath. Chee had given her too much of that goddamn drug.

"God," she moaned. "It won't stop. Why won't it stop?"

"It will, Angel, soon, I promise." He slipped away from her and crawled to his saddlebags. He didn't have the strength to stand.

"Matt?"

"I'm right here, Angel."

"Oh, God, Matt," she sobbed. "Don't leave me like this. You can't leave me like this!"

"It's all right, Angel, I'm coming." He found a clean rag and wet it from the water jug, then returned to her side. "This is going to be cold, but it should help the soreness."

Angela was long past blushing. She was so ashamed of her actions she just wanted to die. When the cold, wet cloth touched her heated flesh, she sucked in her breath sharply. He pressed the cloth firmly against her. Her eyes flew open wide, and her climax came almost immediately.

Matt rained tender kisses across her face, ending at her lips. "Better?" he whispered.

Angela turned her head away and bit back a sob of mortification. He forced her face around.

"Look at me," he ordered. "Whatever has happened, whatever has been said or done, by either of us, is nothing to be ashamed of, Angela. It wasn't you, and it wasn't me. It was the drug. You have nothing to be embarrassed about. It was only the drug that made us act this way."

Angela lowered her eyes, unable to hold his steady gaze. No matter what he said, she was still ashamed of the way she'd behaved.

But it was over now. That burning need no longer consumed her. As Matt held her in his arms, she fell into exhausted sleep.

Chapter Eleven

Angela drifted awake slowly, aware of a tremendous heat on her legs. She opened her eyes and glanced down. It was the sun, shining through the smoke hole. But why were there so many legs? She was only supposed to have two, wasn't she? So where had those other two come from? And why were they so hairy?

She tilted her head back and found herself trapped by a pair of sleepy brown eyes that took her breath away.

"Good morning," Matt whispered hoarsely.

He ran a hand down her bare back. She shivered. Memory swamped over her. *Oh, God!* she thought. Fiery heat swept from the tips of her breasts to the roots of her hair as scene after scene of last night played across her mind. Shame lent her energy, and she thrust herself away from Matt and huddled on the edge of the bearskin in misery. She groaned as a thousand tiny needles of pain shot through her abused muscles.

"Angel?" Matt sat up behind her.

"Don't call me that!" she cried, tears clogging her throat.

"Why not?" he asked quietly.

She couldn't answer. She was remembering the things they'd done to each other, whispered to each other, throughout the long, dark night. My God, she'd even *begged* him! *More than once!*

If a girl could will herself to disappear or die, she would have done it right then and there. She could never face him again. *Never.*

"Angela, look at me." He tugged lightly on her shoulder, but she wouldn't turn. "Angela."

His fingers burned like a brand on her bare skin. She shook her head and buried her face in her hands.

"Look at me."

"I c-can't."

"Yes you can. Just turn around and look at me."

"I d-don't think I c-can ever look at you a-again. Oh, God, Matt, I'm s-so ash-ashamed. Wh-what must you think of me? I-I've never done anything like . . . that . . . before in my life!"

"Don't you think I know that?" Matt cupped both hands over her shoulders and buried his face in her glorious hair where the sun beat down and warmed it. "I'm not usually like that myself," he admitted, remembering the lessons a few years ago taught to him by the widow, several years older than himself, right here in this compound. She'd taught him to be a kind and considerate lover. Last night he'd been anything but that.

"It was the drug, Angela. It made us both do things we wouldn't normally do. I'll admit I wanted you last night, from the minute I saw you walking toward me with your hair shining all around you like some magical cloud. God, you were beautiful. You *are* beautiful. But I wanted you honestly. I wanted you to come to me willingly, even though I knew you wouldn't. But, Angela, I swear, I had no idea what Chee was planning. I would never have gone along with it."

"Why did he do it? I thought he was my friend, your friend. Why would he do such a thing?"

"I'm not sure, but I think he's decided we should stay together. He knew what we were planning. I guess it was his way of making sure we didn't get that annulment. And we won't be getting one now."

"What?" She looked at him then, a stunned expression on her face.

He gazed steadily into wide, green eyes. "You heard me. I even remember saying it last night. There'll be no annulment, Angela."

"But . . . you said . . . we agreed. . . ."

"Things have changed. You're my wife now, in every sense of the word, even though it didn't happen quite the way either of us would have planned it."

"But you promised!"

"I know what I promised, but that was before last night. Is it really such a terrible idea, being my wife?"

Angela turned her back to him again. What could she say? She'd never had any serious thought of marriage, only those vague dreams a young girl has about a handsome man coming along, rich, well-dressed, from a good family, to sweep her off her feet. Now here she was, apparently firmly bound to a stranger who spent his time with Apaches and went by the name of Bear Killer. Her mind shied at the thought. She studied the jagged circle of sunlight slowly creeping up the grass wall before her.

"Come on," Matt said, startling her. "I know a small pool up in the rocks where no one ever goes. Let's take a swim and cool off. It's hot in here."

She heaved a troubled sigh, and he asked, "What's wrong?"

What's wrong? What isn't wrong? she wondered, a sense of panic threatening to overwhelm her. Her mind was filled with so many bewildering thoughts, each fighting for supremacy, each demanding an explanation from her apparently nonfunctioning brain, all she could think of to say was, "I can't swim."

"That's all right," Matt said, his nonchalance making her want to scream. "It's not really deep enough to swim there anyway. But you could have a bath if you wanted." He reached into his saddlebag and tossed something down in front of her.

Soap.

It seemed like years since she'd seen soap, but in reality it had only been just over a week. The idea of being able to scrub away the sweat and smell of the past night lifted her spirits a tiny bit, but not enough for her to look Matt in the eye. She reached for the coveted bar, allowing her hair to fall forward and form a curtain around her face. "Thank you," she whispered past the lump of mortification in her throat.

Matt came and stood in front of her, and she refused to raise her eyes above his feet. But even looking at his feet was difficult; they were so big and . . . and masculine. He held out his hand to her. After a long, silent moment, she placed her palm in his and tried to rise. She gritted her teeth against the protesting muscles in her legs and back, and finally stood, still refusing to look at him.

He left her there and tied his breechcloth around his hips. Angela noticed the buckskins he'd worn last night lying in a heap beside the bed, then glanced back at the strip of bare thigh and hip where the front and back flaps of his skimpy attire didn't meet. "Why do you dress like that?"

"You mean like an Apache instead of a white man?"

Angela shrugged, then nodded.

"Because," he said, "when I'm here, I'm one of them. In this compound I'm not Matt Colton, I'm Bear Killer. Besides," he added with a quirk of his lips, "I feel conspicuous being the only man in camp with pants on."

To hide a sudden grin, Angela turned sideways and took a step. She gasped and bit her lower lip as her muscles screamed in protest.

"Angela? Are you all right?"

She took another painful step, then suddenly found herself swept up in Matt's arms. He ignored her cry of surprise and lowered her to the bearskin again. "Stay there," he ordered gruffly.

He pulled on a pair of moccasins. "Where are your clothes?"

Angela pulled a blanket up to cover her nakedness, then looked around the wickiup. "I don't know. I think Nod-ah-Sti had them last."

When Matt swung toward the door, Angela gasped at the sight of the long, red welts across his back. He was covered with the marks she'd given him during the night. "Where are you going?"

"To find you some clothes," he tossed back over his shoulder.

"Matt, wait!"

"What is it?" Matt was impatient now. He was in a hurry to get to Huera. She was the only one he could ask about what to do for Angela. He'd used Angela shamelessly all night, and now she was so sore she could barely walk. Maybe Huera knew of something to ease the soreness.

"Before you go, could you, I mean, would you . . . please put on a shirt?" she asked in a shaky voice.

Matt swung around to face her, a sick feeling in his gut. "Christ," he swore in disgust. He stood with his legs apart, hands on hips, and glared at her. He'd thought she was different. She'd never stared at the scar on his face like other white girls. He cursed himself for a fool. He should have remembered.

Men, even strangers, seemed not to notice the scar on his face at all. But girls, they were different. He'd always hated to be talking to a girl and have her eyes keep straying to his cheek, whether in fascination or revulsion. They either loved the scar or hated it. Angela was the first girl he'd ever met who'd just accepted his looks without comment.

But the scar on his face was nothing. Even the three curving, parallel marks on his chest weren't so bad. His back, however, was another matter. Even grown men had been known to quail at the mass of scars on his back.

His family was used to the sight. So was the tribe. Angela was not.

He should have remembered.

The self-consciousness he thought he'd conquered years ago reared its head, then anger took its place. He would not apologize or make excuses for the way his skin looked, damn it.

She'd seen him around camp the last few days without his shirt, and she'd said nothing. She hadn't said a word last night when he'd undressed. Now she wanted him to wear a goddamn shirt. "Everyone here is used to my scars. You'll just have to get used to them, too."

Angela's eyes lowered to his chest and traced the three parallel scars running from his shoulder to the opposite hip. She'd noticed them before, and knew there were more on his back, but she'd seen so many men with scars since she was a child during the war that she'd thought nothing of them. "Matt, I—"

"Like I said—get used to them."

"Matt—"

But he'd already stormed out of the wickiup. Now everyone he passed would see those scratches and know exactly what they'd been doing. She'd never be able to face anyone again. Huddling there under her blanket, she wished she could just disappear. Maybe the ground would open up and simply swallow her.

She lay there listening to life going on all around her, wishing hers would end. Children laughed; a woman scolded; dogs barked; hoofbeats pounded across the camp; a hand slapped against bare skin; a man spoke a few words, then roared with laughter. A moment later the hide over the door fluttered, and Matt entered. She lowered her eyes quickly to hide the gathering tears.

Matt's smile died. He laid her blue gingham dress down and pulled on a shirt. Cautiously, as if she were a rabbit he might frighten with a sudden movement, he knelt beside her and rested an elbow on his upraised knee. "Tell me why you wanted me to wear a shirt."

Angela picked at a ball of lint on the blanket and refused to look at him. "Since you went without one, it really doesn't matter now. The whole camp probably saw you."

"Tell me."

"You know why."

"It wasn't the scars, was it."

"You know it wasn't."

"Angela, I'm sorry I yelled at you like that." He caressed one fiery red cheek with the backs of his knuckles. "I guess I'm just a little sensitive. I'm sorry. Come on," he said. "I promised you a bath."

Before she could protest, he placed her clothes, shoes, and soap in her arms and wrapped her in the blanket. He picked her up and carried her outside, then ducked behind the wickiup and slipped into the woods.

A half hour later, Angela still in his arms, he stood at the edge of a small pool that was fed by a tiny waterfall trickling down between two boulders. The place was entirely surrounded by huge rocks and thick brush.

In minutes Matt had removed his clothes and her blanket and carried her into the warm water, the bar of soap resting on her stomach. He set her down in a shallow, sandy spot and proceeded to bathe her. He ignored all her protests, but he knew how embarrassed she was when he washed the dried blood from her inner thighs.

Angela was more than embarrassed; she was mortified. She tried to appreciate his tender concern, but the gentle touch of his soap-slicked fingers sliding across her inner thighs (and more!) brought sharp images to mind of herself as she had writhed and

110

moaned beneath him last night. Against her will, she closed her eyes and remembered the intense pleasure of his deep thrusts.

Her lips parted and her breath came in little gasps, and Matt knew what he was doing to her. He cursed his own body for its refusal to cooperate with his desire, but she was too sore for that anyway. However, there were other ways.

He moved carefully, afraid of breaking the spell that held her. He lowered her hips into the water until the lather floated away. Her eyes were still closed, her mouth open. He maneuvered her slowly, gently, until her head lay in the sand at the water's edge. Her shoulders and hips rested in a mere inch of warm water. Her knees were at the edge of a shallow, two-foot drop-off, and her feet drifted down to rest on the sandy bottom. He knelt there, between her feet.

The silky feel of his soapy hands as he washed her feet and legs only added to the fire building in Angela's veins. She was so ashamed of her reaction to his touch that she didn't dare open her eyes. But if she was so ashamed, why did she feel such pleasure?

She stopped thinking altogether when he began washing her stomach. His strong fingers kneaded her waist, then slid up her sides and down her arms. He touched her everywhere, except her tender breasts, which begged for his touch.

When his lips touched her thigh she jerked. Then she lay still again, afraid to encourage him, more afraid to discourage him. His fingers drew slick, soapy circles around her breasts, smaller and smaller circles, until he reached her already hardened nipples. She flattened her palms against the wet sand and arched against his teasing fingers.

She cried out, a mixture of protest and pleasure, when his tongue flicked between her legs. Her head snapped up, her eyes flew open, and she saw him there, between her thighs. His hot brown eyes devoured her.

"No!" It was indecent! It was broad daylight! They were out in the open! In the sunshine! And he had his mouth on her, *there!*

But, dear God, what he was doing to her with that mouth! Her protest died a quick death as he kissed and licked, sucked and nibbled. His soapy hands trailed down from her breasts to her hips, and he lifted her to meet his lips and tongue.

Angela didn't care anymore about anything. She didn't care that this was the most indecent thing she could imagine. She didn't care that she'd *never* be able to face him after letting him do this to her. She didn't care if the entire rest of the world disappeared. *Only please, God, don't let him stop!*

The pleasure and the pressure built to such heights, she didn't think she could bear it. Tears seeped out from beneath her tightly closed eyelids. She clutched at the wet sand beneath her hands as if it could steady her spinning world. But she didn't want her world to steady. She wanted it to spin and spin and spin, until it spun so fast she flew right off, out into the sky.

And that's exactly what happened.

She felt herself breaking free of the earth, and her cry of release was nearly a scream. Her climax was so powerful that she sobbed aloud as the spasms shook her.

Matt quickly rinsed the soap from her before it dried, then pulled her into his arms and held her in his lap. He cradled her there for a long time, until she stopped crying. Then he gently kissed the tears from her wet cheeks. Without saying anything, he set her down in the water and began to wash her hair.

Angela was drained. Her limbs drifted in the water wherever Matt directed them. Even her scalp relaxed under his massaging fingers; her head rolled on her limp neck. She made no protest when he carried her from the water and dried her with a rough blanket. She stared at the water trickling down from the rocks and let Matt comb the tangles from her hair.

The last person to do that for her had been her mother. Matt was much more gentle.

She just sat there, staring at the ripples in the water, then finally asked, "Why did you do that?"

"Do what?" Matt sat down beside her and smoothed loose tendrils of pale hair from her face.

She blushed and kept her eyes lowered. "You know."

"Because I wanted to, and you wanted me to."

She felt his gaze on her face as he ran his fingers through her hair. A denial sprang to her lips, but she swallowed it when he spoke again.

"Because I wanted to show you how good it can be when there's no drug to cloud your mind. Because I wanted to be the one to make you feel that way, just me, no drug."

Angela pulled the blanket tighter around her. She glanced up at him, then away, the heat in her face nearly suffocating her. "But why didn't you . . . I mean . . . you didn't. . . ."

"Why didn't I take my pleasure, too? Is that what you mean?"

"I-I guess so," she whispered.

He chuckled and squeezed her shoulder gently. "A man's body doesn't always cooperate with his mind, especially after a night like the one we just spent. You're too sore for that kind of loving anyway."

Beneath the curtain of her long hair, Angela felt herself blushing fiercely.

"Here," Matt said, handing her clothes to her. "Get dressed and we'll head back. I, for one, am starving. You must be, too."

When she reached to accept her clothes, the blanket slipped. She felt his gaze burn into her bare shoulder, sending tingling waves of awareness clear to her toes. She didn't move.

"Hurry up and get dressed, woman," he said with a smile in his voice. "I'm hungry."

He expected her to dress in front of him? While his gaze burned her like a flaming torch? Of course he expected it. After last night, and just a few minutes ago in the pond, what secrets could she possibly have left? But a lifetime of modesty held her motionless. "Would you . . . turn your back, please?" she managed.

"Would I what?" Was that surprise or anger in his voice? "After last night, and then just now, you want me to turn my back while you get dressed?"

She finally looked at him then, but kept her gaze trained on the only thing he wore, the bearclaw necklace, not daring to look at his face or the tall, naked, beautiful length of him. Through eyes brimming with tears, she could see the wet, spiky clumps of her own lashes. "Please?"

The curse died in his throat when Matt saw her woeful expression. "All right," he said with a reluctant nod. *Damn.* He'd hoped she'd be over her embarrassment by now, but then, he shouldn't expect her to go from virgin to wanton in less than twenty-four hours.

Soon, he told himself. No woman as passionate as Angela could remain shy for long.

"How is it a girl your age never learned to swim?" he asked, his back to her as he tied on his breechcloth and slipped into his moccasins.

"There aren't any swimming holes in downtown Memphis."

"Memphis?" It was the first piece of personal information she'd given him. "You're sure a long way from home."

"Don't I know it," she said with a sad little smile.

Later, on their way back to camp, Matt tried again to ease her mind. "Is there anything I can do to make things easier for you? I meant what I said last night. There won't be any annulment now, so you don't have to feel like I'd . . . use you, then just . . . walk away."

Angela stepped ahead of him on the narrow footpath and let her hair fall forward to cover her face. Each step she took was painful, yet she knew she had to walk the soreness out of her body. But what of the soreness in her heart? Every word Matt spoke only served to remind her again of her shameful actions of the night before, and then again today. The more he tried to get her to talk, the more she wanted to scream at him to leave her alone.

"Damn it, Angela, talk to me."

"What am I supposed to say?" she cried, flinging her hair back over her shoulder to finally look at him. "Am I supposed to say it's all right? Don't worry about me, I'll be fine? I didn't have any plans for the rest of my life anyway? I really don't mind being the butt of some cruel joke between you and your so-called friend?" *That I don't catch fire when you look at me, when you touch me?* Her eyes stung with the threat of tears. "I just want to forget it ever happened."

Matt shook his head slowly. "I can't do that." He reached to touch her cheek, but she jerked away. "Neither of us planned on any of this, Angela, but it doesn't matter now. The fact is, you're my wife. It happened, it's done, and all the pretending in the world won't undo it."

Angela stopped and sat down on a low rock, her muscles burning in protest in places where she didn't even know she had muscles. "You go on without me," she said. "I'd like to sit here awhile."

Matt looked at her a long moment, then nodded. "All right, but don't leave the trail. Camp is just around that next bend, so you don't have to worry about getting lost. But this isn't Memphis. There are wild animals in these woods, so don't stay too long, and don't leave the trail," he repeated.

Angela held her breath until Matt disappeared around the bend and out of sight. She just couldn't believe all this was happening to her. Had the entire world gone crazy? She was supposed to be in Tucson by now, with her mother and father, at their new store. Instead, her parents were both dead, the money from selling the Memphis store was a pile of ashes, along with everything else she owned, she had been held captive by Apaches, and now she found herself married to a total stranger. A white man who called himself Bear Killer.

And he could turn her inside out with just a touch.

She took a deep breath and stood up slowly, then began to pace back and forth trying to figure a way out of this mess. There really wasn't much she could do as long as they stayed with the Apaches. She hadn't the slightest idea where she was. If she tried to run away, she knew she'd become hopelessly lost. She had to stay with Matt until he took her away from here. Then maybe her chances for escape would be better.

The thought of leaving him, of never seeing his smile or hearing his voice, never feeling his hands and lips on her body again, left her cold and empty. And where would she go? How would she live? Would she ever be able to forget him?

Behind her, a twig snapped. She was surprised to find herself in the woods, several yards away from the path. Matt's warning came back, and she slowly turned her head to peer behind her. A sharp, sudden pain exploded in her head. She felt herself fall. The last thing she saw was the ground, tilted at an odd angle, rushing up to meet her.

Then everything went black.

Chapter Twelve

It took Matt over an hour to find Chee. It seemed everywhere he went, Chee had just left. He finally found him tending the horses.

"Is it coincidence that I've 'just missed' you for the last hour? Or have you been hiding from me?"

"Why should I hide from you?" Chee asked innocently.

"Maybe you don't want to hear what I have to say about your little stunt last night."

Chee smirked as he released the hoof he'd been inspecting and straightened to face Matt. "And what do you have to say?"

"Just this." In the blink of an eye, Matt swung at his friend and dropped him with a solid right to the chin, then turned his back and walked away in grim satisfaction.

He stopped for a while at the boys' playing field, where Pace and some friends were running races. A dozen or so men stood on the sidelines placing bets with each other. Gambling was a favorite pastime for these people, many of whom would bet everything they owned on the outcome of a single race or game.

And white people thought Apaches weren't civilized!

The sun was sinking low when Matt finally returned to the wickiup, but Angela wasn't there. He checked next door with Huera, but she hadn't seen the girl. Neither Serena, Nod-ah-Sti, nor either of Cochise's wives had seen Angela since last night. He went back to the wickiup, but again found it empty. Could she still be sitting on that rock in the woods?

When he neared the edge of camp Alope hailed him, but he ignored her.

As Matt followed the trail to where he'd left Angela, a sense of unease crept over him. She'd been embarrassed and upset. He shouldn't have left her alone. He reached the rock, but she wasn't there. A cold feeling settled in the pit of his stomach.

A low snarl came from the woods to his left. He whirled to find a *ńdíí*, a mountain lion, crouched, ready to spring from its perch on a high rock. Matt scanned the ground beneath the cat, and his heart jumped to his throat. Barely visible at the edge of a thick clump of shrubs was a small patch of blue gingham, directly beneath the cat's perch.

Matt automatically reached for his pistol. It wasn't there. He never wore it in camp. The only weapon he had was his knife, and he wasn't as good as he'd like to be at throwing it.

Still unaware of Matt's presence, the cat shifted its feet and twitched its tail, ears flat against its tawny skull. Any second it would spring. Without taking his eyes off the cat, Matt squatted, ran his hands along the path at his feet and came up with three fist-sized rocks. With a shout, he hurled them one after the other at the mountain lion. The cat yowled in rage and turned toward the man, but reversed itself and bounded into the woods when the third rock struck it in the ribs with a hollow-sounding thud.

Matt practically flew the few yards to the spot of blue gingham and dropped to his knees beside Angela's limp form. In the growing darkness he saw a frighteningly large pool of blood staining the ground beneath her. He pressed his ear to her chest and listened for a heartbeat, but his own heart was pounding so loud he almost missed it. When he did finally hear her heart, it was so faint it was barely audible at all.

Darkness spread rapidly. Matt searched, frantic to find where the blood was coming from. Then he saw it, and his own blood left his face at once, as though it would join hers there on the ground. The small, thin cut on the inside of her wrist from the wedding ceremony was now a deep, ugly gash that ran up her inner arm almost to her elbow.

"My God," he whispered. She must have been more horrified and upset over last night than he thought, to have taken such drastic measures to escape him and their marriage.

With a jerk, he bolted into action, tearing off what remained of her petticoat and wrapping it tightly around her lower arm. He picked her up, but she didn't stir. As fast as possible, he made his way out of the woods and back to their wickiup.

Triple C Ranch
Near Tucson, Arizona Territory

Travis Colton located his wife's shawl in the bedroom and returned to the salon. "Dani, I found your—"

"Ssh!" Seven-year-old Spencer Colton put a finger to his lips to quiet his father. "She's doing it again," he whispered loudly.

"Who's doing—"

"Ssh!" lisped Jessica, Spence's three-year-old sister. It sounded like, "Thh."

"What's—"

119

"Ssh!" they warned in unison.

Travis looked to Daniella for an explanation, and the shawl slipped from his fingers. He'd seen this before, but it still frightened him every time it happened.

"Is this how she did it when I got lost that time?" Jessica whispered to her brother.

"Yeah. Now ssh!"

Daniella sat in her chair, her hands poised in midair above the spinning wheel she used more for nostalgic reasons than out of necessity, and stared, unblinking, into the cold fireplace. Her eyes were glazed. She was totally unaware of what went on around her.

Spence and Jessica stared at their mother in awe. Spence remembered last spring when Jessica had wandered away from the house and got lost for several hours. He'd been with his mother when she'd suddenly dropped the flowers she'd been carrying and stared off at nothing for several moments. It was like she was in a trance or something, and it had scared him half to death, he remembered. But when his mother had snapped out of it, she'd said she had seen Jessica in the creek with her foot caught beneath a rock.

Less than half an hour later, Jessica had been found, cold and frightened half out of her wits, almost a mile from the house, just like Mama had seen her.

And now Mama looked just like she had that day, and Spence knew she was "doing it" again, "seeing" something.

Travis knelt before his wife and waited. That was all he could do. He should be used to this after ten years of marriage to her, but he wasn't. It scared him when her face turned so pale and her skin so cold.

120

Suddenly she blinked, and her eyes focused.

"Dani, are you all right?"

"What?" She stared at him stupidly for a moment, then shook herself.

"What'd ya see, Mama?" Spence asked.

"Is thumbody lost?" Jessica whispered.

Daniella glanced at Travis, anxiety written on her face.

"Mama's fine now, you two, and I think it's your bedtime," Travis said.

"No!" they both protested.

"I beg your pardon," Travis said in that tone he had that meant someone was about to catch it.

Spence heard, and obeyed. He took his sister's hand without a word and tugged her unwilling little body toward the door.

"We'll be there to tuck you in in a minute."

"It's not fair," Spence mumbled as he went out the door. "Every time sumpin' excitin' happens around here, us kids gotta go to bed. How's a fella supposed to know what's going on if he has to keep going to bed all the time?"

Travis took Daniella's cold hands in his warm ones. "What is it, love?"

"Oh, Travis, it's Matt."

Travis felt the blood leave his face. "Matt?" The last time she'd "seen" Matt was several years ago, when he'd been mauled by a bear. "What? What did you see?"

"He's all right," she assured him. "But I saw him in the woods. There was a girl with long blond hair, wearing a blue dress. She was lying on the ground in a pool of blood, and Matt was kneeling over her. Oh, Travis, he's so upset!"

"What do you mean, upset?"

"I don't know for sure, but I think she might die, and I think . . . Matt somehow feels responsible. We

121

have to go to him, Travis; he needs us."

"Then, we'll go." Travis brought her hands to his lips and kissed them. "We'll leave first thing in the morning."

Matt knelt inside the wickiup beside his wife of one day and watched, every nerve tensed, as Huera cleaned and bandaged the deep cut on Angela's arm.

"*Shimá*, will she be all right? Why is she still unconscious?"

"She's lost a lot of blood, *shiye'*, so she is very weak. And she must have fallen hard to have such a large knot on her head."

Matt gently fingered the lump the size of a hen's egg on Angela's scalp just above and behind her ear. She must have grown weak from loss of blood and struck her head on a tree or rock when she passed out.

Huera left, then returned a short time later with a pot of broth. "Feed this to her as soon as she wakes. It will help her recover her strength quickly."

Matt sat beside Angela and held her hand, willing her to wake up. If she didn't recover, he'd never forgive himself. His rational mind knew he wasn't to blame for the events leading to her attempted suicide, but in his heart he felt responsible. He should have realized how upset she was, should never have left her there in the woods, alone.

It was hours later before her eyelids finally fluttered. She rolled her head and moaned, then blinked several times to clear her vision.

"Matt?"

"I'm right here." He squeezed her left hand, then reached for the pot of broth.

"My head hurts." She strained to see him in the near darkness and blinked again. "What happened?"

122

"Don't try to talk. Here, eat some of this. It'll make you feel better."

"A spoon?" She eyed the utensil carefully, as if to make sure that's what it really was.

"It's probably the only one for miles around. I brought it from home," Matt explained.

He propped her head up with an extra blanket, then began spooning the warm broth into her mouth.

She shuddered as it went down. "It's awful!"

Matt shifted his squatting position and leaned back to give her a breather between spoonfuls. He saw her lower her gaze and blush. *Now* what did she have to blush about?

Her gaze darted away from him, then back. He followed her line of sight as her blush deepened. His lips twitched involuntarily.

When he'd shifted his weight, his new position left his breechcloth gaping open, giving her what he was sure was a clear view beneath. The smile he'd been fighting died.

The last thing he wanted just then was for her to be reminded of last night or this morning. She'd been embarrassed enough lately to last a lifetime. He didn't want to add to her distress. He shifted again; the gap closed.

He made a big show of taking a sip of the broth and making a face. Then he grinned at her. "You're right," he said, grateful to see her relax slightly. "It's awful. But I swear it works. You'll be on your feet in no time." He pushed another spoonful into her mouth.

"What makes you so sure?" she asked, wrinkling her freckled, sunburned nose.

"Because it's what they fed me when I got these scars," he said, surprising himself. He'd never spoken about that with anyone before.

"How did you get them?" she asked, swallowing another mouthful of the bitter stuff.

"From a very angry bear."

Angela jerked her gaze from the broth and studied the scar on his face. "A bear did that?"

"Uh huh." Right now he wasn't worried about her reaction to his scars, as long as he could keep her mind off what she'd tried to do to herself this afternoon.

"I'd say you're lucky to be alive."

"Uh huh." He kept spooning the broth into her between her words.

"What happened to the bear?"

He grinned slightly. It was probably the first time he'd ever thought about that long-ago day with anything close to humor. "You're lying on him right now."

She glanced down at the bearskin beneath her, then at the yellowed claws around his neck. "Is that why they call you Bear Killer?"

"Uh huh. Want to know what they call you?"

"Me? What do they call me?"

He pushed another spoonful of broth between her lips and gazed deeply into her eyes. "They call you Eyes Like Summer Leaves."

Angela felt trapped by his dark gaze. "They do?" she whispered.

"Uh huh. They've never seen a person with green eyes before." Then he added softly, "Neither have I."

Angela gripped the blanket with her right hand, then gasped as a deep, throbbing pain shot up her arm. Her throat clenched at the sight of the bandage from her wrist to her elbow. "What happened to my arm?" she cried.

"Take it easy," he said. "It'll be all right in a few days."

"But what happened? It feels like it's on fire."

"You cut yourself. Don't you remember?"

"No . . . I—"

"It's all right, Angela. All you have to worry about right now is resting and getting better. Just forget what I said earlier. As soon as we leave here, we'll get that annulment, and I'll see to it you get wherever you want to go, I promise."

Her mind couldn't make any logical connection between her arm and an annulment, but of the two, the annulment was much more important. "But you were so adamant about it. What made you change your mind?"

Matt set the broth aside and took her hand, gazing earnestly at her. "I know I was, and I'm sorry, Angela. So sorry. I had no idea it meant that much to you. I had no idea you'd rather—well, that you felt so strongly about it."

"What do you mean? How do you know I feel that way?"

"How do I—? You slit your arm open from wrist to elbow and nearly blead to death, and you ask how I know?"

"Is *that* what happened to my arm?" she cried, her eyes widening in alarm.

"You don't have to pretend, Angela. I said I'd get you out of here, and I will, just as soon as you're well."

"I appreciate that. You're right, I do want to leave here, but not enough to do what you think I've done! You actually think I . . . that I tried . . . to kill myself?!"

Matt looked at her in confusion. "What else am I supposed to think? You were embarrassed and upset. You wouldn't talk to me. Then I find you lying in a pool of blood. The reason your head hurts is probably because when you passed out, you fell and struck it on something."

Angela stared at him in astonishment. She knew her mouth was hanging open, but she couldn't seem to help it. "You really think I'd do that? For heaven's sake! If I were going to do something that drastic, I'd have done it when Tahnito and his friends had me!"

"You mean you didn't—?"

"Of course I didn't!"

"Then, what did happen to your arm?" Matt wanted to believe her. Lord, how he wanted to believe her.

"I don't know. I was standing in the woods, and I heard a noise behind me. That's when I realized I'd left the trail. The next thing I knew, something hit me on the head and I fell. Everything went black."

With each word she spoke, Matt's eyes grew wider, and his blood grew colder. "Are you sure, Angela? Are you very sure?"

"I'm positive. I'll admit I was trying to think of a way out of here, but Matt, I would never have done anything quite so drastic, I swear."

It was impossible for him to doubt her sincerity. "If what you're saying is true, that means someone here in this camp struck you from behind, then slit your arm open and left you to bleed to death." He gripped her hand tightly. "Knowing the Chiricahua the way I do, I find that almost impossible to believe. But I'd rather believe that than think you tried to . . . kill yourself . . . because of me."

Angela shuddered. "I don't want to think someone tried to kill me either, but I think you've overlooked the obvious," she said.

"What's that?"

"What did I use to cut myself with? I don't have a knife."

Matt swore at his own stupidity for not realizing it sooner. "You're right. I'm sorry," he said with a small grin. "But you still have to eat the rest of this broth."

While he spooned the rest of it into her mouth, he spoke, his voice grim. "Since it's apparently not safe for you to wander around alone, you're to stay with me at all times. I don't even want you going to the bushes or to bathe or anywhere, unless I make sure it's safe first. I don't want you out of my sight for even a moment. Do you understand?"

Angela nodded. It was finally sinking in that someone had actually tried to kill her and make it look like suicide, and she was scared. She didn't need to be told twice to stay close to Matt.

Chapter Thirteen

When Angela was up and dressed the next day, the throbbing pain in her arm was nearly unbearable until Matt fashioned a sling for her. When they stepped out of the wickiup Serena came running up to them.

"Matt!" she called. "Grandfather's back! What happened to your arm, Angela?"

Angela looked at Matt. What was she supposed to say?

Matt answered for her. "She took a fall in the woods yesterday and cut it."

"I hope it's not bad. I've gotta go!" Serena dashed off in a breathless hurry.

"And who is your grandfather?" Angela asked.

"He's not my grandfather, he's the twins' grandfather. Cochise."

Angela's eyes widened. "Cochise? I don't understand. I thought his two sons were around your age. I didn't know he had any other children old enough to have children the twins' age."

"He has an adopted daughter," Matt explained as they walked through camp. "She's Pace's and Serena's mother."

"Your father married an Apache?"

"And if he did?" Matt asked tightly.

"I didn't mean anything by it, Matt, I was just asking."

"Look. If we're going to get along at all until we get you out of here, you're going to have to forget everything you ever heard about Apaches and pretend to like them. You met three bad ones, but there are bad white men, too. These people have accepted you, or at least most of them have," he added, looking down at her arm. "What happened yesterday could have happened to you just as easily in Memphis as here. So just keep your prejudices to yourself."

"I'm not a child, Mr. Colton," she gritted out between smiling lips while nodding to a passing woman. "I'm supposed to be your wife, so stop acting like my father. Even he never treated me like an idiot.

"I've been kidnapped, forced to walk — sometimes run — miles and miles across the desert, nearly raped, forced to marry a stranger with more than one chip on his shoulder, drugged, hit over the head, and stabbed. You'll pardon me if I don't feel exactly welcome."

Matt stared straight ahead, jaws clenched. "And for those things, you hate all Apaches."

"I never said that!" Two could play his game. She refused to look at him. "I hate the three who kidnapped me, and I'd like to murder Chee for what he did. I'd hate whoever attacked me yesterday if I knew who it was."

"And me? Do you hate me, too?" he asked quietly, a hint of tenseness in his voice.

"No." Angela kept her eyes straight ahead. "But sometimes you make me very angry."

Matt let out the breath he'd been holding. The tightness around his mouth and in his chest relaxed. He didn't want her to hate him.

She was really something, this wife of his. In the space of a few days she'd lost everything she'd ever known, including her parents, had been thrust into a world more foreign than any she could ever have imagined, and found herself married to a stranger. In the course of all this she'd been captured, scared half out of her wits, drugged, used so harshly on her wedding night she could barely move the next day, and nearly killed. Yet she walked beside him, her head held high, and argued with him, expressing her anger.

Most women in her position would have been reduced to a quivering mass of hysteria by now. But not his Angel. Such courage was rare in a woman. And whether she knew it or not, she was *his* woman. No matter what he'd said before, he had no intention of letting her go.

They walked on in silence for several moments before Matt spoke again. "Dani's not an Apache."

Angela let out her breath, unaware she'd been holding it. "Who's Dani?"

"My stepmother, Daniella. We call her Dani."

She looked at him them. "Now I'm really confused. If she's not an Apache, and your father's not an Apache, how did the twins get to be half Apache?"

A boisterous group of young boys and yapping dogs cut across their path, forcing them to stop for a moment. When the path was clear Matt seemed more relaxed, even though his voice remained grim. "Remember when I told you I'd only known of one woman who'd lived through what those three had planned for you?"

Angela shuddered at the thought. "Your stepmother was captured?"

"She wasn't my stepmother then, but yes, she was captured."

"What happened? How did she get away?"

"She didn't. At least not the way you mean. There was no one to save her. She was beaten, tortured, raped, and left for dead."

Angela's eyes widened, and she felt faint. It could have been her. *Would* have been her, except for Chee and Matt. It was too horrible to contemplate. She forced the thought away and took a deep breath. "She obviously didn't die, so what happened?"

"No one really knows for sure." Matt kept his eyes trained on the ground as they continued through the compound. "After they . . . finished with her, they left her at the base of an old pine. Sometime during the night lightning struck the tree and split it in two. The next time Dani was seen, she had a white streak down the middle of her hair, which hadn't been there before. Dee-O-Det said it was a mark of favor from Yúúsń."

"Who?"

"God," Matt explained. "Dee-O-Det said the streak was put there by the hand of God to show the world that Dani was favored by Him."

Angela didn't know what to think. What was one supposed to think about a story like that? "What happened then?"

"The Apaches found her, gave her a new name, took care of her, and Cochise adopted her."

"What did they call her? Did she ever get to go home? How did your father meet her?"

"Just full of questions, aren't you?" Matt said, darting her a look from the corner of his eye. "They called her Woman of Magic. When she got home to her real family there was some trouble, so she moved away to a ranch right next to ours."

"And that's where she met your father?"

"Sort of." Matt hesitated, then finally turned to face her. "Look, Angela, I'm telling you about Dani

131

because there's every possibility she and my father will be here any day now, and I want you to understand."

"Understand what? You didn't tell me before that they were coming."

Matt hesitated again. It felt strange telling someone about Dani. He'd never done it before. But he wanted Angela to know, even though he wasn't sure why. "Let me show you something."

He took her by the hand and led her to the east edge of camp and showed her the remains of the pine, where Dani had lain that night over ten years ago. It had decayed a great deal since then, but the blackened, jagged stump was still there.

An eerie feeling swept over Angela. She shivered in the hot afternoon sun.

"Dani was left with three things that night that have remained with her, will always be a part of her. That's the night she conceived the twins, she got the white streak in her hair, and she started having visions."

"Visions? You mean . . . like second sight or something?"

He shrugged. "Yeah, I guess so. Anyway, right after that, Dad and I were on the stagecoach, coming home from New Orleans, when the Apaches hit us. I was captured. That was Dani's first vision. She saw it while it was happening."

Angela shuddered. *Good Lord! Has everyone in this godforsaken country been captured?* What had her father been thinking of to bring her and her mother to such a place?

"Then," Matt continued, "she kept seeing me with the Apaches, and kept seeing Dad looking for me, so even though she didn't know who he was she set out to find him. She found him, brought him to Cochise, and arranged for my release. That's how we met her. She and Dad were married not too long after that."

"May I ask another question?"

"You don't have to. I can guess what it is, so I'll tell you. Yes, Dad knew she was expecting before he married her, and he knew how it happened."

Angela was quiet for a moment, digesting all he'd told her. "Your father must be a very special man to marry a woman under those circumstances. I would imagine most men wouldn't want a woman who'd been through something like that."

"You're right, I guess. Dad is special. But so is Dani. And unless I miss my guess, you'll be finding that out for yourself any day now."

"You're sure they're coming? What will we tell them?"

"I'm not sure they're coming, but Dani still 'sees' things. She may have 'seen' you. I just don't know. But I've learned not to be surprised when she shows up unexpectedly. As far as what to tell them, they may already know the truth. Neither one of them is very easy to fool. And speaking of someone not easily fooled, I think it's time I introduced you to Cochise. He'll be offended if I don't. But no matter what he says, or guesses at, we can't admit the truth to him."

"I understand," she said with a nod. "But I have another question."

"What?"

"How do Huera and Hal-Say fit into all of this?"

"They adopted me after I was captured, before Dani and Dad came to get me."

"And your real mother?"

"She died right after I was born."

Angela was silent then, and Matt took her to meet Cochise. He greeted the chief in the Chiricahua language, and the two men talked for several minutes.

133

Angela didn't understand a word, of course, but she knew by their gestures they were talking about her.

She carefully studied the man who was said to be the scourge of the Southwest. He was a couple of inches taller than Matt's six feet, which made him the tallest man she'd seen since coming here. The other Apache men were several inches shorter. He had broad shoulders and a thick, muscular chest. In fact, his entire body was covered with hard muscles beneath bronze skin. And she could see nearly every muscle, because he was dressed like the other men in camp: all he wore was a loincloth and tall moccasins. His black hair was long and thick, streaked with gray.

When his gaze met hers, Angela sucked in her breath sharply. His eyes were deep, dark brown—almost black—fringed by thick, black lashes. But what held her attention was the intelligence, the power, and the hint of sadness in his gaze. It was a commanding, compelling gaze. The look of a great leader. She'd seen eyes like that once before in her life, years ago.

"Beauregard," she whispered.

"Angela?"

Matt had been talking to her, but she hadn't heard him. "I'm sorry," she said with a start. "What did you say?" She felt a blush stain her cheeks.

Matt frowned at her in disapproval. "I'd like you to meet Cochise, chief of the Chidikáágu'."

Angela ignored Matt's frown. She turned back to Cochise in awe with a slight smile curving her lips. "Please tell him I am honored to meet such a great leader of men."

Matt looked at her strangely for a moment, then translated her greeting to Cochise, who acknowledged with a smile.

A few minutes later they left Cochise and headed

back to their wickiup.

Cochise watched them go, the smile fading from his lips. His heart was saddened for what the young white girl was going through and for the lies Bear Killer was forced to tell, yet warmed by what the two were willing to do to keep the tenuous peace he himself had finally established.

Did Tahnito and his friends, in the supreme arrogance of the young, think their chief so old and feeble-minded he would not know of their treachery? The same chief who had led all the Apache nations in war since the death of his friend Mon-ache, who whites and Mexicans had called Mangas Coloradas — Red Sleeves? Did they think a man who for years had known the movement of every white man within hundreds of miles would not know of their actions?

The young pups must think him a fool. But he would allow them their deception. This time. For the sake of peace.

"What was the matter with you?" Matt hissed as soon as they were away from Cochise. "And who the hell is Beauregard?"

"I'm sorry. I didn't mean to stare like that, it's just that he reminded me of a man I met during the war, when I was a child."

"Beauregard?"

"General Pierre Gustave Toutant de Beauregard. He was a Confederate general."

"Cochise reminds you of a Confederate general? I think you've been in the sun too long."

"No. He really does. General Beauregard came through Memphis looking for supplies and recruits on his way to Shiloh. I don't know, it's just that they have the same look in their eyes, Beauregard and

Cochise. A look of pride and determination. A look that makes men want to follow them. But at the same time, there's a look of weariness, even sadness, like they both know something the rest of us don't want to know. They've both done things they didn't want to do, fought battles they didn't want to fight, because they had no choice. They did what they felt they had to do. Beauregard directed the bombardment of Fort Sumter," she added softly.

Matt was stunned at the depth of her insight. He began to see her in a new light. His admiration for her, as well as his determination to keep her as his wife, grew. "I don't know about Beauregard, but you certainly seem to understand Cochise. You could tell all that from just meeting him?"

Angela shrugged. "It was in his eyes."

Matt paused outside their wickiup and spoke. "Maybe Beauregard knew he was fighting a losing battle. Maybe he saw the defeat and destruction of what he considered to be his country."

"And Cochise? Does he see those things, too?"

"He sees them. That's why he's allowed no raiding for over a year now. He wants peace very badly for the Chúk'ánéné. He's come to realize that if something isn't done soon, it'll be too late. No Apache is afraid to die, but they also don't want to see the Apache wiped off the face of the earth, either. Peace with the government is their only chance."

"Is there much chance of a treaty?" Angela asked, stooping to enter the wickiup.

"I don't know," Matt replied as he followed her through the low door.

Angela straightened up, then swayed on her feet. The grass walls of the wickiup swam before her eyes.

"Angela!" Matt grabbed for her and steadied her before she could fall. "Are you all right?"

"Just . . . dizzy," she murmured, leaning against

him. It felt good to lean against him, feel his warmth, his strength surrounding her.

Matt picked her up and carried her to the bed. "You're still weak. I shouldn't have kept you up so long."

Angela closed her eyes as he placed her on the bearskin. After a few minutes, the dizziness passed. When she opened her eyes, Matt was kneeling next to her, a worried look on his face.

"I'm okay, really," she said. "I guess I'm an awful lot of trouble, aren't I?"

"Yeah," he said with a grin. "But don't worry about it. You just lie there and rest. I'll see about something to eat."

Angela groaned when he came back a few minutes later with more of Huera's horrible-tasting broth, but insisted on sitting up and feeding herself this time.

After the first few mouthfuls, Angela began to eat faster, then started laughing. "Heaven help me, I think I'm starting to like this stuff." She smiled up at Matt, then her breath caught in her throat when their eyes locked. His gaze was so intense she couldn't look away, didn't want to.

Finally, after an eternity, his lips curved up. "That's the first time I've heard you laugh."

Angela felt her cheeks heat up and knew another adolescent blush covered her face. "It is?" she whispered, still staring at him.

"I like it."

Angela felt another flush, and knew her face had turned an even deeper shade of red. Her heart pounded against her ribs. She wondered if she'd be dizzy again. If so, it wouldn't be from her wound this time, she knew.

Good heavens! How could she react so strongly to a man she barely knew? She'd been around men every day of her life, waiting on customers in the store, but none had ever affected her in the slightest . . . until Matt Colton. But then, she'd never shared with them what she'd shared with him.

Stop it! she told herself. *That's over and done with and won't happen again. It was a mistake.*

Matt tore his gaze away and resumed eating. Later, he helped Angela out of her dress, much to her embarrassment. She slept in her chemise, the only garment she had left besides the blue gingham. Without her petticoat, which had been torn up in stages to use as bandages, and her drawers, which she'd lost that night they'd been ripped off her, she felt positively naked.

More tired than she realized, she fell asleep quickly.

Matt waited until she was sound asleep before he joined her on the bearskin. He lay next to her, gazed at her lovely face, her silky hair that looked like a mixture of daisies and moonbeams, and remembered their incredible wedding night. His loins tightened. There had been a few passionate women in his life, but they all paled next to his Angel. He knew she was even more passionate without the drug, then cursed himself for even thinking of it. He'd sworn to leave her alone.

It wasn't going to be easy.

But it wasn't going to be for long, either, he vowed.

Chapter Fourteen

The next morning Huera brought them corn cakes and honey for breakfast.

"I feel like a worthless ninny," Angela said after Huera left.

Matt laughed. "Why's that?"

"I see the other women working all day, and here I sit. If it wasn't for Huera, we'd probably both have starved by now," she said, dipping a golden brown cake into the honey pot. "She's even been doing my laundry. It's not fair. She has enough to do, I'm sure, without taking care of me."

"Don't worry about it," Matt said. "She understands. When your arm's better you can help her cook. In a day or two, when you're stronger, we'll take Huera into the woods and get some more honey. She'll like that."

As they finished eating, Angela noticed Matt had fallen unusually silent. "You're awfully quiet," she said softly.

He kept his gaze lowered and finished licking honey off his fingers.

"Is something wrong?" she asked.

He looked at her then and gave her a sad half-smile. "You mean aside from everything that's happened to you since we met?" He shook his head. "I . . . if you don't want to talk about it I'll understand, but I was wondering . . . what happened to your parents."

139

Angela felt her heart lurch and lowered her gaze. Her parents were never far from her thoughts, but she hadn't spoken of them, of what had happened. Not with anyone. The wounds were still too raw.

Matt touched her shoulder. "It's all right. You don't have to talk about it."

But suddenly she did have to talk about it. She wanted to. Her eyes stung and her jaw quivered. She looked up at Matt, at the tender concern in his eyes, and wasn't sure she could get the words out around the ache in her throat.

"It's all right. Come here." Matt gave her shoulder a slight tug.

The next thing Angela knew, she was in his arms, her cheek pressed against his hard chest, her tears soaking his skin. She swallowed and concentrated, and finally stopped crying. "I'm sorry."

"No," Matt said, running a hand down her hair. "It's okay. You don't have to talk about it right now."

But she did. She had to. "Mother got sick right after we left Camp Bowie. . . ." She told him everything, from how she met Chee to turning from her father's grave and finding Tahnito and his friends surrounding her.

She finished with a shudder. Matt held her close. His fingers trailing through her hair soothed her. Then she felt him press his lips to the top of her head.

"Angel, I—" She felt him swallow. "I'm so sorry for everything you've been through. I can't imagine losing even one of my parents, let alone both of them in one day."

He held her tighter, and she relaxed in his arms. Talking about it had been the right thing for her, but she didn't want him feeling sorry for her. Still, she couldn't bring herself to pull away from his warmth, until a few minutes later when running footsteps pounded close. Then a shout.

Angela sat up. When Matt's arms slid from around

140

her she felt the loss of his warmth and shivered.

"Matt! Matt!" Pace barreled into the wickiup, out of breath from running. "Taglito's coming!"

Matt sucked in his breath sharply. He jumped up, his heart thumping with eagerness. "Are you sure?" As far as Matt knew, Tom Jeffords, known to his Chiricahua friends as Taglito, hadn't been to the stronghold in years.

"Yeah, I'm sure. Last night the trail guards spotted a ring of five fires, and this morning they recognized Taglito."

"I'll be damned!" Matt clenched his fists at his sides, excitement surging through him. "Five? Who's with him?"

"There's Taglito," Pace began, counting on his fingers. "Then, there's two bluecoats, and two Apaches—Army scouts, probably. Cochise's goin' down into the hills to meet 'em. He wants you to come, too."

"What about Tahza and Naiche?"

"They didn't come back with him. They're still out hunting somewhere. Cochise is taking Juan, Nali-Kay-deya, Tesal-Bestinay, and you." Pace's mouth twisted down at the corners in disappointment. "The rest of us have to stay here."

"Do you have time to do something for me, or has he got you running errands, as usual?" Matt asked.

"No, I've got time. Whacha need?"

"I need you to saddle the pinto for me and bring him here. Would you do that?"

"*Dá'ndiide*. Sure. Anything else?"

Matt shook his head, his mind already rushing forward. "Just holler when you get back."

When Pace was gone, Matt turned to Angela. "How are you feeling this morning?"

"I'm fine. What's going on? Who's Taglito?"

"You don't feel weak or anything do you? Dizzy?"

"No, of course not. Why?"

"I hate to keep bringing this up," Matt said, ignoring

141

her question, "but remember the promise you made about not telling anyone how you came to be here?"

Angela pursed her lips. "How can I forget, when you keep reminding me all the time? Are you going to tell me what's going on, or not?"

Matt paced the narrow confines of the wickiup and absently fingered the bear claws hanging around his neck. "Aside from my father and me, Taglito is the only white man Cochise has ever really known. He and Cochise are good friends—closer than some brothers. If Taglito's bringing soldiers here, the only thing I can think is that it has to be some sort of peace mission." He stopped and looked directly at her as she rose.

"That's why I brought up your promise again. It's more important now than ever." He grasped her shoulders tightly. He had to make her understand. "I can't begin to tell you what this means, Angela. Nothing is more important than that Cochise and his people make peace with the United States. Nothing! Not you, not me, not anything else in the world. I've been praying for this for ten years. You've got to swear to me you won't say a word to these men about how you got here. Swear it."

"Matt, you're hurting me."

He quickly let go of her shoulders, then took a deep breath and clenched his fists at his sides. "Swear it."

"I've already sworn it a dozen times," she said, rubbing her shoulders where he'd gripped her. "But if it'll make you feel any better, I'll swear it again."

Matt stared hard at her for a long moment, studying the look in those bright green eyes. Could he trust her? Did she realize the enormity of what was at stake? She couldn't. She couldn't understand. Not the way he did.

But she would keep her word. He read that truth in her eyes. This was his Angel. He could trust her. He had to. Forcing himself to relax, if only a little, he took her by the hand. "All right, let's go."

Angela resisted. "If you trust me so little that you

think I won't keep my word, why don't you just leave me here? That way I can't say anything."

"No." A sudden coldness seeped down his spine. "I can't leave you here alone, not after what happened to you in the woods."

"I won't go in the woods, I'll stay right here till you get back. All the men will be off playing or hunting or something, as usual, so there won't be anyone around but women. I'll be perfectly safe."

"No. You're coming with me."

"Why? Why can't I just stay with the women?"

Matt took a deep breath to calm himself and grasped her hand more tightly in his. "I wasn't going to tell you this, because I didn't want you to worry, but I guess you need to know."

"Need to know what?"

He took another deep breath and ran his thumb over the back of her hand, forcing himself to loosen his grip, marveling at the smoothness of her skin. "I went back to where I found you in the woods, to look for tracks. They'd been wiped out—even yours. Someone was being careful. But whoever it was wasn't careful enough."

"You found something?"

He saw her shiver, felt it through their joined hands, and tightened his fingers around hers. "I found part of a footprint."

"And?"

"And . . ." He swallowed heavily, his heart full of remorse as he met her questioning gaze. "It was too small to belong to a man, and any boy that small would be too young to do something like that. That means whoever attacked you was a woman."

Angela gasped. "Couldn't it have been my footprint?"

"No. Whoever it was wore moccasins."

"But who could it have been? Who would want to kill me?" she cried, confused, obviously frightened. He couldn't blame her. He was frightened for her. "All the women I've met have been so nice to me," she said.

143

"I don't know who it was. That's why you're not staying here alone. You're coming with me."

Angela agreed wholeheartedly. After what he'd just told her, she wasn't about to stay in camp without him.

Pace brought the pinto. Matt lifted Angela to the saddle, then mounted behind her. They rode out with Cochise, his two wives, and his brother, Juan.

It wasn't nearly so scary being on top of a horse this time, Angela realized. Maybe she was getting used to it. But she would have felt a whole lot better about it if Matt had worn some clothes. For heaven's sake! She was sitting on the front flap of his breechcloth!

Naiche, Cochise's youngest son, must have just returned from his hunt, for he joined them as they were leaving camp. Matt explained that Naiche would ride ahead to make sure it wasn't a trap, then they would follow him. Cochise trusted Taglito completely, but he'd never had any reason to trust bluecoats. They could have forced Taglito to bring them. There might be more soldiers on the way. It wasn't likely, but it was possible.

Angela did her best to concentrate, knowing Matt expected her to understand what was happening. But it wasn't easy, what with his bare chest pressed against her back, his heart thudding against her ribs, his thigh rubbing the back of hers, his arms wrapped around her. It all felt so familiar . . . so right . . . and made thinking difficult.

But when she realized what Matt was saying she straightened abruptly. "Cochise sends his own son into a possible trap?" Angela was shocked. She had the impression Cochise had more integrity than that.

"It's safe enough for Naiche," Matt said. His right hand released the reins and rested on the knee she had wrapped around the saddle horn, while his gaze remained on the trail. The gesture, the touch, seemed totally unconscious on his part, and for some reason she didn't understand, Angela felt like smiling.

"None of the soldiers will know he's Cochise's son, and Taglito would never tell them if it would cause Naiche harm. It's really just a formality. Besides, the only thing the Army could accomplish by harming Cochise's son would be an all out war, and they don't want that any more than the Chúk'ánéné do."

"But what if they took Naiche and held him hostage?" she managed. Heat radiated from his hand on her knee, making thought and speech difficult. "Couldn't they force Cochise to surrender?"

"They tried something like that back in sixty-one," Matt said, his thumb brushing absently along the inside of her knee.

Angela shivered and barely held her train of thought. "What happened?"

"Some shavetail lieutenant fresh out of West Point invited Cochise into Apache Pass and tried to arrest him for something he hadn't done. Cochise made the mistake of believing the U.S. Army would honor the flag of truce the good lieutenant was flying, and took one of his brothers, a couple of nephews, a woman—I don't remember who she was—and a couple of kids."

Matt's thumb caressing her inner knee jerked to a halt as he seemed to finally realize what he was doing. He gripped the reins tightly in both hands. Angela breathed a sigh—was it relief, or regret?—and once again concentrated on his words.

"When Lieutenant Bascom ordered them all arrested, Cochise managed to escape, but the others weren't so lucky. Bascom held them hostage, so Cochise went out and got his own hostages. Neither side would give in, so Cochise killed his hostages, and Bascom hung Cochise's brother and nephews."

"How horrible!" She grew chilled at the thought of such violence. "What happened to the woman and the children?"

"Bascom eventually let them go."

"What did Cochise do then?"

"He went to war. He started raiding supply trains, stagecoaches, farms, ranches, you name it. And he didn't stop until just over a year ago. Ten years, all those people killed—red and white—just because some idiot from back East wanted to make a name for himself by capturing an Apache chief."

"You think the war could have been prevented if it hadn't been for that Lieutenant Bascom?"

"Oh, probably not," he replied with a trace of sadness. "There were too many whites moving in and taking their land, running off their game, leaving those who were here first with barely enough to make it through the winter." He closed his eyes briefly and shook his head. "No, I guess it was inevitable. But we'll never know, will we?"

Angela longed to offer words of comfort to ease him, yet the very idea confused her. She shook the notion away. "Whatever happened to the lieutenant?"

"Bascom?" Matt grunted. "He got what everybody thought he deserved. The Army thought he deserved a promotion, so they made him a captain about a year later. Not too long after that, I heard he finally got what the Apaches thought he deserved. He got killed in the War Between the States."

They'd been riding slowly, giving Naiche time to go ahead. Now Naiche signaled to come on, so Cochise motioned the party forward. They arrived at the campsite a few minutes later. Matt lifted Angela to the ground, and she watched Cochise embrace a tall, older man with red hair and beard. They greeted each other like old friends.

"Taglito?" she asked Matt.

"Uh huh."

"Let me guess," she whispered. "Does his name have anything to do with his red hair?"

"You're learning," Matt said with a chuckle. "It means Red Beard."

With a quick grin and nod, Tom Jeffords acknowledged Matt's presence. For an instant Jeffords let his mind wonder who the white girl was, then he dismissed the question as unimportant. He had business to attend to. Important business.

It was with a great deal more self-control than Jeffords ever realized he had that he held himself in check. He knew he had to give this occasion the seriousness it was due, but it was a struggle to keep from jumping and shouting and laughing in his excitement. For Cochise himself to ride out to greet them, knowing his friend Taglito had brought a bluecoat "star chief," meant Tom's hunch had been right: Cochise was ready to talk peace!

Nervous now and trying with all his might not to show it, Tom Jeffords introduced Cochise to General Oliver Otis Howard. The two powerful leaders—one tall, strong, muscular; the other shorter, older, one-armed—shook hands in the white man's fashion. Or as close to it as possible, since Howard's missing arm was his right one.

The two leaders greeted each other in Spanish. But since *"Buenos días, jefe* Cochise," was the extent of Howard's Spanish, Tom acted as interpreter for them.

General Howard, through Tom, told Cochise he'd been sent by President Grant specifically to talk peace with the Chiricahua.

"No one wants peace more than I do," Cochise said.

"Then, sir," Howard replied, "let's make peace."

Tom Jeffords felt his heart whack against his ribs. *Hot diggity! Here we go.*

"My people have been at peace for more than a year," Cochise said. "Our horses are poor and few. We could have had more by raiding, but this we did not do."

General Howard nodded his head and pursed his lips. "There's a place where you could live much better than you do now, a big reservation on the Rio Grande."

"I've been there," Cochise said. "I've seen that country, and I like it, but it is too far from our home. If that's the only way for us to have peace, I will go there, but many of my people will not. It will break up our tribe."

The tall Apache chief looked the shorter, one-armed man directly in the eye and spoke earnestly, yet with great dignity. "Why not let us stay here, and give us the place you call Apache Pass? Give us that, and we will protect it. I will personally see that no one is harmed or robbed by any Indians, even those of other tribes."

"Perhaps we could do that," Howard said, obviously surprised by the idea. He seemed to think it over a moment, then went on to talk about the reservation on the Rio Grande.

But Cochise was no longer interested in living there. "Why keep us on a reservation?" he asked. "When we make peace, we will keep it and honor it. Why won't we be allowed to go around as free Americans? When you made peace with Mexico, you did not keep Mexicans on a reservation. You allow them to live wherever they want. They can travel freely. Why not let us do the same?"

Sweat popped out all over Tom's face. He knew Cochise would resist being kept on a reservation. He also knew the resistance would do Cochise no good if he really wanted peace. But Howard, it seemed, was a born diplomat. Tom eased a bit—but only a bit—as the general spoke.

"Perhaps some day that will be possible," Howard said. "But there has been so much hostility between our peoples, on both sides. I'm afraid the first time you tried to go somewhere where there were Americans, they'd attack you on sight. For the time being, I believe all your people will be safer if they stay together on a reservation. It's true you won't be allowed to come and go freely, but we'll also keep the white men from entering the reservation."

When Tom had translated, Cochise reluctantly saw the wisdom in the suggestion but insisted the reservation for the Chiricahua be established in the Dragoon Mountains, rather than on the Rio Grande.

"How long can you stay, General?" Cochise asked. "Do you have the time to come to our *rancheria*? Can you wait for others to join us so we may talk about this?"

"My mission is to meet you and your people, and make peace. I'll stay as long as it takes," the general stated firmly.

A lump of pure emotion lodged itself in Tom's throat as the two leaders shook hands again and smiled at each other. He had to look away quickly or risk making a complete fool of himself.

Raising his face to the sky, he blinked rapidly. When his vision cleared he noticed the sky was a brighter shade of blue than he'd ever seen before. The white glow of the sun touched his skin and warmed his soul.

The Apaches, if they were preparing for battle, would say it was a good day to die.

But these were not battle preparations; these were peace talks.

It's not a good day to die—it's a good day to live. To live, and make peace.

Tom lowered his gaze from the sky and met Matt Colton's eager, hopeful expression.

Matt returned the look, finally relaxing the tight control of his facial muscles and allowing his excited grin to break loose. It was the only concession to his emotions he could allow himself without screaming and laughing and making a total ass of himself.

His grin widened a little when he read the same struggle for control in Tom Taglito Jeffords' eyes.

It was a sign of how eagerly everyone here sought peace that the only introductions that had been made so far were between Cochise and Howard. Taglito was only now introducing everyone else. The second soldier was General Howard's aide, Captain Joseph Sladen.

The two Chiricahua scouts were Shanta and Fletcher, both from Camp Bowie.

"Fletcher?" Angela questioned.

Matt gave her a smile. "Well, his real name is Fle-Cha-Ka-Eda-Ty-gee."

"Right," Angela said. "Fletcher."

"Matt! How the hell are you?" Taglito called as he finally broke free and approached. "And more important, who's this pretty little thing with you?"

"Tom!" Matt grinned and shook hands with his old friend. "It's good to see you. I'd like you to meet my wife, Angela. Angela, this is Tom Jeffords, an old friend of my family and of the Chúk'ánéné, known to some as Taglito."

"Your wife! Well I'll be da—Well, this is a surprise!"

Jeffords personally introduced them to the rest of his party. General Howard was a soft-spoken man whose white beard quivered when he smiled. His aide was young, nice looking, and overly serious. Fletcher was quiet and shy. Shanta, too, was quiet as he stared from Matt to Angela, then back again.

Matt quickly nudged Angela forward and introduced her as his wife. He felt her tremble beside him as Shanta eyed her carefully. There was no doubt the scout who'd taken the twins to the post that day at Camp Bowie recognized her. Something other than surprise passed across the Apache's face. Something more like doubt. It passed quickly. "You wouldn't be Angela Barnes, from the Hargrave wagon train, would you?" he asked softly.

Matt held his breath.

Angela's face went white. "I-I . . ."

"We'll talk later," Shanta said, eyeing them both. Then he turned his back and walked away.

Matt let out his breath, but Angela's trembling increased. Neither spoke as he lifted her to the saddle and mounted behind her.

By the time they returned to the compound the entire camp was in chaos. A peace delegation directly from the President of the United States was big, welcome news to most. Runners had already been sent to the other camps to call in those leaders who'd ridden with Cochise over the years. The visitors were made welcome and appeared to be enjoying themselves. Pace and Serena volunteered their services as translators, and General Howard seemed delighted with them.

We'll talk later.

The ominous words spoken that afternoon by the Apache scout she'd first seen at Camp Bowie filled Angela with dread. Her nerves stretched so taut she felt like her whole body was ready to snap. She spent the rest of the day tensing at every footfall behind her, starting at every shadow that loomed near, jumping nearly out of her skin at an accidental touch.

Now it was late, the entire camp dark and silent for the night, and still she couldn't relax. A small blaze crackled merrily within its circle of rocks beneath the smoke hole of the wickiup, mocking her with its cheerfulness.

Next to her, Matt sat staring toward the doorflap. He tried to hide that he was every bit as tense as she was, but she read the signs in his silence, his clenched jaw, his furrowed brow.

She heard a slight sound outside and stiffened. Matt placed a hand on her arm, she assumed to calm her. It didn't. It merely let her feel his tension through his tight grip.

Low and soft, a voice came from just beyond the door. "Bear Killer."

Angela choked back a cry, knowing instantly it was Shanta. Shanta, who somehow knew her name and that she'd been with Mr. Hargrave's wagon train. What else did he know?

Tahnito and his friends had burned her wagon—a

sure sign she hadn't left peaceably. Shanta must know she'd been captured. And if he knew, did that mean the Army knew? Did General Howard know some of Cochise's band had captured her? Would he question Cochise about her?

She felt all the lies, hers and Matt's, tremble beneath their own weight and threaten to tumble, destroying the one thing Matt, as well as Cochise and others, wanted most in the world. Peace.

Angela straightened her shoulders and forced her trembling to a halt. There had to be a way out of this maze of lies. There simply had to be, and she'd find it. *Even if it takes more lies?* a little voice demanded.

Yes. No matter what it took, she couldn't let Matt down.

Matt called for Shanta to enter. The scout squatted across the fire from them and started in with a rapid, guttural stream of Apache.

"In English, Shanta. Angela needs to hear this."

"All right," the scout said, his face as unreadable as a rock. "I wanted to warn you, Captain Sladen is going to start asking questions."

"About what?" Matt asked.

"About your wife, and how she came to be here."

Angela inhaled sharply and held her breath.

"Why?"

"Because nearly two weeks ago, a man rode in to Camp Bowie to warn the commander that the wagon train he scouted for had been attacked by Apaches."

"That's a lie!" Angela said hotly, forgetting momentarily about her own lies. "That had to be Abe Miller who carried that tale. He saw one lone Apache, Chee, and shot him. That's what he calls an Indian attack!"

"Take it easy," Matt said. "Let him finish."

Shanta continued. "This man left the fort, then showed up again the next day. He said he'd found where one wagon, belonging to the Barnes family, had evidently turned back toward Bowie, but hadn't made

152

it. The commander sent me to check it out. I went out, scouted, and reported my findings."

In a corner of her mind Angela vaguely noted Shanta's English was every bit as good as Chee's. She wondered where he'd learned it.

"What did you report?" Matt asked heavily. His tone gave Angela a sick feeling in the pit of her stomach.

"I reported a burned wagon, two fresh graves, the footprints of one survivor, and tracks from three unshod horses. It was Tahnito, wasn't it?"

Angela felt the blood drain from her face. "What makes you say that?" she whispered.

"I'd recognize that troublemaker's trail anywhere. I followed. It was a girl they took. They swung north, as if to leave a false trail, but made no attempt to cover their tracks. They were drunk. They made her run on foot the second day as they turned south. That night when they made camp, there was a struggle, and a fourth rider, Chee, joined them. They rode toward the hills and camped among the rocks. Chee left, met you, Bear Killer, and you returned with him."

Good heavens. How could he know so much?

"The next morning you put the girl on your horse and brought her here."

"And you reported all of this?" Matt asked.

"I reported losing the trail in the rocks the first day. And I didn't mention any names."

Angela nearly sagged with relief. He was on their side.

Of course he was. He, too, would want peace for his people. He hadn't told the Army all he knew.

She licked her lips nervously. All she had to do was come up with a plausible reason for the things he saw and reported.

A reason other than the truth.

She could feel Matt's gaze on her, hear his unspoken question, feel his silent plea for her to keep her word.

153

After a long silence, she took a deep breath and stiffened her spine.

"My mother was very sick," she said softly. "Chee knew I was to meet Matt in Tucson, but he saw that our wagon turned back toward the fort alone, so he sent Tahnito and his friends to make sure we got there safely."

Angela locked her fingers together and forced herself to stare straight into Shanta's eyes. She had to clear her throat three times before she could speak past the huge lump of fear. "But my mother never made it," she whispered. "She died that night." Tears gathered, but she blinked them back. "The next morning my father and I buried her. I went back to the wagon while he stood over her grave. The next thing I knew, there was a man in the trees pointing a gun at my father."

"What man?" Shanta asked.

Angela shook her head and cleared her throat again, this time of sadness. "I don't know. All I could see was the hand that held the pistol. He . . . shot my father, killed him. I shot back, somehow hit him in the hand, and he ran."

Tears rushed again, nearly blinding her. Matt loosened his tight grip on her and ran his hand up and down her arm, soothing her, giving her courage.

"I buried my father, then Tahnito and his friends came. They knew they couldn't leave me there alone, so they took me to meet Matt. Chee had gone after Matt to tell him my family and I had turned back. When Matt found me, we came here and got married."

After an endless moment of silent tension, a slow grin spread across Shanta's face. "You were meeting Matt in Tucson to get married?"

Angela glanced at Matt, then nodded.

Shanta's grin faded. "Why did you act like strangers at Camp Bowie?" he demanded. "Why didn't you go with him then?"

Angela's eyes darted nervously from side to side,

154

then met Shanta's piercing gaze. "Because . . . because I hadn't told my parents about him yet. They didn't know who he was or that we were getting married. I'd planned to tell them once we reached Tucson."

Shanta let his breath out loudly. "Stick to that story. It might just work." Then he was gone, and Matt and Angela were alone. She was too sick with worry to even be glad the questions were over.

"Are you all right?" Matt asked.

Angela shivered, then nodded.

Suddenly Matt grabbed her and drew her to his chest, his lips crushing hers. She forgot the lies she'd just told, forgot her fear of being trapped by them, forgot everything as he kissed her thoroughly. His tongue danced in her mouth, and her bones seemed to melt. Her arms wound around his neck of their own accord. Her heart slammed against her ribs, then seemed to stop altogether as the kiss continued.

Matt pulled away, and they both opened their eyes in shock at the emotions they each felt. "Keep looking at me like that," he whispered, "and our annulment's off again, Angel."

Angela continued staring at him, her eyes wide, her wet, tender lips slightly open. Finally the fog in her brain began to lift, and she shook herself and turned away.

My goodness! Was that all it took, just one kiss, for her to completely lose control? She knew right then she was in trouble. This man who called himself her husband was too much for her. If he hadn't stopped kissing her, she'd have done anything he wanted.

"You were perfect," Matt said. "Thank you."

It was a long moment before Angela realized he wasn't talking about the kiss, but about what she'd said to Shanta.

"Perfect! I was scared to death. And besides, he didn't believe a word of what I said, and you know it."

"Of course he didn't. He knows exactly what happened. But he's on our side, Angela. He knows if the truth comes out it could blow this whole peace mission to hell and back. If that captain asks questions, all you have to do is tell him what you told Shanta. It'll work, I know it will."

Angela thought hard while she removed her dress and crawled beneath the blanket. So much depended on her keeping her story straight. What if she couldn't? What if she stumbled over all the lies? She shuddered at the thought.

In the dim glow of the dying fire, Matt chuckled.

"What's so funny?"

"I was just wondering . . . is your name really Barnes?"

They looked at each other a minute, then burst out laughing.

In another wickiup, located near the center of the *rancheria,* two old friends passed a jug of *tiswin* back and forth.

Tom Jeffords took a swallow of the thick, yeasty corn beer and remembered. It had been over ten years since he'd sought Daniella Colton's help in locating Cochise. As Cochise's adopted daughter, known to Apaches as Woman of Magic, she'd been hesitant to give him any information that might harm Cochise.

But when she'd found out he'd gone to the unheard-of trouble to learn the language of the Chúk'ánéné, and that he planned to ride alone into the stronghold to ask Cochise to let the mail carriers ride through the territory unmolested, she'd reconsidered.

Goddamn, he'd been scared that first time he'd come here. He took another swig and passed the jug.

Cochise accepted it and took a swallow. He, too, was remembering. He remembered the first time this tall, thin white man with red hair on his face as well as his head rode into camp, alone, unarmed. Cochise's first instinct had been to have the man killed when the trail guards first reported him two days earlier. He grinned at the memory.

He'd never regretted his decision to let the man ride in.

He might never have made that decision but for his adopted white daughter. Woman of Magic, her husband, Yellow Hair Colton, and Colton's son, then known as Little Bear, had shown Cochise that some whites, few though they be, were honest and trustworthy. Cochise had gambled that Taglito would prove to be as honorable a man as Yellow Hair Colton. And he'd been right.

Cochise accepted the tobacco pouch and papers Taglito handed him. He couldn't remember the last time he'd had real tobacco. And white man's paper to roll it in. This ban on raiding had its drawbacks.

"So, my friend," he said after he'd exhaled his first drag. "How is it that after staying away from us for years, you come after all this time and bring with you that which you could not know I wanted, but that which I have prayed for with all my heart?"

"It wasn't so hard to know your mind," Taglito told him. "I knew you were tired of war as soon as your band quit raiding last year. But I've not brought you any sure thing. All I've brought you is a chance."

Cochise nodded solemnly. "A chance, my friend, is all I ask."

Chapter Fifteen

No one had an opportunity to question Angela the next morning, because all the women were busy preparing a huge feast in honor of the visitors. Even with the limited use of her right arm, Angela was run ragged.

There was corn to be ground for corn cakes. There was fresh meat to clean and spit, then turn slowly over the many cook fires. There were herbs to be gathered for seasoning, fresh water to be hauled from the stream. There were wild, exuberant children to be kept out of trouble, and dozens of dogs to be kept from the roasting meat.

Huera and Serena stayed with Angela every minute, so Matt decided it was safe for him to leave her. Angela was relieved. His constant presence in the face of the questioning looks several women gave him only served to remind her that someone had tried to kill her. Besides, it would have looked odd if he'd hung around with the women all day, especially when Cochise requested his presence.

Everything went well until Matt came to her in the late afternoon wearing a tense look. "Angela's tired, Serena. Why don't you go see if you can help Nod-ah-Sti?"

"But, Matt, we were just getting ready to —" Angela began.

"Your arm's hurting. Put your sling back on. We'll see you later, Rena."

"What was that all about?" Angela asked once they were inside the wickiup.

"The trail guards just spotted my parents. They're on their way in."

"Your . . . your parents?" A sick feeling settled in her stomach like a rock in a pond. "What'll we do?"

"They'll run into the visitors before they get here, so we have to be there to meet them before anybody starts talking about you, congratulating them on their new daughter-in-law."

"But—"

"And put that sling back on. It'll give us something to talk about besides how you got here and where you came from."

"Is this going to work, Matt?"

"I don't know. They already know something, or they wouldn't be here. We'll just have to play it by ear. Come on."

Angela had to practically run to keep up with him. It was either that, or fall down and be dragged, for he had a tight hold on her hand, and his stride was long. They reached the central campfire just as two riders came in, and Angela stared at them openmouthed.

The man was big and blond and handsome, and very obviously Matt's father. The two men looked so much alike it was remarkable. If they were closer in age, they could have passed for identical twins, right down to the scar each bore on his cheek.

Angela recognized the woman from Matt's description, but he'd failed to say how beautiful his stepmother was. Her long, black hair fell over her shoulders in waves and hung to her waist, the white streak down the side glowing in contrast.

Travis and Daniella Colton.

Angela's knees weakened. Her parents-in-law! Not that she really considered herself married to Matt, but everyone else did. His parents would. What would they think? Her hair was mussed, her face was streaked with sweat and freckles, her dress was soiled, and her arm was in a sling. If she'd purposely tried to make herself unpresentable, she couldn't have done a better job.

The two dismounted and greeted Cochise warmly, then walked together toward Matt and Angela. The four of them stood silent for a moment, the older couple looking Angela over carefully.

"Matt, what's—"

Travis Colton's words ended in a pained cough, triggered undoubtedly by the sudden impact of his wife's elbow against his ribs.

Startled by the byplay, Angela waited warily as Matt's stepmother reached toward her with both hands.

"My dear," the woman said, "we're so glad to finally meet you." She grasped Angela's cold hands in her warm ones.

Matt's hand on Angela's shoulder gave Angela the courage she needed to return his stepmother's smile. "And I, you." Angela was proud of herself. Her voice barely shook at all, even though her knees and smile did. "Matt's told me so much about you."

Angela chanced a quick glance at Matt's father. The man's face was carefully blank.

A moment later the newcomers were surrounded by members of the tribe who'd come to welcome them, and there was no more chance for private talk. Angela nearly wilted with relief at having the inevitable questions postponed.

It was later in the evening, while the four adult Coltons sat with Tom Jeffords, before any more questions were asked. Angela felt Matt tense beside her. She followed his gaze to see Captain Sladen heading directly toward them.

Her first instinct was to run. Matt must have read or felt her thoughts, for he grasped her hand and laced his

160

fingers through hers. She held on to him as if she were drowning and he was her lifeline.

"Pardon me if I'm intruding, ladies, gentlemen," Sladen said, doffing his hat and nodding to the women.

"Not at all, Captain," Matt answered easily. "Have a seat. What can we do for you?"

Sladen sat on the ground with them and fidgeted with his hat while Angela held her breath. "Well." He cleared his throat. "I don't know how to go about this. It's going to sound a little crazy. But, mind, I'm just following orders."

"Orders, Captain?" Daniella Colton asked.

"Yes, ma'am." He cleared his throat again, then looked at Angela. "I'm supposed to try to locate a young lady answering your description, Mrs. Colton."

"Really?" Angela said breathlessly. She didn't have to feign the breathlessness at all. This moment had been looming over her all day, stretching her nerves near the breaking point. At least the waiting was over. It was happening.

She forced herself to take a deep breath in an attempt to relax and appear normal. All she had to do was repeat the story she'd made up last night for Shanta. She had to keep it straight, though, so as not to trip herself on all the lies. Matt was counting on her. He'd saved her life. She wanted desperately to be able to do this for him.

And she *could* do it. She *would*. She squeezed Matt's fingers for strength. What was there to worry about? Who here could contradict her story anyway? With that thought came a confidence she'd despaired of ever feeling again. She jerked her mind back to the man before her and gave him her full attention.

"Yes, ma'am. You see . . ." Sladen cleared his throat yet again, the sound grating on Angela's already taut nerves. "You see, a girl named Angela Barnes was kidnapped from a wagon train by Apaches, and the tracks led in this general direction."

"But, Captain," Angela protested, blinking her eyes

161

and swallowing hard. "Surely there's been some mistake."

"How's that, ma'am?"

"I'm Angela Barnes, or I was," she said, casting Matt a tender look. Funny how easily that came, even in spite of the fear ricocheting through her body. "And I was with a wagon train. But I certainly wasn't kidnapped by Apaches."

"But your wagon was found burned, your parents dead, and you missing."

"Maybe you'd better explain to the captain just what happened, Angel," Matt suggested with a soft smile.

"Yes, I guess I'd better." So Angela repeated the story she'd invented last night for Shanta, telling how she was to meet Matt in Tucson, but had to turn back. It wasn't hard to produce real tears when she told about her parents, and she vaguely heard Daniella mumbling her sympathy. "So you see, Captain, I was never kidnapped at all. Someone just jumped to conclusions."

Captain Sladen smiled at her. "You're a lucky man, Colton. This little lady went through a powerful lot just to get to you."

"I know," Matt said, putting his arm around her and hugging her to his side.

"But what do I tell the commander at Camp Bowie about your wagon? What happened to it?"

"Oh," Angela said with a nervous laugh. "That was my fault, and I'm paying for it every day. I knocked over a lantern while climbing out over the tailgate. By the time I realized the wagon was on fire, it was too late to save anything. All my clothes were lost, and my hope chest." She cast Matt a look of despair.

"I told you not to worry about that, sweetheart," Matt said, giving her another hug. "We'll buy you all new clothes when we get to Tucson."

Captain Sladen shook his head. "I'm right sorry about you losing your family like that. Lucky for you you had Colton waiting for you. No telling what might have happened to you out there on the trail, all alone." He shook his head again, then chuckled. "My wife's going to love this story when I tell her. She'll think it's the most romantic thing she's ever heard. But I think I'll skip the part about all your clothes burning. She'd probably set fire to her closet just so she could buy a whole new wardrobe."

Angela felt her heartbeat start to slow to a more normal rhythm. It was working! The captain believed her! She felt weak with relief. Until Tom Jeffords spoke.

"Where are you from, Angela? How'd you meet Matt?"

Angela's heartbeat raced again. She opened her mouth to speak, but nothing came out. Matt squeezed her fingers gently and answered for her.

"She's from Memphis. I met her when I was up there last year."

Just then Matt's father, seated to Angela's left, began to cough and choke. Daniella, sitting on the other side of him, pounded him on the back. "Are you all right, Travis?" she asked. She pounded on him a few more times, frowning, until he scowled and motioned for her to leave him alone.

"I'm fine," he finally managed.

When the captain left, Tom rolled himself a cigarette and took a long drag, exhaling slowly. Angela could practically see his mind ticking away. His eyes said he hadn't believed a word of her story. She held her breath, waiting for his denouncement.

"Well, Matt, you've got yourself the prettiest little bride this side of the Mississippi. If you're smart," he said with a wink as he stood to leave, "you'll keep her."

"What do you suppose he meant by that?" Angela whispered when he was gone.

"Knowing Tom, there's no telling," Matt said easily. "Come on, Angel, let's turn in. I know you're tired and your arm's bothering you. Dad, Dani, we'll see you tomorrow."

163

"Matt?"

"Don't ask, Dad."

Travis Colton wrinkled his brow in frustration and eyed his son. He started to speak, but Daniella cut him off with a hand on his shoulder.

"Leave it for now, Travis. The night has too many ears."

Travis heaved a sigh and nodded. "All right. For now. Good night, you two."

" 'Night, Dad, Dani."

Before anything else could happen, Matt hustled Angela off to their wickiup. A shaft of moonlight streamed in through the smoke hole and cut a swath in the darkness. As Angela entered the streak of light on her way to the bed, Matt gently caught her arm and turned her toward him, then tilted her face up.

Angela's breath caught at the tender touch of his hand on her chin. Only half his face was visible, the other half shadowed. Her heart skipped a beat at the look in the eye above his scarred cheek. It was a soft look filled with many things she didn't understand. When he spoke, his voice was scarcely more than a husky whisper.

"Thank you."

She shook her head and opened her mouth to speak, but he closed her lips with his thumb.

"You held the fate of an entire nation in your hands tonight. With one word, you could have destroyed the Chúk'ánéné, yet you didn't. You lied for them. You kept your promise. Forgive me for ever doubting your word."

His calloused thumb felt rough and exciting against her lips before it trailed over her chin and down her throat. He bent his head, throwing his features into darkness, making it impossible for Angela to read his face. Her lips parted. Surely he could feel her trembling, hear her heart pounding in her chest.

A soft puff of warm breath brushed her cheek, then a softer, warmer pair of lips feathered across her mouth. Her very bones melted, but somehow she managed to

164

stay on her feet. His lips pressed hers again, lightly, gently.

"Thank you," he whispered.

When he lifted his head and backed away, Angela nearly cried out in protest.

Later, when they were lying side by side in bed, not touching, Angela asked, "Were you really in Memphis last year?"

"Huh uh."

"Then, your parents knew you were lying?"

"Uh huh."

Both of them spent hours staring up at the grass dome in the darkness before they finally fell asleep.

Chapter Sixteen

It was several days before all the other leaders Cochise had sent for finally arrived. In the meantime, the *rancheria* was in a constant state of turmoil.

And Angela was in a constant state of apprehension. She kept waiting for Travis or Daniella to ask the inevitable questions, but they seemed content to leave matters alone for the time being. Perhaps Matt had spoken with them privately.

The only good thing to happen during those days was that Angela was reassured she wasn't with child. She'd never dreamed she'd ever be glad for that time of month to come, but she was this time. At least now she wouldn't have to worry about that particular complication. She could put their wedding night firmly in the past . . . where it belonged. She shook off the strange feeling of emptiness that thought produced.

It had been years since Cochise and Taglito had seen one another, so now they took time out to get reacquainted and caught up on the latest news. Travis and Hal-Say joined a group of hunters to provide more fresh meat for the other Chiricahua who were coming in. Matt and Daniella, sometimes accompanied by Angela (whenever Huera didn't need her) or the twins (when they were allowed), took charge of showing General Howard and Captain Sladen around.

General Howard was especially fascinated by the children of the tribe, and he asked Pace and Serena dozens of questions. Those two immediately swelled with their own importance.

Daniella rolled her eyes and groaned. "There'll be no living with them after this."

"That's the second dog I've seen today with its feet wrapped," Sladen noted aloud. "Have they been injured?"

Daniella smiled and shook her head. "That's the same thought I had when I first saw them years ago," she answered. "Those aren't wrappings; they're moccasins." Sladen furrowed his brow and blinked while Howard frowned. Daniella glanced at Matt, and her grin widened. "This is rocky terrain. The moccasins are to protect the dogs' feet."

The two white men looked at each other. "Well, I'll be. . . ." Howard muttered.

Daniella could practically read their thoughts — thoughts about a vicious tribe of murdering savages who made moccasins to protect the feet of their puppies.

Sladen wandered off on his own, and Pace took the general to the boys' playing field. There he showed him the twisted grass target the boys used in their bow and arrow practice. There were a dozen other games going on, on the field. Howard was surprised at how ordinary and universal these games were. One group of boys was playing hide and seek at the edge of the woods. There was also a foot race in progress, and teams were being chosen for tug of war. In the center of the field four different wrestling matches were under way.

"How extraordinary," General Howard said out loud. He ran his thumb over the pebbly leather cover of the Bible tucked beneath his belt and felt blessed at being the one chosen to bring peace to these people. "It's absolutely remarkable that people from two such diverse cultures, Americans and Apaches, should each begin there lives playing the same childhood games."

His idea was reinforced when he saw young girls building their own small wickiups and furnishing them with broken pieces of pottery and scraps of hide. Some of them even had cornhusk dolls dressed in leather, with hair from a horse's tail sewn into the dolls' heads.

"They're playing house!" Howard said.

He even saw two girls playing with a string. They were making a cat's cradle! "My mother taught me that when I was just a youngster," he muttered.

Matt and Daniella looked at each other and smiled. No matter what he'd thought about Apaches and their way of life when he came here, the children of the tribe had won the general over as nothing else could have.

Daniella blinked back the sudden rush of tears that came to her eyes. Long before the twins were born, Dee-O-Det had told her that her children would be important to the People. They would be a bridge between the white man and the Apache.

As if her thoughts had conjured him up, she saw Dee-O-Det out of the corner of her eye. She looked at him fully, but he was watching Pace and Serena with General Howard. The old shaman wore a pleased, knowing look on his weathered face. He looked at Daniella then and raised his brows as if to say, "Did I not tell you? A shaman knows these things."

One by one, the other Chiricahua leaders arrived. Juh came up from the south, and with him were Golthlay and old Nana. From the west there was Mangas-Chee, son of Mon-ache—Mangas Coloradas—who'd been murdered years ago after asking for peace and surrendering to the bluecoats. Chihuahua came in from the east.

When all the leaders from the outlying camps were assembled and the negotiations were ready to begin in earnest, Travis and Daniella decided Cochise had enough on his mind without having to worry about Pace and Serena, so they decided to take the twins home.

"We'll see you soon?" Travis asked when they were ready to ride. "Both of you?"

Matt put his arm around Angela's shoulders and pulled her to his side. "We'll stay till this treaty is worked out. Cochise has asked me to help translate. Then we'll be home. Both of us."

Anyone who wasn't needed elsewhere spent every minute possible listening to the negotiations. Several times General Howard and Captain Sladen were asked to take a walk, and heated discussions ensued amongst the Chiricahua. There were some present who were against any type of treaty with the white man. Tahnito was one of the most vocal.

"Why should we let them tell us where we can and cannot go? Where we can and cannot live? We were here first! It is our own land they want to give us!"

"If you don't have anything new to say, young pup, then keep quiet," Cochise said. "We've already been over that trail."

Tahnito opened his mouth to argue further, but Bear Killer stopped him with a sharp motion of his hand. *"Bini',* Tahnito," Bear Killer warned. "Let it go."

The two men stared at each other, their eyes locked. What Tahnito saw in his foe's eyes turned his anger into a boiling rage. The message was plain. The white girl was safe now. If Tahnito continued to hinder the making of this treaty, Bear Killer would expose him. Tahnito's hatred knew no bounds. It was true he didn't care if there ever was peace. But he could not afford to be the one to prevent it. Cochise would murder him.

Tahnito glanced at his chief, then threw Bear Killer a murderous look before taking his leave.

Someday, my treacherous white friend, I will kill you.

Angela slumped with relief when Tahnito left. She saw Matt's shoulders visibly relax.

Poor Matt. He was working so hard for this treaty. At times it seemed as if it was more important to him than it was to Cochise or Howard. He never left a meeting in progress for any reason. When the meetings broke up, he went from group to group, helping hammer out the myriad differences and misunderstandings. He carefully measured each word he spoke, lest the words lose something in their translation.

When he finally entered the wickiup late each night he was exhausted. One night he didn't make it to bed at all. He'd stayed beside the central campfire with Howard, negotiating for more land for the reservation, going over each and every boundary. He won some points, lost others.

Sometimes, when Angela set a meal before him, he was so exhausted he'd just stare at it like he wasn't sure what it was. Last night he'd been so stiff from sitting long hours without moving that Angela knelt beside him as he lay on his face, and she massaged his shoulders.

Unsure of herself at first, she'd reached for him timidly. But when her fingers came in contact with his warm brown skin, they developed a mind of their own. She traced the length of his spine to where it disappeared beneath the blanket draped over his hips, then each long scar that crossed his back. When she reached for his shoulders and began to massage them, he moaned. Long before she'd worked the stiffness from his muscles, he was asleep. Her sleep had been slow in coming.

Just thinking about how she'd touched him last night made her fingers tingle.

And that wasn't the only strange sensation she was aware of. The hair on her nape had been standing up for the past hour. She felt like someone was staring a hole through the back of her head. When she couldn't stand it anymore, she darted a quick glance over her shoulder.

It was that same girl again. Angela had seen her around camp before, and each time she ran into her, the Apache girl had glared at her in obvious hatred.

Angela sighed and turned back around. She was just another one of Matt's would-be harem. There were at least a half-dozen girls around camp who hadn't been the least bit happy when Angela had married Matt. The others had apparently given up hope and turned their attentions elsewhere. But this one still sent her nasty looks.

There was a full-fledged argument going on among the Chiricahua now, and Tom had given up trying to translate for Angela.

"Tom," she whispered. "Who's that girl behind me who keeps staring daggers at me?"

Tom glanced casually around, then grimaced. "That's Alope, Tahnito's sister. I'd imagine you're not at the top of her list of favorite people since you married the man she's been after for years."

"That's what I thought."

"Just ignore her. She'll get over it. I understand Tahnito, as head of his family, has received several marriage offers for her lately. She'll pick a husband soon and forget all about you and Matt."

Angela wasn't so certain. If she'd been in love with Matt for years, would she be able to forget him just because he married someone else? She ran her gaze over Matt, seated several yards away from her. Her eyes searched out every inch of him. Sitting cross-legged like he was, wearing nothing but breechcloth and moccasins, his bare, muscular thighs gleamed in the afternoon sun. If he were standing, she knew she'd see firm buttocks, lean hips and waist, and a sculptured, muscular chest. His profile was chiseled and strong. Her fingers tingled again at the thought of his bare back.

No, she thought, if she were in love with him, she'd never be able to forget him.

When she raised her gaze to his face, she blushed to

find him watching her, a knowing little grin on his lips.

Later that night, during the feasting, Matt explained to General Howard why some of the Chiricahua were being difficult about the treaty.

"It's that business at Camp Grant last year, General."

"Heard about that," Howard said. "The whole country heard about it. Nasty business. Can't say as I blame them too much for being on edge."

"I don't know what you heard, but did you know the men were away hunting when those hundred and forty men from Tucson attacked?"

"Away, you say?"

Matt nodded. Grimly, he recalled the tragic, barbaric massacre. "All together, one hundred forty-four Aravaipa Apaches were killed that morning. Did you ever hear how many of them were men?"

"No, as a matter of fact, I don't believe I did."

"Two."

"Two?" Howard cried, outrage plain on his face.

"One old man, and one twelve-year-old boy. All the rest killed were women and children. That doesn't include the twenty-seven children who were captured and sold into slavery in Mexico. And those killed weren't just shot. Many of them were tortured."

Angela shivered in the silence that followed. How could people, red or white, be so cruel? Even during the War Between the States, as far as she knew, nothing that terrible had happened.

"If these people are reluctant to trust you, General," Matt said, "it's not necessarily personal. You can't blame them for being bitter. The Aravaipas had been encamped and farming at Camp Grant for months, with no trouble. The news that William Oury and his group of vigilantes got off scot-free for the massacre has never sat too well, either. And they probably know that Lieutenant Whitman, who stood up for Eskiminzin and the Aravaipas, was court-martialed earlier this year. They don't believe it was a coincidence."

"I heard Whitman was acquitted of whatever he was charged with," Captain Sladen said.

"He was," Matt confirmed. "But now he's up on new charges again. And we all know it's because he was responsible for bringing Oury and his men to trial, for what little good that did."

Tom Jeffords stood up next to Angela, yawning and stretching his arms over his head. "That's enough serious talk for now," he declared. He turned and raised his voice in Apache.

Shanta translated for Angela, Howard, and Sladen, telling them that Taglito was explaining the white man's custom of proposing a toast.

"Good idea," said Howard. "What is he toasting?"

"He proposes a toast to the newlyweds, Matt and Angela."

Angela blushed fiercely and wished the ground would open up and swallow her. She was greatly disappointed when it didn't.

Someone handed her a gourd of *tiswin*, the Apaches' homemade brew. She glanced up to see Chee grinning at her.

"If you think I'm going to drink anything you've been within ten feet of, you're crazy!" she hissed at him.

Matt smirked, Shanta looked puzzled, and Chee burst out laughing.

"I swear, Angela," Chee said. "It's just plain *tiswin*, nothing more. It's the same thing everyone else is drinking. After the bloody nose I got last time, I wouldn't dare try to put something in your drink."

"Angela," Matt whispered. "You have to drink it. Everyone is watching. If you don't, they'll all be offended. It's safe, I promise."

"I'm supposed to believe you?"

But in the end, she drank with the others. She wished instantly that she hadn't. It was the most horrible tasting

173

stuff she'd ever drank in her life! It tasted like pure yeast, with something added—paste maybe—to make it as thick as day-old oatmeal.

Tom started talking again.

"Now he says you're going to show them another American custom," Shanta translated. "Something Apaches don't do, at least not past the age of ten." The scout grinned broadly, his eyes centered on Angela.

"I'm afraid to ask," she said.

Matt laughed as he stood and pulled Angela to her feet. "It's nothing too drastic. All you have to do is kiss me."

"What?! In front of all these people? You've got to be kidding!" Her hands came up to cover her burning cheeks.

"They want to learn about Americans. What better way than for us to show them a kiss? Make it good, Angel. Your country is counting on you."

Matt's arms wrapped around her, and his lips closed over hers. Even with all those people around, Angela felt herself answering him as her arms crept up around his neck.

"Atta boy, Colton!" Tom shouted.

Then others joined in the shouting, and soon catcalls, whistles and war whoops echoed all around them. Matt and Angela broke apart in laughter. Her face was so hot she knew she'd never been so red in her life. She swore that if she didn't die of embarrassment, she'd strangle Tom Jeffords.

The only reason Alope even attempted to keep her passage quiet was she was too filled with rage to be bothered with answering questions about why she was traipsing through the rocks and brush so late at night. Never had she felt such anger.

Even Bear Killer's ceremonial joining with that pale-haired white girl hadn't made her this angry. What did

Alope care for some white girl? Bear Killer would soon grow bored with a wife so ignorant she couldn't construct a wickiup, couldn't even cook.

And when he grew bored, he would turn to Alope, a woman who knew what a man wanted, what a man needed.

It had upset her to hear Chee say that Bear Killer would follow his white upbringing and take only one wife. Somewhere in her heart she knew Chee spoke the truth.

She clutched her new basket and its nearly finished lid to her chest and grimaced at the thought of her earlier failed attempt to rid Bear Killer of this wife of his. But even that bungled effort had not been performed out of anger. No, it had simply been the most practical thing to do at the time.

But tonight at the campfire, Alope had seen the look on Bear Killer's face as he'd gazed at the girl with the strange-colored eyes. She'd seen that look before on other men — that look that came straight from a man's heart and promised a lifetime of love.

That was what she could not abide. That he should marry the girl was one thing. He had been forced into it by Tahnito and his stupid, drunken friends. But that Bear Killer should actually care for the girl! It was not to be tolerated!

Alope's fury did not cool as she climbed higher into the dark rocks, nor did it cool when she found a spot to sit and lean back against a boulder. It raged so fiercely that she stayed awake all night planning ways to dispose of her white rival.

By the time the sun was up she'd not arrived at any workable plan. Angry with herself now, in addition to life in general, she picked up the unfinished lid to her basket and concentrated on weaving the grasses into her own particular style. But her mind kept returning to Bear Killer and the problem of his wife, and she lost track of what she was doing. The finished lid fell into the basket. She'd made it too small.

With a muffled oath, she jerked the offending lid out and threw the basket against the rock at her feet. If it had been a clay pot, she would have felt better, for it would have shattered into a satisfying thousand pieces. But the basket, as if purposely adding to her frustration, merely bounced once, then rolled a few feet down the path, where it came to rest on its side in a tangle of brush.

Alope took a deep breath and started over on the lid, dreaming of various methods of torture for Bear Killer's bride.

Finally satisfied with her finished lid, Alope got to her feet and noticed the lateness of the morning. She would have to think of something to tell her mother about where she'd been all night.

When she approached the brush down the path, she picked up a small rock and threw it at the basket to scare off any snakes that might be lurking. She picked up the basket, then paused. A slow smile curved her lips.

With a soft chuckle, she bent and carefully placed the basket back at the edge of the brush in a spot that would get several hours of sun.

Yes. That would do nicely.

Chapter Seventeen

Everywhere Angela went the next day she was met with grins from the men and giggles from the women. They all remembered last night's public kiss. Even Alope had given up her hateful glaring, but Angela wondered at the new expression the girl wore. It was a look of smug superiority, as if to say, "I know something you don't know."

Angela puzzled over Alope's attitude, but finally shrugged away her uneasiness. The girl was just jealous, that was all. She was only trying to worry Angela, and Angela determined not to let it bother her.

Angela spent the entire day either blushing or trying to hide from everyone. Matt laughed at her embarrassment. He laughed when others grinned and giggled; he laughed when Angela blushed; he laughed when she tried to hide. And when she remembered the taste of his lips and the feel of his arms, he must have read her mind, for he laughed then, too.

By the second day, most people seemed to have forgotten all about that kiss, and Angela was able to walk around camp again without the desire to crawl into a hole.

In the late afternoon, Angela and Matt returned to their wickiup. Out of the corner of her eye Angela caught a glimpse of Alope standing nearby, an unmis-

177

takable look of triumph on the girl's face. Angela stopped and stared at her. What in the world was that look supposed to mean? The girl was as unpredictable as the wind.

Matt followed Angela's gaze and cursed under his breath. Alope had been following him around for days, trying to catch him alone. He'd made damn sure she was not successful.

Alope was a beautiful girl and had been his friend for years. But if her brother ever caught her alone with Matt, Tahnito would kill her. Didn't the little fool know that?

Angela had the strongest urge to play the child and stick her tongue out at Alope, but instead, she managed to smile politely and enter the wickiup.

When she knelt before the remains of the fire and saw another new basket, she sighed. "Oh, Matt, I wish you'd tell them to stop."

Matt raised a brow in question.

"The women, Matt. Huera, Nod-ah-Sti, Cochise's wives. They're always sneaking new things in here while we're out. I know they're trying to be helpful and nice, and make me feel welcome, but . . . I already do less than my share of the work, and, well, these gifts are just too much."

Matt looked around at all the baskets, gourds, and various utensils. He'd never really thought about where they came from before. They were simply things that belonged inside a wickiup. Now he realized that Angela surely had no idea how to weave a basket, and even if she did, she couldn't possibly have made so many in the time she'd been here. His heart warmed toward Huera and the others for their thoughtfulness.

He smiled at Angela. "You're right, of course. They are just trying to help."

"I know, and I'm grateful. But, Matt, *another* basket? And this one is so finely made, with a fitted lid."

178

Matt looked at the basket as Angela reached for it, and something nagged at the back of his mind.

"And there's something in it, too. It's heavy," Angela said as she picked it up, then set it back down.

Matt watched her reach for the lid, and it seemed as if she moved in slow motion. A dozen images crossed his mind as she began to lift the cover. He remembered watching young girls learning how to make their own baskets. Each girl, as she gained experience, brought her own unique design to the craft, and only a few made lids of this type.

He remembered finding Angela lying in a pool of her own blood, with a small moccasin print nearby.

A sharp tingling started at the base of his spine and raced upward. Something was wrong. *What? Who?* He mentally went over each face in camp, each pair of eyes that had looked at Angela with anything other than curiosity or friendship.

As Angela lifted the lid, he suddenly remembered where he'd seen that particular basket design before. Then everything happened at once. He heard what sounded like a cicada, but the noise came from the basket. His instincts told him, though, that it was not a cicada. In that instant he knew without a doubt what was in that basket, and his blood ran cold.

With one hand, he reached for the knife at his waist. With the other, he thrust Angela roughly aside. At the same time, the harmless-sounding buzz came from the basket again, louder this time. The name of the basket maker burst in Matt's brain.

Alope!

Angela fell on her side with a cry of alarm just as a dark blur followed by a silver flash swept past her hip. It was a full moment before her mind acknowledged what her eyes saw. There on the ground next to her writhed a small but vicious-looking two-foot-long rattlesnake, its head pinned to the ground by Matt's knife.

Angela's mouth worked in a silent scream; her lungs labored to draw breath. Her eyes bulged, but remained glued to the thrashing, dying form of the snake. Her ears heard nothing but the terrifying sound of the small rattle as it gave a last defiant buzz before falling silent. The sound lingered in her ears, blocking out everything else.

She began to tremble violently, and then Matt was there, holding her, soothing her with his strength, kissing her face. "You're all right, Angel. You're all right. It's dead; it can't hurt you."

Tears of relief stung her eyes, then rolled down her cheeks. She buried her face against Matt's shoulder as the sobs shook her, for she understood what this all meant. Someone had tried to kill her. *Again!*

Much later, when her tears had dried and her trembling had almost stopped, Angela watched, mesmerized, while Matt finished severing the snake's head and stuffed it back into the basket, along with the body. It was strange, she thought, but that body was pretty, beautiful even, with its double row of matched splotches running down it's back.

"I saw a rattlesnake once in New Mexico," she said. "But it didn't look like that; it was much bigger."

"This is a twin-spotted rattlesnake," Matt explained, trying to keep his voice calm. He was so filled with rage at Angela's brush with death—her second since coming here—that all he wanted to do was put his hands around Alope's throat and squeeze until her treacherous eyes popped. "This one's full grown, I'd say. His kind doesn't get very large."

Angela hunched her shoulders against another shudder. "Who could hate me so much?"

He replaced the lid on the basket, hiding the snake from her sight, then took her in his arms again. "Don't worry, Angel, nothing like this will happen again. I know who it is now, and I can stop it."

"You know? How can you? Who is it?"

"I recognize that basket," he said. "It's Alope's."

Angela jerked upright and sucked air in through her clenched teeth. "Of course!" But what could be done about her? These people had no marshal or sheriff, as far as she knew. "What do we do now?"

"Don't worry," he said grimly. "I have a little something in mind. When we get through with her, she'll be so afraid of you she won't get within a dozen yards of you again."

He explained his plan, and Angela swallowed heavily. Her part wasn't going to be easy. "I don't understand what good it will do," she said, hoping he'd come up with another idea.

"It'll work—trust me. Alope is terrified of snakes. In fact, I can't imagine how she got this one in the basket in the first place, but it doesn't matter. She's even afraid to *talk* about snakes, much less what I have in mind. Can you do it?"

Angela nodded reluctantly. She'd do what was necessary. Matt had explained that because of the peace negotiations, it was impossible to openly accuse Alope without causing serious problems. Since Angela could think of no better idea, Matt said this was their only choice.

Some choice.

Two hours after dark, Matt and Angela made their way through camp to pay a visit to Alope. Angela was grateful for the darkness. She hoped it hid her pale, bloodless face and trembling hands. Why in the world had she ever agreed to this?

She had thought she would scream when Matt slipped the rawhide thong around her neck. Now the rattles from the tail of the snake hung between her breasts and made a faint whisper of sound with each step she took. And if that weren't bad enough, the light brown snake skin, with its double row of darker brown spots, now encircled her forehead.

Talk about primitive!

But when they found Alope in her mother's wick-iup, all Angela's misgivings disappeared, and she was filled with devilish delight at the look on the other girl's face. Alope was clearly stunned to see Angela at all, but when she recognized the necklace and headband for what they were, she was visibly shaken.

"Duuda'!" Alope whispered as she backed away, her hand in front of her to ward off the evil. *"Duuda'! Nuushkaa!"*

Angela ignored the words she didn't understand. Her voice rang with confidence when she began the prearranged speech Matt had insisted upon. He said it would look more real if she spoke for herself, then he translated for Alope.

"Please tell Alope I'm grateful for the gift of the snake," she said, holding the basket toward the terrified girl. "Since we had some left over, I'd like to share the meal with her."

When Matt translated this last statement, Alope stifled a scream behind her hand and stumbled backward, her eyes nearly popping from her head.

Angela took a step toward Alope and slipped the cover from the basket. Alope's horrified gaze darted everywhere, as if seeking a quick escape. She refused to look into the basket.

"Have you never tried it?" Angela asked. She was the picture of innocence, she was sure. "It's really quite good." She waited until Alope's huge, terrified gaze reluctantly slid to the basket; then Angela tore off a small hunk of the cooked snake meat and brought it to her own lips. She popped the meat into her mouth and chewed with relish, then thrust the basket toward Alope again. "Try some," she urged.

Alope didn't need a translation. She was stunned and horrified. Not only had her plan failed, but Bear Killer's white she-devil of a wife must have used some sort of magic to avoid being struck by the *gúú'*. Powerful magic.

Terror streaked along every nerve. Not magic. *Witchcraft!*

Alope looked to Bear Killer for help. "Make her go away! Make her take that thing and go away!" she cried in Apache. She reached out and slapped the basket away, knocking it from Angela's hand and spilling the meat to the ground.

"Náhalá! Matt ordered. "You pick it up! You are more evil than any snake for what you have tried to do. Be warned, you viper in woman's skin. If anything happens to Eyes Like Summer Leaves, *anything,* you will pay. If she so much as stumps her toe on a rock, I will find you, and I will kill you. Hear me, Alope, for you know I do not lie."

"You did good," Matt offered once he and Angela returned to their wickiup.

Angela ignored his words of praise. She tore off the hideous necklace and headband and flung them against the grass wall. "Do you think it worked? Will she leave me alone now?"

Matt came up behind her and put his hands on her shoulders, squeezing them gently. "Oh, it worked, all right." He laughed. "She's terrified of you now. You won't have any more trouble out of her, I promise. Why don't you get into bed? I need to talk to *shimá* and *shitaa* for a minute, but I won't be gone long."

A few minutes later Angela tumbled gratefully to bed. The ordeal of finding the snake, then confronting Alope, had exhausted her, and she was asleep in moments.

Matt told Hal-Say and Huera what had happened, and they agreed to keep their eyes open for any further trouble. When he returned to find Angela already asleep, he crawled in beside her. A sudden trembling seized him, and he had to clench his fists to keep from reaching out and crushing her in his arms. How had she come to mean so much to him in such a short time?

If that rattlesnake had been facing just a few inches in the other direction. . . . Matt's mind refused to finish the thought.

Chapter Eighteen

Finally, ten days after General Howard's arrival, the Chiricahua were in agreement.

Cochise stood solemnly, his people behind him, the bluecoat "star chief" before him. The crowd quieted.

"You came to us seeking peace," Cochise said. "No one wants peace more than the Chidikáágu'. Over the seasons, for every one of us who has died, we have killed ten white men, but still the white men are no less; they are only more. The white man grows more numerous while we, the People, grow fewer and fewer. If we do not have a good peace soon, we will disappear from the face of the earth.

"If you can give us these mountains as our reservation, we will have peace. Hereafter, the white man and the Chiricahua will drink of the same water, eat of the same bread, and be at peace.

"Nzhú! It is good!"

General Howard nodded his agreement, and Taglito grinned at Cochise. Then the star chief brought up a new aspect of the treaty.

"In order for this new reservation to be legal, so white men will honor it, you must have a white man as your agent, someone to be in charge of seeing that you get the food and supplies you have coming to you."

"There is no question," Cochise said without hesitation. "Before you came, I knew three white men. Two of them are tied to their land and family. That leaves one. Taglito will be our Agent."

"Hold on there, *amigo*," his old friend protested. "I don't know the first thing 'bout being an Indian agent. I'm sure the general can find somebody else who'll know what in tarnation he's doin'."

"I'm sure he could," Cochise replied. "But if we don't have someone all the Chidikáágu' know and trust, there may be trouble. You would not want there to be trouble, would you?"

Taglito grinned. "Are you threatening me?"

"Me? We are like brothers, you and I. Would I threaten my own brother?"

Tom Jeffords wasn't eager to tie himself down to what he considered a "regular job" like Indian agent. But he knew as sure as his mother's eyes were blue that neither one of the Coltons, Travis nor Matt, could leave their ranch to live on the reservation year-round. And Cochise was right. The agent had to be someone Cochise and his people trusted.

There were a few men Tom Jeffords trusted, but he trusted no one as much as he trusted himself. *Hellfire.* He had to do the job, and he knew it.

With considerably less reluctance than he knew he should feel, he agreed to his old friend's request.

Angela felt a thrill shoot through her as she watched Cochise, chief of the Chiricahua Apaches, shake hands with General Oliver Otis Howard, representative of the President of the United States of America, and then with Tom Jeffords, Indian agent for the Chiricahua Reservation.

She reached out and squeezed Matt's hand, and he returned the pressure. His eyes were suspiciously bright, and he swallowed heavily, his Adam's apple bobbing up and down.

* * *

When it was all over and the treaty was signed, the celebration started almost immediately. The story of the day's events would be told around Apache campfires for generations. This day Cochise and the Chidi-káágu' made peace with the white man!

Tom Jeffords raised his hands for silence, then shouted an Apache phrase that brought a round of cheers. Matt translated for Angela: "Drink now, talk tomorrow."

The crowd concurred.

Cochise had been strict about how much *tiswin* his men consumed each night . . . until now. He hadn't wanted any drunken brawls to interfere with making peace. But now there was peace. All restrictions were lifted. The women had been brewing *tiswin* and stocking it up for days. Tonight his warriors—should they call themselves that now that there was no more war? At any rate, tonight they would drink the camp dry. Tomorrow they would try to drink the stream dry.

"Just look at this place!" Angela stared around her in amazement at all the feverish activity. The pace had been hectic, at least for the women, for days, but nothing compared to this. People ran back and forth, women checking the food, men racing their horses through camp, boys shouting, imitating the men, but on foot. "If God is looking down from the heavens, He must think this place is a busy anthill, with all this running around."

General Howard, walking next to her, clutched the Bible tucked under his belt and smiled. "God is most assuredly looking, Mrs. Colton. This treaty wouldn't have been possible otherwise."

"Once again you agree with our people on something, General," Chee said, walking on Howard's other side.

"How's that, young man?"

"Dee-O-Det, our shaman, dreamed one night that Yúúsń—God—would send us peace and let us keep

187

our land. And then you came."

"No offense, but I had no idea the Apaches even knew about God," Howard said, astounded at the idea.

Chee smiled. "I know what white men think of us. But as far as we're concerned, we're much more religious than white men."

"What do you mean?"

"Well, for instance, most white men who even admit to being religious only admit it one day a week, if that often. We pray every day. Yúúsń told our people, way back at the beginning of time, to face the rising sun each morning and pray. You'll notice the door to every wickiup faces east for just that reason."

"Tell me more," the general commanded.

"I'll do better than that. I'll take you to Dee-O-Det. You've not had the chance to talk much with him, and I think the two of you will like each other."

Chee and Howard left to find Dee-O-Det, and Angela went to help with the food. Matt hung around nearby to keep an eye on her. He still didn't like having her out of his sight, even though no one had made any further attempt to bother her.

That afternoon Angela saw a different Matt Colton. As the celebration progressed, the lines of tension in his face eased. His eyes glowed, his shoulders were straight for the first time in days, and he held his head high. He laughed and joked with those around him. He even smoked a cigarette with Chee. She'd never seen him smoke before. And he watched every move Angela made.

She watched him, too. She knew he hadn't had enough *tiswin* to account for this sudden buoyancy, and correctly attributed this new side of him to the just-signed treaty.

Near sundown, Matt grabbed Angela by the arm and led her toward the edge of camp. "Come with me. I want to show you something."

"What is it?"

"You'll see."

They climbed up a narrow path through the trees. Oak leaves and twigs crackled under foot, and jays and sparrows took flight, scolding the intruders with every flap of their wings. Soon the woods gave way to rocks. A scraggly bush sprang from a crevice here and there, and from an occasional, deeper crevice a juniper or a scrub oak grew. After a short climb through the rocks, they emerged on a flat shelf. The entire *rancheria* was spread out below them. Overhead a red-tailed hawk soared in the waning sunlight.

Angela craned her neck to look up at the tall, rugged peak that loomed above them.

"Signal fires are set up there," Matt explained. "They can be seen for miles."

He led her around the base of that towering monolith to where another ledge hung, seemingly in midair. It felt like the edge of the world. It was the most peaceful place Angela had seen in her life. The shadows cast by the setting sun made black holes out of the deep crevices below them. It was a fearful place, yet wonderful. Only the wind and her heart moved.

"Oh, Matt," Angela whispered. "It's so beautiful here."

He put his arm around her shoulder, obviously pleased with her reaction. She leaned against him, and together they watched the sun sink below the horizon.

"It'll be dark soon. Shouldn't we head back now?"

"In a minute. You haven't seen the best part yet."

"The best part?"

"Just wait," he said. With his hand on her shoulder, he turned her around to face the east. Soon the sky began to darken. But before the dusk turned completely dark, a mysterious orange light glowed along the eastern horizon. It looked as though the sun had sped around in a hurry to rise again.

Angela held her breath as she watched a huge, red-orange disk rise and light the whole eastern sky. She was unaware of the bruising grip she had on Matt's hand. She stared in wonder at a sight she'd never even heard of, much less seen.

"It's . . . incredible! It has to be the moon, but I've never seen anything like it!"

Matt pulled her back against his chest and draped his arms around her. He rested his chin on the top of her head, and they watched the moon break free of the horizon.

"The Mexicans call it an Apache moon," he said quietly, his deep voice rumbling in his chest and sending shivers through Angela's body.

"Why?"

"Because this is the time of year when the Apaches usually raid below the border for horses. They say the moon is covered with the blood of their victims. Over in Texas folks call it a Comanche moon, because the Apaches aren't the only ones who raid this time of year."

"How horrible." Angela shivered, and Matt tightened his arms around her. "What's the Chiricahua word for moon?"

His answer was no more than a short series of grunts to her. She had yet to learn any of the language. She asked him to repeat it.

He obliged with, *"t'lééʼnaaʼáí,"* then chuckled softly at her lame attempt to pronounce the word.

They watched silently for a while; then Matt turned her in his arms. "The Apaches have another name for it," he said softly, running an index finger along her jaw.

His dark gaze held her captive. His touch sent her heart into an erratic dance. "They do?"

"Uh huh." Matt lowered his face until their breaths mingled and their lips almost touched. "They call it a lovers' moon."

190

He tasted her lips and ran his tongue across her teeth. Angela melted instantly. *Why does he affect me this way?* she wondered. Then she was beyond wondering. Beyond thought. She was a mass of tingly sensations. She pressed herself against him, trying to get closer. He invaded her mouth with his tongue, and she tasted the tang of smoke and tobacco from the cigarette he'd shared with Chee earlier. With both hands, he brought her hips flush against his. The hard ridge of his arousal brought vivid pictures flashing behind her closed eyes. She moaned and moved against him. The kiss deepened and became fierce, demanding.

Suddenly Matt tore his mouth from hers and buried his face in her hair where it draped across her shoulder. His harsh breathing seemed to echo in the stillness of the night, but Angela barely heard it over her own pounding heart.

He ran his hands over her and clutched her tightly for a moment, then stepped back and took a deep breath. He reached out and smoothed a strand of hair from her cheek, and Angela's eyes widened. His hand was trembling!

Without a word, Matt took her by the hand and led her back around the base of the signal peak, across the flat shelf, down through the rocks, then woods, and back to camp. All the way down, she wondered what it would be like if they were really married. Would it be like it was just now up on that ledge? Would he always take her breath away? Would she always be able to make him tremble?

They ate roast venison, and Matt devoured her with his eyes. There'd been more than one comment made in the last couple of weeks about Matt rarely leaving Angela's side. Tonight he took more ribbing because he refused to let go of her hand. Public demonstrations of affection between man and wife were not common among Apaches.

Even as she grew more nervous with each hot look

Matt gave her, Angela took pleasure in his ardent attention. But even so, his constant nearness made her as jumpy as a jackrabbit. She never knew what to expect from him. He promised her an annulment; then he'd do something like he did tonight, kiss her in a way that said he wanted more — a lot more — and made her want more.

And she *did* want more.

The rowdy crowd began to wear on her, as did the constant conversations all around her in a language she didn't understand. She was tired. She was confused. And her lips still tingled from that blistering kiss. When Matt let go of her hand to gesture to one of his friends, she took the opportunity to slip away unnoticed and head for their wickiup.

But her departure didn't go unnoticed. Matt knew instantly when she left his side, and he turned to watch her go. He let her leave, but followed close enough to keep her in sight. He breathed easier when he saw her duck into the wickiup. He'd give her a little time to herself. Apparently she was as shaken by that kiss as he was.

The question now was, what was he going to do about it?

Chapter Nineteen

Angela threw dried leaves and small sticks on the glowing embers. She fanned until the flames caught, then added a single short log to the blaze.

It had been days since she'd had a chance to bathe. She didn't know how much time she had before Matt would come, but she simply had to feel a cool, damp cloth against her skin. She peeled off her dress and knelt beside the water jug after locating a rag to use for washing. She lowered her chemise to her waist and wet the rag.

The cloth was cool. It soothed her heated flesh, but did nothing for the ache in her breast, put there by a longing for something . . . wonderful . . . some kind of life with Matt. Something impossible.

She closed her eyes and wiped the valley between her breasts. A whisper of sound made her open her eyes. She froze. Crouched just inside the doorway, halted in mid-stride with his mouth half-open in surprise, was Matt.

Angela gasped. She flung her arms across her breasts and spun around on her knees, presenting her back to him. She fumbled with her chemise and tried to pull it up to cover her nakedness. She was about to succeed when Matt knelt behind her and gently pushed the garment back down.

He stroked a feathery touch across her shoulders,

grasped her hands, then enfolded her in his arms, with her back pressed to his chest. Angela shivered. It felt so right, being in his arms this way, but she was frightened by the intensity of her feelings. This was no way to conduct a mock marriage.

For the longest time, all he did was hold her. Then he slowly forced her to turn around, and his knees straddled hers. He held her gaze steadily, refusing to let his eyes drift lower, and spoke softly.

"I've waited since I was ten years old to see peace between Apaches and whites. I always thought when it happened my life would be complete. But it's not. Cochise has his peace, and I have my home and my family. But I need one thing more for my life to be complete. I need you, Angela."

Angela's eyes widened. She swallowed heavily when he trailed a finger down between her breasts without taking his eyes from hers.

"I want you, Angel. I want you so much. I want you beside me by day, and beneath me by night."

His deep voice and the picture painted by his words started a trembling sensation deep in the pit of her stomach.

"But this time," he said, "I want it to be just you . . . and me. No drug. This time when your eyes turn dark with passion and you cry out your release, I want to know that I'm the reason for it, not something you drank." He lowered his lips to hers and whispered, "Love me, Angel, love me."

Their bodies didn't touch, only their lips and his hands on her shoulders. Angela was lost to the torrent of emotions he stirred in her. When he pulled back, she felt the heat of his gaze travel over her naked breasts.

"You're so beautiful," he whispered hoarsely.

His fingers traced downward and circled the pale globes until Angela thought she might die from the

194

pleasure of his touch. She gasped and arched when he ran the backs of his fingers over her nipples. They puckered and hardened, and her eyelids grew heavy. A fierce but tender heat rushed through her.

"You want me," Matt said with wonder. "I can see it in your eyes."

He kissed her then, pulling her flush against his chest. The contact of skin against skin was like a bolt of lightning. The kiss was desperate, hungry, searching. They clung to each other in mutual need. Angela shuddered at the intensity of her feelings. This was what she'd been wanting for so long.

Matt tore his mouth free and pressed his forehead against hers. His breathing matched hers for raggedness. She moved against him, trying to get closer.

"Easy, Angel," he whispered hoarsely. "Don't rush it. We have a whole night . . . a whole lifetime." He pulled back to look at her and ran a thumb across her swollen lips. "That's what I want from you, Angel. A whole lifetime of loving."

Angela couldn't speak, couldn't breathe, couldn't think. All she could do was feel. She felt the crisp hair on his chest teasing her breasts, felt his calloused thumb brushing her lips, felt the magnetic pull of his eyes and his words. Amazed at her own actions, she pulled his head down and pressed her lips to his while her fingers traced the scars on his back.

His mouth remained motionless beneath her kiss. Matt wasn't sure what he had expected from her, but an argument, or at the very least, shyness, would not have surprised him. He'd been prepared to overcome her resistance or reluctance. He'd not been prepared for this teasing encouragement of her lips against his, her soft, slender fingers on his back. Every muscle in his body jerked when she ran her tongue along his upper lip. His mouth opened slightly at her urging, and she sucked gently on his full lower lip. His control snapped.

Angela thrilled to the knowledge that she had the power to make his heart pound as hard and fast as her own. Her world began to sway and spin under the onslaught of his ardor, and when she finally opened her eyes again, she and Matt were both lying on the bearskin, their clothes strewn across the wickiup. The heat from the golden flames in his dark brown eyes took her breath away. She wanted him. Lord, how she wanted him.

"Matt—"

"Ssh. Don't say anything," he said between kisses. "Don't talk, just love me, Angel." He continued raining kisses across her face and down her throat. Against her ear he whispered, "I'm going to make you love me."

You don't have to. I already do.

But his lips on hers kept the words from leaving her mouth. And then, as his mouth trailed down her neck to her breast, she lost all ability to speak, or even think. She became a mindless mass of sensation, and a deep, guttural groan was all she was capable of when his tongue flicked across a hard, erect nipple. She dug her fingers into his shoulders and arched against him, feeling her breast throb and swell as he began to suckle.

Another throbbing and swelling began, this time at the juncture of her thighs. As Matt kissed his way from one nipple to the other, his hand slid down her stomach and came to rest on the triangle of golden curls, his fingers teasing lightly between her legs. Angela writhed beneath his touch, arching, trying to press herself against his fingers, but he slid his hand up to rest at the curve of her waist.

Angela was beside herself. She cried out in protest of his denial.

"Look at me, Angel."

Slowly, reluctantly, she opened her eyes. His face loomed above her, golden bronze in the firelight. His lips were full and firm with passion. His nostrils flared. His eyes, black with desire, met hers and held them captive. Angela knew without a doubt that he was feeling the same exquisite sensations she was nearly drowning in.

Matt met her gaze steadily, staring deep into her eyes. He slid his hand down her stomach again and watched in triumph as, with each inch he lowered his hand, her eyes grew darker. They were nearly black by the time he slipped a finger into her warm, moist folds.

Angela gasped. Her eyes fluttered shut. She couldn't have opened them again if her life depended on it, the pleasure of his touch was so intense.

But Matt didn't mind that she'd closed her eyes. He'd seen what he wanted to see. He'd seen how his touch affected her. Emotions stampeded through him. This was his woman. She was given to him; she belonged to him. This was the woman he wanted to spend the rest of his life with, if only he could convince her to stay with him.

He meant to take his time loving her, but was thwarted by his own thoughts. The very idea that she might leave him made him desperate to hold on to her. Frantic now, he positioned himself between her thighs and joined his flesh to hers. Then there was no holding back, for either of them.

Angela welcomed his aggressiveness and met him thrust for thrust as they each sought release from the blinding, building passion. Only she didn't want it to end, not yet. It was too exquisite to end so soon.

At that moment, they were so in tune with each other that Matt knew what she wanted. It was what he wanted, too, and he pushed his fear of losing her

197

aside and slowed his pace in order to extend their pleasure to the limits. But he couldn't hold back for long, and his words, whispered harshly in her ear, spurred her to new heights.

"Don't hold back, just let go, let it happen. Come with me, Angel, come with me."

And she did. She clung to him with all her might as wave after wave of red hot pleasure washed over her, and she cried out her release.

But her cry was drowned out by Matt's hoarse, "Angellll!" as he threw his head back and shuddered violently. She welcomed his weight as he collapsed on top of her.

Sometime later, maybe an hour, maybe only a few minutes, Matt raised up on his elbows and looked down at her. The dark passion in her eyes had exploded, leaving them once again the color of summer leaves.

"I said it once before, then foolishly took it back," he told her. "But now I'm saying it again, Angela, and nothing will ever make me take it back this time."

Angela's heart began to pound at his ominous words. She held her breath, afraid of what he might say.

"There'll be no annulment."

Her heart stopped. "No?" she whispered.

"No."

"Are you sure that's what you want, Matt?"

"I've been sure since the first time I laid eyes on you."

Angela swallowed heavily, afraid to believe what he was saying. "Then, you . . . you want us to . . . stay married?" Hope coursed through her veins at his tender smile.

"More than anything in the world, Angel."

"Oh, Matt!" Angela threw her arms around his

neck and tried to hold back her sobs of relief. He wanted her! He wanted them to stay together! He wanted her for his wife!

"Does this mean you approve?"

"Yes!" She laughed with delight. "Oh, yes!" She covered his face with kisses, and he laughed with her.

"It's just as well, since I wasn't going to give you a choice anyway."

"You weren't?"

"No, I weren't," he said with a crooked grin.

"Why?" She held her breath and waited. Did he love her? Would he say it?

"Because a man would have to be a complete fool to let a woman like you slip away from him."

Angela quickly lowered her eyes to hide her disappointment. *It doesn't matter,* she told herself. *He must feel something. He must care for me if he wants me for his wife.*

What was love, anyway? Was it this constant craving for his touch, the desire—almost a need—to be with him all the time? Before she could comment, his lips took hers in the most tender, loving kiss imaginable, and she couldn't help the tears that seeped from beneath her closed eyelids.

Matt tasted the tears and gently kissed them away. "The last thing in the world I wanted to do was make you cry," he whispered.

"It's all right," she answered, her voice shaky with emotion. "They're happy tears."

He kissed her again; then his hands started roving. The care he took to arouse her stripped away any fear she had that he didn't care for her. They loved each other deep into the night.

The next day was like a holiday. Nearly all the

men and well over half the women were suffering too much from the previous night's celebration to do more than lie around and moan. The streams and creeks did a brisk business all day, as the *tiswin* consumed till near dawn created a powerful thirst in those who overindulged.

The hunt Hal-Say and Matt had planned for that day was postponed, since Hal-Say seemed intent on spending the entire day snoring away in his wickiup. It was just as well, for Matt didn't think he was capable of tearing himself away from Angela's side after the incredible night they'd just spent together.

The two young lovers walked in the woods, teased, held hands, laughed, and made love beneath the sheltering limbs of a willow. It was a perfect day.

"Tell me about your home," Angela asked as they wandered back toward camp near dusk.

"Our home," he said, pausing to press a tender kiss to her lips. Then he told her about the Triple C and its people, some of whom she'd already met.

But as interested as Angela was in everything that touched his life, she barely heard him over the singing in her heart.

"It sounds wonderful," she said. She smiled at him as their entwined hands swung idly between them.

"It is wonderful. You'll love it there, and everyone there will love you."

Anxiety suddenly seized her. "I do want your family to like me."

"You've already met most of the family, and they adore you. So do I." He pulled her into his arms for a long, searching kiss that left her trembling.

Matt devoted himself entirely to Angela for the next two days, ignoring everyone and everything else. It was a special time for both of them, sharing

200

their new-found closeness, exploring it, reveling in it. But finally he was forced to consider practical matters.

When he was in camp, food for Hal-Say and Huera was his responsibility. He couldn't take Angela home until there was enough food to last his adoptive parents for a while, and he wanted to take Angela home. So he must hunt.

Of course Hal-Say was more than capable of supplying for his wife and himself; he was a noted hunter and warrior. But it was the custom of Chidikáágu' that any adult son who wasn't responsible for providing for his in-laws should provide for his own parents, and Matt had always honored the customs of the People.

Angela sighed as she picked up the heavy basket filled with dried locust pods. She and Huera and Klea, Tahnito and Alope's mother, had come to gather the pods just after Matt and Hal-Say left that morning.

When the women returned to camp, they would strip the pods away. The beans within would then either be boiled, roasted, or crushed into flour for use in thickening soups and stews, or baking. Locust beans were a good nutritious addition to the Apache diet, and each fall every available pod was harvested.

Now their baskets were full, and the women headed back to camp. Unsure of the way, Angela walked behind the other two women. Not speaking their language, she kept quiet.

She kept her eyes on the trail before her and thought about what she always thought about these days — Matt. It seemed incredible that he had come into her life at its darkest point and, by his mere presence, gave her the greatest joy she'd ever known.

And even more incredible than that, he seemed to receive that same joy from her.

She couldn't wait to see him again. He'd only been gone half a day, but she missed him terribly. Her lips still tingled from his good-bye kiss. Perhaps, after a time, when they were both more secure in their feelings, she wouldn't have this powerful need to be with him every single moment. Perhaps.

When Matt left that morning, he'd said he might be gone as long as several days. It just depended on how soon they found adequate game. But when he returned to the *rancheria* he would take her home, to the Triple C. She looked forward to that, even if the thought of living with his family did make her a bit nervous.

Angela halted when she noticed that the two women in front of her had stopped and fallen silent. Huera turned to her with a stricken look, and Angela was puzzled. Then, over her mother-in-law's shoulder, she saw the reason.

"No," Angela breathed in denial. The heavy basket slipped from her numb fingers. Locust pods crackled and hissed, scattering everywhere as the now empty basket bounced to the edge of the trail.

Her ears rang with the silence of pain and betrayal. Her heart stopped. Her breath stopped. Her knees threatened to buckle. She wanted to scream, to pull her hair out by the roots, to cry . . . to die.

A few yards ahead, where the trail broke into a small clearing, stood Matt, his arms wrapped tightly around Alope's shoulders as the beautiful young woman stretched up to receive his blistering kiss.

Chapter Twenty

Matt waited at the edge of the clearing for the women to return. Finally he heard voices, one of which belonged to Huera. He was glad he and Hal-Say had downed that buck so soon and had been able to return to camp. He'd dreaded the possibility of spending the night away from Angela. She was in his blood, like a raging fire, and he smiled when he spied her walking behind Huera and Klea.

"Bear Killer, I am glad you are back so soon."

Matt turned, surprised to see Alope approaching him from the opposite direction. She must have come to meet her mother. In the next instant, however, that assumption was proven wrong.

"I have missed you." She kept coming toward him, her eyes staring boldly into his.

Before he could guess her intent, Alope glanced quickly down the path at the approaching women. Huera and Klea stopped and looked. Behind them, Angela did the same. Then Alope took a step back, launched herself through the air, and landed against Matt's chest. Her arms wrapped themselves tightly around his neck, and she pressed her open mouth to his.

For a brief moment, Matt was too stunned to react, except to catch her when she flew at him. For an Apache maiden to behave so wantonly was practically unheard of. He put his hands on her shoulders to push her away, but she just held on tighter. He finally managed to tear his mouth free. The first thing he saw was Angela, standing in the middle of the path, feet buried in a pile of locust pods, face as white as the collar on her blue gingham dress, and her eyes, dear God, her eyes. Her eyes screamed of pain and betrayal and the death of dreams.

"Duuda'!" bellowed an angry voice. "No!" Tahnito stomped into the clearing. "Unhand my sister!"

Matt was furious. He knew how everyone would view this incident, and he looked down at Alope in disgust. He dropped his hands to his sides, which left her clinging rather obviously to his neck.

Alope stepped back. The smile she gave Matt sent chills of dread racing down his spine. *"Duunndii' edida, shilahúkéne,"* she told Tahnito. Matt was grateful Angela couldn't understand Alope's lies. "Don't be foolish, my brother. Bear Killer has promised to set aside his wife and take me in her place."

"Duuda'!" her brother objected. *"Shishxéná!* I shall kill him!"

Matt stiffened and faced Tahnito. "You may try . . . *again,*" he taunted. "You have taught your sister well how to lie."

To call an Apache a liar was one of the deepest insults possible. Their rigid social code demanded honesty from everyone, and anyone who did not adhere to that quickly became an outcast. It was not an accusation to be made lightly, nor had Matt intended that it be taken that way.

Tahnito looked ready to explode. "First you dishonor my sister by sneaking around in the woods with her; now you call her a liar! I will kill you!" The Apache crouched low and pulled his knife from the sheath at his waist.

"She is a liar, and you, my *friend,* are a fool if you think you can kill me." He shoved Alope away roughly and drew his own knife.

"You may be a killer of bears, but I doubt you can do so well against a man. I'm not some poor, defenseless animal. *Núuká, 'indaa.* Come, white man, come and die."

By this time another group had also reached the clearing. Among them were Chee and Shanta. They passed a knowing look between themselves. This fight had been coming for years, they knew.

Shanta and Chee had been present the day of her wedding over ten years ago when Woman of Magic had nearly been killed by Loco, Tahnito's father. Travis Colton had barely arrived in time to save his wife's life. Loco and Travis had fought, and Loco had died. Now the two men's sons would fight each other. It could not be stopped, and Shanta and Chee did not even try to interfere.

"That bear was far from defenseless, as you well know," Matt said as he and Tahnito began circling each other, each looking for an opening, a weakness in the other. There was none.

"How would I know such a thing?"

"I wonder." Matt grunted and dodged when Tahnito lunged.

"I wonder, too, why you have kept silent all these years," Tahnito questioned.

"I've been waiting for you to tell the story, *friend.*" Matt stayed just out of reach of the other's knife. He wasn't ready to fight in earnest yet. He wanted to see Tahnito squirm first. "After all, you're the only one who really knows exactly how my foot got trapped under that rock, and where the bear came from, and how I ended up in that place alone."

Tahnito screamed in rage and ran at Matt, but

Matt sidestepped at the last second and received only a small nick on his side instead of the full blade in his ribs.

"Which bothers you more, I wonder," Matt said, grinning. "That I didn't die, or that I never told what happened?"

"You were supposed to die!" Tahnito raged. He knew others were watching and listening, but he no longer cared. "This time you will die. This time I leave nothing to chance."

Somewhere in the background a woman cried out. It was Klea, but neither man paid any attention; they concentrated on each other. They came together with a grunt and a clapping of bare chests. Sweat glistened and rolled down their backs. When they pulled apart, breathing heavily, they were both covered with trickles of blood.

Alope watched with excitement while the two men fought. It had started because of her, but they'd both forgotten her almost instantly. She, too, knew this fight had been coming for years. Her brother had always hated Bear Killer because that one's father had killed their father. Now, as she saw her brother tiring rapidly, she was torn between him and the man she loved and wanted.

Remembering what she'd just done, and what Bear Killer had said about it, she realized that no matter what happened, he would not want her. For that, she could hate him. He had spurned her! Called her a liar!

In the end, blood and hate proved stronger than her desire for Bear Killer. She saw her brother stumble, saw Bear Killer move in for the final blow. Alope pulled her knife from her belt and joined the fight. With a sob of rage and frustration, she threw herself at Bear Killer's back. Her knife glanced off his shoulder blade and cut a long gash down his back, across the scars left by that long-ago bear.

Klea went wild with grief that her children could shame her so. She rushed in, grabbed her daughter by the hair and tried to wrest the knife from her.

Matt felt the slicing pain in his back. He staggered under the impact of the two women who knocked into him from behind. He fell toward Tahnito, and both men crashed to the ground. It was sheer luck that Matt's knife struck and pinned Tahnito to the ground by the skin of his upper arm, but Matt wasn't in any shape to quibble with luck. He could feel himself getting weaker from loss of blood. He would rest a minute before he loosed his foe.

Angela couldn't believe this was happening! Why didn't someone try to stop it? So many emotions hit her at once that she could only stand and stare at the blood pouring down Matt's back.

First, there was a real and tangible fear for Matt's life. He was on top right now, but she could see him growing weaker every second. The light of madness in Tahnito's eyes said no simple thing like exhaustion or loss of blood would keep him from killing Matt. Angela had never seen such hate on a person's face in her life.

Second only to her fear for Matt's life was the devastating sense of loss she felt, mixed with shame. Matt and Tahnito were fighting over Alope. The humiliation and heartbreak were almost more than she could bear.

The clearing was full of people now, all shouting encouragement at the two combatants. Since she hadn't learned their language, she had no way of knowing what was said, but wouldn't most of them favor Tahnito, one of their own blood, rather than a white man?

And if Matt lost—God forbid!—what would happen to her if he died? She'd be left here, alone, among strangers. Would Tahnito claim her then? *Dear God, no!*

Behind Matt, Klea and Alope fought over the knife for only a moment. Alope had no desire to fight her mother; she had more urgent things to tend to. She released her grip on the knife and shoved Klea away. But now she had no weapon! She saw Bear Killer reach to pull his knife from her brother's arm. *Now he's going to kill him! But not if I can help it!* she vowed.

She bent down and grabbed a three-foot length of broken tree limb. Before anyone could stop her, she swung with all her might. Rage at being rejected and fear for her brother's life lent her abnormal strength. The blow struck Matt in the left temple and knocked him cold.

Tahnito roared with rage. He jerked free the knife that had him pinned to the ground and leaped for Alope. That she should dare interfere! He could not think of a bad enough name to call her. His hand closed around her slender throat, and he lifted her off the ground.

"Get you from my sight!" With that, he flung her away from him.

What happened next would be talked about in hushed tones around winter campfires for years to come. It was such an unlikely thing and so horrible that some unearthly, unholy force must have had a hand in it.

Klea was just struggling to rise when Tahnito threw Alope toward her like a rag doll. Alope tripped over her mother and fell hard, striking her head on a stone at the base of a tree. A sickening thud echoed through the sudden silence. Her neck was broken. Klea stumbled and fell to the ground again, facedown. The knife she still held in her hand, her daughter's knife, plunged into her chest.

Alope and Klea, mother and daughter, lay together with arms and legs entangled.

The only two people in the world Tahnito had ever cared about were dead. A savage howl erupted from deep within him and broke the sudden stillness of the clearing. He turned in a circle with a dazed look. His knife was still in his hand, and he kept turning, staring at the stunned faces around him. Then his eyes lit on the source of all his troubles— Bear Killer.

"Shishxéná!" Tahnito screamed. I shall kill him!

It was not honorable to kill a man who could not defend himself, but Tahnito knew, as did those around him, that he had no honor. All he wanted to do now was kill his enemy—kill Bear Killer!

But Chee and Shanta were there, bending over their white friend, lifting him, carrying him away. With a final scream of pain and rage, Tahnito turned and ran the opposite direction, deeper into the woods.

Cochise witnessed the scene from the shadows of the woods, saddened but resigned that it had come to this. He had known it would. He made no attempt to interfere.

All life is a circle. Sons grow as their fathers, and the past lives again in each of us.

Chapter Twenty-one

Angela stretched her shoulders and arched her back to relieve her cramped muscles. Matt's several nicks and scratches, and the long gash down his back, had been cleaned and bandaged, as had the cut on his head. But that had been several hours ago, and he still hadn't regained consciousness. It did not lend anything to Angela's peace of mind that Huera, Hal-Say, and Dee-O-Det shared her vigil. Worry was etched on each dark face.

Dee-O-Det had sent Hal-Say back to the clearing for a piece of bark from the limb Alope had struck Matt with. Several times since then, the old shaman had left the wickiup for a while. Each time he came back, he sang a song over Matt and sprinkled some kind of dust around him. Then he sent Hal-Say back for the entire branch, instructing that it be cut up in small enough pieces to fit in the fire.

When that was done, Dee-O-Det cleaned the fire-pit of all ashes, then set fire to the pieces Hal-Say brought him. The new fire burned slow and long. It was nearly sunup and the coals were still glowing. And Matt was still unconscious.

The sky turned light just before Chee came. He spoke briefly to Dee-O-Det, listened to the old man's answers, then turned to Angela.

"What does he say, Chee? Matt should have been awake by now."

"Do not worry, Eyes Like Summer Leaves, your man will live." Chee bit back a smile at her fiery blush. "When the coals from the offending branch die out, Bear Killer will awaken."

"What do coals have to do with anything? He's been out far too long. He needs a doctor, Chee."

"You are the wife of my friend, but you do not understand our ways. I will assume your ignorance is not meant as an insult to our shaman. You must trust him. He knows what he does. If the bear could not kill your man all those years ago, then Yúúsń will not allow the one who sent the bear to be the cause of his death now."

"What are you talking about? This has nothing to do with a bear!"

"It has everything to do with the bear whose fur he now rests upon."

"That was years ago. You're not making any sense."

"That's because you didn't let me finish. Yesterday's fight has been brewing for years. We all knew Tahnito and Bear Killer, who was then Little Bear, had gone out together that day, and only Tahnito came back. Little Bear wasn't missed until after dark. None of us knew, until yesterday, exactly what had happened, except that Little Bear had been trapped in a rock slide, then attacked by a bear."

Chee's eyes roamed over his unconscious friend. Why had Bear Killer never told what had happened? Or at the very least, why had he never confronted Tahnito?

"But yesterday you found out?"

"Yes. Apparently Tahnito and Little Bear had been together during the rock slide. Little Bear was knocked out, and his foot was trapped beneath a boulder. Then the bear came, and Tahnito ran. When he got back to camp he said nothing about it to anyone."

They were interrupted then by Shanta. Angela tuned out the words she didn't understand and watched Matt's chest rise and fall, assuring her he still breathed.

The next time she looked up, Chee and Shanta were gone.

It was the first time she'd been alone with Matt since the morning before, when he'd left for the hunt. Her control slipped a notch. She felt the tears gather and sting. So much had changed in the past twenty-four hours. Matt lay there, for all she knew at death's door, and she could do nothing to help him beyond tending his wounds, most of which were not serious. The gash on his back was the worst of the cuts, and it wasn't very deep. It was the blow to his head that kept him so still.

She prayed fervently his wounds would heal, even as she prayed for her own wounds to heal. His were of the body; hers were of the heart. How could she have been so foolish as to think he really cared for her? Her own feelings must have blinded her, leading her to believe what she wanted to believe.

What had she done, she wondered, that was so terrible that she should lose not only her mother and father, but now she'd lost Matt? Whether he lived or died, she'd already lost him. Even if he lived, and as far as she could tell, it was doubtful that he would, she could never spend her life with a man who couldn't remain faithful for more than the few days they'd been together. And if he . . . well, if he didn't live, her last vivid memory of him would be with his arms around another woman.

She'd heard stories, of course. Some men just couldn't confine themselves to one woman. But Angela knew she'd rather never see him again than stay with him knowing he was betraying her. She wasn't strong enough to live with that kind of torture day after day.

Angela stared dully at the dead fire for a long time before she realized the coals were black and cold. She looked again at Matt, and her heart began to pound as his eyelids fluttered, then opened fully.

"Angel." Her name on his lips sounded like a sigh of relief.

Angela couldn't speak. Her emotions were at war with each other: relief that he was finally awake, awe and a little fear that the old shaman had predicted the timing of it so well, anger that Matt should call her Angel after being with another woman, and a choking pain in her chest at the reminder that once she left him, she'd never hear him call her that again. But she bit back her cry of anguish and blinked away her tears. Now was no time to talk about any of that.

It was two days before Matt was well enough to sit up. His injuries hadn't seemed that bad at first, but a slight infection settled in the gash on his back, and with it, a fever.

But he was sitting up now, awake and alert, much more alert than Angela wished.

"What's that for?" Matt nodded to the separate bed she'd made herself across the fire from him.

"You were sick and hurt. I didn't want to disturb you, so I slept there."

"Well, I'm not sick now, so you can move your blanket back where it belongs." His back hurt, his head hurt, his ribs hurt. He was miserable, and he wanted her next to him.

"I think it's better that I stay over there." She suited her actions to her words and went and sat on the far blanket.

"Angela."

"It's no use, Matt. We made a m-mistake. I've admitted it, now you have to admit it, too."

"What the hell are you talking about?"

"I'm talking about us. It won't work. I think an annulment will be the best thing all around."

"No!" Matt winced. He never realized a man used his back muscles when he shouted. "I've told you before, Angela, there'll be no annulment. I thought you loved me. Was I wrong?"

"I never said it, did I?" Angela cried. "And what about you? You kiss me good-bye to go hunting, and the next time I see you, you're wrapped up with that . . . that. . . . What were you trying to do, swallow each other's tongue?"

Matt laughed outright at her description of a simple kiss, then wished he hadn't, both for the pain it caused him physically and for the look of outrage his laughter brought to Angela's face. "I'm sorry," he gasped.

"I'm glad you're so amused."

"I said I was sorry. Angela, that whole incident in the woods with Alope meant nothing."

"Kissing other women means nothing to you?"

"That's not what I meant. What I meant—"

"I don't care what you meant! My father didn't go around kissing other women, and my mother never kissed other men. My parents are the only example I have to go by as far as what a marriage should be. That's the only kind of marriage I want, and apparently you can't give it to me."

214

"Angela, you're—"

"No!" She held up a hand to stop him. "Just let me say what I have to say. You're right about the annulment. We don't need one. No one outside this camp knows anything about this *supposed* marriage of ours. There's not even a marriage certificate. For all I know, we're not even really married. When we leave here, we'll just go our separate ways, and that'll be the end of it."

Matt stared at her in stunned silence for a long moment. She wasn't even asking him for an explanation. She'd already tried him and found him guilty, and now she was ready to hang him, without hearing his side of the story.

"You've thought it all out, have you?"

She lowered her eyes to stare at her hands. "It's not my intention to make you look foolish in front of your friends here. They don't have to know about any of this. We can take care of it after we leave here, when you're well."

"Don't you think we ought to talk about this first?"

"No. My mind's made up, Matt."

"Your mind's made up. Great. I thought we had something pretty special going for us. I thought *you* were special." He curled his lip in disgust. "You were good, Angel, I'll give you that. All those sweet kisses and soft sighs . . . the way you'd cling to me when we. . . . It was all a lie, wasn't it? A goddamned lie. You lied with your words, with your lips, with your body. And I fell for it like a green school boy."

He didn't wait for an answer. Hurt, angry, he lay down on his bearskin and threw an arm over his face, pretending to sleep. He never saw the effect of his words.

Angela bit her lip to keep from crying out. How could he think she never meant it? It was him! He was the one who lied! He was the one who ran to another woman the minute her back was turned! He was the one who couldn't be trusted, who couldn't be faithful for even a week!

She wished with all her might that his words were true, that she didn't love him. But she knew better.

Bitter tears gathered in her throat. He hadn't even bothered to deny her accusations. She'd been prepared to hear all sorts of flimsy excuses, but he'd offered none.

The silence within the wickiup lengthened.

Matt was forced to lower his arm from his face by the protesting muscles in his back, but he kept his eyes closed. If he opened them, he was afraid he'd look at Angela, and he couldn't trust himself to do that just yet.

When she'd first mentioned an annulment again, he honestly hadn't had any idea why she was upset. In fact, she hadn't seemed upset, only . . . convinced. Even when she mentioned his kissing another woman it had taken a moment for him to remember.

Alope.

His first thought then had been that Angela was merely jealous. That hope had died when she went on calmly discussing her plans to leave him. If she were jealous, she wouldn't have been so calm, would she?

Damn. How could he have been such a fool as to fall into this trap. He'd let himself be taken in by her soft, helpless looks and sweet words. He would have sworn she cared for him, was even starting to love him. Obviously he'd been wrong.

The kind of love he wanted was considerably stronger than the kind that shattered over a simple kiss. True, he could imagine how it must have

216

looked to her, but she hadn't even asked him for an explanation, or given him a chance to volunteer one. She'd jumped to her own conclusions and wasn't interested in hearing his side of the story.

If her feelings could die so easily, then she wasn't the kind of woman he wanted to spend the rest of his life with. The sooner they parted company, the better.

The next day Chee came. It was the first time he'd come since Matt had awakened. Matt hadn't been told about Alope and Klea yet, so Chee told him.

From Angela's place by the fire, where she tended a pot of stew, she saw Matt's stricken look when he heard the news. Her heart twisted painfully. She didn't consider that Matt had known the two women since childhood, that he and Alope had been playmates until they reached the age when strict Apache custom forbade the mingling of the sexes. She didn't consider that he might simply feel it was a tragic loss of lives, a terrible, horrible, avoidable tragedy. She only saw the brief flash of pain across his face, which he quickly concealed.

"What about Tahnito?" Matt asked.

"He's dead, too."

"Dead? How? What happened?"

Chee uttered a harsh bark of laughter. "He got what was coming to him."

"How's that?"

"When he realized his mother and sister were dead, he turned back to you, but by then Shanta and I were picking you up to carry you here. Tahnito saw his chance was lost to finish you off while you were still out of it, so he ran into the

217

woods. Some boys found him this morning, dead."

"But how'd he die?"

"He met up with one of your guardians."

"What?" Matt was stunned.

"*Shash*. We found tracks. The bear followed him more than a mile before it attacked. Tore him up pretty bad, then broke his neck."

Matt shuddered. "Good God, that poor bastard."

"I hope those words are for the bear," Chee said sharply. "You can't possibly have any sympathy for the man. He had every chance that he didn't give you. He left you wounded, trapped beneath that rock, alone. He came back to camp and said nothing. He even denied knowing where you were. The stinking *maintu'é* had it coming!"

"Maybe so," Matt said with a shake of his head. "Still —"

"Still nothing. Don't trouble yourself about him. I said he had every chance, but he didn't even try. He wanted to die, after killing his own mother and sister."

"That was an accident. It was terrible, but it was still an accident. No man wants to die."

"He must have. He didn't even draw his knife. It was still sheathed."

Matt ran a hand over his face and shuddered again. "Good God," he whispered.

Chee left a short time later, and Matt slept.

His recovery over the next few days was slower than it should have been. His mind wasn't on recovering; it was on Angela. As long as he lay in bed, she stayed near him. She'd erected a wall of ice around her, and he was curious as to why.

If she didn't care for him at all, there should be no need to hide her feelings from him. When she fed him Huera's broth or tended his wounds, which

218

healed much too quickly for his purposes, her touch was gentle, even tender. Her face, however, was another matter entirely. She held it rigid, letting no expression cross it at all. What could she possibly have to hide from him, except that she really did care about him?

Hellfire! What did he care how she felt anyway? If she'd loved him even just a little, she would have let him explain about Alope. She might even have gone so far as to demand an explanation.

And so it went, back and forth. One minute he cursed her for her lack of faith, for not loving him, the next he was convinced she still cared. What he needed, he realized, was an excuse to keep her from leaving him long enough for him to better judge what her true feelings were.

Why he wanted to bother with someone who treated him with such icy politeness, he had no idea. Well, that wasn't exactly true. He'd told himself she was too shallow; she'd tricked him into loving her, then threw it back in his face. But the fact was, he did love her, and there didn't seem to be anything he could do about it.

Chapter Twenty-two

Matt purposely stretched out his role of invalid. As long as he was unable to get around, Angela stayed with him. She brought him food and water and carefully tended his wounds. The way the blood drained from her face whenever an incautious movement caused him to wince told him a great deal about her feelings—much more than she would have wished, he was sure, had she realized what she was revealing to him.

In spite of everything she said, or didn't say, Matt became convinced she still cared for him. All he had to do was get her to admit it to him and to herself. But no matter what he did or said, Angela refused to discuss their personal situation. Sometimes she simply refused to answer his questions. At other times, when he tried to get her to talk about how she felt, she left the wickiup.

Since he was supposed to be so gravely ill, he couldn't get up and follow her, which put him at a distinct disadvantage.

Matt finally determined that his present course of action was getting him nowhere. He needed more time with her, but not when he was flat on his back. He wanted to take her home, to the Triple C. If he could find a way to keep her there for a while, maybe he could convince her they belonged together.

Maybe he could somehow teach her to trust him again, since lack of trust seemed to be the heart of her problem.

Now that he'd decided to quit playing sick and take Angela home, Matt discovered a new trouble. Lying around doing nothing for over a week had sapped his energy. He lost patience with himself and everyone around him several times during the few days it took him to regain his strength, but the day finally arrived when they could leave.

Matt had already said his good-byes to Hal-Say and Huera and his friends. Huera suggested they leave their wickiup standing where it was, so that it would be there the next time they came to visit. Angela had cringed at that, but she held her tongue. Matt had been cool as a cucumber when he'd agreed to that bit of nonsense.

And nonsense it was. They wouldn't be coming back. At least, *she* wouldn't.

A lump of sadness surprised her by lodging in her throat. She'd made friends here, despite her short stay and the language barrier. Friends. Huera and Nod-ah-Sti and Cochise's wives. Even Chee. Friends she'd never see again. It was ridiculous to realize that this good-bye was nearly as painful as the ones with Mary Lou and Jennilee in Memphis.

Since Angela had nothing of her own to pack, and Matt had taken care of his own belongings, there was nothing left to do but leave. Matt had told her to wait for him, and now he returned leading two saddled horses and a packhorse. The pinto was his, and the gray pack horse didn't worry her. But the brown one. . . . She began to panic.

"What's that?" she asked stupidly.

"I believe they're called horses," Matt answered with a mocking smile.

221

"I-I can see that. But what's the brown one for? Where did it come from?"

"It's Pace's, and *it's* not *brown*. *She's* a *chestnut*. Pace left her here for you to ride home. Unless, of course, you'd rather walk. Now come on, let's go."

Angela swallowed. He actually expected her to ride! The only times she'd ever been on a horse in her life, other than facedown on Tahnito's, were when she'd ridden double with Matt or Chee. She'd never been on one by herself and didn't have the slightest idea what to do. Before she could confess her lack of experience, Matt tossed her into the saddle and mounted his own horse.

Angela sat perfectly still, trying to get used to the idea of being perched on the back of the huge brown animal. *Excuse me,* she thought with disgust, *chestnut.*

She wasn't sure what she had expected, but she hadn't expected to be able to feel every flick of muscle, every breath in and out of the deep lungs, every blink of the horse's eyes. When the horse snorted, Angela grabbed the saddle horn with both hands. When it—no, when *she*—shuffled her feet, Angela swayed dangerously and held on for dear life.

She might have been all right then, but she tried to put her foot in the stirrup. She missed. She didn't fall off, due to the deathlike grip she had on the saddle horn; but it was a very near thing, and she cried out in alarm.

"Now what?" Matt demanded.

Angela took one look at his stormy face and swallowed her words. She knew he'd intended on leaving at first light, and it was well past that now. It wasn't her fault that her friend Nod-ah-Sti came this morning for a last visit. It wasn't her fault that Huera made Matt wait while she presented Angela with a new pair of knee-high moccasins, or *kébans,* to replace her worn slippers. It wasn't her fault that Cochise came personally to bid her good-bye, delaying them yet again.

To give Matt credit, he'd borne the delays fairly well, considering he couldn't wait to get rid of her. But one more delay would fix things for sure. And now she had to tell him she didn't know how to ride a horse. If he didn't murder her right on the spot, it would be a miracle. Just as she opened her mouth, three more men came to bid them farewell. At least this time it was Matt they wanted to talk to.

Chee laughed to himself as he watched Matt grit his teeth at another delay. Natzili-Chee, son of the great warrior Natzili, did not speak three languages fluently and understand the American and the Mexican cultures nearly as well as he understood his own because he was stupid. As soon as he'd seen the look on Angela's face when she realized she was expected to ride, he knew what was wrong.

He also knew Bear Killer was in no mood to deal calmly with the situation, so Chee had sent this latest group of young men to divert Matt's attention while he gave Angela brief tips on how to control her mount. It was no substitute for real instruction or experience, but he hoped it was enough to get her by until she grew used to the idea of riding.

Matt glared in their direction. "Are you two finished? Can we go now?"

Chee grinned back at him, the picture of innocence. "Of course. Have a good trip. See you next spring." To Angela he said, "Come back to us, Eyes Like Summer Leaves. Your next visit will be better, I promise."

"Chee." Angela grasped his hand and squeezed

tightly. This man had saved her life and been her friend. She would miss him. "Thank you for everything, Chee. I wish there was some way I could repay you for what you did for me."

"You can," Chee answered for her ears alone. "Be good to my friend. I don't know what's happened between the two of you, but I know he loves you, and he needs you, no matter what you may think. Go now." He released her hand and turned to Matt and said, "May we live and see each other again, my friend."

Matt's mood lightened. He smiled at Chee and repeated the words of the formal parting phrase of friends. This parting, however, was easier for Matt than others had been. In the past, he'd always worried about the raiding and the killing. Each time, he'd wondered if his adoptive family and his friend would be alive the next time he came.

But all of that was over now. Now there was peace.

Once they were out of the stronghold and on the trail, Matt's mood seemed to improve, although he didn't talk. It was just as well as far as Angela was concerned. She was concentrating so hard on staying in the saddle she didn't have any thought left over for conversation. Thank God Matt kept the pace to a walk. Luckily her horse just followed the other two. But the unaccustomed position of sitting astride, as well as the constant swaying in the saddle, kept her mind and body fully occupied.

Most of the time she stared at the line on her mount's neck where the mane fell to one side. Once in a while, when she felt particularly brave and confident, she raised her eyes to stare between the two upright ears. Scrub oak, stunted juniper, and strange rock formations passed in and out of her view. So did Matt.

At least he was wearing clothes again, but that didn't do much for her peace of mind. The buckskin pants and brown cotton shirt fit him like a kid glove, contouring each and every muscle, leaving only the color of his skin to the imagination, and Angela already knew every subtle shade of it.

Slowly, unconsciously, her body picked up the rhythm of the horse. Riding became easier, less fearful. She began to notice things, like a covey of quail darting away at their approach, the deep, clear blue of the sky, the buzz of the horsefly tormenting the packhorse in front of her.

Matt led them out of the woods and into a narrow canyon surrounded by sheer rock walls. The mouth of the canyon widened gradually until it poured out into a broad, flat valley, so broad it seemed to go on forever, except for the jagged line of mountains to the east.

When they reached the valley floor they turned north until they came to a pass, then followed it west through the same mountains they had just left. The grass grew so tall in places that it tickled the horses' bellies. When they left the pass, they followed a runoff stream out into another broad valley. Along the stream, the grass gave way to rocky ground, more scrub oak, and cottonwoods.

They stopped in a small grove of willows for a short rest in the early afternoon, and Angela watched to see how Matt dismounted. Copying his motions, she managed it without too much difficulty, except that it was farther to the ground than she'd thought. If she hadn't been holding onto the saddle so tightly, she would have fallen.

She nearly fell anyway. Her legs and buttocks were numb, her back and arms ached miserably, and her inner thighs had been rubbed raw. She gritted her teeth and forced her legs to move.

The rest of the afternoon was a repeat of the morning, and they still hadn't reached those distant mountains. By the time they stopped for the night Angela was trembling from head to toe with fatigue. Matt tended the animals and set up the camp while she sat in a stupor, too tired even to lie down and sleep.

The first thing she was really aware of was the smell of food when Matt handed her a plate of biscuits and beans. She had no idea where it came from and didn't take the time to ask. She'd just realized she was starving!

The food revived her somewhat, so when they finished eating, she took the tin plates the few yards to the stream and washed them. She had just finished and taken one step back toward camp when she heard a tremendous crashing in the trees to her right, followed by a loud snort. She was paralyzed for one brief instant, just long enough for the moonlight to show her the huge, furry outline of a bear coming straight for her.

Angela screamed for all she was worth.

Then suddenly Matt was there, wrapping his strong, warm arms around her, telling her everything was all right. She struggled against him, trying to free herself.

"Bear! It's a bear, Matt! A bear!"

"Ssh, ssh. It's okay, Angel. He won't hurt you. See? He's leaving now. It's okay."

Angela was shaking so hard she knew she'd fall if Matt let go of her. But he didn't let go. He picked her up and carried her back to camp, talking softly to her the whole time. He sat beside the fire and held her until she stopped trembling.

He was sorry she'd had such a fright, but he wasn't sorry at all to be holding her. He silently thanked the bear for chasing her into his arms. It had been so long since he'd held her. For the past week he thought he might never get the chance again. And if he didn't come up with a very good reason why she couldn't leave him, this might very well be the last time.

His arms tightened at the thought of losing her. He couldn't stand it. It couldn't happen. He'd think of something—he *had* to.

Angela's thoughts weren't too far from his. The terror slowly slipped from her mind to be replaced by the feeling of security provided by Matt's arms. She closed her eyes against the pain of their parting she knew would take place in just a day or two.

But she'd made up her mind. She would stand firm in her decision. She couldn't live with a man she didn't trust, even if she did love him.

When Angela woke the next morning, not one single muscle in her entire body would move. Even her eyelids refused to open. But the smell of coffee was a strong lure, so she forced herself to sit up. She gasped involuntarily at the sharp, screeching protest of each separate joint and muscle. She'd never felt such pain in her life.

She raised her eyes to gauge the distance to the coffeepot—she'd never needed coffee like she needed it now—only to find Matt sitting cross-legged before the fire, laughing at her.

"Good morning."

His cheerfulness grated on her nerves. "Go away," she mumbled.

Matt laughed again, then rose and came toward her. "Lie back down and I'll see if I can't loosen up some of those muscles."

Angela watched him warily. She didn't trust that gleam in his eye. "My muscles are just fine. Leave me alone."

"Come on. You just spent an entire day astride a horse for the first time in your life. You're stiff as a board."

He pushed her back and rolled her facedown on the blanket and started rubbing her neck and shoulders. Oh, God, but it felt heavenly. She could feel herself loosening up almost immediately. What would it be like to stay with him, to be the recipient of his tender care each day?

But how many others would he lavish the same care on?

"How did you know I'd never ridden before? Was I that bad?"

"No," Matt said with a laugh. "You did very well, as a matter of fact. Most women would have been screaming their heads off and crying to stop after the first mile. Why didn't you?"

"In the mood you were in? You've got to be kidding."

"I see your point. It didn't help any, though, that you wouldn't tell me you'd never ridden before."

"How did you know I hadn't?" God, but his hands felt good. Matt worked his way down an arm and was now massaging her stiff fingers.

"I can always tell when you're doing something for the first time," he said quietly.

Angela felt the blood rush to her cheeks. She looked at him sharply. That knowing little grin on his face made her want to scream. Instead, she turned her face away. He laughed again.

When she finished with her other arm, he made

his way down her back with strong, deep strokes that brought life back into her body and relaxed her at the same time.

His hand touched her buttocks. She tried to roll away in protest. "Matt!"

But Matt was ready for her and held her down. "Don't get excited, Angel. I'm only giving you a rub-down."

She struggled until he swung his leg over her and straddled her back to keep her still. Facing her legs and feet, he now had both hands free again to tend to business. It would have been easier on him if the "business" wasn't quite so pleasurable, but his hands had ached for days with the need to touch her. Her soreness gave him the perfect excuse.

Angela, too, was having trouble keeping her mind off the pleasure of his touch. But her muscles were so sore, and his hands felt so good. She gave up her struggle and let him have his way.

When he finished with her legs and feet, he left her lying there while he brought her breakfast. She felt something terribly close to disappointment at the loss of his touch. Then he had to help her sit up. She grew uneasy when he sat down to watch her eat. She tried to think of something to say, then remembered last night.

"Why didn't you shoot the bear?"

"Apaches don't kill bears, except in self-defense."

"But you're not an Apache."

"Part of me is," he replied candidly.

Angela merely shrugged. She thought she understood how he felt about the Apaches. "But it would have been in self-defense anyway."

"No it wouldn't. He wasn't hurting anything."

Angela shook her head in confusion. "I don't get it. Tahnito was just killed by a bear; you nearly were once. And yet you don't mind when they wander right up to camp that way?"

So then he told her about bears. He told her that when an Apache dies, the only reason he would be denied heaven would be if he had betrayed his people in some way. In that case, he would live again in the body of a bear. If a man killed a bear, he might be killing his own relative.

"That's the most ridiculous thing I've ever heard," Angela claimed.

"Why is it ridiculous?"

"It just is, that's all. Besides, what happens when someone is forced to kill one, like you were?"

"In my case, according to Dee-O-Det, all the bears everywhere were sorry that I had to kill one of them. So now instead of attacking me, the bears follow me around and protect me. Everywhere I go, there's always a bear nearby. Dee-O-Det calls them my guardians."

"You're not serious. You don't actually believe that, do you?"

"Why shouldn't I? How else do I explain the fact that everywhere I go, there's always a bear? If a mountain lion jumped us right now, a bear would probably rush in and kill it. That happened to me once."

"I don't believe a word of it," Angela announced. "I think you're teasing me." The look he gave her sent a shiver down her spine. Maybe he wasn't teasing.

Once they were mounted and riding, Angela had no more energy to think or talk. She felt more confident about riding than she had yesterday, but today she hurt so bad it was a real effort to keep from crying.

At midday they reached the San Pedro River. It

230

was muddy and wide, reaching clear up into the trees on either side. Matt picked his spot carefully, then took Angela's reins. "Hold on tight, Angel," he warned.

Angela pushed her feet firmly into the stirrups and gripped the saddle horn with both hands. Crossing a river from the high seat of a wagon was bad enough, but this!

She was about to decide it wasn't really so bad — after all, the water was flowing swiftly, but it wasn't deep — when she saw the water rise rapidly around Matt's boots, then her own moccasins. In a matter of seconds it was up to her thighs, pulling at her, tugging on her dress, trying to tear her off the back of the horse and send her shooting downstream. After an eternity of terror, the water receded as the horses lunged up the west bank and onto dry ground.

Matt dismounted and lifted her down. "Are you all right?"

Too relieved to even speak, she merely nodded, then sank to the ground at the base of an old cottonwood and leaned her head back against the rough bark.

"The river's not usually so high, even after the August rains. Must have had a lot of rain south of here."

How odd, she thought. The river flowed north! She'd never seen a river that flowed north before.

A few minutes later, Matt brought her canteen, a biscuit, and a strip of dried beef, then sat down beside her.

Was he always this polite to women, she wondered, or did he really care about her? If she could only be sure of him. She was torn in two by her inability to believe in him and the equally painful problem of her inability to stop loving him.

Deep down she knew Alope had meant nothing to him. What in the world had possessed her to claim it was over between them, and that she was leaving? And why had he let her? Maybe he didn't really care after all. Maybe she was right to leave him.

I don't want to be right. I want Matt.

Angela stopped chewing on the tough jerky Matt had given her when she saw him stiffen. He trained his eyes on the dry ravine before them and cocked his head. Then he suddenly became a blur of motion.

"Mount up," he ordered.

From his look, something was wrong, so she didn't question him. She tied her canteen onto her saddle, led her horse to a fallen log, and pulled her protesting body up onto the horse's back. As they crossed the ravine and headed for a thick stand of mesquite and boulders, Angela finally heard what Matt was listening to. She heard, but it made no sense, for what she heard was a loud clicking sound. It sounded like a hundred little boys, each one running a stick along a picket fence at top speed. "What in the world?"

"Ssh," Matt cautioned. "It's cattle."

"Cattle?" she whispered.

"Longhorns. It's their horns clicking together."

"Why are we hiding up here?"

"Because in this part of the country, it's just as likely to be rustlers as ranchers. We'll just wait and see."

Matt could see the dust raised by the herd now. He peered from behind the trees and looked down into the ravine just as the lead steer came into view. It wore the Circle M brand. Matt breathed easier. Then the rest of the thirty to forty head rounded the bend, and Matt's ease slipped away when he spied the riders.

They were most definitely not Circle M riders, unless old man McMahon had changed his hiring practices drastically. Matt doubted if there was a more bigoted man in the territory, and these men with the Circle M cattle were decidedly Mexican. In fact, they were dressed like typical bandits, with crossed bandoliers loaded with cartridges, Mexican silver spurs and broad sombreros.

Then something else caught Matt's eye. All the cattle were not from the Circle M. Some of them bore the Shattucks' Lazy S brand. It was possible that the two ranches had sold some cattle, but McMahon would never have sold to a Mexican.

When the herd was out of sight, Matt and Angela left their hiding place. He explained the situation and told her they were riding to the Circle M to let McMahon know what they'd seen.

"You think those men are stealing those cattle?"

"It sure looks that way," he said. "We'll tell McMahon about it and let him take care of it."

"Is it far?" Angela asked.

"A couple of hours, if we hurry. Are you up to a little fast riding?"

Angela looked at him skeptically. "How fast?"

"Not too fast," Matt promised with a laugh.

Angela didn't see any more of her surroundings after that. She was too busy hanging on.

Chapter Twenty-three

The Circle M Ranch was just like a dozen other ranches Angela had seen when coming through New Mexico: a small, flat-roofed adobe house, with a few adobe outbuildings and a rough corral. As she and Matt rode into the yard, three dogs rushed out to greet them, barking and yelping. A half-dozen scrawny chickens squawked and scattered out of harm's way. Angela had to concentrate on controlling her mount, which didn't seem to appreciate having its heels nipped at.

"What d'ya want?"

The rude greeting startled her. She looked up to see a big, barrel-shaped man with a pipe between his teeth glaring at Matt.

"Afternoon, McMahon," Matt said. His voice sounded calm and cool, but Angela noticed the tense muscles of his jaw ticking with irritation as he dismounted.

"Ya didn't ride all this way to tell me that," McMahon said, puffing on his pipe. "What d'ya want, Colton?"

A pretty girl about Angela's age, with long auburn hair, joined her father in the yard. "Papa, that's no way to treat company. If Mama could hear you now, she'd be ashamed." Her father's face flushed as he glared at her, but she just turned away from him.

"Hi, Matt. We're kinda off your beaten path, ain't we?"

"Only a little, Marthy. How've you been?" He relaxed some when he spoke to the girl.

While Matt spoke, Marthy McMahon approached him, rolling her hips like a riverboat floundering on the Mississippi. When she reached Matt's side, Angela gasped. The brazen hussy placed a dusty hand right smack on Matt's chest! Bold as brass!

"I've been pretty good," Marthy said with a wink. "Who's *she?*"

Angela bristled. The impertinent little twit asked it like she had a right to know.

"Angela, this is Marthy McMahon and her father, Mac," Matt said. He took a step back, and Marthy followed, running her grubby little hand up over his shoulder and down his arm. Angela seethed.

"Marthy, Mac, I'd like you to meet my wife, Angela."

Angela gritted her teeth and thought her face would crack when she smiled. "Miss McMahon, Mr. McMahon." She nodded to each of them.

The girl and her father both looked surprised. Marthy's surprise turned quickly to bitter disappointment, plainly visible on her face. She finally took her paws off Matt. *And about time, too!* Angela thought. Her attention was drawn away when Marthy's father began to laugh.

"Goddamn, Colton, I didn't know ya had it in ya, to marry up with a white woman. Always figured you'd take up with one of ol' Cochise's squaws."

Matt tipped his hat back and stood with his hands low on his hips. "I've got a couple of pieces of news you might be interested in, but if you'd rather stand there and run off at the mouth than hear about the new treaty or your stolen cattle —"

235

"Hold on, boy. Didn't say I didn't want any news, did I? What treaty you talkin' 'bout? What stolen cattle?"

"Thought that might get your attention," Matt said with a smirk. "Cochise just signed a treaty with the government."

"No shit?"

"McMahon!"

"Oh, sorry, ma'am." He nodded at Angela. "I mean, no foolin'? The old son-of-a—I mean . . . he did?"

Matt nodded. "Just a few days ago. The Chiricahua have been given the Dragoon Mountains as their reservation."

"The Dragoons? Why the hell . . . I mean . . . why the heck didn't they ship 'em off to New Mexico? Can't say as I like the idea of all them 'Pachees bein' so close ta hand."

"In the first place, Mac, the Dragoons are their home. Why should they leave? And in the second place, they've been there this whole last year and not caused any trouble; you know that. Yours would have been one of the first places they would have hit if they'd raided for horses or cattle, and I happen to know they haven't."

"Look here, Colton." McMahon stuffed his hands in the pockets of his worn trousers and hunched his shoulders. What ever it was he intended to say seemed to be taking a lot of effort. He cleared his throat twice. "I know you and your folks have takin' a lot of heat over the years 'bout them twins bein' breeds an' all, and I know I done more than my share of the talkin'. But, well, dammit, I know you and yours had a hand in this here treaty, and I jist wanna say that, well . . . it's good. It's real good."

"Thanks, Mac," Matt said with some surprise.

236

"But you've got to give credit where it's due. Nobody around here wanted peace more than Cochise did."

"Well, I guess you'd be the one ta know," Mac said.

"I'm afraid you're not going to like my other news so much."

"How's that?"

"Have you sold any cattle lately?"

"Sold some to the Army a couple o' weeks ago. Why?"

"Earlier today we came across thirty or forty head, some yours, some wearing the Lazy S. They were being herded east by three Mexicans, looked to be banditos."

"Goddamn, Colton. My cattle's bein' stole an' you stand there jawin' 'bout 'Pachees an' treaties!"

"You're the one who brought up the Apaches, old man. When we spotted your cattle, we rode straight here."

"Marthy," Mac said, "ride out west of the creek and round up Frank an' Harve. They was headed east, you say?" he asked Matt.

"They were getting ready to cross the river where that dry ravine hits it about five miles south. You need any help?"

"I reckon me an' the boys can handle it, but I thank ya jist the same, Colton. You're welcome to light an' set a spell, if you've a mind to." Then he turned to his daughter. "I'll ride north over the hill and get the rest of the boys an' meet ya on the east range, Marthy."

"All right, Papa." The girl was already saddling her horse, and a few minutes later she and Mac rode out.

"My goodness," Angela said after the dust of their departure cleared. "What . . . interesting people."

237

"That's one way to put it," Matt said with a laugh. "Come on, let's get out of here."

"Is that girl some special friend of yours?" Angela asked as they headed out.

"Who, Marthy?" Matt looked surprised at first; then he laughed. "Why? You jealous?"

"Of course not!" Angela snapped, much too quickly.

The rest of the day was even more exhausting than the previous one, if that was possible. Angela spent the remainder of the afternoon and most of the night chastising herself for ever having a kind thought about Matt Colton. She had almost convinced herself to forget about Alope and to trust Matt again. Then, right before her eyes, he let that little Marthy hussy rub herself all over him.

No. She'd been right in the first place. She couldn't trust him. If he'd do that in front of her, what would he do when she wasn't looking?

No. She could never trust him. Never.

When she finally closed her eyes to sleep, she was unaware of the tears seeping out from beneath her lashes. But the man across the fire saw them.

By the fourth day, which Matt said would be their last day on the trail, Angela had high hopes of actually living through this ordeal. She made a vow then, that if she did live through it, she would never again mount a horse for any reason, even if her life depended on it.

According to Matt, they were only a couple of hours from the Triple C when he asked, "Are you still determined to leave?"

The question startled Angela. Since that one discussion they'd had, on the subject, neither of them had mentioned it again. She'd assumed by his silence that he agreed with her plan. With vivid pictures in her mind of Alope and Marthy, she gave the only answer she could. "Yes."

"Why?"

"Why? I told you why. I won't marry a man I can't trust."

"But we're already married. Why don't you trust me?"

"You know the answer to that." She gripped the reins tighter and fought a sudden rush of tears. "Every time you were out of my sight I'd wonder what other woman you were with."

Matt uttered a word Angela had never heard before; then he glared at her. "For Christsake, Angela, Alope threw herself at me from five feet away. It was no more than a reflex that made me catch her. And I was not kissing her. She was kissing me."

Angela wanted to believe him with all her heart. In fact, she did believe him. Then she shook her head. "It doesn't matter. You have no idea what it was like for me to stand there and watch you hold Alope in your arms. Even if you did love me, and I loved you, I'd always be afraid of something like that happening again. And it did, just yesterday. I know it wasn't really your fault, but I hated it. It's not you, Matt; it's me. I just don't trust you, and there's nothing I can do about it."

"Even if? Are you saying you don't love me?"

She bit the inside of her lip and refused to answer.

"I think there's one thing you haven't considered in all this planning of yours."

"What's that?"

"What if you're carrying my child?"

Angela sucked in her breath, a confused mixture of horror and hope warring inside her. *What if . . .* "Well, I'm not, so just forget it."

"You don't know that yet. It's too soon since your last monthly flow for you to know."

Angela felt suffocated with embarrassment. Never had she heard such talk from a man before. But she wouldn't let him have the last word, no matter how embarrassed she was. "You don't know what you're talking about."

"Of course I do," he said with a laugh. "I knew the first day, about a week before Dad and Dani came."

"You don't know anything about it." This wasn't happening. It simply wasn't happening.

"Sure I do," he insisted. "You were uncomfortable. Your face was as white as a sheet for two days, you had dark circles under your eyes no matter how much you slept, and you walked like you had a corncob—"

"Matt!" She couldn't believe he was saying such things. And she couldn't believe he was so observant and accurate. Good heavens!

"You asked how I knew. I was just telling you. Don't tell me you hadn't considered you might be pregnant?"

Angela squinted into the lowering sun, cringing at the word *pregnant*. Such a crude-sounding word. "If I am, it's none of your concern. I can take care of myself."

"You'd deny me my own child?"

That shut her up. What could she say to him, anyway? Besides, it didn't matter, because it wasn't true. She wasn't with child. She wasn't.

"You'll stay with me at the ranch until you know for sure."

240

"I'll do no such thing."

"You will. I mean it, Angela. I'll have you watched every minute of every day. If you try to run off, I'll bring you back. If it turns out you're not carrying my child, and you still want to leave, then I won't stop you."

"And what if I am with child?" She had to at least consider the possibility, didn't she? "What happens then?"

"Then you stay till the baby is born. If you want to leave after that, you can. But the child stays with me."

"What?!" She jerked on the reins, and her horse came to an abrupt halt. Matt reined up beside her.

"You heard me."

"You'd take a helpless child away from its mother?"

"You'd take him away from his father? My child will be a Colton. He'll be raised as a Colton, with all the advantages I can provide. You don't have any place to live, no way to support yourself, much less a child. You'd be a fool to even try."

Angela cringed inwardly. Everything he said was true. How could she expect to earn a living and take care of a baby? But give him up? Never. She just couldn't be expecting. She just couldn't, that's all. "This entire conversation is ridiculous."

"We'll see, won't we?"

An hour later they crossed a creek and topped the rise beyond it. Matt reined in to look around. He loved this first view of home when he'd been away for weeks. Every time he sat here like this, drinking it all in, he remembered that day ten years ago when his dad had brought him home from the Apaches' summer stronghold east of the Dragoons.

He and his dad had stopped right here and looked

241

back to watch as Dani disappeared over the hills to the north, onto El Valle de Esperanza, her ranch. Simon, Dani's friend and partner, was still up there in that little valley, still taking care of his sheep. He'd bought the place a few years back, then surprised everyone by marrying Lucinda, who had been in charge of the Colton's nursery since the twins were born.

Matt went to El Valle from time to time to visit. So did his parents. The Valley of Hope had a special place in Dani's heart, and so did Simon. Dani went often to tend the grave of her old friend, Tucker, who'd helped her run the place before she married Travis. Tucker took over after that — Tucker and Simon — until five years ago next spring, when a rattler had come out to sun itself.

Matt breathed in the scent of sage and cedar as he faced west again. Home. It had changed a bit since that day he'd sat here with his father all those years ago. The adobe ranch house was larger now. They'd had to build two new wings, making the structure into a U shape, to accommodate the children and still leave room for guests.

They'd built a new and larger barn and added two more corrals, plus a cookshack and bunkhouse for the extra hands they'd hired over the years as the ranch increased its operations. These were located just beyond the four small adobe houses for their married hands, and as usual, all the little adobes were occupied.

Benito, Carlos and Jorge, with their wives, Consuela, Davita and Pilar, had lived in those houses and worked on the Triple C for as long as Matt could remember. And they would stay, no matter what. The boys' father, Luis, was ranch foreman, and their mother, Rosita, was in charge of the Coltons' kitchen, as she had been for years. Her daughters-in-law took care of the ranch house since her sister, Juanita, died back in sixty-four.

Good people, all of them. They were like family, and Matt knew they would love Angela, if only she stayed long enough to let them.

Angela watched Matt and saw his love for the land shining in his eyes. This must be the Triple C, she decided. She was humbled by the look on his face. He was drinking in the landscape like a man straight off the desert drinks water.

Memphis had been her home all her life, and she'd been sorry to leave it. But if it lay before her now, she doubted she would feel what Matt was feeling. She'd never felt that strongly about her home. It was just three rooms above the store on a busy, crowded street in the heart of town.

Would she ever learn to feel strongly about a place, a home, the way Matt did? Would she ever have a real home?

Finally instead of getting mad at me and telling the
to let you go he'll probably spend the next two
months telling they ways to make you happy or you to
stay.

Chapter Twenty-four

A footstep sounded in the hall, then the door rattled and swung open. Angela closed her eyes, feigning sleep. It had worked every night during the week she'd been at the Triple C. The pattern had been set that first day, when Angela pleaded tiredness and went to bed early, then pretended to be asleep when Matt came. She'd got away with it so far; Matt hadn't tried to touch her.

When Matt had announced his intentions of keeping her a virtual prisoner until they knew whether or not she was with child, Angela's plan was to reveal everything to his parents in hopes they would make Matt let her go. The more she thought about what Matt was doing to her, the angrier she got, until, as they rode toward the house, she finally told him what she planned.

"Go ahead, if that's what you want to do," he said calmly. "It won't make much difference, except to cause bad feelings all the way around. But Dad and Dani are going back East after Christmas to settle Dani's grandparents' estate, and they're taking the kids with them, so, if you're still here, it won't make any difference then what they think."

"Why shouldn't I want to cause you as much trouble as you're causing me?"

"Because it wouldn't work. We're a pretty close

244

family. Instead of getting mad at me and telling me to let you go, they'll probably spend the next two months before they leave trying to convince you to stay."

Angela's hopes crashed as she realized the truth of his words. His family would undoubtedly side with him.

"My parents, actually everyone on the ranch, will protect you from any outside threat, but no one will interfere between you and me, Angela," he said. "If you keep quiet and play the part of my wife, you'll be accepted as one of the family."

By the time they arrived at the Triple C, Angela still thought she might take the chance and ask his parents to help her. But then, why should they side with her, a stranger, over their own son?

And it would be embarrassing in the extreme to confess all that had passed between her and Matt.

What was she to do?

In the end she had kept quiet. She was welcomed like a long-lost daughter by both Daniella and Travis. The twins were glad to see her and made her feel at home. She found she didn't have the heart, or the nerve, to take a chance on losing the affection of this family.

That night she'd had her first hot bath in over six months. She lay back in the tub with bubbles and steamy hot water up to her ears, and closed her eyes and laughed out loud with pleasure. Then she cried.

She cried for a thousand reasons. For the loss of the only home she'd ever known, for her parents, for the fear she'd suffered at the hands of Tahnito and his friends, for the loss of her girlhood innocence, for relief that the physical danger was past, for the warm and undeserved welcome she'd received from Matt's family. She cried for Matt, for the love she'd come to know and lost. She cried for herself, un-loved, unwanted. She cried for the child she may or may not carry.

As the tears flowed out of her reddened eyes, so did the tension flow out of her exhausted body. That, combined with the hot bath, stripped her of what little strength she had left. As soon as she left the tub and crawled into bed, she slept.

When she finally awakened and remembered where she was, she felt refreshed and depressed at the same time. The sleep had been just what she needed, but it was time to face the family, and Matt, and act out the lie of her marriage.

She stared at the ceiling and tried to talk herself out of bed. Her musings were interrupted by a giggle, punctuated with a little hiccup at the end of it. A young girl of about three peered at her from the foot of the bed.

"Hello," Angela said.

The child grinned, then giggled again. And hic-cupped. When she calmed, she spoke in a loud stage whisper. "Are you Angela?"

"I am." Angela answered the girl's big smile. "You must be Jessica, am I right?"

"Uh huh," Jessica acknowledged with another gig-gle-hiccup.

Just then the bedroom door creaked partway open, but Angela couldn't see who was there. A young boy spoke from behind the door.

"Jessie, you pea-brain, you're gonna get it! You know you're not s'posed ta be in there."

"I am *not* a pea-brain, Spencer Colton!" In spite of the defiance in her voice, the young girl's slight lisp made her brother's name come out sounding like "Thpenther." On top of that, her feelings were hurt; her lower lip trembled, and her eyes watered.

"There you two are," came another voice from the hall. It was Daniella. "If you wake up Angela," she continued in a loud whisper, "I'll skin you both!"

Jessica's big, gray eyes darted from the doorway to Angela. Angela put her finger to her lips, motioning for Jessica to remain quiet. Then Angela winked at her and lay down, pretending to sleep. Jessica giggled again and hurried from the room, a little hiccup echoing behind her.

"It's okay, Mama, she's still asleep. But Spence called me a pea-brain. I'm not a pea-brain, am I, Mama? Daddy says I'm smart as a whip, even if I am as spoiled as last year's bacon."

"No, sweetheart, you're not a pea-brain. Spencer, I thought I told you you're not to call your sister names. It's really very rude, you know, and rude people don't get blueberry muffins for breakfast."

A small ache blossomed in the region of Angela's heart as she lay there listening. What would it be like to be a part of such a large, wonderful family?

It didn't bear thinking about, she reminded herself. She was only here temporarily, and against her will, at that. She couldn't afford to get close to these people.

And on that depressing thought, she got out of bed.

Someone had laid out a lovely pink dress for her, along with all the other necessities, and Angela was surprised at how well the clothes fit. She brushed her hair, tied it back with a ribbon, took a deep breath, and left the room.

The smell of coffee and bacon led her to the dining salon, where breakfast was well under way. Until she smelled the food, she hadn't realized how hungry she was, but she hadn't eaten since her arrival.

The family greeted her with pleased surprise.

Matt came forward, took her hand, and led her to the empty chair beside his.

"We thought you were going to sleep forever," Serena said with a grin.

"I feel like I have," Angela answered with a laugh. She winked across the table at Jessica, who tried unsuccessfully to hold back another giggle. "That hot bath last night must have relaxed me more than I realized. Why didn't someone wake me?"

Her last question was addressed to Matt, who sat beside her laughing. As if it were the most ordinary thing for him to do, he put his arm around her shoulders and dropped a light kiss on her forehead. She tried to hide her reaction, one of pain and pleasure mixed with considerable surprise, but the surprise won out when Matt spoke.

"You were more tired than you know. That bath was night before last."

Her rosy blush of confusion brought a round of pleasant laughter, then everyone started passing food her direction. Little Jessica wrinkled her freckled nose at Spencer as she made certain Angela had plenty of blueberry muffins. Spencer had none. He responded by sticking his tongue out at Jessica. Angela simply concentrated on filling first her plate, then her empty stomach.

Later that day, Matt took Angela to the bedroom down the hall from theirs and introduced her to his grandfather, Jason. Angela was grateful that Matt had warned her of what to expect, but still, what she saw wrung her heart. Jason Colton was an older version of Matt and Travis. He was in his early sixties but looked much older, due to the stroke he'd suffered two years ago which had left him paralyzed on his left side.

The effects even showed on his face, leaving the

muscles on the left hanging slack, that side of his mouth loose, while the other side smiled. His left eye was dull, and the lid drooped slightly. But his right eye sparkled with life.

"Grandad, this is Angela."

Angela smiled and held out her hand as she approached him. He sat in a large wicker chair mounted on wheels. "How do you do, Mr. Colton. It's a pleasure to meet you."

"Please, call me Jason," he said, his speech only slightly slurred.

"All right, Jason, I'd like that."

"I was about to decide Matt had made you up when he told me how pretty you were. But now I see he was telling the truth. Welcome to the family, Angela."

Angela felt herself blush slightly. From the corner of her eye she caught Matt's grin. Confused and a little embarrassed, she answered, "Thank you." Jason's crooked grin warmed her heart.

That day had set the tone for the days to come. When they were together in the presence of others, Matt and Angela were easygoing and carefree, sometimes even affectionate with each other. When they were alone together, they spoke only when necessary, and never touched.

Now, as she'd done every night, she lay in the dark, pretending to sleep as Matt came in.

Angela realized, as she listened to him undress, that he had purposely been giving her plenty of time to fall asleep before he came to bed each night. She was both hurt and grateful. She bit back a sigh as the bed dipped with his weight.

Matt steeled himself as he crawled into bed, being

careful not to touch Angela. He couldn't touch her, not like this, not alone, in the dark, in bed. He'd never be able to stop himself with just a touch. His longing and frustration were eating him alive.

And it wasn't any great help during the day, either, when they touched each other so casually before others, laughed, smiled. It was becoming sheer torture for him to be in the same room with her. It felt so natural, so right, to reach out and touch her with casual confidence. But it left a bitter taste in his mouth knowing Angela didn't feel the same. Or at least, she wouldn't admit it.

That was what kept him from giving up and letting her go, that little suspicion that she was lying to herself, that she *did* still care for him. After all, love wasn't something she could turn on and off at will.

It was his belief that how she acted toward him in front of others reflected her true feelings, and the silent tension between them when they were alone together was false.

It was his hope that her easy acceptance of him during the day would eventually spill over into the night.

It was his fear that it would work the other way around.

Yet if she was carrying his child, he might have enough time to soothe her fears and jealousies and regain her trust and love by the time the child came. He didn't think it could be accomplished in just a week or two if it turned out she wasn't expecting.

Someone else might say it was an awful lot of trouble to go to for just a woman. But she was *his* woman, and he loved her. He would never let her go unless he became thoroughly convinced she didn't love him and never would. Even then, he wasn't sure he could let her go.

Chapter Twenty-five

Angela was frantic. Until now she'd managed to convince herself that just because her flow hadn't come since the Apache peace conference, over two months ago, that didn't really mean anything. Until now. The terrible, sickening churning in her stomach, brought about by simply raising her head from the pillow, was impossible to ignore. This was the third morning in a row she'd been hit with nausea. She was only grateful Matt wasn't in the room to witness her distress.

Oh, God . . . oh, God. What am I going to do?

Was she to stay here in this house, continue to endure Matt's warm embraces and tender glances in public, his cold shoulder in private, until she gave birth to his child? And then what? Stand calmly by and let him tear her baby from her arms? Would he really do that?

He would. The way these people clung together as a family, there was no way any of them would let one of their own be taken away by an outsider. And Angela was the outsider.

The trouble was, she didn't feel much like an outsider. In all instances, except when she and Matt were alone, she was treated as a member of the family. She oddly felt like she really belonged, like this was her home. But how could she feel that way when it was all a lie?

What wasn't a lie was her feelings for every member of this family. Each and every one of them was so special to her, had come to mean so much to her in the past few weeks. They all accepted her, and she more than accepted them. How could she leave them?

Who would read to Jason every afternoon out in the courtyard? Who would help the twins and Spence with their math? Who would little Jessie follow around all day and get to retie the pretty bow in her hair?

Well, someone had obviously done these things before she had come, so things would just go back to the way they had been before. But the thought of never seeing any of them again took her breath away.

And then there was that one question that hurt the most.

Who would lie beside Matt each night in his big, soft bed?

She was so confused she didn't know what to do. But one thing was certain: she wouldn't be able to keep her condition a secret indefinitely. How much longer could she go on eating a regular meal at the table, then hiding out in the kitchen to eat half again as much where no one would see, without getting caught?

Once Matt knew she carried his child, there would be no way out for her. She would either have to stay here and be tortured by his nearness, or give up her own child. Either way, it would destroy her. What to do?

The nausea passed, and she knew the one thing she had to do right now was put in her usual appearance at breakfast. She must act normal. But she had to get away from here before it was too late!

The penciled figures in the account book blurred. Travis's voice faded to an indistinct murmur as Matt let his attention stray from the matter at hand.

Why hasn't she told me yet? he wondered for the thousandth time. She must realize by now that she carried his child, but maybe she was hiding from the truth.

He breathed an uneasy sigh. At least now he would have more time with her, but at this point he wasn't sure what good that would do. His hopes were dashed a little more each day as more and more of their nighttime tensions and awkwardness spilled over into the days. And that was as much his fault as hers.

Lying beside her night after night, feeling her warmth next to him but unable to touch her, hold her, was driving him crazy. He was jumpy and irritable most of the time. Good God. He'd even yelled at Jessica yesterday, for no good reason. He'd regretted it and been ashamed of himself even before she started crying, but before he could soothe her, Angela had run into the room, picked up his sister, glared her defiance at him, and took the child away.

If he acted this way with the Chiricahua, they'd change his name again. Instead of Bear Killer, he'd probably be known as Bear With A Sore Paw. And the analogy wouldn't be too far off. The pain of Angela's rejection pierced him like a thorn. His reaction to the pain angered him. He was damn good and mad at Angela for inflicting it, and at himself for being so vulnerable.

Slowly he became aware of a subtle difference in

the room. It was quiet. His eyes jerked guiltily to his father, who sat with his arms folded, watching him patiently.

"You want to talk about it?" Travis asked.

"About what?"

"About whatever it is that's bothering you." Travis looked at his son expectantly. "About Angela?" he prodded.

"What about Angela?"

Travis leaned forward and rested his elbows on his knees. "We haven't asked, Dani and I. We've never asked you about Angela. We've been waiting ever since you brought her home with you—longer than that, really—for you to tell us." Again, he paused. "I guess you'll tell us when you're ready," he finally said with a sigh.

Matt echoed his father's sigh. "I will, Dad, but not yet. I'm not ready yet. I don't have any answers for you, only more questions I have to answer for myself."

Travis flicked the ashes from the end of his cigar, then nodded. "All right, son, I won't pry. But I know things aren't quite what they seem between the two of you. If you'll take a bit of free advice from someone who's been there, talk your troubles out with each other. Nothing breeds misunderstanding quicker than silence."

Matt's mouth twisted into a crooked grin. "Thanks, Dad."

The heavy tread of a man's boots sounded in the hall and stopped at the open door to the study. Matt and Travis both looked around expectantly as Jorge stood there twisting his hat.

"Excuse me, *señores,* but . . . I'm supposed to tell you, Matt, that your wife, she took a horse and went for a ride."

Matt's stomach tightened into a knot. The pencil in his hand snapped in half. "Did anyone go with her, so she wouldn't get lost?" Matt asked.

Jorge shifted his stance. "No, *señor,* she went alone."

Matt rose from the desk with a casualness he did not feel and started toward the door. "Then, I guess I'd better go after her before she loses her way, hadn't I? Did you see which way she went?"

"*Sí, señor,* she took the road toward town."

Travis stared at the empty doorway and listened as Matt and Jorge left the house. His brow creased in a frown. Angela hadn't been on a horse since she arrived here. In fact, she often swore she'd never ride another one after that grueling trip from the mountains.

And now, she took a pleasure ride? And Matt broke pencils and worried that she'd get lost on a road that led straight to Tucson. Those two seemed to have more problems than he or Dani realized.

Chapter Twenty-six

After eating a generous breakfast, Angela sneaked off to the kitchen and ate three more rolls, then went outside for a walk. The morning was clear and bright, and warmer than it had been lately. She didn't even need her shawl, so when she entered the barn, she draped it across the stall door as she leaned to look in on a new foal.

Horses were fine, she thought, as long as she didn't have to ride one. Then she sobered, realizing if she was ever going to get away from here, it would have to be on a horse. That in itself would present a problem, since she knew she couldn't saddle one on her own, nor could she ask anyone else to do it for her. Matt had probably told the *vaqueros* to watch her every move. A request for a saddled mount would be reported to him.

She turned to leave the barn, kicking idly at some loose straw, when a movement beside her caught and held her attention. Standing there like a gift from heaven was a horse—nothing chestnut about it; it was just plain brown—all saddled and ready to ride. Angela quailed at the thought of actually mounting and riding out.

But there was no other way. *Damn Matt Colton for making me go through this.*

Angela blocked all other thought from her mind

but that of escape. Here was her chance, perhaps her only chance. She had to take it now or lose it. With determination, she led the horse to an up-turned crate and mounted. The animal shifted rest-lessly beneath her while she clung to the saddle and tried to arrange her skirt.

Then, as if she were out for a Sunday ride in the park—as if she actually knew what she was doing, where she was going—she trotted the horse out of the stable and headed northwest, along the road she'd heard led to Tucson. If she didn't make a spectacle of herself as she left, it might be hours before Matt learned she had gone.

After about a half mile, the road curved around a low hill, which put Angela out of sight of the house. She kicked the horse into a gallop and hung on for dear life. The wind stung her eyes and ripped her hair loose from its pins. The ground sped by in a blur. Her skirt slipped from beneath one leg and billowed out like a balloon. She tried to stuff it back beneath her and nearly lost her seat in the process.

The horse tossed his head and snorted, then kicked out with his hind legs.

Angela flew at least a foot in the air, shrieking with every inch. She landed hard. Scared now, she pulled back on the reins, trying to slow her mount, but he didn't respond. Instead of slowing, he jerked his head forward sharply. Angela lost her grip on the reins. Her heart thudded in terror as the thin leather straps slipped through her fingers and dangled dangerously to the ground, bouncing around the horse's hooves.

Angela screamed and clutched the saddle horn until her knuckles turned white and her nails dug gouges in the leather. She couldn't control the horse without the reins! The horse ran faster and faster, and there was nothing she could do! If she jumped, she'd surely break her neck at the very least, even if she could command her fingers to loosen their deathlike grip, which she couldn't. She couldn't do anything but hang on.

Terror weakened her. She wouldn't be able to hold on much longer. Already her fingers were getting numb and her arms were beginning to ache. Tears blinded her. The wind roared in her ears. Her head throbbed so that the beast's hoofbeats seemed to echo all around her.

It seemed the most natural thing in the world for her to look around and see Matt riding close beside her. Without even thinking, she let go of the saddle horn and reached out both arms to him.

As soon as he rounded the low hill, Matt spotted her, and recognized the horse. *Damn.* That particular horse was saddle broke, but just barely. Matt was amazed Angela had even been able to mount a skittish, green-broke mustang like that.

Having rushed out without his spurs, Matt used his boot heels with force to urge his own horse faster.

He saw her skirt fly up, then saw her shift in the saddle, trying to hold it down. He was still many yards behind her when he heard her scream and saw the reins dangling loose between her mount's hooves. Christ Almighty! Any second now the horse could step on them, stumble to the ground, break a leg, and throw Angela. Matt's mouth went dry. At that speed Angela was sure to break her neck.

It seemed to take forever to pull up beside her, his heart in his throat the whole time, praying her horse wouldn't stumble.

258

Several alternatives raced through his mind like lightning. He could pull up and try to turn her horse, but that wouldn't necessarily slow the beast down. He could grab for the bridle or the loose reins, but the horse had its ears laid back, and its eyes were rolling in fear. That kind of move might scare the half-wild mustang worse and make it rear or buck. He could throw a rope over the horse's head, but he feared the same results.

What he wanted to do was reach out and grab Angela, but she had a death grip on the saddle horn. If she was too scared to let go—and she was definitely scared. The goddamn fool girl even had her eyes shut!

Her mount swerved off the road into the cactus and brush, but Angela didn't seem to notice. He had to do something!

Just as he decided he'd make a grab for the bridle, Angela opened her eyes and saw him. When she turned loose of the horn and reached for him, he reached out with one arm, circled her waist, and pulled her over in front of him. Before she even touched his saddle, she had her arms locked around his neck so tight he thought he might choke.

But he didn't object. He slowed his horse to a stop, knotted the reins, then wrapped both his trembling arms around her. God, but it had been close!

Angela buried her face in the curve of his shoulder and soaked his shirt with her tears. If she hadn't been shaking so hard with her own sobs and terror, she would have told him how thankful she was for being alive and in his arms.

He spoke to her, soft and low, unintelligible words. Gradually she regained a modicum of self-control, and her sobs quieted to an occasional shudder.

"You're all right now, Angel. It's over. You're safe now. You're not hurt, are you?"

"No," she managed past her aching throat. "I-I'm okay. I was just scared."

"So was I, sweetheart."

His soothing words, the endearments, and his arms holding her close against his chest were all so wonderful that she stopped crying altogether. For a moment she even forgot what had just happened, and how it came to happen, her need to escape, his threats, everything. She just burrowed deeper into his embrace, longing to stay there forever.

Matt nudged his horse into a walk until they reached a clump of scrub oak. After assuring himself Angela was really all right, he left her there so that he could go after her horse.

Left alone, Angela watched Matt ride off, then lost sight of him over a rise. What would happen when he came back? He certainly didn't seem angry. It seemed like he'd actually been worried about her. Well, that was okay—she'd been worried herself. She'd been scared witless.

Witless. That was a good word to describe what she'd tried to do. Grab a horse on the spur of the moment and head out for town. *Just great, Angie Sue,* she thought with disgust and a remnant of panic. She could have been killed!

A shot sounded in the distance, from the direction where Matt had gone. Angela froze, and her mouth went dry. Had something happened to Matt? Was he in trouble? What should she do?

Then she picked out the sound of pounding hooves and held her breath until she saw Matt galloping toward her. Thank God he was all right!

He reined in so sharply the horse's hooves rose from the ground and dust swirled in the air, choking her. Matt jumped from his horse and reached her in two angry strides. He grabbed her by the arms and shook her roughly.

"Why, goddamn you? Why'd you do it, Angela?"

"Matt, you're hurting me!" she cried.

"I'll do more than hurt you. I oughta turn you over my knee and beat you till you're black and blue."

"What for? Why are you so angry?"

"Why? Do you know what they do to horse thieves in this part of the country?" He glared at her, and she just stared at him, open-mouthed. "They hang them. You still want to go to town? Maybe the marshal would like to hear how you stole a horse."

"You wouldn't dare. That's ridiculous. You would have got the stupid horse back. I would have left it for you."

"Oh, you left him for me, all right—left him with a broken leg. He tripped on the reins you dropped."

Matt turned loose of her and gave her a little shove before turning his back on her. He took several deep breaths, trying to get his temper and his fear under control. If she'd been on the horse when it stumbled. . . . And he was nearly as upset that Angela had tried to leave him. That was no pleasure ride she'd taken.

He whirled and faced her. "I just had to kill a perfectly good animal that showed every sign of becoming one of the best cow ponies in a long time. It was a waste, a stupid, terrible waste. What in the hell did you think you were doing?"

His anger scared her, but she refused to let him know. She tossed her head in defiance. "I was getting away from you, that's what I was doing."

"Damn it, I know that. What I want to know is why."

"Why? You expect me to just calmly go along with whatever you say? You expect me to stay here and let you steal my baby?"

"Is there a baby, Angela?"

She lowered her eyes and stubbornly refused to answer.

"Is that what you think I'm trying to do? Steal your baby?"

Her vision blurred. She opened her eyes wide to keep the tears from falling. "Isn't it?"

"In the first place, *wife*, it isn't *your* baby, it's *our* baby. In the second place, if you give birth to our child and then leave, I won't be stealing anything, you'll be abandoning your own child. I told you before, it's your choice whether you stay or go."

"That's some choice, isn't it?" she said with disgust.

"Just out of curiosity, what were you planning on doing when you got to town? You have no money, you don't know anyone there, you've never been there before. Were you just going to walk up to the first person you met and ask them to take you in? And what about the baby? How were you going to raise it?"

"I could have got a job."

"Doing what?" he demanded. "You wouldn't last an hour in that town on your own."

"And just why is that?"

"Tucson is not Memphis, Angela. There might be five, maybe six white women in the whole town, and every one of them is a respectable married lady. If someone like you showed up alone, men would be all over you like flies on shit. And these aren't your fine, upstanding Southern gentlemen, either. Most of them are thieves and murderers hiding out from the law. They'd just love to get their hands on a juicy little piece like you. You'd be on your backside so fast you wouldn't know what happened."

Angela didn't say anything as she stood there and glared at him. He was lying, just trying to scare her so that she wouldn't try running off again.

Matt swung up into the saddle and extended an arm down for her. She made no move to accept it.

"Come on and get up here, unless you'd rather walk home."

No, she thought reluctantly, she'd not rather walk home.

Chapter Twenty-seven

By mid-December the days were still on the mild side, but the nights were cold. The entire family enjoyed the warm fire in the salon after the evening meal.

"Matt, have you forgotten your promise to Angela?" Daniella asked one evening.

"What promise is that?" Matt asked warily.

"I distinctly heard you say, in front of witnesses, I might add, that you intended to replace Angela's wardrobe that was lost when her wagon burned."

Angela flushed with embarrassment. She'd been wearing borrowed clothes since she got here. Apparently Daniella was getting tired of sharing.

"Oh, that promise," Matt said. "No, I haven't forgotten."

"Good. I'm sure Angela hasn't forgotten either." Daniella turned her attention to Angela. "I know you must be tired of having to wear whatever's available, dear. Don't misunderstand me. We all share gladly everything we have with you. But you must want things of your own. I have some shopping to do before Christmas and before we leave for Boston. Tomorrow we'll go to town and see what's available."

Daniella was sure there was a reason Matt hadn't already seen to replacing Angela's clothes. It wasn't likely he would forget her need, yet every time someone mentioned a trip to town, he shied away from it, making first one excuse, then another.

She and Travis had talked about what could be wrong between Matt and Angela, and about why neither of them had mentioned how they came to be married. Well, that was their business, she supposed.

It was almost as if Matt didn't trust Angela for some reason. At least when it came to going to town. So Daniella pushed the issue. She wanted it resolved before she and Travis left for Boston right after Christmas to settle her grandparents' estate. Matt and Angela obviously loved each other very much, but there was a definite strain between them. Maybe if she took Angela to Tucson for the day, it might help.

Later that night, while Angela lay in bed alone, waiting to hear Matt's footsteps in the hall, she wondered why he hadn't tried to stop it. He'd voiced no objections about the trip to Tucson; he'd only looked at her strangely, almost sadly. She didn't understand.

During the weeks since her ill-fated horseback ride, the tension between Matt and Angela had increased. When he worked outdoors, he always stayed near the house. If she so much as poked her nose out, he was there. Even if she'd wanted to try again, she'd never have made it to the barn without him spotting her.

When they were with the family, there was no more pretense of a loving couple. No more lingering touches. No more long, soft looks. No more affectionate smiles or pecks on the cheek. Only silence . . . and distance. Always distance.

If she had it to do over again, she'd have kept her fool mouth shut after that scene in the woods with Alope. Angela knew now, probably knew even then, that Matt hadn't betrayed her. She'd betrayed herself. Her irrational fear and petty jealousy had destroyed whatever it was they'd had.

Each night she relived those few precious days after the treaty was signed. How she longed to go back to that time, to erase what happened afterward. Even amid this kind, loving family, she felt alone. They accepted her, they cared for her, and she loved every one of them. But she knew what Matt meant that night of the Apache moon. The love of his family wasn't enough. She wasn't complete.

Matt Colton's child grew inside her, but even that wasn't enough. Not without the man himself.

She didn't want to live this way anymore. If they couldn't have a real marriage, then she didn't want one at all.

She shuddered when she remembered her attempt to get to Tucson on her own. She certainly wouldn't try that again. Now it appeared she was going to be delivered there by her own mother-in-law. Why hadn't Matt objected?

Damn you, Matt! Why are you letting me go?

It was later than usual when Matt finally entered the room. She closed her eyes and tried to keep her breathing even. Would he hear her heart pounding?

She nearly cried out when his boots hit the floor one at a time with a loud *thud*. The rattle of buttons on the bare floor told her he'd dropped his shirt. His belt buckle clanked next, the sound dulled slightly, as if the buckle had landed on the shirt.

Instead of crawling into bed beside her, he sat on the edge, elbows on knees, his head in his hands. A cloud of whiskey fumes surrounded him. She hadn't known him to take a drink since they'd left the Apaches. Something compelled her to speak.

"Matt?"

He jerked as if he'd been shot, then took a deep

breath. "It's late. I thought you'd be asleep by now."

"Is something wrong?"

Matt snorted in disgust. "What makes you say that? My wife is taking our unborn child and leaving me in the morning. What could possibly be wrong?" He laughed harshly, then flopped down beside her on the bed.

"I'm beginning to realize what you meant when you said you couldn't live with someone you couldn't trust," he said quietly. "You don't trust me to be faithful, and now I don't trust you not to run off the first chance you get, which will be tomorrow."

She swallowed. "Then, why are you letting me go? You could have stopped it, you know."

"I know," he said with a deep sigh.

A deep ache grew in her chest. "Then . . . you want me to go?"

"Did I ever tell you about my mother?" he asked. "No, I guess I didn't. Before I was born, Dad brought her out here, much against her will. She hated it here, he said. She wanted to live in New Orleans so she could buy fancy gowns and go to big parties. She hated it here so much that as soon as I was born, she took me and ran off."

"Is that what you think I'll do? Take my child and run off?"

Matt acted like he didn't hear her. "The only thing was, she was so desperate to leave here, she didn't wait until she recovered from having me. The trip was too hard on her. By the time Dad caught up with her in New Orleans, she was dead."

It was quiet for a moment before Angela spoke. "Are you saying you think that's what will happen to me if I try to leave here?" *Would you care?*

"I'm saying I don't want to take that chance, Angela, but I don't know what to do. If you want to leave badly enough, I guess you will. But unless you

267

have family or friends somewhere to stay with, I don't see how you can hope to survive. At least here, with me, you're safe."

"A prison is safe, too, Matt," she said quietly.

Matt winced inwardly at her words. "I know. I was wrong to force you to stay here. But, Angela, you really don't have any idea what it's like out here for a woman alone, especially someone as beautiful as you. You might stand a chance back East somewhere, where things are more civilized, but not here, not in Tucson.

"To answer your question, yes, I want you to go tomorrow. Go to Tucson. Look around carefully at what kind of town it is. It's rough and it's dangerous. Even most men are afraid to go there alone, most decent men, anyway, and with good reason. There are stabbings and shootings every single night, and sometimes in the middle of the day. Go to Tucson, then come home, Angela."

"Home?"

"I'd like you to feel like this is your home, because it is. But I'm like you in one respect. I don't think I can live with the constant threat hanging over my head that any day you might change your mind and walk out. So if you come back tomorrow, I'll take that to mean you plan to stay."

Angela was stunned. He was giving her a choice. He was offering her the chance to leave. He was letting her go! And in that instant, she knew she couldn't do it. She couldn't leave him.

"I know you don't trust me," he said softly, "but if it'll make you feel better, I'll make you a deal."

Her voice was breathless when she spoke. "What kind of deal?"

"I won't touch another woman, and you won't run away. You trust me, and I'll trust you."

"Matt, I —"

"Don't say anything, Angela. Just think about it. Sleep on it. When the wagon comes back from town tomorrow, I'll have my answer, one way or the other."

Sleep on it? It was hours before she was able to sleep. The next morning, when she was dressed and waiting in the front hall, ready to go, Matt tossed her a leather pouch that landed heavily in her hands with a metallic clink. She looked inside and gasped. No wonder it was so heavy! It was full of twenty-dollar gold pieces! She looked at Matt questioningly.

"For whatever you need."

Angela took a deep breath, for courage. "Matt, I've made my decision."

"Well, don't tell me," he said, his expression strained. He kept his eyes on the bag of coins and didn't look at her. "You might change your mind. Women have been known to do that from time to time."

Just then Daniella joined them. "You won't need that money, Angela. We have accounts at all the stores. But I'd keep it, just the same," she said with a mischievous grin. "A wife never can tell when a little money of her own might come in handy."

Daniella's attempt at humor failed miserably with Matt and Angela. The air between them nearly crackled with tension.

Matt didn't dare stand and watch them leave. He was afraid he might make a fool out of himself by doing something stupid like begging Angela to stay. So he turned his back and walked away.

When Angela turned to wave good-bye, he was gone.

Travis drove the wagon, and Benito rode beside them on horseback. Serena had persuaded her mother to let her come along, but she had to ride in back, as there wasn't enough room on the wagon seat.

"One rule about living out here," Daniella said as they bounced along, "is never, ever go into Tucson alone. If for some reason you have to go without Matt, take at least one of the men along."

"Is it really that bad?" Angela asked, wondering if Matt had put his stepmother up to this.

"It's worse, but you'll see for yourself when we get there. There are some very decent people in Tucson, but not enough to matter much when you're in trouble."

"Isn't there a sheriff?"

"Tucson's got lots of sheriffs," Daniella said with a harsh laugh. "In fact, they have a different one every two or three months. They either don't live long, or they skip town in the middle of the night. It's not a very pleasant town, my dear. It's changing, though. Some day, maybe in not too many years, it'll be a nice town. Even now, as bad as it is, it's a thousand times better than it was when I first came here ten years ago. Back then there was no law at all. At least now they have a jail and a courthouse."

To emphasize her point, Daniella motioned toward the northeast. "Look at the land between here and the mountains," she said.

The land she indicated stretched for miles before the ground rose into the foothills, then the dark, purple mountains in the distance. Like toy soldiers, giant saguaro cacti stood tall and erect. Their spines and arms reached toward the sky while smaller cousins, chollas and prickly pears, guarded their feet.

"Tucson's not nearly as hospitable as the desert," Daniella said.

When they reached Tucson, it was obvious Daniella and Matt both had spoken the truth. It was a larger town than Angela expected, but it should be

270

large, she reasoned, since it was the capitol of the territory.

But no railroad? No telegraph? Good heavens! And the saloons! She'd never seen so many saloons. And all of them seemed to be doing a roaring business, even though it was the middle of the day. She noted a post office and the jail, but not much else that denoted civil government. The courthouse must be on another street.

There was garbage lying in the streets, and what appeared to be a good deal of two-legged garbage walking around. Men were everywhere. Dirty men, sleazy men, evil-looking men, all with pistols and knives sticking out of their belts, holsters and boots.

There were a few — very few — nicely dressed Mexican women going about their business, and Daniella and Travis occasionally waved at someone they knew.

And dogs. The streets were full of dogs. Most of them were skin and bones, rooting through the garbage for food.

There were no laughing groups of young ladies dressed all in ruffles and lace, with parasols resting on their slender shoulders, out for an afternoon of shopping. No dashing groups of young men with walking sticks out eyeing the young ladies. No mothers with children hovering around their skirts. No baby carriages being pushed along by proud parents out to show off the world's most beautiful child. No old men gathered to whittle and chew and solve all the world's problems.

No fine, red-brick buildings; no cool verandas with wicker chairs; no shaded green parks or tree-lined avenues. Good heavens. No parks or avenues at all. And not a single tree in sight. At least nothing she was willing to dignify with that name.

What on earth had her father been thinking of? Had he even known what it was like out here in this desolate, violent country? She was suddenly, sadly, glad her parents hadn't lived to see this Tucson. How they would have hated it.

The wagon pulled up at a spot in front of a general store as soon as there was room. Travis helped the three ladies down, and Daniella sped them along on a whirlwind tour of the stores. Angela had intended to buy only a few necessities and some material for a few dresses, but Daniella had other ideas.

Soon the boxes and packages made a sizeable pile beside the wagon where Benito stood guard.

Travis met the ladies for lunch at the Hodges Hotel, which made good its boast of "fine food." The group was personally greeted by Mr. Levin, the owner. Having had Christmas on her mind lately, Angela thought the fat, jolly, outgoing German would make a perfect Saint Nicholas if he grew his beard a little longer.

Later in the afternoon, when the wagon was loaded and Travis was helping the ladies up onto the seat, Angela heard Benito talking to his employer.

"Señor Travis, do you know that man in the red shirt there, in front of the saloon?"

Travis glanced across the street without seeming to do so. "Not that I recall. Why?"

"He has been watching *las señoras* ever since you came from the hotel."

Travis snorted. "Him and about fifty other men on the street. Wouldn't you watch them?" he added with a grin.

"*Sí, señor,*" Benito responded. "But this one, he watches only them, no others."

Travis didn't say anything as he climbed up and sat next to his wife. Then, softly, "Do either of you know that man?"

Daniella turned around as if to check on Serena in the back, and let her eyes pass over the man in question. "No," she said. "I've never seen him before."

"Angela?" Travis asked.

Angela was a bit unnerved by the tension around her, but felt sure she wouldn't know the man. After all, she didn't know anyone from around here. But she glanced anyway, and her breath halted in her throat as her eyes locked with those of the man across the street. His eyes were angry, triumphant, and threatening, all at the same time.

"Miller!" she gasped.

Travis didn't wait for more. He slapped the reins, and the horses pulled out, taking the lumbering wagon down the street. He didn't speak until they were out of town on the road home.

"Who was he, Angela?"

"I-It was a man named Miller," she said. "He was the scout for our wagon train."

"Any particular reason why he wouldn't just come over and say hello, instead of standing back and watching like that?"

"I-I don't know. He's a mean, vicious man. He didn't like me much, said I thought I was too good for him. He's the one who shot Chee."

Miller nearly laughed out loud when he saw the Barnes bitch ride into town on the wagon. He'd been hanging around this hellhole of a town for months trying to get a line on her. All the Army had said was that she'd married some rancher who lived over near Tucson.

The minute he saw her, his gloved right hand began to throb. But that was ridiculous. His right hand was dead, had been for months, would always be dead, according to Tucson's only doctor.

But for what he had in mind for that scrawny

little bitch, his left hand would do just fine. His left hand, and another certain part of his body that jumped up and got hard just thinking about what he was going to do to that slut. She'd got in his way once too often, and it was time she paid.

Now he knew where she was, knew how to find her. But not yet, he thought with grim determination. He'd seen the look of fear in her eyes just now when she'd turned and spotted him. Let her think about him for a while. Let her worry. When the time was right, he'd have her; there was no doubt about that. He'd have her right where he wanted her.

He pushed himself away from the wall and entered the saloon. As soon as his eyes adjusted to the dim light, he spotted what he was looking for. He strode across the dirt floor, grabbed Rosalita by the arm, and dragged her toward the stairs. Just thinking about what he would do to one Angela Barnes Colton when he had her created an urgent need in him, and if there was one thing Miller believed in, it was satisfying his body's needs. Rosalita would do for now.

But soon, he'd have the other one.

Chapter Twenty-eight

Matt was in a cold sweat. It was almost dark, and he could hear the wagon returning from town. Was she on it? Had she come back, or had she—

His mind shied away from finishing the thought, even though he knew it was a very real possibility.

He sat in the salon with his back to the door, like a complete coward. Light, feminine footsteps tapped their way across the floor. Angela? Or Dani, coming to tell him . . . ?

The footsteps stopped behind his chair. Metal clinked against metal. In the next instant, a leather bag dropped into his lap. It was his bag, the one he'd given Angela that morning, and it was still heavy with coins.

Inch by inch, he forced the muscles in his neck to turn his head around. She stood there, behind him, with a slight smile on her face. His total relief left him speechless, but his heart asked a thousand questions.

Angela shrugged. "I didn't need it after all. I charged everything."

Matt stood slowly and came around the chair. He stopped inches in front of Angela, his heart pounding, his mouth dry. "You'll stay, then?" he whispered.

Angela trembled. Her voice shook when she said, "I'll stay for as long as you want me."

Matt took her hand in his, inhaled deeply, and closed his eyes, trying to hold his emotions in check. When he opened his eyes, he half expected to find this was a dream. But she was there; her hand was still in his.

They looked at each other solemnly for a moment, then gradually, they both began to smile. Warm, radiant smiles. Loving smiles. He pressed his other hand to her cheek and started to lower his lips to hers.

"Oh, there you are, Matt," Serena called from the doorway. "Dad says come help with the unloading. He says us women bought out the stores." Unaware of what she'd interrupted, Serena spun away and skipped down the hall to her room.

"Bought out the stores, huh?" Matt said with a slight grin.

Angela tried to shrink into her skin. "I hadn't really planned on getting much, but Daniella kept insisting I get this, and get that. I hope you don't mind."

He gazed at her with such tenderness that it affected her breathing. "I'd buy you the world if I could."

"The only world I want or need is right here, with you," she whispered as he lowered his mouth once more.

"Matt!" Travis's voice boomed from down the hall.

Matt groaned in frustration, pressed a quick kiss to her ready lips, then forced himself away. "Coming, Dad!"

Later that night, after supper, after her bath had been removed, the packages opened and their contents put away, Angela stood before the long mirror in the bedroom and fingered the lace edge of her new nightgown. It had been part of a new shipment, just arrived in Tucson the day before. Daniella had spotted it first, remarking how rare it was to find such a thing in Tucson without having to order it. She insisted that Angela have it.

It was the one thing Daniella suggested she buy that Angela hadn't felt guilty about. Good heavens, she'd bought so much! But this was something special, it was for Matt. He'd never seen her in anything really nice before, and she wanted him to be proud of her.

Uncertainty plagued her when she thought of him coming through that door. What would he think? Did he still want her the way he had before? Before she'd been so stupid as to turn him away? Or did he only want her to stay because of the child she carried?

She thrust the fearful thought away. He'd said the child was only an excuse to keep her here. He'd asked her to stay.

Angela squared her shoulders and picked up her hairbrush. She was tired of being a timid little mouse. A man like Matt Colton deserved better than a mouse for a wife. He deserved a woman. She was determined to be that woman. She didn't want a pretend marriage; she wanted a real one, with Matt. Since she was the one who'd put a stop to it, it was up to her to set things right between them.

She brushed her hair vigorously until it hung in loose, shining waves to her hips. Her skin smelled like roses, the scent of her bath soap. The delicate fragrance hung in the air as she waited eagerly, nervously, for Matt to come. She hadn't realized — mercy! The gown was so thin she could see right through it!

Maybe she should change into something a little less revealing. A little less blatantly inviting. *No.* If she wore this gown for him, it would speak for her. She wouldn't have to tell him in words what she wanted; the gown would say it all.

She looked up quickly as the door opened and Matt came in. Her cheeks were hot from the realization of her own boldness. Matt's sharp intake of breath and the sudden heated glow in his eyes caused a fluttering in her stomach.

With slow, deliberate movements, Matt closed the door, his gaze devouring the vision of loveliness across the room. The bolt shooting home into the lock echoed the pounding in his veins. He clenched his fists so that his shaking wouldn't be obvious.

Her skin glowed golden in the lamplight, and he could make out the rosy tips of her breasts through the sheerness of the gown. His heated gaze roamed lower, to the dark golden triangle where her thighs met. Her hair fell down her back and over one shoulder in a soft cloud of sun-streaked blond. Daisies and moonbeams. It had been so long since he'd seen her hair loose. For one brief instant, he was struck with fear.

My God, she's so beautiful. She's too beautiful. She can't really be mine.

Then he saw the look in her eyes. His heart soared. Everything about her, her eyes, her shy, hesitant smile, her new wispy, see-through nightgown, all said welcome.

"Angel."

Neither of them was sure he actually spoke, but she felt him call her. They met each other in the middle of the bearskin rug, which now lay on the hardwood floor instead of on a straw bed in a wickiup. A sudden, shivering weakness overcame Angela. But when his arms came around her, she echoed his deep sigh of satisfaction. She felt so safe, so cared for. This was home to her, in his arms.

Their lips met, softly at first, until the urgency built and their starving senses begged for more. Nothing was denied, nothing held back.

Angela trembled with the power of her emotions. His fevered lips, his searching hands, his big, hard body pressed against her, were all so achingly familiar, yet new . . . wondrous. It had been so long. *So long.* Fueled by weeks of loneliness and pain and denial, her passion soared to new heights. She groaned deep in her throat when his tongue plunged between her lips.

Matt groaned, too, and clutched her even tighter. Like a man too long in the desert, he drank of her, taking all she offered, and giving everything he had in return.

After an eternity, he released her lips and spread heated kisses across her cheeks, her eyes, along her jaw to her ear. "It's a beautiful gown," he whispered.

"You like it?" she asked, her voice husky with passion.

"Uh huh."

"I bought it for you."

He nibbled his way along her jaw to her other ear and whispered, "Does that mean I can do what I want with it?"

"I . . . suppose so."

He grinned against her neck. "Good. Let's see how it looks on the floor." With trembling fingers, he slipped the thin straps from her shoulders and brushed the gown down past her hips. It fell in a pool of shimmering white around her feet. Matt took a step back and drank in the sight of her from head to toe and back again.

His hot gaze took her breath away. She swayed toward him. He scooped her up in his arms and laid her gently on the bed. Before joining her he shed his own clothes in record time, his boots hitting the floor with a solid *thump, thump.*

When he was beside her on the bed, there were no slow, languid kisses, no soft laughter or sweet sighs. There was only fire and passion, a fierce, urgent need, an overpowering hunger. His hands and lips were everywhere at once.

"Christ, Angel, I've missed you."

His hand found the center of her desire as his lips and teeth tugged on a rigid nipple. Angela squirmed and whimpered beneath him, his hot, wet mouth and questing fingers driving her insane. She was ready. Oh, God, she was so ready for him. "Love me, Matt," she begged. "Love me!"

Matt groaned and trailed scorching kisses from her breast to her ear as he parted her thighs with his knee. His voice was harsh with ragged breath. "I do, Angel, I do."

He entered her then, and there was no more need for words. There was only this terrible, urgent need for fulfillment, and that need was satisfied to the utmost a moment later. Angela dug her nails into Matt's shoulders and cried out as release washed over her and bright-colored lights flashed behind her closed eyelids. A few seconds later Matt's shoulders tensed, his head flew back, and he cried out her name as he followed her over the edge.

It was much later before either could breathe properly, much less speak. Matt rolled to his side and curled himself around Angela.

"Was I too rough, Angel?"

Angela opened her eyes slowly. She couldn't keep the grin from spreading across her face. "No."

Matt's gaze followed his fingers as they drew lazy patterns on her stomach. "Our child grows here." He flattened his palm and spread his fingers as if to protect the babe in its warm nest. "How do you feel about that?"

"I feel a thousand different things," she said softly, her eyes luminous in the glow of the lantern.

"Like what?"

"I feel blessed that such a miracle should occur just because we loved each other. I feel like it was meant to happen, that this was why I was born. I feel eager to hold our child in my arms."

Matt was humbled by her soft-spoken reply and the emotions she stirred in him.

The next morning the entire household knew something was different. When Matt and Angela finally came from their room, well past breakfast, they couldn't keep their eyes, or their hands, from each other. Pace and Spence rolled their eyes in disgust. Serena and Jessica giggled. Daniella and Travis smiled and breathed sighs of relief that whatever was wrong seemed to now be right.

The days passed swiftly, but not half as fast as the nights, when Matt and Angela lay wrapped in each other's arms. Christmas came in a hurry, and the house was filled with sounds of laughter and shouts of joy as they all opened their presents beneath the pine tree Travis and Matt had brought down from the mountains the week before.

Matt's present to Angela brought tears to her eyes. It was a solid gold wedding band, and it took her completely by surprise. "Oh, Matt, it's beautiful!"

"You sound surprised. Did you think I wouldn't get my own wife a wedding ring?"

"I just never . . . well, I guess I never thought much about it at all."

Matt took the ring from the box and slipped it onto her finger. Their eyes locked. Hers were brimming with unshed tears. Their lips met in a sweet, tender kiss that lingered, regardless of the watching audience.

"There they go again," Spence said with disgust. "Kissin' and makin' cow eyes. Yuk."

Laughter broke Matt and Angela apart. Matt put his hand on Spence's head and ruffled the boy's hair. "Just wait till you're older, kid, and you'll see how much fun it is."

"Wait till I'm older," the boy muttered. "That's what everybody says about everything."

Matt's eyes returned to Angela, and they communicated silently. "We have an announcement to make," he said a moment later.

Travis and Daniella exchanged curious looks, then waited for Matt to continue.

Grinning from ear to ear, Matt announced, "Angela's expecting."

All eyes turned instantly to Angela. She blushed and laughed.

"Well, congratulations!" Dani and Travis cried at the same time.

"What's espettin?" Jessica demanded.

"You know," Spence explained. "Like Sheba."

"You mean Angela's gonna have puppies?"

"No, dummy."

"Pace," Daniella scolded. "Don't call your sister a dummy."

Chapter Twenty-nine

The new year was a week old when the entire family, except Jason, set out for Tucson. Baggage had been shipped ahead, traveling clothes were crammed into carpetbags, and a bench had been added to the wagon bed for extra seating space. Matt rode horseback beside the wagon to ease the crowded conditions, and Angela held little Jessica in her lap. Travis and Daniella, with Serena, Pace, Spence, and Jessica, were headed for Boston at last.

Angela hugged Jessica to her, realizing she was going to miss the little imp. She was going to miss them all. She'd been with this family, day and night, for over three months now, and there wasn't one of them she didn't love with all her heart. It would be impossible not to love them.

Jessica laid her head against Angela's breast, and Angela wondered what it would be like to cradle her own child to that breast, to feed it, nurture it, raise it.

The bumpy, uncomfortable ride took over two hours; then there was a mad scramble to make sure no bags were left behind. When the stage driver announced it was time to leave, a dozen hugs and kisses and good wishes were exchanged, then the family piled into the coach. There was only room for one more passenger, but no one else showed up, so the Coltons had the stage to themselves, at least until the next stop.

Abe Miller pushed himself away from the bar when he saw the wagon full of Coltons come down the street and stop at the stage station. He passed through the swinging doors and leaned against the post that supported the saloon's overhanging roof. He had to squint until his eyes adjusted to the bright sunlight, but that didn't keep him from recognizing Angela right away.

The man on horseback was a younger version of the man driving the wagon. From what he'd been able to learn from gossip, that would be Matt Colton, Angela's husband.

Husband. He'd still like to know just how that came about. He'd heard what the young officer had reported at Camp Bowie after General Howard's meeting with Cochise, but he wasn't buying it. There'd been no gossip on the wagon train that Miss Angela Barnes was on her way to meet her fiancé, and he was sure there would have been if it were the truth. Just what was the little bitch up to? Had she found herself a rich sucker?

Colton was reportedly rich enough for three or four wives, but no one in town even hinted that he was a sucker. Folks didn't like to talk much about the Coltons at all. It had taken him weeks to get what little information he had, and that wasn't much.

But he did know where the Triple C Ranch was. He'd been out there last week to scout the place out. It was a sizable spread. Miller couldn't see why anyone would want to tie himself to land like this.

Now Tennessee, that was different. It was green, there was plenty of water, and it was home. Abe might have stayed on the family farm the rest of his life and been content. Would have, probably. Except when neighbors drive up and see a son choking his father to death . . . well, that's the time for that particular son to hightail his ass outta Tennessee.

Course Pa had deserved choking, no doubt about it. Abe would have done it years ago, but Ma wouldn't hear of any of her boys raising a hand to their father. Even if the old bastard did knock her and the boys around a lot—half the time just for pure meanness.

Abe figured maybe he could have gritted his teeth and stuck it out till the old man killed himself with his infernal drinking. But Pa had hit Ma too hard that last time. Knocked her down. She'd hit her head on a rock and broke her neck.

So Pa's neck was what Abe had grabbed. And he hadn't let go till his two brothers, Ben and Caleb, and three neighbor men had pulled him off. By then it didn't matter. Pa was dead, like he should have been years ago.

When Abe heard one of the neighbors talking about going for the county sheriff, he'd lit out and ended up in Memphis.

Memphis. Where Miss Busybody had poked her nose out that damn alley window and seen what she shouldn't have seen.

She'd admitted she'd told her old man about that night, but Abe had taken care of him. Now it was time to make sure she didn't tell anyone else. Ever.

'Sides all that, he told himself as he tugged the glove on his useless hand, *she owes me, by God.*

He stepped away from the post he'd been leaning on, crossed over to a side street, went around the block and came up the alley next to the stage depot. Everyone had boarded the stage except for the man who must be Travis Colton, Matt Colton's father.

285

He and his son were having a last word with each other, and those on the stage couldn't see Miller where he stood. That uppity bitch, Angela, was a mere three feet from him, with her back to the alley.

With his one good hand, he massaged the dead souvenir she'd given him.

If he wanted, he could reach out and grab her, pull her into the alley, and slit her throat before anyone even missed her. It was tempting, and he actually took a step in her direction before he realized it was too easy. She wouldn't even know who had her, or why, and he wouldn't get to take his revenge.

He had to stick to the plan, that was all. Then everything would work out. He'd have her, he'd have his revenge, and then he could kill her whenever he wanted.

Miller did reach out and grab Angela, but it was only to pull her back against the corner of the building. If her husband looked at her, he'd think she was just leaning there waiting for him.

Angela was so surprised when she felt the hand on her arm that she didn't even cry out. She was dragged two steps backward; then her shoulder was shoved up against the building.

"Don't make a sound or I'll start shooting into that there stage full of brats."

The blood left Angela's face when she heard that voice. She'd forgotten that Miller would likely be in town. She tried to step away, but he had a grip on the back of her dress. Unless she wanted to leave some of it behind, she had to remain where she was.

"That's a good girl," Miller sneered. "Just stand there and act natural. If that man of yours comes over here before I've had my say, I'll kill him."

"What do you want?" she hissed.

"Tonight at midnight, you meet me in that big fancy barn of yours, and we'll have us a little talk."

"You're crazy. I won't do it."

"You'll do it, missy, or I'll set fire to every building on that ranch, including the house, and I'll stand back in the dark and shoot everybody who runs outside."

Angela gasped with outrage, then shuddered with terror. She remembered this man well. He would do as he threatened. Her throat thickened with fear. "What do you want with me?"

"I just want to talk to you, that's all. You'll find out what about tonight."

Angela felt him turn loose of her dress. A moment later she dared a glance over her shoulder, but the alley was empty. He was already gone.

What should she do? If she told Matt, he'd go to the barn himself tonight. He could be killed.

No. She wouldn't tell Matt. Miller said he just wanted to talk, so she'd just slip out and meet him. They'd talk, she'd find out what he wanted, and that would be that.

But she was scared. Miller wasn't the kind of man a person could trust. What could he possibly want to talk to her about?

Her knees shook as she pushed herself away from the corner of the depot and pasted a wavering smile on her face.

Chapter Thirty

"You're awfully quiet tonight," Matt said over supper. "Is something wrong?"

"N-no, of course not. I . . . guess I'm just tired, after the trip to town and all."

"Are you feeling all right?"

"I feel fine. Like I said, I'm just a little tired." Angela had been doing her best to act normal since the stage pulled out this afternoon, but apparently she'd failed.

She just couldn't get over the feeling that she was about to do something wrong . . . something dishonest. But that was ridiculous. She was just going to walk out to the barn tonight at midnight for a few minutes; then she'd come right back to the house. There couldn't be anything dishonest in trying to keep Matt from being hurt, could there?

For the most part, any fear Angela had felt at the prospect of meeting with Miller tonight had fled. If anything went wrong, all she had to do was scream, and Hans would hear her. Miller couldn't know that Hans slept in the barn. So she felt relatively safe from harm, but a nagging sense of guilt about not telling Matt still plagued her.

Her mind went around in this same circle again and again. She knew she should say something to Matt, but she was afraid he'd get hurt. His safety was a thousand times more important than her peace of mind. She wouldn't tell him.

Moonlight streamed in through the bedroom window as Angela lay wide-eyed, listening to Matt's deep, even breathing. She smiled in the darkness and caressed his arm that rested across her ribs. It was no wonder he was asleep. After coming back from town, he'd worked with the horses the rest of the day, coming in late in the evening, hot, dirty, sweaty. He claimed he was so tired all he wanted to do was eat and go to bed. But once they were together behind the closed bedroom door, sleep was not what he had in mind. She had no idea where he found the energy for the hours of lovemaking that followed, but she was thrilled.

Their lovemaking was still just as special as it had been that night the treaty was signed, that first night they'd come together willingly. Every time they made love now, it was just as exciting, just as passionate and wonderful. She had no doubts at all that he still desired her as much as ever, even though her waist was beginning to thicken and her stomach was growing rounder.

But . . . there was always a *but* to mar one's happiness, wasn't there? And the *but* that worried her on a daily basis was the fact that from the very beginning, a profession of love was never spoken by either of them.

Did he only desire her, and want their child? Or was he still too sensitive over her rejection of him to admit he loved her? And what about her? There wasn't a doubt in her mind that she loved him, would always love him, but she hadn't said it either. She was too afraid her love wasn't returned.

His hand moved down and rested on her stomach.

Angela tensed, then relaxed as his breathing continued its regular rhythm.

She was surprised she could even hear him over the pounding of her own heart. It was nearly midnight.

Angela slipped carefully from beneath Matt's heavy arm and left the room, being as quiet as possible. Earlier in the evening she'd hidden some clothes in the room Serena and Jessica normally shared. She let herself into the room and dressed hurriedly in the darkness, then crept silently from the house.

The moon was so bright the trees, bushes and buildings all cast dark shadows across the ground. She kept to those shadows as much as possible and made her way to the barn, hoping Sheba would recognize her scent and not bark.

The big double barn doors were partially open. Angela stopped just outside. She turned around to make sure no one was about. A hand clamped roughly over her mouth. She screamed behind the hand. She nearly fainted when a pistol cocked loudly in her ear. It seemed to echo in her head as she was dragged into the dark interior of the barn.

"Don't make a sound, or I'll kill you here and now. Understand?"

The hand across her mouth was so tight she could barely nod her head.

"I'm going to take my hand away now, but you can feel the gun."

She could! My God! It was Miller, and he had the cold barrel of his pistol pressed against her neck. Angela began to tremble like she'd never trembled before.

She was still hearing the echo of the pistol being cocked, so she didn't hear the match strike; but she saw it flare.

290

Miller lit a lantern and hung it from a hook on the wall after he closed the barn doors. Angela opened her mouth to speak, then closed it with a gasp when the pistol came up between her eyes.

"Don't say a word," Miller growled. "And don't think that Swede who sleeps in the tack room is gonna help ya any. He's sleepin' *real* hard." Miller chuckled at his own wit. "If he manages to wake up in the morning, he's gonna have one hell of a headache."

He nudged Angela toward the shelf next to the lantern. "Pick up that pencil and paper. You're gonna leave your husband a note; then you and me are gonna take a little ride in the moonlight. Won't that be romantic?" he added with a half sneer, half leer.

"Wh-what do you w-want me to write?"

"Tell him you're leavin' and not coming back. Make him think you left on your own. If he comes after you, I'll kill him."

"I—"

"Shut up and write."

Dear God! What was she to do? He obviously meant to take her with him. He said he'd kill Matt! Matt may or may not love her, but she carried his child. Of course he would follow. Nothing she could say in a note would stop him.

As panicked as she felt, her brain was still functioning, and she knew what she had to do. She had to warn Matt somehow that if he followed her, he would be walking into a trap. He would still come, she knew, even if she said she hated him. She had to say something that sounded innocent to Miller, but that Matt would take as a warning.

Then, like a gift from God, it came to her, and she knew what to say. She scribbled a few hurried lines and even managed to sign her name before

291

Miller grabbed the note away from her. He held it up in the light to read.

" 'Matt, it's been fun, but now I'm leaving you, just the same way I married you in the first place — of my own free will. Angela.' " Miller snickered. "You done real good."

He moved the lantern to the shelf and stuck the note on the hook on the wall. He swung the big door open a crack and dragged her through, then clamped his hand back over her mouth. He practically carried her around the far side of the barn and threw her into the saddle of his waiting horse, then mounted behind her.

Miller removed his kerchief and gagged her with it. He also took a short length of rope and tied her hands to the saddle horn. He started his horse out at a slow walk and followed the trees for several hundred yards. When the cover veered away from the road, he left the sheltering shadows and kept to the middle of the road, still at a walk, until they rounded the hill. Once they were out of sight he spurred his horse into a mile-eating gallop toward Tucson.

The ride was a nightmare. The wind in her face was cold, but that was nothing compared to the cold she felt when Miller's hands started roaming over her thighs, her stomach, her breasts. She squirmed and leaned forward, trying to scream behind her gag. Miller laughed at her useless efforts and pinched her breast so hard it brought tears to her eyes.

Finally he wrapped the reins around his right hand and settled his left hand between her legs, digging his fingers between her and the saddle.

If it had been Matt's hand there, she was sure she would have swooned with pleasure, but now she felt nothing but revulsion. Her stomach heaved in protest, and she fought down the nausea. If the contents of her stomach came up while she was gagged, she'd choke to death.

And if that weren't enough, he pressed his crotch against her buttocks and wiggled, making certain she felt the hardness of his arousal with each pounding beat of the horse's hooves. She tried to scoot forward, but it was impossible.

In spite of the fear of not knowing what Miller intended to do to her, a terrible weariness swept over her. It was the middle of the night, and she'd ridden most of the day on a hard, uncomfortable wagon seat; then she and Matt had made passionate love — more than once. She began to doze in the saddle, but each time she nodded off, her back came in contact with Miller's chest, forcing her to lean forward again. She couldn't stand any more contact with him than she already had.

The night seemed to go on forever. When they finally reached the outskirts of Tucson, the sky was still black, giving no hint that dawn would ever come. Thick, heavy clouds now covered the moon. Miller guided the horse off the main road at the edge of town and cut across an empty lot toward the dim outline of a small shack.

The horse shied suddenly as something small, a rabbit maybe, darted across the path. Angela was jostled in the saddle. She tried to find some place to brace her feet, but there was no such place. All she got for her efforts was a growl from Miller to be still, and a bare foot when one of her shoes slipped off.

When Miller pulled up in front of the shack, he swung down from the saddle, tied the reins to a hitching post, and left Angela there while he went inside. After a few minutes, the dim glow of a lantern shone through the open door. Then he came back and untied her from the saddle horn. He threw the short rope he'd used on her wrists over his shoulder and pulled her roughly to the ground. Her legs were so weak she stumbled and fell against him.

Miller laughed. "Hot for me, aren't ya?"

Angela cringed away. He grabbed her hands and dragged her into the shack. She wrinkled her nose at the stench of the place. In the center of the one-room adobe hovel stood a table covered with dried bits of food. Next to it was one whole chair, and strewn about the floor were pieces of others. There was a fireplace along one wall, piled high with cold ashes. The only other thing in the room was a single bunk opposite the fireplace.

He pushed her toward the bunk. Fear overwhelmed her. The leer on his face sent shivers down her spine. She fought him then, trying to get away, but she was no match for his strength. He managed to get the rope around her wrists again. When she kept struggling, he landed a backhanded blow across her face. She felt her lip split, then a second later tasted her own blood in her mouth. She screamed behind her gag. He hit her again. Everything went black.

Chapter Thirty-one

The sky was just turning gray when Matt woke up. The bed had an empty feel to it. He reached out to draw Angela closer, but met only her pillow. Startled, he raised up quickly and peered across the gloomy darkness. Was she sick again? He fumbled beside the bed for a match and lit the lamp.

No Angela.

As tired as she'd been last night, he was surprised she was up this early. She never woke up before him.

The air was chilly against his bare skin when he threw back the covers and got up. She was probably in the salon, warming herself before a roaring fire. He dressed in a hurry, eager to join her.

But she wasn't in the salon. It was dark and empty, the hearth cold. Nor was she in the dining room. When he reached the kitchen Rosita was there starting breakfast, but she hadn't seen Angela.

He started back through the house again, but was interrupted by a frantic pounding on the front door.

"Matt!" Carlos yelled from outside. "Matt! Open up!"

Matt swung the heavy front door open. "What's going on?"

"It's Hans! Come quick!"

The urgency of Carlos's voice left no doubt in Matt's mind that something was wrong. He'd have to find Angela later.

He followed Carlos at a run through the side door of the barn, past the tack room, past the stalls, toward the large, double-doored front entrance.

Benito was bending over Hans, their voices low, indistinguishable. They both looked up when Matt and Carlos approached.

"What happened?" Matt demanded. A rope and a dirty rag lay next to Hans. The big, gentle Swede was holding his head as if it pained him.

"Some stinking, no good coward clobbered him from behind. Tied him up and gagged him!" Benito was outraged.

So was Matt. Nothing like this had ever happened on the Triple C before. "Did you get a look at him, Hans?" Matt asked.

"No, boss. I was in the tack room. Thought I heard the big door squeak. It was late, nearly midnight I guess. I came out here and the door was open. Next thing I know, Ben here was telling me to wake up."

"Damn!" Matt couldn't begin to imagine who could have done such a thing.

"Matt, I think you'd better come here," Carlos said from behind him.

Matt hurried to his side and saw the note. He tore it from the wall. As he read it the blood drained from his face. She'd left him! *No. It's impossible.* He read the note a second time, then a third. *. . . of my own free will.*

When the meaning of her words finally penetrated the fog in his brain, he inhaled sharply. She'd been taken!

"Get Hans to the house and have Rosita look at

his head. Hans, you take it easy till your head clears. Are there any horses missing?"

"Not from in here," Carlos said. "You want me to check the corral?"

"Yes. I'm going to have a look around. And just so you don't get the wrong idea, this note doesn't mean what you think it means. Go!"

Matt swung open the big doors and studied the ground. There were too many tracks and prints. Dozens of people and horses came and went through this door every day. He let his eyes roam over the terrain. If he were coming here in secret, where would he hide his horse?

Who? his mind screamed. *Who? Why?* And how had the man grabbed Angela when she should have been sleeping beside him? Matt was certain she wasn't taken by force from the house. He would have heard something. She must have come outside. But why?

One thing was sure: he wouldn't find out anything by standing around wondering. He circled the barn, studying the ground as he went. When he reached the west side, he found what he was looking for. A horse had been here, recently, where no horse should have been. The droppings weren't even a day old. Up next to the building were three clear boot prints. In between two of them was a smaller print. The print of a woman's slipper.

Matt forced himself to remain calm, and it wasn't easy. All he wanted to do was ride out after them, but he made himself wait. He studied the ground again.

There. That's what he was looking for. Something to set the man or the animal apart. Now he had it. One horseshoe was worn completely down on the front edge, leaving a distinctive, telling imprint.

297

The bastard doesn't take very good care of his horse.

Matt ran back to the house, calling for his pinto to be saddled. He strapped on his six-shooter and tied the holster down to his thigh. He stuck one knife behind him, in his belt, and another in his boot. He slapped on his spurs, grabbed his rifle and an extra box of cartridges, and went for his horse. Not knowing how long he'd be gone or how far he'd have to travel, he tied his bedroll behind his saddle, praying all the while he wouldn't need it. He added hastily stuffed saddlebags, grain for the horse, and a full canteen.

"Tell Luis he's in charge till I get back. I don't know how long that'll be."

Matt picked up the trail where it led from the barn to the trees and followed it to where it joined the road. The pinto sensed his impatience and fretted at the slow pace, but Matt couldn't afford to race headlong toward Tucson. He had to keep an eye out in case the one he followed had left the road somewhere between here and town. The bastard had a six- or seven-hour lead on him, and Matt knew he couldn't afford the time to backtrack.

He shied away from the thought that Angela had been gone that many hours. So much could happen in that amount of time. Then he forced himself to admit she could even be dead by now. If she was, he'd find the one responsible if it took him the rest of his life. The man would die a very slow and painful death. Matt hadn't been listening at the Apache campfires for over ten years and not learned something about torture.

In fact, even if Angela was all right, and he *must* believe she was, the bastard deserved to die. Unless Angela went willingly, but he didn't believe that for a minute. As willingly as she'd married him in the first place, her note had said. She chose him willingly, all right. Her only alternative was death. So the man, whoever he was, had threatened her.

But who? Why? his mind screamed. Angela didn't know anyone around here. Maybe some drifter in town saw her yesterday and took a liking to her. But why did she go to the barn?

Something Travis had said a few weeks ago struck his mind now. The man who had been watching the women while they were shopping. Angela had known him. Miller—the one who shot Chee.

Chee had told Matt how Angela had stood in front of the white man so that Chee could get away. Could this be some sort of attempt at revenge?

Around and around the questions went. Matt finally forced them to the back of his mind, afraid he would miss some sign on the trail. None of it really mattered anyway. All that mattered was getting Angela back, safe and sound.

They'd had such a short time together, he and Angela. Things had been so sweet between them since she came home from Tucson that day just before Christmas. She was his wife, and she carried his child. The only thing lacking in the past few weeks was that little phrase, "I love you." Neither of them had said it.

But they were there, those words, even though they weren't spoken. They were there in every touch, every glance, every kiss. Why had he not told her in words? Why had she not told him? Pride, he supposed, or fear of rejection. How stupid; how sad.

When he got her back, he swore the first thing he was going to do was tell her, in words, how much he loved her. He just hoped and prayed he wasn't too late.

It was daylight now, but it was hard to tell, the

299

sky was so overcast with heavy gray clouds. He figured it was around nine when he neared the outskirts of Tucson. His eyes continued to dart from one side of the road to the other. Something off to his right caught his attention.

He swung his mount off the road to investigate. It was blue, and it didn't belong on this brown, hardpacked earth. He got down and picked up a woman's blue slipper. His heart thundered in his chest. Angela had worn a pair just like this only yesterday.

Matt began to search for tracks, and found them. They led in a straight line from the road to a tiny, rundown adobe hut standing all alone just ahead. A bay gelding stood tied to the hitching rail out front, saddled, as if ready to leave any minute.

Or left saddled all night by a man who didn't take care of his horse.

Chapter Thirty-two

Angela came to with a groan. When she tried to move, every muscle in her body protested. She opened her eyes, but it was several long seconds before she remembered where she was and how she got there. She was on the floor; her hands and feet were tied. Miller stood over her with a sneer on his face.

"Not quite so high an' mighty now, are ya?"

He turned his back on her and proceeded to shave in front of a tiny broken mirror hanging on the wall near the bed. There was something odd about the way he shaved, but Angela's dazed mind couldn't figure it out. She concentrated on watching him to give her mind something to focus on besides what he might have planned for her.

The glove. That was what was odd about his shaving. He wore a glove; just one — on his right hand.

Who ever heard of a man wearing a glove when he shaved?

A sharp tingling began at the base of her skull and spread outward. A new feeling of danger assailed her.

This was different from the terror she'd been experiencing since he'd first grabbed her last night.

Different. Stronger. A feeling of dread settled in her stomach. But why?

Her gaze remained locked on that gloved hand while her mind tried to discern why the glove should upset her so.

It was then she realized the glove wasn't the only peculiar thing. He wasn't using his fingers on that hand. They never bent or curled or grasped.

Miller finished shaving and tossed the razor onto the table behind him. It landed on a dried bread crust, but he never even looked. His eyes were all for her. The look in them made her skin crawl.

"What happened to your hand?" she asked to distract him.

He changed instantly from a wary beast to a maddened animal. "You think that's funny, you goddamned bitch?" he shrieked at her.

Angela tried to sit up, but her hands were tied behind her back and had long since gone numb. Her feet, too, were dead. She couldn't even feel the difference between the one with the shoe and the one without.

"I-I'm sorry. I was just curious, that's all." She cringed at the fear evident in her voice. *Trying to show him what a coward you are, Angie Sue?*

Miller cursed and kicked the remains of a chair from his path. "Don't play cute with me, you little slut! You know goddamn good an' well what happened to my hand." He whipped a knife from his belt and cut the bonds at her feet, then sheathed the knife, leaving her hands still tied behind her.

"What are you talking about?" she demanded. "How would I know . . ." Images exploded in her mind. His threat that day she helped Chee. Her father standing over her mother's grave, falling dead on her mother's grave. The pistol, held in a man's

302

right hand. Her shot that somehow hit true. "You?" she shrieked. She struggled to rise without the use of her hands. "You killed my father?"

Miller merely grinned at her, a slow, evil grin that chilled her blood. "Get up."

"It was you!" she screamed. "You killed my father! You murdered him!"

"And you crippled me, you bitch! You're gonna pay for what you did to me that day!"

"What I did to *you!* You stinking, crawling, lowlife worm! You didn't get half of what you deserved!"

"I sure didn't, sister, but I aim to get what I deserve right now. Get over there on that bunk and lay down, *now!*"

Angela was so outraged by what she'd just learned that she forgot to be afraid. She'd never been really angry in her life, but now she purposely allowed it to boil in her veins. She wanted revenge! She wanted him to pay! Who did he think he was, to go around ordering people, kidnapping people, killing people! "I will not!"

"You'll do what I say, or it'll go just that much harder on you."

"You want to know what I think of your threats?" She worked her dry mouth for all it was worth, and spit right in his face. "That's what I think of you and your threats."

Just as Miller swung at her, striking her full across the face and cutting her lip again, the weathered door exploded inward. The tiny room was filled with the roar of Matt Colton's rage.

In one quick glance, Matt took in Angela's battered face, bleeding lip, and the awkward way she held her arms behind her. Rage like he'd never known before filled him, a deep, smoldering, murderous rage. He'd never seen this man before, but for the first time in his life, Matt hated. He'd never even really hated Tahnito. But this man who hurt Angela, this man he hated with all his being.

Matt launched himself at the object of his hatred, casually knocking aside the knife swinging at his head. The knife clattered against the adobe wall and fell with a soft thud to the dirt floor, leaving Miller unarmed, since his gunbelt hung on a peg beside the only door.

Miller's gaze darted frantically around the room, searching for a weapon. With his good hand, he scooped up a broken chair leg and moved in for the attack. Matt caught the blow on his forearm without so much as a blink. He snatched the chair leg away and tossed it behind him without looking.

Matt continued to advance. "I'm going to take you apart limb by limb, you bastard." But he had to wait to make his move, because Miller was directly in front of Angela now, and Matt didn't want to take the chance of either one of them, or both, landing on her.

Miller reached sideways and grabbed the only good chair. He sidestepped quickly, enabling himself to swing the thing like a club. On his backswing, the chair rammed forcefully into Angela's stomach.

When the chair struck her, Angela felt several things at once: a terrible, wrenching pain deep inside, a sudden loss of breath, and her head striking the adobe wall behind her. Her world went dark again, and she slumped to the floor.

On the rebound, the chair struck Matt. It was so old it shattered against Matt's solid form like it was made of matchsticks.

Miller growled. This was no greenhorn tenderfoot he was up against, even though Colton was a good six or seven years younger than himself. Colton was big and muscular, a full head taller. Miller's chances didn't look so good; but he'd never run from a fight yet, and he'd never lost one, either.

Of course, he'd never been forced to fight fair before, and his useless right hand left him at a distinct disadvantage. Sweat beaded across his forehead. His eyes skimmed the table, and he remembered the razor. The only problem was, it looked like he might have to go right through Colton to get it.

Miller swung a hard left to Matt's jaw, knocking him back a couple of steps. Just enough so that Miller could reach the razor. He grabbed it, flipped it open, and waved it in front of Matt.

Matt made a dive for the hand that held the razor. He'd already noticed Miller didn't use his right hand, so he grabbed at the left wrist. Both men went down, rolling on the dirt floor, struggling for control of the thin blade.

Miller's right hand might have been almost useless, but there was nothing wrong with his arm. He swung it at Matt's head, clipping him on the ear with the heal of his hand, once, twice. Matt was forced to loose one hand from Miller's other wrist to keep from being bludgeoned to death by the right arm being used like a club.

Matt's grip was so tight Miller lost control of his left hand, and the razor slipped from his fingers. Matt quickly rolled over on top of the razor and, using his feet as well as his hands, threw Miller up and off of him. Miller came down on the table, scattering tin plates across the room, and rolled off the other side. Matt scrambled to his feet and kicked the razor beneath the bed.

As Matt turned, Miller grabbed the gun from his holster hanging on a peg next to the door. Without hesitation, Matt drew and fired, hitting him in the shoulder. Miller staggered, then straightened. He aimed his pistol again. Matt fired again, this time shooting Miller's gun hand.

Miller bellowed in pain and outrage. "Goddamn you! Goddamn you! Why don't you just kill me, instead of leaving me with two useless hands!"

"Don't tempt me." Matt grabbed a length of rope from the floor and tied Miller's hands behind his back, ignoring the blood pouring from the bastard's shoulder and hand, then turned his attention to Angela. He tossed his gun down on the mattress, rolled her to her side and cut her hands free.

She came to with a low moan, and Matt was there, dabbing gently at the cut on her lip with his handkerchief.

"How do you feel, Angel? Are you all right?"

"Oh, Matt!" She threw her aching arms around his neck and clutched at him desperately. "You came! You found me! I knew you would!" Her tears wet his neck. Tears of relief so sweet she couldn't stop them.

Matt cradled her, held her, kissed her tears away. His hands ran over her, frantic in their search of possible injuries. "Are you hurt?" She only sobbed again and pressed her face deeper into his shoulder. "Angel, talk to me, sweetheart. Are you hurt?"

"N-no," she managed, trying to control her emotions. "I . . . I'm okay."

Matt pulled away and gazed into her puffy, red eyes. "Are you sure?"

She sniffed back her remaining tears and nodded. "I think so. My head hurts some, but I just want to go home. Take me home, Matt."

"I will, Angel, I promise." He kissed her lips, softly, tenderly, afraid of hurting her. "Just as soon as I figure out what to do with our friend here."

Angela sat up carefully, with Matt's help, and glared her hatred at Miller, who lay whining against the far wall. She wiped her face with her palm. "He killed my father," she spat.

"He what?"

"He killed my father! He's the one who came that day, just before Tahnito. I told you about it."

"Yeah, you did," Matt said grimly. He picked up his revolver and placed it in Angela's lap. "I'm going to send someone for the sheriff. If the bastard moves so much as an inch, shoot him."

Matt strode out of the one-room dwelling, spurs jingling with each step. Not far away, he spied three Mexican boys playing with a dog.

"Hey! ¡Niños!" He called the boys over and promised a silver dollar to each if they would go get the sheriff. The boys took off at a run, excited both at getting to talk to the sheriff, and at getting a silver American dollar.

Angela didn't feel well, but for Matt's benefit, she put on a brave front. She didn't want a doctor; she didn't want to lie down and rest. She just wanted to go home, the sooner the better.

It wasn't long before the sheriff came. Matt paid the three boys their dollar each, then explained the situation to the sheriff.

"Well, I'll just drag this varmint on over to the jail," Sheriff Pugh said. "Face looks kinda familiar to me. I'll check my files. Could be a circular out on him. Let ya know, Colton."

All the way home, Matt held Angela carefully, gratefully, in his arms. He finally got her to tell him what she was doing in the barn last night when Miller came.

307

"Angela, why didn't you tell me? I would never have let you go out there to meet him."

"Oh, Matt!" she cried. "I know it was stupid of me, but he said if I didn't show up alone, he'd set fire to all the buildings and shoot everybody as they ran out. I couldn't let that happen."

"My sweet Angel, do you think I would have let him burn the ranch down on top of us? If you'd told me he was coming, I could have posted guards, we would have caught him, and you wouldn't have had to go through all this."

"I—I . . . guess it wasn't very smart of me, was it?"

"Well, it's over now. But, Angel, if anything like this ever happens again, God forbid, if anyone ever threatens you in any way, you come to me."

"All right."

"Promise?"

"I promise."

Just as they rounded that last low hill and the ranch buildings came into sight, a sharp pain caught Angela below her navel and shot clear through to her backbone. She gasped and doubled over.

"Angela! What is it?"

She clutched his arm with one hand and her stomach with the other. "I don't know! Oh, God, Matt, it hurts! It hurts!"

"Hang on, sweetheart," he said urgently. "I'll have you home in a minute. Just hang on, Angel."

He kept the horse at a walk, afraid to jostle Angela around, and it seemed to take forever to reach the house. Benito spotted them first, and Matt sent him on the run for Rosita.

Matt swung down off the saddle, keeping one hand on Angela to steady her. He slid an arm beneath her knees and quailed at how pale her face was. When he lifted her from the saddle, she clung to him and cried.

Matt held her in his arms and stared stupidly, unable — unwilling — to accept what his eyes told him.

The saddle was covered with blood.

Chapter Thirty-three

"What has happened?" Rosita cried. She followed breathlessly behind Matt as he carried his precious burden into the house and down the hall.

He placed Angela on the bed. His arms, when he withdrew them from beneath her, were covered with blood.

"So much blood!" Rosita cried. "Help me undress her, quickly!"

Angela was crying and moaning, and Matt did his best to soothe her with words.

"What's happening? Why does it hurt so much?" she gasped.

"Hang on, Angel, just hang on," Matt said, unable to keep the tremor from his voice.

"The baby is coming." Rosita crossed herself.

Matt's throat tightened, and his hands trembled when Rosita uttered a quick prayer for help from her beloved saints, both for herself, and for Angela.

"Noooo!" Angela screamed. "It's too soon! The baby can't come yet! It can't come till spring!"

"I think you should leave us, Matt," Rosita suggested.

"No," Angela begged. She clutched Matt's hand to her breast. "Don't leave me, Matt. God, please don't leave me."

The pain and fear in her eyes tore at his heart. "I

won't, Angel. I'm right here. Hush, sweetheart. You'll be all right. We'll take care of you."

"Pobrecita," Rosita whispered. "Poor little one."

"Can't you do something?" Matt demanded.

"Not for the baby." Rosita shook her head sadly. "It's too late for the baby. But I will do my best for your little wife, Señor Matt."

Matt's mouth went dry with dread. Rosita hadn't put a *señor* to his name in years. Not since he was a child.

It was a nightmare, one that would haunt him for years. Angela was racked with pain for hours. When the underdeveloped child came, so tiny, so dead, Angela finally lost consciousness.

Later that night, a fever set in. All over the Triple C candles burned in the darkness. Prayers for the young *señora's* well-being were offered to God and all the saints.

Matt sat beside the bed, totally unaware of anything except Angela. She didn't moan, or toss and turn, or rave, as some did when consumed by a high fever. She just lay there, so still, so quiet, barely breathing. He'd never felt this helpless, this scared, in his life. Being mauled by a bear was infinitely easier to endure than watching Angela suffer.

Rosita came several times to change the packing between Angela's legs. After the first few times, Matt refused to look. So much blood! How could one small woman lose so much blood and still live?

The fever finally broke the next afternoon, and Angela slept and breathed easier. Matt, too, finally slept, but he refused to leave her side. He slept sprawled in the chair he'd pulled up next to the bed.

When Angela opened her eyes, the first thing she

311

saw was Matt. He looked so tired! His clothes were a mess. Dark circles hung beneath his eyes, and two- or three-days' growth of whiskers covered his face.

She tried to move and discovered she was as stiff and sore as she'd been after that first full day in the saddle. And weak! The simple effort of trying to move exhausted her. She moaned.

Matt sat up with a jerk. "You're awake."

"What's happened?" she asked, her mind still groggy. "Why do you look so tired? And why am I so stiff and weak?"

"Don't you remember, Angel? You've been ill for two days." He gripped her hand tightly in his. "You lost the baby, Angel."

At first she simply stared at him, trying to make sense of his words. It was a full minute before his meaning sank in. "Noooo!" she cried. "Our baby! Oh, Matt, not our baby!" In her weakened condition, she couldn't even begin to hold back the tears, and didn't try. She ran a hand across her abdomen, felt the terrible emptiness where once there had been a slightly rounded firmness, and knew he spoke the truth.

Matt held her and tried to wipe the tears away, but they came too fast. "I'm so sorry, Angel. So sorry. But we almost lost you, too. I'm just glad you're all right. Don't cry, sweetheart. We'll have other babies, I promise. You'll see, everything will be all right now that you're better."

Angela's tears continued, accompanied by great, wracking sobs. She cried and cried, and finally cried herself into an exhausted sleep.

She stayed in bed for two weeks recovering, regaining her strength. Her spirits improved daily, and Matt was relieved.

He was in his study going over the books one

morning after breakfast when Davita came rushing in.

"Matt! Come quick!"

"What is it?" He rose immediately and crossed the floor in three long strides. "Is it Angela? Is something wrong?"

Davita sobbed once, then covered her mouth. "Just come, Matt!" she cried. "Hurry!"

Matt's heart jumped into his throat. Something had happened to Angela! He ran down the hall and was almost too afraid to open the door, but he forced himself.

He stood in the open doorway and sagged with relief. "You're up," he said with a big smile.

Angela turned from rummaging through a drawer and returned his smile distractedly. "Yes, finally," she said. She turned her back to him and opened one drawer after another in the bureau, spilling the contents of each to the floor. "Where is it?" she hissed to herself.

"Looking for something?" Matt asked. A stupid question, he thought. The room looked like a cyclone had struck. The doors to the wardrobe gaped open; clothes were strewn everywhere. The mattress lay half on the floor. The trunk at the foot of the bed sat open and empty, its contents having gone the way of the rest of the clothes in the room.

"Oh, Matt," Angela cried. "I've looked everywhere, and I just can't find it!"

"Find what? What in the devil are you looking for?"

"What a silly question. I'm looking for the baby, of course."

Matt jerked as if he'd been shot.

Angela looked up at him and laughed lightly. "Oh, Matt, don't look like that. I know you said I lost the

313

baby, but you can't have been serious. A mother simply does not misplace her child. It must be here somewhere." She looked around the room with a puzzled expression. "I just can't seem to find it. But I've only just started to look. I'll find it, don't you worry."

Matt's mind refused to accept what he was hearing. His throat went dry and his stomach heaved.

"I know," Angela exclaimed. "How silly of me. The baby must be in the nursery."

She brushed past Matt and headed down the hall. Matt turned and stared at Davita, dumbfounded. "Get Rosita," he said softly.

Matt found Angela in the nursery, looking under each stack of blankets. "Angela." His voice shook with fear and dread. "You should rest. Come back to bed and lie down for a while."

"But, Matt, I've got to find the baby," she insisted.

When he reached for her hand, his own trembled. "Please come with me and rest."

"He is right, *señora,* you should be resting," Rosita said from the doorway. "Davita is preparing a special cup of tea for you." She eyed Matt deliberately, and he understood.

Rosita's "special tea" would put Angela to sleep and let her rest for a time. And pray God, when she woke —

"Well, all right," Angela said reluctantly. "I guess I am a little tired. I can look some more later."

Rosita helped Angela change back into a nightgown while Matt straightened the mattress. Davita brought the tea. While Angela sipped the hot, fragrant brew, Rosita nodded at Matt. He understood what was needed, but didn't know quite how to start.

"Angela."

314

"Yes?" She looked at him so openly, her green eyes so big and trusting.

"Angel, I. . . . You've got to listen to me, sweetheart."

"I'm listening, Matt. What is it?"

"Angel, when I said you . . . lost the baby, I didn't mean you had . . . misplaced him."

"Him? It's a boy? Oh, I'm so glad, Matt. I was hoping for a boy."

"Angela, listen to me." God. He'd rather face a firing squad than look into her gentle eyes and say what had to be said. He muttered a quick prayer for strength and guidance. "It was a boy, but he died, sweetheart."

"No! I don't believe you." She shook her head, her mouth formed in mutinous lines.

He brought her hand to his lips and buried a long, slow kiss in her palm before raising his head again to look at her. "I'm sorry, Angel, but it's true. You only carried him about four months. It was too soon for him to be born; but he came anyway, and . . . and he was dead, Angel." Matt swallowed heavily. "I know it's hard to accept, but that's what happened."

"Matt," Angela said as if explaining something for the tenth time to a small child. "That's not the way things happen. I carried the baby inside me until he decided he was ready to be born. Babies know these things, Matt. If it was too soon, he would have stayed where he was." She interrupted herself with a huge yawn. Rosita's tea was already working.

"You're tired, sweetheart," Matt said. "We'll talk about it later."

"All right," Angela said, snuggling down under the blanket, her hand still in his. "But I'm right, you'll see. When I find him, you'll see I'm right." Her eyes

315

closed, and she was asleep.

Matt raised his gaze to Rosita and found tears streaming down her cheeks.

"What do we do now, Rosita?" he whispered. "What do we do?"

Rosita took a deep breath and crossed herself. Her control restored, she said, "We let her sleep. Davita, put this room back together, quietly."

Rosita led Matt into the hall. "I don't know what to do, Matt. I've heard of this happening before. I think it just takes time. Time for her to learn to accept the truth. Maybe *el médico* in Tucson knows of some remedy, but I do not, except for time, and prayers."

Matt rushed outside and told Jorge to go for the doctor. "And hurry, Jorge. I don't care what he's doing when you find him. If you have to bring him here at gunpoint, do it."

As it turned out, the doctor offered no objections and went with Jorge readily. Jorge was extremely relieved. It was not a popular thing to do in this part of the country, to threaten a doctor. There were too few doctors as it was. No one wanted them scared off.

But as fast as old Doc Harding got to the Triple C, he wasn't much help. He, too, had seen it before, but knew of no sure cure. "Sometimes having another child helps them forget," he offered.

"Another child!" Matt was appalled. "She almost died losing this one. She's not recovered from that yet."

"I know, son, I know. I didn't mean right away. I meant later on, in a few months. The only other thing you can do is talk to her. Try to get her to accept the truth. Don't humor her, Matt. Don't go along with her on this, or she might not ever get

316

over it. What did you do with the child, by the way?"

"Do with it?" Matt clenched his jaws, then his fists, fighting the memory of the tiny casket . . . the tiny grave. He blinked rapidly and tore his gaze away from Doc Harding's piercing blue eyes. "We buried it — him."

"Good." Doc gave a sharp nod. "If she doesn't come around soon and face the truth, you might try showing her the grave."

Just the thought of it made Matt quail. "Isn't that a bit drastic?"

"It can be, yes. But sometimes a severe shock like that will get through when nothing else will. Give it some thought."

Matt nodded reluctantly, but doubted he'd ever find the strength to do it.

Chapter Thirty-four

Three days later Sheriff Pugh rode out from town. "Interestin' fella you turned over to me, Colton."

"I don't think I'd call a kidnapper and murderer *interesting*," Matt spat.

"Oh, this 'un is. Got a list of aliases as long as yer arm. Abe Miller, Miller Scott, Abe Stockton, Sam Miller. List goes on and on. Wanted in Tennessee for assault and robbery. And git this—wanted for stranglin' his own pa. A real cold bastard, he is. And sittin' in his cell just like butter wouldn't melt in his mouth. Judge'll be here the first of February, and we'll have us a trial. After we're through with him, Tennessee gets him. We'll need your testimony, and your wife's, too."

"I'll be glad to testify," Matt said. "But I don't know if Angela will be up to it or not."

Pugh wanted to know why. Matt reluctantly explained, making sure the sheriff knew her condition was only temporary. It had to be temporary!

"Real sorry to hear that, Matt, real sorry," Pugh said, shaking his head. "I'll send word out when I know the exact date of the trial. We oughta be able to nail him on kidnapping with just your testimony, but without your wife, we probably won't be able to make the murder charge stick. We'll just have to do the best we can."

* * *

The days passed slowly, with Angela doggedly insisting that she would find her lost baby. The atmosphere over the entire ranch was one of hushed waiting. Matt, too, waited. He waited for Angela to accept the truth. But no matter how many times he explained it to her, it didn't help.

She didn't cry or yell or argue. She just quietly insisted that Matt was wrong.

About everything else, Angela was totally reasonable and rational. But not about the baby. He was simply lost, and she would find him.

Matt tried everything. He tried cajoling, pleading, praying, yelling. Nothing got through to her. He wished Dani were home. Maybe she'd know what to do.

Angela soon went back to reading to Jason every day, and it broke the older man's heart every time she talked about finding the baby. He, too, had tried to convince her of the truth, to no avail.

"I'm really embarrassed by all of this," she confessed one afternoon.

"Embarrassed by what?" Jason asked cautiously.

"Well, this is your first great grandchild, after all, and I have to go and do something stupid, like lose him." She fiddled nervously with the pages of the book in her lap.

"Angela—"

"But don't worry, Jason. I promise I'll find him, and when I do, you'll be one of the first to know. In fact, if you don't mind, that is, I'd like to name him after you. I mean, if it's all right."

Jason had to clear the lump from his throat. "I'd be honored, honey." He just couldn't tell her again that the baby was dead. He just couldn't. With the half of his face that still worked, he forced a smile.

When he blinked the moisture from his eyes, he saw Matt standing a few feet behind Angela, a grim, tortured look on his face.

If the prayers of an old man carried any weight at all in heaven, then this terrible ordeal would soon be over, for Jason had never prayed so hard in his life.

The next day dawned as cold and gray and dismal as Matt felt. Despair and helplessness weighed on him, threatening to overwhelm him. With heavy steps and a heavier heart, he met Angela for breakfast.

"Have you seen my quilt?" she asked right off.

"What quilt is that?"

"The little one," she explained patiently, as if any idiot would have known. "It's for the baby. I haven't put the ruffle around the edge yet, and when I find him, he'll need his quilt."

Matt laid his fork down and stared at his plate. God, how much more of this could he take? And Angela—what must it be like for her?

"Matt," she insisted. "Have you seen my quilt?"

There was one thing he hadn't tried yet. He didn't want to do it, but he'd tried everything else. With dread and hopelessness—and fear—making his stomach churn, he answered. "Yes," he said. "I know where the quilt is, Angel."

"You do?" She smiled. "Good! Now I can finish it. Where is it?"

"It's . . . with the baby."

"The baby?" Her green eyes grew large in her face. "You found him? Oh, Matt! How wonderful! Where is he?"

"Get your shawl, and I'll take you to him."

"My shawl?"

"Your shawl."

With no further questions, Angela went to get her shawl. Matt spent the brief moment she was gone praying this was the right thing to do. When she came back, he led her out into the dim, cloudy day, across the courtyard, and on toward the low hill past the bunkhouse.

"It's awfully cool out here for a little baby, Matt. It's a good thing he's got his quilt, or he might catch a chill. But Matt, the quilt wasn't finished yet. It wasn't ready."

Neither was the baby, Angel. Tears stung Matt's eyes and throat, and he fought to hold them in. "He's not cold, I promise."

He held her hand as they walked. When she saw where they were headed, she tried to pull away.

"No!" she cried. "I don't want to go there. You said you were taking me to the baby. My baby's not there."

"Trust me, Angel." Matt wrapped his arm around her shoulder and held her close to his side. "If you want to find the baby, we have to go this way."

They walked on, but as they approached the low adobe wall around the family cemetery, Angela's eyes darted all around. She looked everywhere except at the grave markers. Matt led her a few steps beyond the gate and stopped. Angela buried her face against his shoulder.

"Angel," Matt whispered.

"No!" She tried to pull away and run, but he held her tightly. "Let me go! My baby's not here! He's not here, Matt! He's not! I won't look! You can't make me look!"

"I'm sorry, sweetheart." His throat thickened. Tears finally overflowed and ran down his cheeks. "So sorry."

When Angela saw the look of utter pain and help-lessness on his tearstained face, her eyes closed tight over her own tears. "No, no, no," she whispered. She went limp for a moment, then jerked free of his arms. She turned to run, but her legs wouldn't hold her, and she fell, landing hard on her hands and knees. She raised her head, preparing to get up, and stopped cold at the sight before her.

It was something she would never forget for as long as she lived. Burned into her mind, just as they were burned into the wooden marker over the tiny grave, were the words:

Matthew Jason Colton
Infant Son
Born and Died, January 9, 1873

Angela faced it then, the truth, just as she faced that marker. It was true. Deep down inside, maybe she'd always known it was true, but it was just too cruel to think about. Her son! Hers and Matt's! He never even had a chance at life!

"Oh God oh God *oh God!*" Angela clutched at her empty womb and rocked back and forth as the tears came, then the sobs, quietly at first, then more forceful. The grief and pain took over completely, and Angela screamed out her anguish to the gray, uncaring sky.

Matt dropped to his knees beside her, and she fell against him. He felt her sobs and shudders to the core of his being, and his tears mingled with hers as they dripped down onto the tiny mound of bare earth.

Matt wiped his face on his shirtsleeve. He tightened Angela's shawl around her shoulders, then carried her back to the house. He lay down on the bed

322

with her and held her until they both slept. The fact that it wasn't even mid-morning yet made no difference. They were both emotionally drained.

As his eyes closed to the sound of Angela's soft, even breathing, he sighed. Now they could put this all behind them and go on with their lives. And he swore to himself that if it was at all within his power, he'd see that nothing and no one ever hurt his Angel again.

But there were hurts he couldn't prevent, simply because he didn't know they existed. From the moment Angela acknowledged the death of their child, she began to draw up inside herself. To a passing stranger, she might appear to be a normal wife going about her daily routine. But to those who knew her — Matt in particular — she wasn't Angela.

There was no light in her eyes, no ready smile on her lips. There were no more lingering touches or looks of longing. There was only a shell of the bright and beautiful woman he'd fallen in love with just a few months ago. Matt felt lost, abandoned, and he didn't know what to do about it.

He made the mistake once of asking her what was wrong. He would never do that again, he thought with a shudder. Her eyes had glazed over and turned inward, and the hideous travesty of a smile she'd given him was so false, and so obviously for his benefit, it made him want to cry.

Time. Maybe she just needed more time.

But Angela never thought of time as her friend. She'd proven herself a failure in every way, and her time with Matt was running out.

She'd failed her parents by letting them die.

She'd failed to keep herself from falling in love with Matt. She'd failed to keep him from another woman. She'd failed to keep from conceiving his child.

323

And once with child, she'd even failed at that. And what tormented her now was the reminder that the only reason Matt had brought her home with him was the baby.

Now there was no baby.

She'd been trying to work up the courage to broach the subject with Matt, certain he would want her to leave soon, but she just couldn't do it.

At any rate, she knew he wouldn't ask her to leave until after she testified at Miller's trial. That was supposed to have been several weeks ago, at the first of February, but had been postponed twice. First because the judge who was to hear the case had died. Then, when a new judge was appointed, some irate witness at one of his first trials had smuggled a gun into the courtroom and proceeded to shoot up the place, managing to wound the judge during the fracas.

They were now waiting for his recovery. The new trial date was set for mid-March, which was next week. Her time was running out.

There was proof enough for her that Matt didn't want her anymore. They used to sit together in the evenings on the sofa in the salon and watch the fire blazing away in the fireplace. Now, if he didn't lock himself away in his study, he sat across the room in a chair, leaving the space beside her vacant. As vacant as her lifeless womb. Occasionally they touched by accident, and when that happened, Matt would jump like he'd been scalded and move away.

No, he didn't want her anymore at all. He used to put his arm around her, hold her hand, tease her, kiss her. Now he mostly just watched her, or left her completely alone.

Another week went by. The trial was tomorrow.

Angela was as nervous as a long-tailed cat in a room full of rocking chairs. She couldn't stand it anymore! She couldn't just wait for him to tell her to leave. After all, she had *some* pride.

Matt came to bed earlier than usual that night and caught her packing.

"Angela?"

She stiffened, her back to the door, when he entered. She didn't turn around. After taking a deep breath, she finished folding the last dress and stuffed it into the carpetbag on the bed.

His footsteps sounded as hollow as she felt when he crossed the room to stand beside her. "I doubt we'll have to spend the night in town, but you're probably right. Better to be prepared, just in case."

He gathered an extra shirt for himself and added it to her bag.

Tell him. Tell him, you coward. But in the end, she couldn't tell him she was only packing because she wouldn't be coming home with him after the trial. She couldn't. She just couldn't come back here to this place that felt so much like home and wait for him to tell her to leave.

But she couldn't say the words.

Coward.

Chapter Thirty-five

They left the wagon at the livery stable and walked the several blocks to Courthouse Plaza. They were early, but a crowd was already gathering. There wasn't much for entertainment in Tucson, outside of the saloons and "Maiden Lane," the area where the brothels were located, so trials were quite popular.

Benito had come with them. He and Matt shouldered a path through the crowd into the courtroom for Angela.

After being seated, Angela stared at the witness stand, where she would be asked to tell what had happened to her father and then to herself. She gripped her hands together to still their icy trembling. She'd never been in a courtroom before, and here she was, the star witness for the prosecution.

Matt noticed her pallor and put his arm around her shoulders. "You'll do fine, Angela. Don't worry about anything. All you have to do is answer the questions and tell what happened. It'll be all right. Trust me."

For the first time in weeks, he was touching her, holding her. And she couldn't even respond. She couldn't take her eyes off that chair where she would have to sit and face a room full of strangers. Before she realized it, the judge had entered, the charges had been read, the opening arguments had been given, and the district attorney was calling her to the witness stand.

Her knees didn't shake nearly so bad as she thought they would. That was reassuring. Maybe she could survive this after all. She *could* face her father's murderer and see him convicted. She could. She could. *She would.*

After being sworn in, Angela seated herself in the witness chair. She searched the spectators and found Matt. He smiled as their gazes met and locked, and nodded his head in encouragement.

"Mrs. Colton," the district attorney began, "when did you first see Mr. Scott?"

Angela stared at the prosecutor, her mind momentarily blank. "Who?"

"Mr. Abraham Miller Scott, the defendant."

"Oh." Her eyes traveled to Miller for the first time. She noticed that instead of one glove, he now wore two. And both hands rested awkwardly on the table before him. "I'm sorry. I only knew him as Mr. Miller."

"That's quite all right, Mrs. Colton, just tell us about the first time you saw the defendant."

And so Angela told the court about that night in Memphis, when she'd watched Miller break a man's leg so that Miller could have his job as scout. Then she told about the trip, about how he had shot the dog, how he'd shot Chee, then threatened her."

"It wasn't nothin' but a thievin' Apache!" Miller cried.

Most of the spectators in the room seemed to agree that there was no harm in shooting an Apache. Judge Titus banged his gavel and called for quiet.

Angela straightened her spine and faced the onlookers. "Chee is a man, not an animal. He was alone, and he was minding his own business."

District Attorney McCaffery frowned at her and asked her to continue with her story.

So Angela continued her story. She told how sick her mother had been, how they'd been forced to turn back toward Camp Bowie, and how Miller, too, had headed for the fort to report being attacked by Apaches. He'd told her that much the night he'd kidnapped her. She told about her parents' deaths, and about shooting her father's killer.

"That was quite a remarkable shot, Mrs. Colton."

"Yes, it was, Mr. McCaffery, but it was either sheer luck or God's will that I hit him in the hand like that."

"Why do you say that?"

"Because I had my eyes closed."

One of the spectators let out a whoop. In the back, someone called out, "Atta way, girlie! The scum had it comin'!"

The judge pounded his gavel and called for quiet again.

Angela then told about seeing Miller in Tucson, both the time he'd watched her from a distance, and the time he'd threatened her. Then she told about the night he came and took her away, about how he'd confessed to killing her father, about how Matt had saved her, and about losing the baby because of Mr. Abraham Miller Scott.

By the time she returned to her seat between Matt and Benito, she was exhausted, but relieved. She'd been afraid of what the defense attorney might ask her, but he'd simply shrugged his shoulders and said, "No questions."

Matt testified next, telling how he tracked Angela's abductor to the tiny adobe on the edge of town. Then other witnesses were called. District Attorney McCaffery was a thorough man. A bartender told how Miller had been asking a lot of questions about the Colton family and the location of the Triple C. The barber said he saw Miller sneak up behind Angela at the stage depot. Three other citizens said they saw the defendant ride out of town just before sundown, in the direction of the Triple C, the same day the rest of the Coltons had left on the stage.

The only defense presented was three rather questionable-looking men who swore Miller was playing cards with them the night Angela was abducted, and Miller's own testimony that he was at Camp Bowie the day her father was killed.

"Would you mind telling us what happened to your hands, Mr. Scott?" McCaffery asked.

"My hands?"

"Yes. I couldn't help but notice you don't move your fingers. Could you tell us about that?"

"Objection, Your Honor," came from the defense attorney. "My client's physical handicaps have nothing to do with this case, except to prove that he couldn't have shot anyone, since it's obvious he can't even hold a gun."

"Your Honor, Sheriff Pugh and Doctor Harding are both willing to testify that when Mr. Scott was arrested the morning after Mrs. Colton was abducted, he was suffering from a bullet wound in his left hand, plus, incidentally, one in his shoulder. That corroborates Mr. and Mrs. Colton's testimony of what happened that morning on the edge of town. It is my contention that his right hand, too, bears the scars of a bullet wound, and I am prepared to call in Doctor Harding to confirm this."

"Objection overruled," Judge Titus said. "Answer the question, Mr. Scott."

"No!" Miller's attorney shouted. "My client cannot be forced to testify against himself. That's according to the Fifth Amendment of the Constitution of the United States of America."

McCaffery smirked at the defendant. "And do you refuse to answer the question on the grounds that it might incriminate you, Mr. Scott?"

Abraham Miller Scott looked to his attorney and received a reluctant nod. Miller wasn't a stupid man.

He knew it would make him look guilty as sin if he didn't tell about his hands. But to tell would be to remove all doubt from the judge's mind. It would be a confession. "Yes," he said. "I do refuse."

"No further questions, Your Honor."

And that, such as it was, was the end of the testimony.

Judge Titus announced a ten minute recess while he deliberated. He didn't really need the ten minutes, but he took it anyway, just so the records would show he at least thought over his decision.

"This court finds the defendant, Abraham Miller Scott, guilty of murder and kidnapping. You are hereby sentenced to ten years at hard labor in the Territorial Prison at Yuma."

Miller sagged in his chair while the on-lookers hooted and hollered, some pleased, some angry. The judge once again pounded his gavel for quiet in the courtroom.

"The prison sentence will be postponed until the State of Tennessee has a chance to question you about some crimes you're suspected of committing there. But when they finish with you, you will be returned to Yuma to serve your time — provided Tennessee doesn't hang you first."

Miller spun around, and his cold, gray eyes pierced Angela with sheer hatred. She gasped at the force of it.

"This is your fault, bitch! I'll see you in hell for this!" he screamed. "I'll get you if it's the last thing I do, even if I have to come back from the grave to do it! You hear me, bitch?"

The sheriff managed to handcuff the raving lunatic and started dragging him out of the courtroom. "You hear me, bitch? I'll get you for this! I'll get you!"

Angela shuddered. She'd never imagined such hatred could exist, much less that it could be directed at her. Matt put his arm around her, shielding her from curious eyes, and took her from the room.

"It's over, Angel. It's all over now. Don't let him get to you. It was just talk. He can't ever hurt you again."

Angela's brain went numb. The only part of Matt's words she heard was, "It's over." It echoed in her mind like an Apache drum. It smothered her. It robbed her of all thought. It matched itself to her footsteps. Left foot, *over*. Right foot, *over*. Left foot, *over*. . . .

She panicked briefly when the world went dark, then realized Matt had led her into the livery stable. The sweet smell of clean straw and fresh hay penetrated her numbness and calmed her screaming nerves. Even the horse manure smelled good just then. She paused beside the wagon to take a deep breath. Anything to delay the inevitable.

Matt turned away and talked with Benito. Angela took another deep breath. *This is it*. She climbed up and retrieved her carpetbag from beneath the wagon seat, then jumped down.

"You won't need that," Matt said, reaching to take the bag from her. "We won't be staying." His hand closed beside hers on the wooden handle, but she refused to let go. "Let me put it back and we'll go home."

"I—" Her throat swelled shut and trapped the words she needed to say. She forced herself to take slow, even breaths, then tried again. "I . . . I'm not . . . going with you, Matt."

Matt stared at her and blinked. "What?"

"Do I really have to say it again?" She took another deep breath to screw up her courage. Maybe if she didn't look at him it would be easier. She stared at the wagon wheel beside him. "It's time for me to leave, don't you think?"

"Time? What do you mean, *time?* You're my wife."

"But I'm your wife for all the wrong reasons, don't

you see?" She looked at him then, and if ever there was a face carved of granite, it was his. "We ended up together by accident. A marriage shouldn't be by accident, should it? Two people shouldn't stay together just because it's easy or convenient. That's all we're doing and you know it. You don't love me; you never did. Now that there's no baby there's no need for me to stay. I have nothing you want."

Matt stared at her for a long moment, then released his hold on the carpetbag so abruptly she almost dropped it. "You're right," he hissed between his teeth. "You don't have anything I want. I want a woman who'll stick by me, not a little girl who runs away every time the ride gets a little bumpy."

Despite the sick feeling in her heart and stomach, she felt the tiny spark of anger his words ignited. Felt it, and fanned it. "I'm not a little girl! If that's how you see me, that's your problem. I see myself as a woman. A woman who can take care of herself."

Stop me, her mind screamed. *Don't let me do this, Matt. Tell me to stay.*

Matt shook his head. "Either way, it doesn't make much difference now, does it, since you're leaving. Unfortunately for me, I happen to be in love with you. I thought the feeling was mutual." He paused a moment, then went on. "That first time you came back from Tucson, you said you'd stay. Forever, you said. Your exact word. I had no idea forever was so goddamned short."

Without another word, Matt spun on his heel and walked out into the sunshine. When he turned the corner and disappeared, Angela stared, stunned, at the spot where he'd been. Always before, he'd either forced her to stay, or asked. This time he was doing neither. He was letting her go!

She'd been right all along. He didn't want her. His words of love just now hadn't meant a thing. The man she thought she knew would have dragged her home kicking and screaming if he'd really wanted her. But that must have been some other man. This one was letting her go.

Her feet carried her out the door and into the street, but with each step, she no longer heard just the word *over* in her dazed mind. Now the word had company. *Forever* had joined it. Left foot, *over*. Right foot, *forever*.

Nothing else penetrated. Not the bright afternoon sunshine or the noise of the street. The wagon barreling down on her made no impression. Nor did the driver, who bellowed at her to get out of the way as he sawed back on the reins, trying to keep his team from running her down.

The only thing that jarred her was the strong arm that swept her from the middle of the street seconds before four sets of iron-clad hooves would have trampled her to death. Realizing what had nearly happened, Angela blinked and looked up to thank her rescuer. The words died in her throat as Matt released her.

"Take care of yourself, ha," he claimed with disgust. "You can't even cross the goddamned street."

Angela's eyes burned. She clamped a hand over her mouth to stifle a sob. When she turned to flee, the carpetbag swung out and caught on a large splinter protruding from the hitching rail beside her. She yanked, then yanked again. Matt shook his head and stepped forward to help. On the third yank the splinter snapped and the bag came loose. Carried along on momentum, it swung back and struck Matt in the stomach.

The sound his breath made as it left his body made Angela cringe. "Oh!" she cried.

By the time Matt opened his eyes, she was gone.

merantile. It was ... adobe wall with
... She wiped her sweaty
... departing from one

Chapter Thirty-six

Angela leaned against the rough adobe wall of the building behind her, then pressed her trembling hand to her face. She couldn't cry now. She just couldn't. After several minutes she calmed enough to look around. She was in an alley. Three doors down a pig rooted in a pile of garbage. Over its head, a woman emptied a slop jar from a second-story window.

Gagging, her hand over her nose now, Angela rushed around the corner, out of the filthy, garbage-strewn alley and into an unfamiliar street. It was quieter, less busy than where she'd left Matt. It was the wrong street for her. She needed a job, and for that she needed a street with stores, not houses.

At the end of the block she peeked cautiously around the corner. She wasn't sure exactly where she was, and she didn't want to run into Matt again. Across the street and down a few buildings stood a mercantile. She could work in a store like that — she'd done it all her life.

The thought of walking up to a stranger and asking for a job started her knees trembling. *Good heavens. What will I say?* It was silly, of course, to be so nervous. People asked for jobs every day. It wasn't as if she'd never worked before. So why was her heart pounding? Why was her stomach churning?

After first looking for oncoming wagons, Angela forced herself across the street, then down to Stone's

Mercantile. It wasn't one of the stores she'd visited with Daniella, but that didn't deter her. She wiped her sweaty palms on her dress. Switching the carpetbag from one hand to the other, she opened the door. An overhead bell jingled; so did her nerves.

The familiar sights and smells inside the store welcomed her, from the oiled leather of saddles and harnesses to the crispness of fresh-dyed cotton fabric. The bright bolts of calico were stashed on the top shelf directly above a row of cast-iron pots. Barrels of flour and oats and pickles stood against the near wall beneath the large, fly-specked window. It had been ages since she'd smelled pickles. The tangy aroma somehow reassured her.

Until she looked at the counter. The man on the other side was big and fat and dirty. It was hard to tell which had more grease, his hair or his apron.

"Hep ya, missy?"

Angela jumped when he spoke, and her eyes widened. He sounded like a sweet, old grandmother! "I . . . uh . . . that is, well. . . ."

The man stalked slowly from behind the counter, and that was when Angela noticed his eyes. Watery, black, and as hard as coal. When he grinned, yellow, crooked teeth leered at her. She took a step backward.

"Ain't you jist cuter'n a speckled pup."

Angela swallowed heavily and took another step back. "I . . . I was just . . . uh . . ." She groped behind her for the door handle and met nothing but air.

"Yeah?" the man said, coming closer. He was close enough now that she could smell him. She instantly thought of that pig in the alley. And the slop jar.

"I . . . I'll be going now," she managed in a rush. As she spoke, she spun and threw open the door, escaping into the sunshine. She was two streets away before she dared to slow down.

It took half an hour before she had the nerve to try another store, then another fifteen minutes to find one.

But she didn't fare much better. Even though the proprietor was somewhat cleaner, and a lot more pleasant, Angela still couldn't get the words out. Once again, she panicked and ran.

Out on the street, she berated herself sharply. This was ridiculous. She squared her shoulders and went down the street to Koelsche's General Store, lecturing herself every step of the way. Mr. Koelsche was a pleasant-looking, white-haired man with a friendly smile.

Without a single stammer, Angela managed, "I've worked in a store like this all my life. I'm new in town and need a job. I can read and write and do bookkeeping, and I'm honest to a fault. If you can use my help, I'd like to work for you."

She said it all so fast, at first the man merely blinked in response. Then he smiled. "Well, young lady, I surely wish I could help, but if I hired you, I'd have to fire my wife!" He laughed loudly at his own joke. "As pretty as you are, that might cause more trouble than a man could handle."

Angela tried to smile back at him. "I understand," she said slowly. "Could you give me an idea of where else I might look for a decent job?"

The man rocked back on his heels and scratched his chin with short, stubby fingers. "Well," he drawled, "ya might give Tully and Ochoa a try. Don't know as they need any help, but they're the biggest store in the Territory."

Angela managed a smile and a soft, "Thank you."

"But if ya want my advice," he went on, "you'll go on home before that husband of yours finds out what you're up to."

Her heart instantly tripled its speed.

"The wife came downstairs and ran the store so's I could watch the trial," he explained.

Stupid, stupid, stupid. Of course people were going to recognize her. Why hadn't she thought of it sooner? What was she going to say?

"The Triple C's a darn sight better — and safer — place for a pretty little thing like you than this rough ol' town. You're better off at home, Mrs. Colton. Home where you belong — with your husband."

His tone and manner were kind, but the words still stung. With burning cheeks, Angela mumbled a swift good-bye and left.

Out on the dusty street once again, panic threatened. How many people would recognize her on sight as Matt Colton's wife?

Dozens, she thought with despair. She'd been to town twice with the family, although as far as she could remember, they hadn't been in this part of town.

Then there was the trial. It had looked like half the town had been there.

Well, she just couldn't let it bother her, that's all. She had to have a job. And soon. The sun was going down; the stores would be closing. She simply must find something. She didn't even have a place to sleep tonight.

She located the Tully-Ochoa store on the next street and recognized it at once. Daniella had taken her there.

But the store was closed. Dispirited, she turned up a side street and nearly ran head-on into a woman standing there.

"Whoa there, honey," the big woman said, smiling.

"Excuse me. I guess I wasn't watching where I was going."

"Didn't find what ya was lookin' for?"

Angela blinked. "I beg your pardon?"

"Seen ya go in an' outta purt near ever' store in town. Guess none of 'em had what ya was wantin'."

"No," she answered with a sigh. "They didn't."

"Wall, ain't that somthin'," the woman said. She stuck out her large, work-worn hand. "Name's Sadie. Sadie Horton."

Angela shook the sturdy, rough hand and introduced herself, without thinking, as Angela Colton.

"What in the world could a body want that cain't be bought in one of them stores?"

Angela sighed again. "A job."

"Lookin' ta git rich, are ya?"

Angela studied Sadie Horton, the gray, frizzled hair slipping from its pins, the broad, toothy grin, the dark mole on the woman's forehead just above her left eyebrow. It wasn't any of those things in particular that gave off an aura of friendliness. It was the eyes. Blue, faded with age, but alert. And twinkling.

Get rich? Ha. She knows better. "Just trying to feed myself and put a roof over my head," Angela answered.

"How would you feel about waitin' tables an' cleanin' up a bit?"

"Waiting tables?"

"Course, I cain't pay ya nothin' but room and board at first. I'm a widow lady, an' I had just enough money for this place here." She indicated the door behind her, over which hung a rough board with the words "Good Food" painted on it. Next to the door was a large set of double windows, and through them Angela could see about a dozen table-and-chair combinations and one long plank table with benches on either side.

"You mean you're . . . offering me a job?" Angela asked hesitantly, hopefully.

"I can use the help, and you can keep any tips. There's a spare room upstairs with a bed in it, and all yer meals is free. Whad'ya say?"

Angela blinked, then smiled. The sweet smell of steaming onions wafted out the door before her, and she realized she hadn't eaten since breakfast. "I say, if your food tastes as good as it smells, you'll soon have more business than the two of us can handle."

The woman grinned and motioned her inside. Angela followed her broad beam into the dim room, through the stifling but clean kitchen and up a back set of stairs. Sadie threw open the last door on the left.

" 'Tain't much, but it's yours," she said.

She was right — it wasn't much. But it was clean. Angela stepped into the room and glanced around at the bare, hardwood floor, the single threadbare blanket on the small cot, and the curtainless window, which overlooked the alley. "It will do just fine, really," she assured Sadie as she dropped her carpetbag on the floor and her hat on the bed. "Now, what do I do first?"

"First," Sadie said with a toothy smile, "you come downstairs and eat."

The meal was one of the best Angela had ever eaten. Afterward, she helped Sadie clean up the kitchen. The real work wouldn't start until the next morning. Sadie wanted to be open for her first day of business by noon, and there were a few last-minute things to do.

Upstairs in her room that night, Angela removed her dress and hung it on a hook behind the door. Her spirits were in good shape, compared to this afternoon. What an eventful day. She'd been the star witness in a murder trial; she'd left a husband who didn't love her; she'd found a job with room and board. No wonder she was tired.

She carried her candle and set it on the floor beside the bed. The room might be small and bare, but it was hers. In time, perhaps she'd be able to make it a bit more homey. Curtains would come first. Meanwhile, it would certainly do.

Intent on finding her nightgown, Angela knelt beside her carpetbag and reached inside. The first thing she came up with was Matt's shirt. With trembling fingers, she pulled it out and pressed it to her cheek. *Matt, oh, Matt, I miss you already. Why didn't you love me? Why?*

She slipped the shirt on, crawled into bed, and cried herself to sleep.

Chapter Thirty-seven

All the next morning Angela and Sadie were busy with last-minute cleaning and arranging. In a crate in the alley, Angela found a three-foot square blackboard. She carried it to the end of the street and propped it against the outer wall of the barbershop on the corner. With chalk she'd found in a small box, she wrote, "Good Food!" Underneath, she drew an arrow pointing down the side street toward Sadie's. Below that she wrote, "Beans & Ham, Cornbread, 2 bits."

By the time she finished writing, she'd attracted quite an audience.

Sadie pressed her nose against the front window and grinned. The interest Angela had aroused was exactly what Sadie had in mind when she hired her. The girl would draw hungry men like cow chips draw flies.

When Angela walked back down the street, more than a bit nervous about the seven men who followed, Sadie threw open the front door. The aroma of simmering beans met those men like a long-lost friend. Three of them stepped around Angela and ran through the door hollering.

Within ten minutes of opening, Sadie's Good Food had twelve hungry customers chowing down like they hadn't eaten in a week.

Angela was leery at first. All their customers were men, and she had to thread her way past them, between them, around them, in order to serve the food and clean up the tables. But as mean-looking as most of them were—guns and knives sticking out of nearly every belt and boot—they were, for the most part, polite.

As the first week passed, she began to understand that under everyday circumstances, no matter how rough the man, he generally still respected a lady. (Abraham Miller Scott must have been the exception.) Angela wouldn't give two cents for her safety if she ran into any of these same men in a dark alley some night, but inside Sadie's they were friendly and polite.

At first the work was difficult and exhausting. She climbed the stairs to her room each night worn out, asleep almost before she could put on Matt's shirt and crawl into bed. She was glad, because she was usually too tired to lie awake and think of him.

But as one week stretched into two, Angela grew used to the work, and it wasn't so tiring. The results of her new-found stamina were not all good, however. True, it did give her more self-confidence and a small but growing feeling of independence, but it left her with too much energy to think.

And when she thought, she thought of Matt. What was he doing? How was he? Did he miss her? Was he sorry she left? She thought about him so much at night, it began to seep into her days. Sometimes, when she'd step into the dining room to take an order or serve a meal, her heart would flutter in her chest. She saw Matt in every pair of broad shoulders, every blond head, heard him in someone else's deep laugh.

Naturally, it was never him. Matt wouldn't come to this place to eat. When he ate in town he ate at nice places like the hotel. No, he'd never come here.

Of course he wouldn't come here.

But, of course, he did.

It happened late in the second week. Angela set two

341

tall stacks of flapjacks down in front of a couple of breakfast customers and turned to go back to the kitchen. The light in the room suddenly dimmed. She glanced toward the front door, propped open to let in the morning breeze and let out the aroma of sizzling bacon, and froze. Her heart stopped and her throat swelled.

Matt!

Even without seeing his face, cast in shadows by both the light behind him and the wide brim of his hat, she recognized him. Every dear, familiar inch of him. From his height, to his broad shoulders and trim waist, to the way he stood, tall and straight, weight balanced on both feet. She'd always liked the way he stood so erect, not slouched, his weight not thrown to one hip like so many of the tinhorns she saw these days.

Along with shock, sheer joy at seeing him surged through her. Until she remembered he hadn't loved her enough to ask her to stay. After a brief flash of pain, she carefully schooled her expression blank.

But when she spoke, her voice gave her nervousness away. "Ha-have a seat. I-I'll . . . get you some c-coffee." She wiped her sweaty palms on her apron and turned toward the kitchen once again. And ran smack into Sadie. "Oh!"

"Whoa, there!" Sadie said with a chuckle, putting a hand out to steady Angela. "Howdy, stranger," she said to Matt. "Name's Sadie, and this here's my place. Ain't seen you around before. Welcome!"

Matt grinned as the robust woman pumped his hand in a firm shake. "Matt Colton," he said.

"Colton, huh? Any relation to our Angie here?"

With her back to Matt, Angela stiffened. She'd never mentioned a husband to Sadie. And none of the customers had ever said they recognized Angela from the trial.

If Matt claimed to be her husband, everyone would think she was a runaway wife. Women simply didn't leave their husbands. It wasn't at all the thing.

When Matt didn't answer immediately, Angela glanced at him over her shoulder.

"Only distantly," he answered. "By marriage."

Even as she felt relief take hold, her cheeks burned.

One of the two men she had just served snickered. The other hooted. *They know. They know I'm his wife.* Yet no one had mentioned it. She blushed fiercely and left the room as fast as she could.

Only distantly . . . by marriage. Well, what had she expected him to say?

It was several moments before she felt capable of picking up the coffeepot, but then she shook so badly the scalding liquid sloshed out of the spout. Sadie, who'd followed her, stood by silently, watching, a speculative look on her lined face.

Angela forced herself back to the dining room. Matt was seated at the far corner table. On her way with cup and coffee, she stopped at the now-disappearing stacks of flapjacks and filled the men's cups. She dared a look from beneath her lashes, but neither man met her gaze. No hint of humor crossed their features.

When she reached the corner table and got her first good look at Matt, she nearly gasped. His ravaged face, with sunken cheeks and darkly circled eyes, practically screamed *exhaustion.* She would have commented, but the hard look in those tired, dark eyes stilled her tongue.

So he was angry. *Good,* she thought. *Serves him right for letting me leave.*

She poured his coffee and followed the steam with her eyes as it rose against the wall. "Flapjacks?" Was that her voice, sounding so calm and businesslike?

He pulled his hat off and tossed it on the table. "Fine."

Like a coward, she hid in the kitchen until his breakfast was ready. *What is he doing here?* she wondered frantically.

The scrape of chairs, the clump of boots followed by silence, told her the other two men had left. Matt was the only customer now. She would have left Sadie to serve him, but when Sadie stacked the flapjacks on a plate, she tossed down her spatula and headed out the front door, closing it behind her as she left.

Angela served him his food, refilled his coffee, then retreated to the hot kitchen and began cleaning up. He hadn't attempted to speak with her, which was just as well, for she didn't have the slightest idea what to say to him. Conversations with one's estranged husband had not been part of her schooling.

If she ever lived through this episode, maybe she'd write a textbook on the subject. "How to Leave Your Husband in Three Easy Steps." *Step Number One: Be an idiot. Steps two and three will follow naturally all on their own.*

The jingling of the front bell brought her back to reality. When she stepped from the kitchen, the dining room was empty. He was gone.

Well, so much for their first encounter.

With hands and knees trembling, she began cleaning up the tables. When she found the silver dollar he'd left, a choked, desperate laugh escaped her throat.

At least he's a generous tipper.

Chapter Thirty-eight

The rest of the day stretched into an eternity for Angela. Would it never end? The lunch crowd seemed hungrier and thirstier than usual. Three times during the day she had to go out to the barbershop at the corner and repair her sign. Some prankster kept changing her arrow so that it pointed in the opposite direction.

When the dinner crowd rushed in things got rowdy. Three men got into a fight. When two of them swung and hit the third simultaneously, he crashed into the table so hard its legs broke off. Food flew everywhere.

Angela was so tired by then, the sheer violence of the event didn't even faze her. All she could think of was the extra energy it would take to clean up the mess. Sadie helped by hauling the broken table pieces out the back door.

By the time Angela was finally able to climb the stairs to her room that night, she was numb.

Matt hadn't come back.

In her loneliness and exhaustion, she admitted she'd rather be at the ranch, taking whatever crumbs of affection he dropped for her, than here, learning life's lessons of independence.

No, that wasn't quite true, she realized. There

was one thing she'd learned about herself lately, and that was that she suffered the sin of pride.

She was too proud to humble herself that way, to live on the scraps of his goodwill. For her, it was all or nothing. He either loved her, or he didn't.

And he didn't.

Out of sheer stubbornness, she donned her white cotton nightgown and left Matt's shirt hanging on its peg. This would be the first night — and about time! — she hadn't slept in it since leaving him.

She was startled out of her reverie by a high-pitched squeal that ended in a grunt coming from the alley below. She blew out her candle and crept to the window. What she saw in the dim light from a window somewhere down the street drew a gasp of outrage from her. It was a fight — a very uneven fight. A large, burly man pummeled his fists into the stomach and face of a girl.

Angela froze, her mind going back to that other time she'd seen someone beaten outside her window. She'd done nothing then, and because of her cowardice, her father was dead, and so was her baby.

"Not this time, by heavens," she muttered. She wouldn't sit here cowering in the dark this time. This time she'd do something.

But what?

Sadie. Sadie would know what to do.

Without even putting on her robe, Angela felt her way across the dark room and eased open the door. Down the hall, she stopped at Sadie's door and was met with the rattle and spurt of Sadie snoring the night away. She moved on to the stairs, determined to do this on her own.

Careful, so as not to knock anything to the floor, she felt her way around the kitchen until she came up with a cast-iron skillet big enough to do some damage, but light enough for her to swing.

Her quiet precautions were unnecessary. The man in the alley was yelling. He probably wouldn't have heard if she'd whacked the skillet against the iron cookstove.

"You work for *me*, goddammit. You don't take off on your own 'les I say so. And I don't say so." He punctuated his statements with his fists. The girl moaned and begged him to stop, but he didn't. "I'll teach you, you little slut."

They were right outside the back door. Angela, heart pounding in her throat, threw open the door and ran out screaming, "Stop it! Get away!" with the skillet held over her head in both hands.

The man dropped his victim. The poor girl fell to a groaning heap at his feet. He swung around just as Angela rushed at him, screeching all the way. With all her might she swung the skillet toward his head. He dodged at the last second. The skillet took him in the shoulder with a dull *thud*.

"Get away!" Angela shrieked. She swung the skillet again, but this time the man was ready for her and grabbed it from her hands. He flung it behind him, and it crashed into the back door of the house across the alley.

Angela was too caught up in what she was doing to panic. A dog barked nearby, then another, and another. As lights flicked on up and down the alley and people poked their heads out of doors and windows to see what was going on, Angela jumped back and grabbed one of the broken table legs Sadie had thrown out earlier. She held it in both hands like a club and dug her bare toes into the dirt to brace herself.

The man took a step toward her and snarled, "Mind your own business, missy, if you don't want to get hurt."

With his next step, Angela swung at him. Again,

he yanked her weapon from her hands and tossed it aside.

"What's goin' on down there?" someone shouted.

"Nothing!" the man before her yelled, advancing closer, not taking his eyes off Angela.

"Then, keep it down, will ya? There's folks tryin' to sleep around here." The statement ended with the slamming of a window.

Now Angela faced him, weaponless. She began to shake all over and had to fight for every breath. The enormity of what she'd done suddenly dawned on her. Now she was terrified. Now, when it was too late to do her any good. If she was going to be terrified, why couldn't it have been before she'd rushed out into the alley? Why couldn't she have been terrified enough to have kept her nose out of it?

No. Not this time. This time I don't back down.

The girl on the ground tried to crawl away; but the effort was too much for her, and she collapsed. Her new position left her lying in the man's way. He kicked her aside, wringing another moan from her bloody lips.

The man's hand came out, reaching for Angela's throat, but stopped in midair, frozen there as if by magic. Through all the clatter and noise echoing down the alley, the metallic click of a pistol being cocked rang out as if it were the only sound.

Matt had been hanging around on the street corner for over an hour waiting for the lights downstairs at Sadie's to go out. A few minutes after the big double windows darkened, a light flickered in an upstairs window. Was it hers?

His question was answered a moment later when a large bulky shadow crossed the drawn shade. Even allowing for the distortion a flickering lantern might cause, that was *not* Angela's shadow.

348

When no other light appeared after several minutes, Matt figured her room must be in the back. He hesitated, not sure what he was doing there in the first place. So what if her room was in the back? She certainly wasn't about to invite him in. She'd made that plain with her coolness this morning.

But still, his feet began to move. Instead of just crossing the street and taking the alley, he forced himself to walk all the way down the street, past Sadie's, to the other end of the block before entering the alley.

He grunted with disgust. It was a typical Tucson alley, all right. There was a fight going on. As he drew nearer, he realized what an uneven fight it was. Thinking to mind his own business, which was the best way to stay alive in this town, he raised his gaze to the lighted window above.

The light went out. A second later a pale face appeared at the curtainless window. Not wanting to be seen, in case that was Angela up there, Matt ducked into the nearest doorway. His gaze was involuntarily drawn back to the fight right outside Sadie's back door.

Christ! No wonder the fight was so uneven. It was a man beating up a woman! Matt tensed to step forward, but in that instant the most unbelievable thing happened.

Barefoot and wearing nothing but a nightgown, Angela flew into the alley like an avenging angel, shrieking at the top of her lungs. It was several stunned seconds before Matt was able to react.

Berating himself for a fool, he slipped the thong off the hammer of his six-shooter. He'd never been so slow to move in his life. The man had already disarmed Angela—twice!

Matt pulled his gun and cocked it.

* * *

The girl on the ground whimpered, thinking her assailant had pulled a gun. Angela stiffened, thinking the same thing. But the man knew, as a man who's been around knows these things, that the gun was pointed at him.

Forty feet down the alley, a tall shadow separated itself from a darkened doorway and stepped forward. In desperation, the man whose hand was halted halfway to Angela's throat continued his motion as if he'd never stopped. In the blink of an eye, he grabbed her and held her in front of him as a shield.

Through the thinness of her cotton nightgown, Angela felt the man's clammy chest against her back as if he and she were both naked. Sheer black terror engulfed her and held her motionless. The smell of him, a mixture of cloying perfume and sweat, gagged her. She was so unnerved, she even imagined the man with the gun, who walked slowly toward them, was Matt. She blinked, then gasped. It was Matt!

As Matt drew closer, the man holding Angela made another sudden move. He thrust her forward, directly toward the gun, then darted around the side of the house across the alley.

Angela stumbled and landed solidly against Matt's broad chest. His arms came around her, and she thought, *Oh, God. Matt. Matt.* Hot, seeking lips found hers in a desperate, all too brief kiss. A tingling thrill shot through her. Then he thrust her away and took off after her assailant.

She stared after him, panting. When she finally turned to check on the woman at her feet, Angela's lips were parted in a wide grin.

Her grin disappeared when she knelt beside the moaning girl. "It's all right now," Angela told her.

"You're safe. He's gone." The girl didn't seem to hear. "Don't move. I'm going to get some light. I'll be right back, okay?"

Angela felt around in the pitch-black kitchen until she located a lantern on the counter. She lit it with a wooden match from the holder on the wall and was back outside in seconds.

A few minutes later Matt rounded the corner and stopped abruptly. Angela was speaking to the girl on the ground and smoothing the hair back from the bruised brow. But what halted Matt in his tracks was the outline of her body, cast in sharp relief by the lantern on the ground beside her. As he drank in the outline of her full, unbound breasts through the thin fabric of her nightgown, sweat broke out on his palms, and the rhythm of his breathing changed.

He must have made some sound, for she turned on her knees and looked at him. He knelt beside her, and their eyes locked. A moment later the girl on the ground moaned. They tore their gazes apart. Matt looked at the girl and swore.

"Hiya, Colton," she said between swollen lips.

"Kali. Did Harvey do this to you?"

Angela leaned forward. "You know her, Matt?"

"Yeah," he answered. Then, "We've got to get her to a bed."

"We'll use mine," Angela offered, nodding toward the window above them.

"Take it easy, Kali." He ran his hands over her carefully. "Nothing seems to be broken. Hold on now. I'm going to carry you upstairs."

Kali rolled her head toward him and tried to laugh, but it came out as a groan instead. "I don't . . . think . . . you'll get your . . . money's worth . . . tonight . . . hon."

Matt chuckled. "You're not supposed to say things like that in front of a man's wife, Kali. A girl in

351

your profession should know better."

Angela gasped as their meaning became clear.

Matt picked Kali up in his arms, but Angela just knelt there, staring at him. He shrugged. "I said I knew her."

Angela grasped the lantern and sprang to her feet. "Yes," she hissed. "But I didn't think you meant *biblically*. And I'm not your wife anymore."

"So you say." He followed her inside. She was right about no longer being his wife, but he wasn't about to admit it to her. Since they were married under Apache law, their marriage was ended when she left him. But he'd never explained Apache divorce to her, so she couldn't know that. It was just wishful thinking on her part, damn it. As far as he was concerned, she was most definitely his wife.

They went through Sadie's back door, climbed the narrow stairs, and headed down the hall. Sadie's snorts and rumbles nearly rattled her door. Matt almost smiled, picturing Sadie's mouth open, lips quivering away.

In her own room Angela lit the candle for Matt, then hurried back downstairs for hot water and rags. Matt gently laid Kali on the narrow cot, then examined the bare room. Depression settled over him. So, this was what she preferred to a life with him. A narrow, lumpy bed, an upturned crate for a night table, and three hooks on the wall which held two dresses and . . . his blue shirt?

He carried the candle closer. It *was* his blue shirt. He remembered placing it in her bag the night before the trial. It had been crisp and clean, and he'd folded it neatly on top of her dress. Now it was wrinkled. It looked like—

A slow grin spread across his face. It looked like it'd been slept in. More than once.

When Angela returned, he held the light for her

352

while she worked to clean up the girl on her bed. The girl Matt "knew." Kali was awake, but kept her eyes closed against the pain of having her cuts and bruises tended. She looked up at Angela once and tried to smile. "His wife?"

Angela opened her mouth to deny the fact, but Matt interrupted. "That's right. Angela, meet Kali. Kali, Angela."

"He's imagining things," Angela said, casting him a glare.

"No," Kali whispered weakly. "I seen you before . . . at the courthouse. But you ain't gotta worry none about me, ma'am. Your man ain't been near me in over a year. He wouldn't cheat on ya. Matt's not that kinda guy."

Angela felt Matt's stare boring into her but refused to look at him. "Hush now," she told the girl. "Just rest and save your strength."

By the time Angela did all she could for the girl, Kali was fast asleep. Back downstairs, Angela heated some coffee without asking, somehow reluctant for Matt to leave.

Seated at Sadie's big work table, he finally raised his gaze to her. "You look tired," he observed.

Angela braced an elbow on the table and rested her head in her hand. "So do you," she said softly.

She should be feeling extremely self-conscious, sitting there in her nightgown. At least she'd put on her wrapper before coming downstairs this time. But her hair hung in snarls down her back, and her feet were bare and dirty. And a woman Matt *knew* was upstairs in her bed.

She must be more tired than she realized, for none of that seemed to matter. Here she sat, at this old scarred table, sharing coffee with Matt, and it felt comfortable. It felt right.

"How've you been?"

His deep voice startled her from her easy thoughts. Tension crept into the room like an unwelcome guest.

"All right," she said with a shrug, staring at the steam rising from her coffee. "And you?"

He shrugged, too. "The same."

Angela cleared her throat. "I'm . . . ah . . . surprised you're still in town."

"Unfinished business." His gaze bored into her as if trying to read her mind. Then, out of the blue, "I was proud of you tonight."

She looked at him then, startled. "Proud?"

He smiled. "You were really something, the way you came screaming out into the alley like that. What was it you hit him with the first time, anyway?"

She gasped and put her fingers to her lips. "The skillet. I forgot about it." She pushed herself back from the table so hard she nearly spilled her coffee. "If Sadie doesn't find it in the morning, she'll kill me."

Matt followed with a smile as she carried the lantern to the back of the house across the alley and searched through the weeds until she found the skillet. Back inside, he watched, and appreciated, the way the wrapper swayed around her backside while she cleaned the pan.

"Looks like you're out of a bed for the night. Where'll you sleep?"

She placed the skillet back on the counter with care. "Sadie's got some old blankets in the spare room upstairs. I'll just make a pallet on the floor."

"Doesn't sound too comfortable."

"It'll do," she said, picking up her coffee.

"I've got a room at the hotel. You could stay there for the night."

She stiffened. "Is that what all this is about? Tired

of sleeping alone? Well, I'd suggest you go upstairs to your *friend,* but I don't think she's in any shape to accommodate you."

"Are you off on that subject again?" he demanded.

"No. The subject is closed. I think it's past time for you to go. I have to get up early."

Matt took a step forward, then changed his mind. It was too soon to force the issue. "All right, Angel, I'll go. But the subject is far from closed." He took another step forward, then turned abruptly and stomped out the door. When he slammed it, the windows shook. So did the pots and pans.

Chapter Thirty-nine

Sadie was disappointed the next morning to learn she'd missed all the excitement. "Next time, by Jove, wake me up! I swing a pretty mean fryin' pan, myself. Between the two of us, we coulda clobbered that varmint good."

Doc Harding came by to check on Kali. Said Matt sent him. The poor girl was so stiff and sore she could barely move, but Doc confirmed that nothing was broken.

Before the dust settled from Doc's departure, Matt showed up for breakfast. Angela was still piqued at him over his suggestion that she sleep at the hotel. She slammed a coffee cup down in front of him loud enough to turn heads and cause stares. "Don't they serve breakfast at the hotel anymore?"

Matt smirked. "I wasn't in the mood to be treated like a valued customer. Friendly service gets boring. Thought I'd come here for a change of pace."

Three men at the next table laid their forks down in slow motion and turned to face him. "Ain't no call ta be pickin' on the little lady, mister," one of them warned.

Another leaned an elbow on the table and said, "Miss Angela's a lady, fella. Don't you be givin' her a hard time."

"Yeah," the third one said. "Nobody else's complain' 'bout the service. Maybe it's just your attitude she don't like."

Matt raised a brow at the three, then turned his gaze on Angela. "My apologies, ma'am," he said.

Angela mashed her lips together to keep the grin from her face. "Apology accepted," she told him with a nod. Then she turned to the other three and smiled brilliantly. "Gentlemen, I thank you."

During the next week Matt turned out to be the most regular customer Sadie's Good Food had ever seen. Angela didn't know what to make of it. Once or twice he asked about Kali. Angela thought for a while that was his reason for coming around, but changed her mind. He didn't really seem that interested in the answers he received. She hoped.

After two days in bed, Kali was bored to tears, saying something about bed being no place to be alone. Angela blushed, but when Kali giggled, Angela laughed, too. The next day Kali started helping Sadie in the kitchen. Not wanting anyone to see her terrible bruises, and not wanting to cause Sadie and Angela the embarrassment of befriending one of "Harvey's girls," she refrained from helping in the dining room and stayed in the kitchen, out of sight.

"But you don't have to help at all, girl," Sadie claimed.

"Of course I do," Kali said. "I owe you for putting me up, and I owe Angela for coming to my rescue like she did."

"Nonsense," Angela and Sadie said together.

Later that day, talk in the dining room was all about some saloon keeper over on Maiden Row named Harvey, who'd had some sort of unfortunate accident and would be laid low for the next several weeks. When Matt came in for dinner the men gave him a wide berth. Kali grinned from ear to ear when Angela mentioned his skinned knuckles.

"Are you crazy?" Kali shrieked at Angela in their room that night. "You're married to *Matt Colton* and you *left* him? What the hell made you do a damn fool thing like that?"

Kali had been trying to start this particular conversation for days. Until now, Angela had managed to avoid it. *Might as well answer and get it over with.* She shrugged to cover up the turmoil inside. "He doesn't love me."

"Love, schmuv! With a guy like him, who cares? He's young, he's handsome, he's rich, and he sure knows how to show a girl a good time, if you don't mind my saying so."

Angela stiffened. She did mind. She minded like hell!

When Matt walked boldly into the kitchen late Sunday morning, Angela didn't know whether to scream, cry, or run. Every day! Every day he'd been in. His presence unnerved her. Whenever she waited on him he never said much, just ordered his meal and asked how she was. He was always polite since that time the three men took offense at his rudeness.

But he watched her. His gaze followed every move she made, while his brow wrinkled in concentration. Once in a while she could even catch him at it, but she tried not to. Whenever their gazes met, he refused to look away. And the looks he gave her were always different. Sometimes friendly, sometimes serious. Sometimes playful, sometimes sad. But what affected her the most was when their eyes would meet and his would smoulder and scorch her with their heat. And the heat was not from anger.

This time, as he stood in the kitchen, he didn't look at her at all. But she looked at him. She'd never seen him dressed like this before. He wore a black, three-piece suit with a white dress shirt and black string tie. And for once, his face wasn't shaded by the brim of a hat. He was bareheaded. The total picture he presented nearly robbed her of her breath. He was without a doubt the handsomest man she'd ever seen.

"Everything ready?" he asked Sadie.

"Sure 'nough. Right over there." She pointed with her chin, since her hands were buried in a pan of bread dough.

He stepped over to the work table and peered inside a large picnic basket Angela hadn't noticed before. "I'll just take this outside," he said with a smile. "Be right back for the rest."

Kali rinsed the plate she'd been washing and set it aside, then hurriedly dried her hands. Biting back a grin, she whirled on Angela and began unpinning the apron top from Angela's dress. Angela was too amazed to object, until she felt the bow at the back of her waist give. She made a grab for it, but it slipped away.

She spun around and watched, open-mouthed, as Sadie folded the apron and set it aside, her shoulders shaking once her back was turned. Behind her, Kali giggled.

"What's going on around here?" Angela demanded. She looked from one to the other as they both grinned from ear to ear and tried to look innocent. When heavy footsteps sounded behind her, she whirled toward the door to face a smiling Matt.

"Good," he said. "You're ready."

She looked from Kali to Sadie again, but they'd both turned their backs. "Ready for what?" she asked cautiously.

"For a picnic," Matt said, as if explaining something to a small child. "And an afternoon off."

"In the desert? What are we going to do, eat in the shade of a cactus? You're crazy. I'm not going anywhere with you. I've got work to do."

Behind her, Sadie mumbled something about too damned much help for such a small business. Matt took a step toward her. "I'm inviting you on a nice, friendly picnic. I have your employer's permission."

"Well, you don't have *my* permission. I'm not going anywhere with you."

Matt's smile didn't even dim as he took another step forward. "There are some things we need to talk about. I'm asking you politely, Angel—"

"Don't call me that."

"You'd rather I called you Mrs. Colton?"

She took a step back, and ran up against the cabinet, her eyes wide.

His smile slipped a little, and he cocked his head to one side. "Are you afraid to go on a picnic with me?"

"Don't be silly," she answered breathlessly, her heart whacking away at her ribs.

"Then, you'll come."

"I will not."

Matt folded his arms and looked like he might be prepared to wait all day for her to give in. His next words, however, dispelled that notion.

"You'll either take my arm and walk out of here with a smile on your face, or I'll drag you out bodily. It's up to you."

Angela stared at him and wiped her sweaty palms

360

on her dress. The only sound in the room was the soft hiss and crackle of the fire in the cookstove. An occasional clank of fork against plate came from the dining room, and somewhere out the back door a dog barked.

She wanted to call his bluff. Oh, how she wanted to. But she was afraid he wasn't bluffing. That smile didn't quite reach his eyes.

Another part of her wanted to go with him so badly her breathing became difficult. To be with him, to spend some time with him away from prying eyes . . . but to what end? Nothing had changed. Her reasons for leaving him were still valid. And he certainly didn't look as if he were about to beg her to come home.

In the end, she decided not to cause a scene. She took a deep breath, then put her hand on his arm and a smile on her face. She'd take this little scrap he was throwing her. She might pay for it later, but she'd risk it.

Matt returned her smile, and with a departing nod and wink to Sadie and Kali, he escorted Angela through the dining room, out the front door to the rented buggy he had waiting. Within a few minutes they were headed out of town on a narrow, rutted track that led only the Lord knew where.

The narrow seat and the overhanging top created a hot, intimate atmosphere that made Angela nervous. She cleared her throat. "What was it you wanted to talk to me about?"

Matt leaned his elbows down on his knees and let the reins thread loosely through his fingers. "We'll get to that later. For now, why don't you just enjoy the ride?"

"I might, if I had some idea of where we're going, and why."

361

"We're going on a picnic," he said, smiling at her over his shoulder.

She gave him a sour look, then averted her gaze. The road, if it could be called that, cut between tall cacti and low, spiny shrubs, skirting large rocks and deep cuts. A roadrunner darted from behind a clump of greasewood and ran along beside them for a few strides before speeding off for new cover.

About an hour from town, Matt pulled up next to a small, trickling stream and lifted Angela to the ground. He spread a blanket beneath a lacy willow, then hauled out the basket. Neither one of them had spoken for the past thirty minutes.

Matt broke the silence when he asked her to sit. Conversation was stilted, at best, while they ate Sadie's fried chicken, potatoes and gravy, biscuits, and fresh-baked apple pie, and washed it all down with lemonade.

"You've got crumbs on your face," Matt said, smiling.

Angela reached up to wipe them away.

"Here, let me." He leaned over and wiped the corner of her mouth with his napkin. His warm breath fanned her cheek. She bit her lip.

He leaned closer. His gaze delved into hers, searching, questioning. Then his lids lowered, slowly, slowly, and he stared, his breathing halted, as her tongue came out and wiped her lips. She held her breath, afraid to move. Any closer and their lips would meet.

He leaned closer. His lips brushed hers, softly at first, then more firmly. He slipped a hand around her neck, and the kiss deepened. She reached up to push at his chest, but instead, grasped the lapel of his coat. Her breath came hot and heavy with the fire that soared through her veins.

362

How she'd missed him! She could feel herself slipping away, becoming part of him, but she couldn't stop what was happening inside her. Couldn't, and for one wild, ecstatic moment, didn't want to.

When he pulled away and looked at her, she opened her eyes and was shocked to realize she was lying down, with him sprawled over her.

Common sense came crashing back with a vengeance.

Chapter Forty

"Is this why you brought me out here?" Her voice was as ragged as her breathing.

"No," he said softly, gazing steadily into her eyes. "But maybe it should have been. It beats the hell out of talking." One hand still held the back of her neck. He wrapped his other arm around her and pulled her close as he lowered his lips again.

Angela tried to ignore what was happening to her body, but couldn't. Heat rushed through her veins, and all her juices flowed to one central spot, creating an agonizingly pleasurable ache. This time, when he finally pulled away, his breathing was as ragged as hers.

He buried his face against her neck. "I'm sorry," he whispered hoarsely. He released her and rolled away to sit up. "You're right. This isn't why I brought you here." He ran his fingers through his hair and heaved a sigh.

Angela was startled, and humbled, to notice his hand was trembling. She sat up, shaken to her core. She fidgeted with her hair and clothes, then took a deep breath and stared at his profile. "Why did you bring me here?"

"More lemonade?" he asked, reaching for her cup.

She accepted it just for something to hold in her hands. "Why did you bring me here?" she asked again.

He filled his own cup before answering. "I wanted to ask you a question."

Angela's heart picked up its beat. She shook so hard the lemonade nearly splashed out of the cup. Would he ask her to come back to him? What would she say?

"Why did you leave me?"

She sucked in a sharp, surprised breath. "You know why—"

"And don't give me that hogwash about how we started out with all the wrong reasons. That may have been true in the beginning, but it changed damned fast and you know it. I want the real reason. I . . . need to know."

He was looking at her now, his gaze steady, his expression unreadable. She tore her gaze away before he could see more than she was willing to admit. "Do you realize that today's the first time you've *really* kissed me since I was kidnapped?"

He closed his eyes briefly, then opened them. "I know."

She jerked her head around in surprise. She held his gaze, bewildered now by his answer. After a moment she shrugged. "Of course, that's only a side effect, not the real point."

"And what is the real point?"

"The baby," she said, staring down at the lemon pulp floating in her cup. Talking about the baby was like probing an open wound. Would the pain, the feeling of loss, ever diminish?

"You left me because you lost the baby?"

"We both know the only reason you wanted me to stay with you was because of the baby."

"Angela, that's—"

365

"When there wasn't a baby anymore, there was no reason for me to stay. You made it quite obvious you didn't want me after that."

"So you left me because you thought I didn't want you. Anything else?"

Her back straightened, and she glared at him. "Isn't that enough? You think I want to spend the rest of my life with a man who doesn't love me?"

"So now in addition to not wanting you, I don't love you, is that it? What about you? You've only talked about how you say I feel. What about what you feel, Angel?"

"I told you before not to call me that. And what I feel has nothing to do with this."

"Nothing to do with it?" He stared at her, amazed. "You walk out on your husband, claiming everything was a mistake, the marriage is over, and what you feel has nothing to do with it? What in the hell does, then?"

Angela started to rise, but he stopped her with a hand on her shoulder. "Just sit still," he ordered. "You've had your say, now it's my turn." He released her and rubbed the back of his neck as if it ached. It did. Everything seemed to ache these days.

"Remember that day you took the horse and tried to run off?" He waited until she nodded, though she didn't look at him. "I told you then that I had only used the baby as an excuse to keep you with me. Christ. I didn't even know there was a baby until that very day.

"You were angry with me because you thought I'd encouraged Alope. I thought if I could just keep you with me for a while, you'd see for yourself how I really felt about you, that I wasn't the least bit interested in other women. I used the idea of a baby to gain some time. You know that. You're just too stubborn to admit it. So just because there isn't a

366

baby anymore doesn't mean I don't want you."

"It's true though, isn't it?" She stared down at her hands and watched herself twist her wedding ring around and around. Why was she even still wearing it? She stopped fidgeting when she noticed Matt eyeing the ring. "What would you want with a wife who can't even produce a child that lives?"

Matt reached out and tilted her head up until she faced him again. "In the first place, losing the baby was not your fault, damn it, and you know it. Miller did that to you. And in the second place, you haven't been listening to me, woman." His voice softened as he caressed her cheek.

"The child you lost was created because we loved each other, Angel. If you'd had the chance to carry him to term, and he had lived, I would have loved him. He would have been precious to me. But not half so precious as you are. It's *you* I want, Angel. You come first with me. Always you."

Angela's spirits soared with hope, then plummeted. She shook her head and turned away. "Your words say you want me, but your actions speak otherwise."

"What actions?"

A brief sound escaped her. It was part laugh, part sigh, part sob. "You did it so much you weren't even aware of it."

"Did what?"

"Moved away from me every time I got near you. And if we accidentally touched, heaven forbid, you acted like I had the plague or something. Usually you left the room entirely, just so you wouldn't have to be near me."

Matt let out a deep breath. "You're right, of course. I did all those things. I even turned my back on you in bed at night, praying you wouldn't reach out and touch me."

She gasped at his admission. The pain of it cut her like a knife.

"But not for the reason you think. Damn it, Angela, you'd just lost the baby. You nearly died, for God's sake! You weren't well enough for . . . for what I wanted. I was *afraid* to get near you, to touch you. I kept waiting for some sign, some word from you telling me you were well, you were ready for me . . . you wanted me. Instead, every time I got near you, you looked like you were ready to bolt. I couldn't bear that wounded look in your eyes. You were still healing, and I was ripe for rape. I *had* to stay away from you."

Angela opened her eyes wide to peer over the tears gathering along her lower lid. God, how she wanted to believe him. If he spoke the truth, did that mean there was a chance for them? Even a small one? Or had she killed it by walking out on him?

He sat there, staring off at nothing, with that jug of lemonade and three feet of empty blanket between them. When he finally spoke again, she held her breath, waiting, hoping.

"So you see, Angel, you were wrong. I did want you. I still do, and probably always will." He turned toward her. Her heart thudded heavily at the look in his eyes. "I love you. It's that simple . . . that complicated."

"Matt, I—"

"No. Let me finish. I love you. I want you to be happy. If you think you could ever be happy with me again, then I want you to come home with me. I want you to give us another chance." She started to speak again, but he silenced her with a wave of his hand.

"Don't answer me now. It's something I want you to think about. I guess I know you well enough to know you wouldn't come back to me just because it might be easier than trying to support yourself. You're not the type to take the easy way out. But if you don't . . . love me . . . if you decide not to come back, I don't want you struggling and scraping for every dollar just to put a roof over your head. I've got more money than I know what to do with. If you don't want me, then I'll give you plenty to live on, and I won't bother you anymore."

"You don't—"

"Don't say anything. Just think about it. Think hard, Angel. I love you, and I want you, but not if you don't feel the same way. I'll be out of town for a few days. When I come back you can tell me what you've decided."

The chirping and twittering of sparrows and an occasional snort from the horse were the only sounds as they repacked the basket and loaded up the buggy. During the entire hour it took them to get back to town, neither spoke.

He wanted her to think about it. What a joke! What was there to think about? She knew what she wanted. But did he really mean it? Did he really love her, want her, or was it only his damaged pride speaking? That's what she had to figure out— whether she trusted him or not. Could she be sure enough of him that she wouldn't suffer a fit of jealousy every time he spoke to another woman?

Then there would be the embarrassment of facing his family again, if she went home with him. She knew Daniella, Travis, and the children had returned from Boston over a week ago. But it was foolish to even think about that. If he loved her, she could face anything.

When he pulled the buggy to a halt in front of Sadie's, the sun was sinking. He climbed down and lifted her to the ground, leaving his hands resting on her waist while he stared deeply into her eyes.

"Think about me, Angel," he whispered. Then, right there on the street, in broad daylight with a dozen people walking past and Sadie and Kali standing behind her in the open doorway, he kissed her. A slow, thorough, devastating kiss. His tongue touched everywhere inside her mouth. She met it, savored it. He groaned, then pulled away slowly, releasing her lips a fraction at a time, making her body beg for more.

But there was no more. He stepped back and brushed the backs of his fingers lightly across her cheek. Without a word, he turned, climbed into the buggy and snapped the reins to head down the street.

Her fingers came up to touch her throbbing lips. By the time he turned the corner and disappeared from sight, her cheeks were wet. She knew what her answer would be when he came back.

Chapter Forty-one

A few days, he'd said. But those few days stretched into an eternity as first one week, then two, passed, with no word from Matt. Angela was beside herself. What did his long absence mean?

Had something happened to him? Was he sick or hurt? Had he changed his mind by now, sorry he'd ever bared his heart that way? Or had it all been some sort of cruel joke, designed to get back at her for leaving him the way she had?

Back and forth, the questions plagued her. It was Saturday night, and Sadie's was packed with cowboys, drifters and businessmen. It was all she could do to keep her mind on her work and deliver the right food to the right person.

And she wasn't doing so well at it either, she realized with a groan. She picked up the two plates she'd just set down and switched them. The man with the beard had wanted his steak rare. It was the clean-shaven one with the broken nose who'd ordered his well done.

Broken Nose scowled at her for her clumsiness when she nearly dumped his meal in his lap. "Sorry," she mumbled as she turned away.

If she didn't keep her mind on her work, there was liable to be a major disaster.

Thinking to appease Broken Nose and his buddy,

she hurried to the kitchen and grabbed up the coffee-pot. When she stepped into the dining room again she halted dead in her tracks. The man who ran the livery had vacated his table in the corner. Matt had taken his place.

Their gazes met. For one long moment, she stood motionless, breathless, speechless. He was here! He'd come back!

"What's a man gotta do ta git a cup o' coffee in this dump?" It was Broken Nose, and he wasn't happy.

Angela tore her gaze away from Matt's grim features and jerked the coffeepot around to fill the empty cup. She was shaking so badly that in the process of pouring, she splashed some of the scalding liquid on Broken Nose's hand. He howled in protest and jerked back. With his action, more coffee slopped over the lip of his cup and burned him again.

"Goddamn!" He dropped the cup. Its contents splattered across the front of Angela's apron when she failed to step back quickly enough. He grabbed her wrist and nearly jerked her clear across the table. She held the coffeepot high to avoid spilling it on the man with the beard. "I'd like it in the friggin' cup, lady, not on my hand!"

Angela heard an angry growl from the corner table. "I'm sorry, mister. It was an accident."

Broken Nose squeezed harder on her wrist. The only sound in the room was the scraping of a chair across the scarred wooden floor. Everyone in the room was staring.

Angela was so embarrassed she wished the floor would open up and swallow her. But her embarrassment turned to anger when the man tugged on her arm and grinned.

"You'll get the whole potful in your lap if you don't let go of me this instant," she warned with narrowed eyes and a stiff jaw.

The man glanced around at the sudden quiet, saw

everyone staring at him, then released her. Angela thought the crisis was over. Then Matt's voice rang out.

"That's it!" he roared, kicking his chair over behind him. He glared at her from three tables away. "I've had it, Angela. I know I promised you plenty of time to make up your mind, but I can't wait any longer. I can't stand the thought of you having to defend yourself against scum like that. You want to wait tables, we've got a great big one at home. I can't stand any more waiting. I love you, damn it. Are you coming home with me or not?"

"Yes," she breathed, setting the coffeepot down in the middle of the bearded man's plate.

"Because if you're not — Yes?"

"Yes!" She stared at his stunned face. Her breath came in swift little gasps through her open mouth.

"Why?" he demanded, returning her stare, oblivious to their hushed, eager audience.

Angela felt light-headed and giddy. She bit her lip to keep from laughing out loud in sheer joy and relief. "Oh, Matt!"

"Oh, Matt," he mimicked. He tossed his table aside like it was made of paper and advanced on her, weaving his way slowly between the other tables. "What the hell does that mean, *Oh, Matt?* I've just said I love you in front of all these people, and all you can say is *Oh, Matt?* What does that mean?"

Angela covered her burning cheeks with both hands, but kept her gaze glued to the man who now stood only an arm's length away waiting for her answer. She lowered her hands slowly, ignoring the onlookers, and stepped directly in front of him.

Understanding dawned slowly. *He's just as unsure of me as I was of him!* It was something she'd never even considered. But she was no longer unsure of anything. She reached out and placed her hands on the sides of his neck.

"I'm sorry. I thought you knew." Her thumbs stroked up behind his ears. "It means I love you. It means I've loved you from the very beginning, and every day since. It means I've never stopped loving you for even a minute." Her fingers slipped to the back of his head where they buried themselves in his hair. "It means I'll always love you, every day for the rest of my life."

She didn't care who was watching or what they might think. This was her husband, her man. They loved each other. She pulled his head down and pressed her mouth to his mouth, her body to his body, her heart to his heart.

When his arms wrapped around her and lifted until her feet dangled several inches from the floor, the customers in Sadie's Good Food broke out in a rousing cheer.

Kali sashayed into the room, hands on her hips and a wide grin on her face. Sadie lumbered up behind her. "It's about damned time!" she hollered.

Matt tore his lips away, and Angela opened her eyes and gasped. The fire in his gaze nearly scorched her with its intensity. Without taking his eyes away, he stood her on the floor and yanked the bow of her apron strings loose at the back of her waist, then rested his hands boldly along the tops of her breasts — much to the crowd's enjoyment — and unpinned the apron's bib.

He tossed the apron to Kali and said, "You've just been promoted from dishwasher to waitress." Then, amid more hoots, whistles and hollers, he swung Angela up in his arms and carried her through the kitchen and up the stairs to her room.

By the time he kicked the door to her bedroom closed behind him he was trembling with eagerness. He lowered her feet slowly to the floor, his eyes having never left hers. She pulled his face toward her again.

"Angel." The word was a sigh on his lips just as they opened to receive her kiss.

It started out as a tender, loving kiss, but after a few seconds, the tone and feeling changed to one of urgency and stark, immediate need.

Matt was trying to hold back. He was too eager. After two weeks of dread, her response was more than he'd dared dream. He'd been a fool to wait so long to come back. He should have come sooner. But the possibility that she wouldn't want him had loomed large in his nightmares. Pure and simple, he'd been afraid.

But he was here now, and she was his. No more fear. No more uncertainty. No more loneliness. Still he tried to slow down. He didn't know anything about women who had miscarried. Would he hurt her? Was it too soon? He wanted to ask her. He had to ask her. But to ask, he had to take his lips from hers, and at the moment, he couldn't. He couldn't bear to lose touch with her tongue as it danced along with his to some inner rhythm they both felt.

One of his questions—was it too soon?—was answered for him when Angela's hands slipped down his neck, over his shoulders, and began releasing the buttons on his shirt with fevered haste. His hands began a similar task on the back of her dress. Then he picked her up, their lips still joined, and carried her to the bed. He laid her down and tore his lips away.

"Are you sure it's all right?" His eyes burned down into hers like fire. "I mean . . . can we?"

"It's not just that we can." Angela's hands shook as she finished undoing the buttons on his shirt. "We should. We must." One hand slid up the scars on his bared chest, then around his neck. "We have to." The other hand went down, over his buckle, and traced the throbbing hardness she found there. "If we don't, I'll die."

Matt thrust himself more fully into her hand and groaned with the pleasure of her touch. He was nearing the point of losing control, but he couldn't bear to move away from her hand. He pulled her dress down over her shoulders and kissed her neck. When he ran a finger across the tight peak of one breast, Angela nearly jumped off the bed.

"Hurry, Matt," she breathed. "Please hurry."

He didn't need any more urging. In seconds their clothes were on the floor, and he was lying half on top of her, kissing her hard, pressing her into the mattress with his weight. He slipped a hand between her thighs. She was as ready as he was.

They came together then, his hardness into her softness, and she cried out her release almost instantly, digging her nails into his back. Matt would have prolonged it, if he'd been able. But the inner contractions of her muscles pulled him right over the edge with her.

"Oh, Matt!"

It was only the beginning of a long, long night of love.

A lifetime of love.

"Oh, Matt."

Epilogue

June 7, 1874
Dragoon Mountains
Arizona Territory

The great war chief of the Apaches, Cochise, lay on his favorite cougarskin rug inside his wickiup. He kissed his three-month-old grandson, Niño, on the cheek, then a woman took the child outside. Cochise looked around him at the people he loved.

There was his oldest son, the next chief of the Chúk'ánéné, Tahza, Tahza's mother, Tesal-Bestinay, and Tahza's wife, Niño's mother, Nod-ah-Sti. Then there was Cochise's other son, Naiche, and Naiche's mother, Nali-Kay-deya. On the other side of his bed sat his faithful shaman, Dee-O-Det, along with his friends, Poin-sen-ay, Skin-yea, and others.

Taglito was not there, but that was all right. He and Taglito had already spoken.

Cochise wished Woman of Magic and her family were here, but it was too late. There was no time.

He picked up a handful of sand and let it sift through his fingers. "Our people are as this sand. These grains escaping are our friends and family who are gone." He opened his hand to look at the few remaining grains. "This is all that is left of us. The white men are too many. Do not try to fight them any-

377

more. Study them. Learn their ways and adopt them as yours, keeping also the ways of our people in your hearts. If we are not all to die away from this earth, you must learn to live with the white men."

Tom Jeffords nearly ran the legs off his bay gelding trying to get back to the reservation with the doctor from Fort Bowie in time, even though he knew it would be too late. He and the doctor reined in on a low hill, still an hour away from Cochise's wickiup. They paused to let their lathered mounts rest a moment before the final stretch.

The breeze cooling their faces suddenly died. Both men wiped the sweat from their brows. Tom raised his head and sat perfectly still in the saddle. Nothing moved around them, nothing at all. There was no movement, no sound — not even a bird.

Suddenly a great gust of wind swept down from the mountains. It swirled around them, then blew off across the valley toward the west. Like a dust devil, but with no dust.

Tom Jeffords shivered in the hot morning sun, then calmed. He was agnostic by nature, but suddenly he felt an inner peace he'd never known before. That wind! What was it? Why should a gust of wind feel . . . friendly?

And then he knew. It wasn't a wind at all. It was the breath and soul of a friend, come to say good-bye.

"We will meet again, my friend," Taglito whispered, "where the cottonwoods stand in line."

The doctor could go back to the fort now. There was no more need for him, Tom knew.

Cochise was dead.

It would be several days before the people at the Triple C received official word of Cochise's death. The family was currently occupied with another great event, this one much happier.

A child was born this morning. Joanna Colton, daughter of Matt and Angela, granddaughter of Travis and Daniella, great-granddaughter of Jason, gave a lusty cry when she entered the world.

Joanna was an hour old, and it wasn't even noon yet. Her mother lay in exhausted sleep, and her father, grandfather and great-grandfather drank toasts in her honor at the other end of the house.

Daniella and her children were in the courtyard enjoying Rosita's lemonade when the strange wind blew over them. It had gained strength as it blew across the land, and now it shook the shutters of the adobe ranch house.

Matt and Travis came outside. Daniella, Serena and Pace stood staring at each other, speaking, without words. Matt and Travis both knew instantly that somehow, the twins had inherited some portion of their mother's strange gift.

"Grandfather!" Serena screamed.

Matt scooped his stepsister up in his arms and held her. Travis went to Daniella and saw that she, too, was crying.

"Pace! Where are you going?" Travis asked sharply.

The boy didn't answer, just kept walking away from the house.

"Let him go, Travis," Daniella whispered.

"What is it, love," he asked softly. "What's wrong?"

"It's . . . *shitaa!*" she wailed.

Travis didn't ask how she knew; he only asked what she meant.

"He's dead, Travis. Cochise is dead."

Travis and Matt did not share Daniella's gift of sight, but they shared a strong bond as father and son. They sought each other now with their eyes, and each knew the other's thoughts.

Two years. They'd had two years of peace in the

Territory since the treaty. And now Cochise was dead. The peace would not live long without him. Tahza would be elected the next chief. He was good and brave, but he would not be able to hold all the bands together as Cochise had. There would be war.

It might not come soon, but it would come. And when it did, it would make Cochise's ten-year war seem like a picnic. There were some truly vicious men among the Apaches, and those men would gain control and lead their warriors on a long and bloody trail.

Jason Colton had always said he wanted to live long enough to see his first great-grandchild born, and he did. He got to hold Joanna when she was only a few hours old.

When Travis entered his father's room the next morning, Jason was dead. He had died with a relaxed, even smile curving both sides of his mouth.

And somewhere far to the north, an escaped convict hunkered beside a small fire high in the Colorado Rockies. No lawman would ever find him here.

He flexed his left hand and grinned. The man hadn't been as good at maiming as the woman. His right hand was still dead, but the left had healed. They would pay for what they'd done to him.

His gaze ranged southward. He looked past the huge rugged peaks, down past the border, through more mountains, across desert, until he pictured a certain adobe ranch house before him.

He could see a man and woman walking arm in arm. The man was tall, broad-shouldered and scarred. The woman was trim, petite and beautiful. Both were blond.

The outlaw's lips moved. "Soon," he whispered.

Author's Note

The Howard-Jeffords-Cochise treaty was signed in late September, 1872. It was filed in Washington, D.C., and the Chiricahua Reservation became official December 14 of that year. The reservation consisted of 3,100 square miles, extending from the Dragoon Mountains to the Mexican border, and had a population of approximately 2,500. Tom Jeffords was the Indian agent.

If giving up one's way of life in the face of insurmountable odds is wise, then this treaty was good. If Cochise's last words to his people can be considered wise, then the creation of the Chiricahua Reservation was good.

And if the Howard-Jeffords-Cochise treaty was a good thing, then it was absolutely the last good thing that ever happened to the Chiricahua Apaches.

The Chiricahua Reservation no longer exists. It was abolished shortly after Cochise's death.

The Chiricahua people do still exist, and that, considering what had already happened to them, and what would happen to them in the years to come, is nothing short of a miracle.

The tale of the Coltons and the Chiricahua, whose lives and fates are intertwined, will continue in the next volume of this series with the story of Serena Colton, as she grows to womanhood and reaches for the love of a lifetime in the turbulent 1880's. The man of her dreams will try to resist the temptation she offers, but Serena. . . .

Ah, but that's another story. When next we share a campfire, you and I, I'll pass you a cup of coffee and tell you of the temptation Serena offers—a temptation of peace and love, of strength and freedom. An *APACHE TEMPTATION*.

Sincerely,

Janis Reams Hudson

KATHERINE STONE —
Zebra's Leading Lady for Love

BEL AIR   (2979, $4.95)
Bel Air—where even the rich and famous are awed by the
wealth that surrounds them. Allison, Winter, Emily: three
beautiful women who couldn't be more different. Three
women searching for the courage to trust, to love. Three women fighting for their dreams in the glamorous and treacherous *Bel Air*.

ROOMMATES   (3355, $4.95)
No one could have prepared Carrie for the monumental
changes she would face when she met her new circle of
friends at Stanford University. Once their lives intertwined
and became woven into the tapestry of the times, they
would never be the same.

TWINS   (3492, $4.95)
Brook and Melanie Chandler were so different, it was hard
to believe they were sisters. One was a dark, serious, ambi-
tious New York attorney; the other, a golden, glamorous,
sophisticated supermodel. But they were more than sisters—they were twins and more alike than even they
knew . . .

THE CARLTON CLUB   (3614, $4.95)
It was the place to see and be seen, the only place to be.
And for those who frequented the playground of the very
rich, it was a way of life. Mark, Kathleen, Leslie and
Janet—they worked together, played together, and loved
together, all behind exclusive gates of the *Carlton Club*.

*Available wherever paperbacks are sold, or order direct from the
Publisher. Send cover price plus 50¢ per copy for mailing and
handling to Zebra Books, Dept. 4005, 475 Park Avenue South,
New York, N.Y. 10016. Residents of New York and Tennessee
must include sales tax. DO NOT SEND CASH. For a free Zebra/
Pinnacle catalog please write to the above address.*

JANELLE TAYLOR

ZEBRA'S BEST-SELLING AUTHOR

DON'T MISS ANY OF HER
EXCEPTIONAL, EXHILARATING, EXCITING

ECSTASY SERIES

SAVAGE ECSTASY	(3496-2, $4.95/$5.95)
DEFIANT ECSTASY	(3497-0, $4.95/$5.95)
FORBIDDEN ECSTASY	(3498-9, $4.95/$5.95)
BRAZEN ECSTASY	(3499-7, $4.99/$5.99)
TENDER ECSTASY	(3500-4, $4.99/$5.99)
STOLEN ECSTASY	(3501-2, $4.99/$5.99)

Available wherever paperbacks are sold, or order direct from the Publisher. Send cover price plus 50¢ per copy for mailing and handling to Zebra Books, Dept. 4005, 475 Park Avenue South, New York, N.Y. 10016. Residents of New York and Tennessee must include sales tax. DO NOT SEND CASH. For a free Zebra/Pinnacle catalog please write to the above address.